EX LIBRIS
ANEITA J.
DE MARKUS

# THE *Best* AMERICAN SHORT STORIES 1948

# THE *Best* AMERICAN SHORT STORIES 1948

*and The Yearbook of the American Short Story*

*Edited by*
MARTHA FOLEY

19 48

HOUGHTON MIFFLIN COMPANY · BOSTON

The Riverside Press Cambridge

The Riverside Press
CAMBRIDGE : MASSACHUSETTS
PRINTED IN THE U.S.A.

To

WALLACE STEGNER

# ACKNOWLEDGMENT

GRATEFUL ACKNOWLEDGMENT for permission to reprint the stories in this volume is made to the following:

To the Editors of *The Atlantic Monthly, Cosmopolitan, '48' the Magazine of the Year, Good Housekeeping, Harper's Bazaar, Harper's Magazine, The Kenyon Review, Ladies' Home Journal, Mademoiselle, Mainstream, The New Yorker, Partisan Review,* Random House, Inc., *Story, Today's Woman,* and *Tomorrow;* and to Sidney Alexander, Paul Bowles, Ray Bradbury, Dorothy Canfield, John Cheever, George R. Clay, John Bell Clayton, Margaret Cousins, M. F. K. Fisher, Philip Garrigan, Martha Gellhorn, Elliott Grennard, Ralph Gustafson, John Hersey, Lance Jeffers, Victoria Lincoln, Robert Lowry, John A. Lynch, Vincent McHugh, Robert Morse, Ruth Portugal, Mary Brinker Post, Waverley Root, Dolph Sharp, Wallace Stegner, Sidney Sulkin, Eudora Welty, and E. B. White.

# FOREWORD

*NOT FOR ONE HUNDRED YEARS,* not since the writing of Edgar Allan Poe, has the short story in America displayed the tendencies it has shown during the past year. *The Fall of the House of Usher* or *The Cask of Amontillado,* if published for the first time today, could be considered, save for some of their antiquated wording, as contemporary as any stories which have appeared in literary or popular magazines in recent months.

The overwhelming tension, the terror, the specter of undefined guilt which permeated Poe's work are the most obvious attributes of today's short story writing. They are attributes present even in those stories which do not actually include ghosts, vampires, mysterious voices, haunted mirrors, little people in bewitched Easter eggs, and similar weird manifestations. In modern atom-bomb-inventing, airplane-traveling, electrically powered United States of America the newest widespread literary development is, of all things, a re-emergence of the old-fashioned ghost story!

This is a startling change from the realistic kind of writing to which we have been accustomed for many years. In England, of course, ghost stories have been written and published continuously for centuries. But we in America turned away from them almost completely, preferring in our reading the natural to the supernatural. There had been an occasional writer in this country, such as H. P. Lovecraft, who specialized in the uncanny, two or three pulp magazines which published such material, and a publishing firm like Arkham House which concentrates on the more literary type of this kind of writing. But they did not prepare us for its incredibly sudden, widespread acceptance.

It certainly has been a hair-raising experience for this editor —

and not hair-raising in the way the author may have intended — to read along casually in one of those big, opulent magazines with lavish advertising and illustrations and encounter a ghost. Yes, a dissatisfied wife, mooning over a man she might have married, is shown what a villain he really is and also saves a young girl's virtue, thanks to a ghost she meets in a department store.

At another publishing extreme, a smart and presumably highly sophisticated weekly published a story in which the main character keeps losing an hour out of his life every time he takes a certain automobile trip. Here it is left to the reader to decide whether the man actually lost that hour or whether it was a mental aberration as a result of wish fulfillment about a certain woman he had met.

This latter variety of story (of which there have been many), where the supernatural and the psychiatric blend, puts the question whether or not preoccupation of writers with the ghostly can be ascribed to the present consuming interest in psychiatry, especially that preached by Jung, with his haunted racial consciousness, or can it be laid to the war? In England, after the First World War there was intensified interest in the psychical. Again, is it, to turn to Poe, the completion of a literary cycle? A friend of mine, a student of history, recently pointed out that many present events, such as the occurrences in Greece, are identical with those of a hundred years ago. Or do such stories show a desperate effort to flee reality, to forget the most horrible war in history and its tragic sequels?

Several years must pass before we know the answers to any of these questions. Certainly, it has been amazing to me, at least, to meet so many ghosts in fiction midway through the twentieth century. And, because so many writers who first appear in print with short stories later write novels, it also will be interesting to see how prominently the supernatural will appear in other forms of American fiction as well.

Since so very many of the stories published this year have used ghosts and their appurtenances, I may have made a mistake in not selecting some of them for reprinting. None of the stories in this particular volume uses a ghost, haunted mirror, or little people in an Easter egg, and I hope I have fulfilled my duty by noting that there have been very many such stories. Many of the stories in this collection do have the same attributes, even if those attributes are psychological and implied rather than visible apparitions.

If I were to be limited to only one word to describe the majority of the stories in this year's anthology, I believe I would use 'tension.' For there is in them definitely a feeling of tension, of expectancy, of breathless awaiting of the unknown. Perhaps a psychiatrist would say they show an 'anxiety neurosis.' Writers reflect the emotions of their countrymen, and therefore this must be a national attitude.

Another unexpected shift has taken place this year. Any reader who has followed this anthology over the years knows that the little magazines have been its richest source of fine short stories. This year, for the first time, it has been otherwise.

The little magazines have been devoting a tremendous amount of space to critical articles. This I regret. It is much easier to be critical than creative. In publishing creative writing the little magazines have been the most constructive literary force in the country. To watch them turn from actual creation to devote entire issues to writing about writing is sad.

It may be that, as one little-magazine editor told me, they have not been receiving as many good stories because popular magazines are now accepting a type of story that they would have rejected a few years ago. I have a theory, which may be wrong, that there is a time lag between publication of new literary form in the little magazines and their appearance in the big magazines. The little magazines do the pioneering, the really creative editing, and then gradually the writing they foster gains wider recognition. If this is true, it is time for the little magazines to regain their crusading spirit on behalf of still newer means of literary expression.

One more curious happening in the literary world should be reported. For a long time the difference between what was supposed to be a 'popular' story adapted to publication in a 'slick' magazine and a 'literary' story due for publication in a non-commercial medium was that the former had a happy ending and the latter an unhappy ending. It was not always true, although generally the big magazines did favor a happy ending, no matter how forced. Now just the opposite is happening. The phenomenon of a forced unhappy ending is becoming common in the popular magazines. Max Beerbohm, in the days of the old Yellow Book, had something to say about that when he declared, 'What is all this talk of happy and unhappy endings? It is a matter of the inevitable ending.'

Like the dishonest unhappy ending is the unreal treatment of real problems in some popular magazines. Problems touching upon racial and religious minorities have become frequent in their stories, but a false approach to them has been almost as frequent. They have served as the core for exceedingly contrived, artificial writing although the authors, and perhaps the editors, may have congratulated themselves that they were being liberal and advanced.

The stories in *The Best American Short Stories* are chosen separately and on their individual merit. I feel that is the only way they can be chosen. If I were composing a collection of stories, rather than selecting from a multitude of magazines what I hope are choice pieces of writing, I would think more of the over-all balance of the book. As it is, each story is a rich, separate substance and should be read and enjoyed that way.

I wish to thank Joyce Hartman for all the help she has given me. I also wish to acknowledge the kindness of the magazine editors of the country who have kept me supplied with their publications. Many of them have done so most generously even though I have not selected any of their stories.

In closing, I pay tribute to the memory of Edward J. O'Brien, the founder of this anthology, who devoted twenty-six years of unselfish service to the short story.

MARTHA FOLEY

# CONTENTS

(From Story)

# PART OF THE ACT

## BY SIDNEY ALEXANDER

TO THE ADULT EYE, it was just the prosaic and none-too-tidy arcade leading into Madison Square Garden. But to the bright-eyed little girl of seven bounding up the slight incline with her uncle, the doors ahead of them were gateways to magic, portals to never-never land. She had never been to a circus before; and for two weeks now (ever since her uncle had told her), the anticipation of it had tinted her days with an unreal glow, and peopled her nights with motley visitors of fancy.

Oh, why does he walk so slowly? she thought; how could this tall, usually playful uncle of hers be so deliberate? She began tugging at his sleeve, urging him forward, and he glanced down at her and gently smiled. Then he clasped her eager little hand as a side current in the throng threatened to separate them. But he did not quicken his steps and it seemed an hour to Helen before they reached the red-faced guard who performed the magic ritual of ripping their tickets in half and returning the stubs, thereby permitting them to pass through the gate.

'Stay close by me, honey,' the man said as the little girl began to wander off into the buzzing crowd. 'You'll get lost and then your mother will have my head.'

She laughed and squeezed his big hand in hers. Why should mother want Paul's head? What a silly idea! But then this uncle of hers was given to queer statements; sometimes he didn't talk like a grownup at all; he built fantasies in the air, knocked them down, concocted the weirdest stories that floated vaguely in all directions like the blue smoke from his pipe.

Now he was standing still for a moment, taking his bearings. The lobby was jammed with children adorned with tasseled sombreros, snapping circus whips, laughing, crying out with piping voices, dragging their heavy-footed parents after them.

It was their world today, he reflected, gay as their floating balloons, raucous as their tin horns, as it had been his world so many years before. When was it . . . fifteen years since he had last been to the circus? But now, as he stood with Helen in the swirling crowd, the years were rolling further back than that, and he was with his father in the old Garden, and Poppa was saying, 'Now stay in your seats. I'll be right back.' Then he had gone to the men's room, leaving the two children alone in the terraced balcony. And after five minutes Paul was certain Poppa was never coming back; oh, they were lost forever and soon a policeman would come to take them away to the station house or wherever abandoned children were taken. And he was crying bitterly, hysterically and a motherly woman was saying 'There, there . . .' and Sister was trying desperately not to cry because she was braver than he was, even in thunderstorms. Of course, Poppa had returned to laugh at him.

But that was long ago. The Garden had changed as he had changed. Somehow it seemed much smaller than the Garden of his childhood, though in reality it was much larger. So had his grandfather once loomed ten feet high, his head in the clouds. . . .

He was back in Madison Square Garden, that was the important thing. He was going to see what he had seen as a child, but through Helen's eyes as well as his own. She was tugging him this way and that, crying out in eagerness. The varnish of good and evil would be stripped from events, the clean, fresh colors would emerge . . . and yet, the varnish would be there all the time. That was why he liked to go places with Helen. The double vision intrigued him.

He looked down at the child. She was trembling with anticipation. Her hazel eyes were darting about the lobby. 'Oh Paul, buy me a sombrero!' she cried as they passed a vendor's stand. 'Buy me a whip!'

'Later,' Paul said, patting her head. No, she is not beautiful, he thought, looking down at her, she's certainly no bisque doll. Her hair was nondescript brown, her features rather ordinary. But what wonderful vitality in her chunky, firm-fleshed body, what gaiety in the quick eyes, what roguishness in the trill of laughter. She wore a starched summery pinafore that flared out from her straight hips. She was always dancing in his vision.

The years melted away when he was with Helen. In contrast to her childish energy, his own movements seemed sluggish, old — older than his thirty-odd years. Sometimes when he sat on a rock in Central Park and watched her cavorting on the grass, he felt a pleasant sense of melancholy, a quietistic acceptance of childhood gone.

But always he descended from this aloof eminence, tumbled to the lawn himself, fell to her world, shared her games, became a child with her. At such times, an ant crawling through the grass was an elephant crashing through a heavy jungle; a precarious pile of dominoes was a skyscraper toppled by the giant hand of Helen or the whirlwind blown from Helen's mouth. It was a wonderful world — this world of Helen's — a world with no cause and no effect, no news and no newspapers; and his ability to enter into it without reluctance — as a child-citizen rather than an adult interloper — was the chief bond of their love.

'We have almost an hour before the circus starts,' he said to her. 'Let's go down to the side show.'

'Oh!' she sighed ecstatically. It was one of those long-drawn-out 'ohs' that bespeak everything — wonderment, thanks, ineffable joy. She held his hand tightly as they wedged through the cackling, perspiring crowd down the spiral staircase to the basement.

The side shows disgusted him.

Was it possible that he had once, like Helen now, shrieked with joy at the sight of such monstrosities? As he stood packed there amidst the gaping crowd, looking up at those abominations on the platform, he felt sticky beads of sweat rolling down his armpits and he longed for escape to clean, fresh air.

But Helen was crying, 'Lift me! Lift me!' She could not see because of the mob; so he hoisted her upon his shoulders where she sat, with her satiny cool thighs brushing his cheeks, ogling the freaks.

They were standing in front of the Tallest Couple in the World. The Tallest Couple were dressed in cowboy and cowgirl clothes, their sombreros as big around the rim as auto wheels. They were selling 'wedding rings' — good-luck charms made of lead — for twenty-five cents.

Paul managed to work his way forward to the platform, where dozens of children were stretching forth their thin stalks of arms for the thrill of shaking hands with the giants.

He gave Helen a quarter and she, too, leaned forward, holding him about the neck with one hand and handing the quarter to the seven-foot girl with the other. The giantess smiled and slipped the good-luck ring over two of Helen's fingers and the child screamed with delight, 'Oh, I can put two fingers in it! Look, Paul! Oh, look at the ring! It's the biggest ring in the world! Look at my ring, Paul! I have *two* fingers in it!'

As she waved her 'wedding ring' before his eyes, there arose unbidden in Paul's mind, like murky underwater growths, images of the giant couple in bed: he heard the titanic threshings and whippings of their love fury, the clinchings of leviathans. . . . And that Lilliputian couple — the next attraction — waiting so sourly on the platform as the side-show barkers waved the crowd on — was their love-making accomplished with mouselike whimpers, sharp nipping of the teeth?

The images persisted, the slimy underwater growths billowed on the ocean floor of his consciousness, and he felt uncomfortable, indecent, that such thoughts should well up in him while he was with Helen. Her thighs were brushing his cheeks, cool and pure.

The midget with the squashed-in face was playing a tune very badly on a midget piano while his wife tap-danced like a marionette. They bowed stiffly, forcing their lips apart in stage smiles, and then retired from the scene.

'She has no arms or legs!' Helen suddenly shouted in Paul's ear. She was bouncing up and down on his shoulders, pointing to the stage next to the midgets. A torso woman was sitting there in a specially built chair; deep, lined with red velvet, and with high side arms to contain her truncated body.

'Shhh. . . .' Paul whispered. 'That's not very nice. You might hurt her feelings.'

A blond woman near by heard his admonition and laughed crudely. 'Augh, she don't care 'bout them remarks. That's what she's gettin' paid for.'

'And now, Ladees and Gentlemen!' the barker cried, 'this *charming* little lady will *deemonstrate* the power of the *yooman* will. As you can see — just draw a little closer there — that's right — let *everybody* see — Miss Sanbras was born without arms or legs' — and he waved his own perfectly good arms toward the charming little lady who was looking at the crowd with the one-eyed somnolence of a cat — '. . . by sheer indom-inable will . . . overcame her handicaps.'

'I can't see,' Helen whimpered. He had put her down, his shoulders aching, and now she was stretching on tiptoes trying vainly to get a glimpse at the magic platform. In her down world, all she saw were backs and feet.

'All right,' Paul sighed wearily, and he hoisted the little girl upon his shoulders again.

A typewriter on a portable table was rolled out, and then to the hand-clapping glee of the spectators, the lady who was just a torso began to peck at the keys with her nose.

'Just like a woodpecker!' the little girl exclaimed, pinching Paul's cheeks in her excitement.

The barker unrolled the paper from the machine and held it aloft for the spectators to see the perfect typing. Meanwhile the torso lady reclined with a bored expression on her pinched, pale face.

Paul was happy when they left her for the sword swallower. The sight of the living torso made his gorge rise in disgust, and he felt an overwhelming surge of sadness for all the truncated people of the world, the half-men and parts of men. . . . He realized already that this visit to the circus would not be a success. Try as he would, he could not look upon these horrors with the eyes of Helen. Too many overtones echoed beyond the walls of Madison Square Garden, the world outside reflected here in a distorted mirror.

But meanwhile, the sword swallower had inserted a wiggly blade like a long bread knife down his gullet, and then withdrawn it, smacking his lips as if he had just devoured a delicious steak.

'Look! look!' Helen cried out as the sword swallower ran his tongue over his lips in anticipation of his next meal. 'He *likes* the taste of swords! He thinks they're *delicious!*' And she broke into a foamy spill of laughter, pleased with her sense of mischief, tickled at the incongruity of feeding upon swords.

Now the sword swallower bent his head back and thrust a lighted blue-white neon tube down his extraordinary esophagus, and the lights on the platform were dimmed to reveal the neon tube shining reddishly through the living scabbard of his flesh. The line of pale light traced upward from the pit of his stomach to his mouth, from which projected — like some mockery of a crucifixion — the cross hilt of the neon sword.

But it was especially when they went to see the elephant that Paul realized what time had done to him, the associations from which he could not free himself but of which the child was free, looking innocently as she did, like Eve before the temptation, at this monstrous garden of freaks.

Hundreds of children with their adult overseers lined the rail behind which, in a malodorous straw-sprinkled enclosure, stood the great beasts, lumbering with heavy grace upon gray tree-trunk feet, their skins the color of fossil rock, folded and creased and pitted like oversized garments on their enormous frames. Their little eyes shone intelligently as they waved their trunks over the rail, begging for peanuts.

Next to Helen, a little boy was throwing peanuts at the elephants, throwing them with a kind of desperation as he backed away from the approaching trunk. It was wonderful the way the great beast would sniff among the straw, find the peanut and loop it back to his mysterious hidden mouth. And then he would be waving his trunk in the little boy's face again, and the boy would cringe and throw another nut at the pink-fleshed opening at the tip of the coil.

It was these bifurcated nostrils — wet, pinkish, quivering, sucking all in — that disturbed Paul. But Helen was not disturbed. He had purchased a bag of peanuts for her, and she was smiling at the sight of these enormous beggars behind the rail, their fat rumps bumping playfully, their ridiculous noses. And here was Helen, courageously feeding them, calmly holding her place as the motile thing reached forward in a begging arc, the delicate pink tips fluttering like a butterfly's wings. Unlike the little boy, she did not shrink away in fright. Instead, she neatly dropped the peanuts into place — one in each nostril — as if she were sorting them into compartments.

And she did this with such assurance while the beast waited, fixing his greedy little eyes at her paper bag, that Paul felt proud. And yet he could not overcome his distaste, and he stood impatiently by as Helen, slowly and with a craftsman's precision, bedded two peanuts at a time into the bifurcated nostrils.

'Kids are sure funny,' remarked a stout, shirt-sleeved man to Paul. He had been observing the little girl and the boy, the contrasts in their behavior. He wiped his pale pink shining forehead with a dirty handkerchief, and grinned. 'You never know what they're likely to do. That one's scared as hell. But that kid of yours . . . she don't seem afraid of nothing. Prob'ly ride on the elephant's back if you'd let her.'

Helen paused in her feeding. She looked up and remarked calmly, without vanity, 'I'm not afraid of elephants.'

'We can see that, dear,' Paul said, while the fat man burst out laughing. 'But you shouldn't brag about it.'

'I'm not bragging,' she said. 'I like elephants. I think they're funny.'

'I tell you, them kids are simply wonderful!' exploded the fat man, loosening the sticky shirt under his armpits. 'Your daughter?'

'Not mine,' Paul said. 'My sister-in-law's. I think she's kind of wonderful too.'

'Hey, Pat! C'mere! Lookit this!' a strident voice called, and the fat man disappeared in the milling throng.

Paul glanced at his watch. 'You'd better finish the rest of the peanuts yourself,' he told Helen. 'We ought to go up and take our seats soon.'

Reluctantly she left the beggars' row of pachyderms, and clasping hands, they crossed to have a look at Gargantua before going upstairs for the main show. As they buffeted their way through the kaleidoscopic crowd, they passed the giraffes. High above the gaping, gabbling mob, their little heads balanced on still precise necks, they looked down upon the people with the aloof Olympian coolness of gods, dwellers of mountain tops, creatures of a higher world.

'Ooh, give me the peanuts!' Helen cried, reaching for the paper bag which he was carrying.

'You're not allowed,' Paul said, pointing to a sign on the bars behind which the lady-footed speckled giraffes stood, motionless as painted statues.

*'For-bid-den to feed the gi-raffes,'* Helen read in a loud voice, spelling out the syllables. She was thoughtful a moment, then looked at her uncle with that bright flash of roguery in her eyes. 'I know why.'

'You know why what?'

'I know why you can't feed the giraffes.'

'Why?'

'Because,' she said gravely, extending one foot and hopping over it with the other, 'their heads are too high to reach.' And she burst out into another rill of laughter, immensely pleased at her little joke.

'Well, if you can't reach *them,* why couldn't they reach *you?*' Paul asked with mock gravity. 'Why couldn't they just bend their heads down?'

'Oh *you!*' said the little girl. 'I was only fooling.'

'Oh. . . .' said Paul, acting very surprised.

'You *knew* I was fooling.'

'No, I didn't,' he said solemnly. 'I thought you really meant it.'

'You did not!' she insisted, troubled now by his apparent naïveté, and he looked upon her upturned sweet face, suddenly so serious, and he laughed loudly and bent to kiss her. 'Of course, silly, I knew it all the time. Come, we've got to hurry.'

There was a large crowd before the glass-enclosed cage of Mr. and Mrs. Gargantua. As Paul and Helen approached, they heard little ripples of laughter now and then, or sudden exclamations, or breathy gusts of 'ahs' as the beasts performed some feat that delighted their watchers.

As they reached the buzzing rim of the crowd, Paul peered over the many bobbing heads into the electric-lighted, air-conditioned, glass-enclosed cage. The two gorillas were squatting on the floor like a couple of bundles of fur. Feces dotted the floor. A trapese was swinging idly.

'I can't see,' sounded Helen's familiar complaint from below, and again he had to lift her to his shoulders.

Impudently, Gargantua was staring at the people through the close-knit bars that prevented him from smashing the glass with a blow of his hairy fist. His black barrel chest was slowly heaving, and his tiny eyes were almost invisible behind the mat of hair, the squashed-up nose, the overhanging beetling brow.

Suddenly Mrs. Gargantua — smaller, but no more delicate than her mate — stood up and waddled to the other corner of the cage. As she passed her huge partner, he slapped her playfully behind the ears. The crowd roared, and the she-gorilla pushed her husband away and then scuttled with an ungainly hop to the other corner where she plumped down, her back disdainful to the audience, and began to search for fleas.

'By God,' breathed a sharp-faced little man who, like Paul, was staggeringly serving as the scaffold for a child. 'They're just like humans, ain't they?'

'Yeah,' said the man's blousy, gum-chewing wife, 'I wonder what they think sometimes, having people stare at 'em all day. What a life! No privacy at all,' she added with a sly chuckle.

'Aw they love it,' said a young woman, entering the conversation. 'They love to show off. See, there he goes again.'

With a catlike bound, surprising for a creature of his weight, Gargantua had leaped onto the swinging trapeze and now he was performing miracles of acrobatics: dangling by one arm, doubling in and out, swinging head downward.

His wife paid no attention to all this, but the crowd was delighted, and Paul found himself being pressed closer and closer to the cage, while Helen clapped her hands in glee.

All of a sudden, the beast leaped from the trapeze and waddled forward, looking with an arrogant expression at the great crowd he had collected by his exhibition. And then, slowly, he bared his teeth in a foul grin, and spat, and they cringed back, momentarily forgetting that between their civilized selves and this uncomfortable reminder of their ancestry there was the saving glass, down which the ugly spittle of his disdain was slowly flowing.

'Let's go, honey,' Paul said, shaking his niece's ankle to distract her attention from the cage.

'Oh, wait a minute!' Helen exclaimed, fresh wonderment in her voice.

As if the spitting were not enough, the ugly beast had now begun to commit an abomination. Slowly, deliberately, with an obscene glaze in his eyes, he continued working in full view of them all, as if by this latest outrage he wished not so much to gratify himself as to indicate his utter contempt for all humanity.

There was a titter of embarrassment among the adults. The thin-faced man next to Paul abruptly lifted his son down from his shoulders and, with his blushing wife, hurriedly walked away. Here and there in the crowd Paul heard complaining cries of children who were being dragged away from this scene of infamy. There was no sound from Helen. Her hands gripped his shoulders.

'Let's go,' he said abruptly. 'It's time for the show to start.'

She made no protest when he put her down. Her face was silent, thoughtful. As they made their way toward the spiral staircase, she twisted around for one last, backward glance. A man laughed gruffly in Paul's face.

After he had watched for what seemed the hundredth time a dizzying procession of white and brown horses prancing round and round in a wooden ring while agile riders leaped upon their bare bobbing backs or somersaulted from one horse to another, Paul fought no more against the ravages of time. For once he, too, like Helen, had been unable to keep his seat for wonder, and had stood as she was standing now, clutching the cold iron guard-rail of the balcony, utterly fascinated by the spinning, whirling, pirouetting three-ringed saturnalia of the circus. Now, he was falling asleep.

For the first half hour she did not speak at all. Her silence was broken only by throaty gurgles of delight, tiny exclamations, spontaneous uncontrolled flutters of the hands.

But Paul was quickly bored at the ever-changing and yet changeless spectacle in the three rings below — the maneuvers of dogs, the dancing elephants, the knotty-calfed acrobats, in sparkling rhinestone tights, the flamboyant showman who caught rubber balls thrown out from the audience upon a peg clenched in his teeth and finally juggled three flaming torches in the darkened arena, while, flanking him, a geometric ballet of half-naked girls (the modern touch) wrote upon the darkness with phosphorescent pencils.

Soon Paul found himself looking less upon the circus than upon the reflections of it in his niece's face. Her emotions were written there like clouds upon a still pool, the blue and green and orange beams of light danced in miniature in her eyes, her mouth opened in round O's of amazement, her lips tightened with anxiety for some daring performer.

He looked upon Helen's face as upon the face of his lost childhood. And now she had broken sufficiently from the spell of rapture to notice her uncle's moonlike observation and she breathed ecstatically, 'Oh, Paul! Isn't it *wonderful?* Only I don't know what to look at first. There's *so* much going on.'

'Look at the seals,' he suggested, pointing. 'There . . . in the middle ring. He's going to play a song.'

'Does he take piano lessons, too? Like me?'

'No,' Paul said. 'He's a natural-born musician.' The little girl laughed appreciatively. 'But watch. . . .'

The star performer of the seals was waddling to the center of the ring, while all his comrades of the act rested their sleek blubbery bodies upon encircling stools, their flippers dangling. Some were still munching chunks of fish which had been awarded them for their virtuosities in balancing red-and-white striped balls upon their noses.

Oily in the spotlight which followed his clumsy progress across the ring, the star seal put his pointy mouth to one of the horns in a rack before him, and suddenly let loose a blast that echoed all over the Garden. Immediately all the seals began furiously flapping their flippers together in applause, and the audience roared.

'They clap too! Just like people!' Helen said.

'Just like people,' nodded Paul.

But the ringmaster was not satisfied. He was snapping his fingers angrily, summoning the seal back to the rack of horns, and now the seal's head was poised like a cobra ready to strike, and he began to blow first one and then another of the horns, darting back and forth faster and faster until Paul recognized a weirdly distorted version of 'My Country 'Tis of Thee,' *prestissimo.*

Again, all the seals clapped their flippers, some of them banging upon the stools like a paid claque. Paul half expected one of them to shout, 'Bravo!'

'Bettuh sit back in yo' seat,' a Negro man said to Helen, who was leaning in her excitement far out over the guard-rail. She drew back at the man's gentle restraining touch, never taking her eyes from the spectacle below.

'Thanks,' Paul murmured, silently reproaching himself.

'These kids . . .' the Negro said with a confiding sigh. 'Yuh gotta watch 'em like hawks.'

Like Paul, like almost all the elders in the Garden, he was chaperoning a child — a handsome little boy about Helen's age, with eggshell-brown skin and eyes of an Oriental cast, shining as porcelain.

'Well,' said Paul, 'I suppose the circus excites them more than it does us.'

'You ain't kiddin'.'

Meanwhile, the two children were looking at each other with the sniffing, tremulous curiosity of strange dogs. And then Helen laughed and the little Negro boy laughed too, and in a twinkling they were comrades, sharing the delight of the strange world below.

Somehow Paul sensed that the Negro, like himself, felt a twinge of envy and sadness and bitterness at the instant blooming of this friendship, destined to wither at the touch of time. He saw them (and he knew the Negro man saw them too) many years hence, when their innocence would have fled, when speech between them would be a guarded mailed joust, a play of swords, implications, punctilio. He knew (and the Negro man knew) that this innocent clasping of hands, pink in eggshell brown, would not survive many more years, and perhaps it was this realization that lent an undertone of sadness to the wary speech between the two men, between all adult whites and adult blacks.

Simultaneously, the children cried, 'The clowns! Oooh, look at the clowns!' and bursting from the doors at each end of the arena came the extravagant shapes of fancy in a long procession.

Oh, the beloved clowns! Paul thought with a lift of his spirit. His boredom was gone. He forgot the Negro man; he forgot Helen; he could not take his eyes from the wonderful clowns performing all the tricks he had seen so many years ago. He was glad the tricks had not changed.

There was the ancient wheeze of the automobile with thirty passengers (the last one out being the Tallest Man in the World with the sour-faced midget on his shoulder). There was the inevitable clown who piled table upon table twenty feet high and then sat on a chair atop the precarious scaffolding, smoking a cigar as he nonchalantly rocked back and forth to the delighted screams of Helen, back and forth until he toppled with a terrific crash, harmlessly. There were magician clowns who waved bull-fight cloths over their colleagues who thereby were transformed into jackasses or goats. There was the prestidigitator clown pulling eggs out of his ears. There was the usual mad scramble at the bargain counter—with the riot call, the frantic whistling, the wig-pulling, the stereotyped chase, the deafening noise of blank cartridges fired by blue-helmeted cops.

There was the Sambo clown whose head suddenly shot off ten

feet into the air, to Paul's needless embarrassment, for his Negro friend laughed uproariously.

And most delightful of all, to Paul's freshly awakened eyes, was the red-wigged baggy-trousered clown who walked on mincing feet, while he delicately fluttered a fan that kept a fragile yellow paper butterfly in the air. Ever so often, he would stop fanning and softly catch the falling butterfly in his outstretched derby.

Around and around the track he went, performing the same wistful little stunt.

But aside from the innocent interludes of the clowns, Paul's afternoon proved a misery. His boredom had given way to terror. By the time the aerialists began their act, he was emotionally spent. In imagination he had flirted with death too many times that afternoon.

When the incredible Chinese tied his feet in a gunny sack and slid blindfolded down the inclined wire the entire length of the arena, Paul had turned his face away. When one obstreperous tiger refused to be prodded by pole or chair, onto his perch, and lunged and roared at the brave man in the cage, Paul completed in imagination the leap, the torn flesh, the blood. No, not even Helen's presence could help him, the wheel had turned too far, not even Helen. . . . As she gaped and gurgled with delight, he winced and sweated out every act. He had begun to doze off from sheer nervous exhaustion when the marvelous aerialists began their flights.

Helen was tugging at his sleeve. 'Paul! how can you sleep? Look what they're doing!'

He knew what they were doing. They were swinging from trapeze to trapeze, somersaulting, gripping the oncoming wrists at the last moment, twisting and diving and turning in a wondrous poetry of motion. All the same, Paul was grateful for the net. And when one of the girls missed and the crowd gasped and she fell deeply into the net and bounced to her feet, he was not even aware that he had averted his face until Helen asked him why.

'Why what?'

'Why did you turn your face away when the girl fell?'

'Oh, did I?'

'Yes.' She was grinning at him, making fun of his fear.

'I don't know,' Paul said. 'I guess I thought she might get hurt.'

'Oh, she couldn't get hurt,' the little girl said blandly. 'She fell on purpose . . . didn't she?' What had begun as a statement ended as a question, as she read some doubt in her uncle's face.

'Sho' she fell on purpose,' said the Negro man, winking to Paul. 'It's just part of the act.'

'Of course,' said Paul. 'Still I'm glad they've got a net.'

'Well, even if they didn't have a net,' persisted Helen, 'they'd do a flip-flop and land right on their feet, wouldn't they?'

'Yeah,' laughed the Negro. 'They got springs in their heels.'

The aerialists were gone, the wonderful aerialists, who had swooped and dived like birds in the smoky upper reaches of the Garden, had folded their wings, their nests were dismantled, the long afternoon was reaching its climax. And now the band flared up in brassy fanfare, and the metallic voice of the announcer cried, 'The Gallos! Death-defying artists of the High Wire!"

Six figures bounded into the spotlighted circle and bowed deeply. There were three men and three women. Their bodies magnificently proportioned: the V-tapering chests and slim waists of the men, the small breasts and firm flat buttocks of the women were clearly defined in identical tights of Lincoln green.

Swiftly they were hoisted to their platforms, more than one hundred feet above the hard board floor. Between the platforms stretched a tightrope almost at eye level with the balcony where Paul and Helen sat. And then began a series of exploits that paled everything that they had seen that afternoon, a performance so audacious that Paul could not bear to look upon it steadily.

O God, where are the nets? he thought, why don't they bring out the nets? But there were no nets. There was nothing between that high wire and the hard floor. The only concession the acrobats made to safety were long flexible balancing poles. And as the gossamer glint of wire trembled with its load of green figures, Helen dwelt ecstatically upon them; but Paul kept turning away, finding relief in the terraced row of spectators, the solid sanity of the iron girders of the Garden.

'Jesus. . . .' murmured the Negro.

Paul glanced again, sucked in his breath. Somehow he felt angry at these Gallos, the indecency of what they were doing, the indecency of holding life so cheaply. For what had begun excruciatingly enough when the first girl inched her away across that wire so high above the floor, continued to mount in intensity, horror piled upon horror, as the Gallos developed new complications in their stunts, just as a composer begins with a simple theme, then introduces a second theme, and weaves and embroiders, inverts and develops until he has achieved a shining fabric of emotional intensity.

So the Gallos wove their themes of danger and courage to the pitch where Paul's brow was dewed with sweat, and he had twisted his handkerchief into a tight grimy ball.

The Chinese who had slid so madly down the wire had stabbed him with fear. But this was worse. This was far worse. For the other fear had been over in a moment, like a flare of lightning, and then there had been the welcome sighs of relief, the laughing, bowing little figure in the distance, the blessed applause.

But this torture was slow, excruciating, endless. As the green figures moved warily across the wire, as man and woman passed each other on that aerial sidewalk attenuated beyond belief, as they mounted on each other's shoulders — they seemed to be deliberately performing all their deeds in slow motion to prolong the agony, to make each feat seem the limit of human courage, only to be superseded by another act even more daring.

No matter how often Paul forbore to look, he found himself returning again and again to the vision of those figures on the wire, staring at them with the fascinated revulsion of a voyeur.

Now they were taxing the very limits of credulity, and Helen clutched her uncle's wet hand and cried, 'Oh, Paul! Look what they're doing now! Do you think they'll fall?'

'Shhh. . . .' Paul whispered as if her loud words would blow them from the wire.

The Negro was leaning forward in his seat, his mouth open, the shadows purplish on his temples. He whistled with disbelief and shook his head.

For two of the Gallos had inched out upon the high wire and hoisted a bar with halters upon their shoulders. And now a girl was cautiously climbing up one of the young men's backs, slowly straddling his neck, creeping tremulously out upon the bar. The silvery wire vibrated like a piano string as she did a split upon the bar, and then she was climbing down, warily down, while the crowd held its breath and all three had slithered back to the platforms.

An audible sigh, a tremendous crackling of applause.

'Phew!' exclaimed the Negro, wiping his forehead as he turned to Paul. 'I'm sure glad that's over.'

'Can you do that, Daddy?' asked the little boy.

'Naw,' he grinned. 'What do you think I am — crazy?'

'I bet my Uncle Paul can do it,' Helen said with competitive pride.

'I bet he can't,' said Paul without a trace of humor. 'I bet he wouldn't even if he could.'

But he had no chance to say more. The trumpets were blowing, the lights were dimming. Soon the entire Garden was in darkness save for the smoke-laden convergence of beams upon the glint of wire. The Gallos had reached the climax of their act.

'Don't tell me they're going to ride out on those *bicycles!*' said a woman's voice behind Paul.

'Aw, that's easier than walkin',' scoffingly replied a man.

'Yeah, wise guy, let's see you do it.'

'Well, that's a damnfool thing to say. . . .'

From both platforms a cyclist had already begun to ride out on that unbelievable roadway, the long balancing poles swaying on the handle bars. And now the four other members of the troupe were slithering out on foot. It was the first time all six had been on the wire at the same time, and the wire tightened with the weight, its slack taken up in a tense arc.

Precariously balanced there in space in their Lincoln green tights and with their long flexible poles, they looked like six strange insects — huge Martian insects — waving their antennae in the air. Slowly the two pairs, a man and woman from each side, inched their way toward the two cyclists in the center. The wire trembled.

Paul was hunched forward in his seat. The roof of his mouth was dry. For the hundredth time during their act, he resented what the Gallos were doing, resented courage expended on so trivial a goal, and he was crying to himself over and over, Why don't they use a net? Why don't the damn fools use a net?

'Look, Paul,' Helen suddenly said, pointing down below. 'Just like firemen.'

Holding a small jump net no more than ten feet in diameter, were a group of assistants, straining their heads upward at the contemptuous Gallos, following their slow green progress across the wire.

Why this fake concession to safety? Paul thought bitterly. Whom are they trying to fool? They were only dramatizing the danger, slapping him harder in the face. The net was obviously inadequate.

But he had no time to reason further. A mounting drum roll heightened tension as the insectlike figures converged. A bar was slung from one cyclist's shoulders to the other; two acrobats were balancing themselves upon the bar. And then the living pyramid of green began to shimmer in Paul's eyes as with disbelief he saw another bar slung across the shoulders of the topmost figures, and the two remaining girls were climbing on their comrades' shoulders, up, up, up, until they stood upon the second bar, slowly swaying in the balance of the twenty-foot poles. It was absolutely incredible — two upon two — the cyclists, the men upon them, the girls upon them — all swaying on that spider strand a hundred and fifty feet above the floor.

And as they stood so, bathed in the rainbow-colored floodlights, a human pyramid of defiance, the crowd roared its approval, the mounting drum roll was punctuated by a cymbal crash, the men holding the fire net strained their tense faces upward, and then the Gallos began slowly to dismount.

When they fell, Paul wasn't surprised. It was logical that they should fall. It was the only possible culmination to the forebodings he had felt all afternoon. Yes, when the woman behind him screamed with such agony, when the Negro gurgled, 'Ahhh,' like a death rattle, and the great crowd gasped like a wounded dinosaur, Paul knew what had happened before his eyes saw it. Yes, it was inevitable that the Gallos should fall at the very pinnacle of their defiance, at the moment of dismounting — it was his childhood that was falling; his faith, his innocence tumbling from the wire in a bizarre conglomeration of green limbs and whirling bicycles.

He heard a rapid succession of sickening thuds — one, two, three, four — as the Gallos hit the floor. One woman landed on her back in the small net which had scurried frantically back and forth beneath the falling green flashes in a pathetic attempt to catch them all.

Another had hit one of the bearers of the net, and the two of them sat on the floor staring into each other's faces with dazed, surprised expressions. The acrobat's green legs were twisted grotesquely backward like a frog's.

But all the other Gallos had smashed upon the boards. Some lay still. Others were twitching in their green tights like grasshoppers squashed under a heel. In the center of the ring, a girl had landed on her back—her head awry, her tights split open at the bosom so that her pink naked breasts lay exposed like the soft flesh within the green shell of a sea creature. Blood was trickling from her mouth.

One body was entangled in the twisted spokes of a wheel. The other cyclist was draped ungracefully across the wooden rim of the center ring. At his feet, a close-cropped dark-haired girl was moaning, her arms reaching upward, her fingers clenching and unclenching in indescribable convulsions.

And now the crowd recovered from its first shock, and Paul felt himself rocking in a litany of mourners—the singsong of hysteria, the Negro crying over and over, 'Jesus Christ! Jesus Christ!' the woman behind him screaming mechanically like a car horn out of order, the herdlike trampling of panicky feet as exodus began, the young man puking on the stony stairs.

Below them in the pit of horror, stretcher bearers had appeared. Doctors were bending over the green broken insects. The mauled parts of the bicycles were being gathered together; tarpaulins covered the pools of blood.

Then all at once, the incongruous blare of the band sounded, playing an exit march. The circus was over. Paul shook Helen's shoulder and said softly, 'Come, darling, the show is over.'

She was still staring silently down at the pit. She had not moved or spoken once since the Gallos fell. Her little hands tightly gripped the guardrail. Paul tapped her shoulder again. She turned around and stared at him. Her eyes were wide open, perplexed, but she said nothing as he repeated, 'Come, darling. It's all over now.'

As they made their way down the steps, stifled in a crowd of solemn adults and squeaking children, Helen suddenly broke her silence. She looked up at her uncle's face with a suddenly radiant smile, as if she had just thought of something, 'It was all part of the act, wasn't it, Paul?'

*'What?'*

'Their falling down. . . . They did it on purpose, didn't they?'

He heard a splutter of cruel laughter near by. A motherly-looking woman glanced at Paul with tear-pinked pitying eyes. *'Oy, Gott! Gott!'* she moaned in Yiddish, her palm flat against her cheek, *'Was weis'n sie, die kinder?'* Paul's lips tightened.

They were out of the Garden at last, standing at the northeast corner of Forty-ninth Street and Eighth Avenue, waiting for the traffic lights to change.

An excited crowd still poured, black and molten, from the front gate, swirled around them, siphoned off down the side streets. Paul stared at the passing figures without comprehension. He could catch scraps of conversation, but even without this he would have known by their gestures what they were talking about. He thought he saw his Negro friend and the little boy crossing the street. He felt drugged, sick with memory. How could they talk so much? Helen's voice shocked him awake: 'You didn't answer me, Paul.'

'What, dear?'

He stooped over her; solicitous, henlike, feeling her small in the shadow of his wings.

'They weren't *really* hurt, were they?' Her hazel eyes were pleading now.

'No,' he said abruptly.

'They fell on purpose, didn't they?' Her birdlike voice trailed off—shreds of questions, of answers, of innocence ravaged by the event. 'It was all part of the act, wasn't it?'

He stared down Eighth Avenue. The afternoon had turned gray. The city was without bulk, one-dimensional. Drizzle hung in the air like dots of a newspaper photograph. In the middle distance he could see the McGraw-Hill Building, dull green against the misty sky. Something was . . . He turned away. At the intersection of Forty-ninth and Eighth, a clown cop was directing traffic. Every time the lights changed, his head shot ten feet into the air. In the neon blaze of a bar, the legless-armless girl was selling pencils on the sidewalk. Gargantua leered from a cheap hotel. From one green parapet of the McGraw-Hill Building, tiny figures appeared, walking on air. The invisible tightrope stretched river to river. The sky grew dark. The acrobats were tottering. . . .

'Of course,' Paul said.

(*From Partisan Review*)

# A DISTANT EPISODE

## BY PAUL BOWLES

THE *SEPTEMBER* sunsets were at their reddest the week the Professor decided to visit Aïn Tadouirt, which is in the warm country. He came down out of the high, flat region in the evening by bus, with two small overnight bags full of maps, sun lotions, and medicines. Ten years ago he had been in the village for three days; long enough, however, to establish a fairly firm friendship with a cafékeeper, who had written him several times during the first year after his visit, if never since. 'Hassan Ramani,' the Professor said over and over, as the bus bumped downward through ever warmer layers of air. Now facing the flaming sky in the west, and now facing the sharp mountains, the car followed the dusty trail down the canyons into air which began to smell of other things besides the endless ozone of the heights: orange blossoms, pepper, sun-baked excrement, burning olive oil, rotten fruit. He closed his eyes happily and lived for an instant in a purely olfactory world. The distant past returned—what part of it, he could not decide.

The chauffeur, whose seat the Professor shared, spoke to him without taking his eyes from the road. *'Vous êtes géologue?'*

'A geologist? Ah, no! I'm a linguist.'

'There are no languages here. Only dialects.'

'Exactly. I'm making a survey of variations on Moghrebi.'

The chauffeur was scornful. 'Keep on going south,' he said. 'You'll find some languages you never heard of before.'

As they drove through the town gate, the usual swarm of urchins rose up out of the dust and ran screaming beside the bus. The

Professor folded his dark glasses, put them in his pocket; and as soon as the vehicle had come to a standstill he jumped out, pushing his way through the indignant boys who clutched at his luggage in vain, and walked quickly into the Grand Hotel Saharien. Out of its eight rooms there were two available — one facing the market and the other, a smaller and cheaper one, giving onto a tiny yard full of refuse and barrels, where two gazelles wandered about. He took the smaller room, and pouring the entire pitcher of water into the tin basin, began to wash the grit from his face and ears. The afterglow was nearly gone from the sky, and the pinkness in objects was disappearing, almost as he watched. He lit the carbide lamp and winced at its odor.

After dinner the Professor walked slowly through the streets to Hassan Ramani's café, whose back room hung hazardously out above the river. The entrance was very low, and he had to bend down slightly to get in. A man was tending the fire. There was one guest sipping tea. The caouadji tried to make him take a seat at the other table in the front room, but the Professor walked airily ahead into the back room and sat down. The moon was shining through the reed latticework and there was not a sound outside but the occasional distant bark of a dog. He changed tables so he could see the river. It was dry, but there was a pool here and there that reflected the bright night sky. The caouadji came in and wiped off the table.

'Does this café still belong to Hassan Ramani?' he asked him in the Moghrebi he had taken four years to learn.

The man replied in bad French: 'He is deceased.'

'Deceased?' repeated the Professor, without noticing the absurdity of the word. 'Really? When?'

'I don't know,' said the caouadji. 'One tea?'

'Yes. But I don't understand . . .'

The man was already out of the room, fanning the fire. The Professor sat still, feeling lonely, and arguing with himself that to do so was ridiculous. Soon the caouadji returned with the tea. He paid him and gave him an enormous tip, for which he received a grave bow.

'Tell me,' he said, as the other started away. 'Can one still get those little boxes made from camel udders?'

The man looked angry. 'Sometimes the Reguibat bring in those things. We do not buy them here.' Then insolently, in Arabic: 'And why a camel-udder box?'

'Because I like them,' retorted the Professor. And then because he was feeling a little exalted, he added, 'I like them so much I want to make a collection of them, and I will pay you ten francs for every one you can get me.'

*'Khamstache,'* said the caouadji, opening his left hand rapidly three times in succession.

'Never. Ten.'

'Not possible. But wait until later and come with me. You can give me what you like. And you will get camel-udder boxes if there are any.'

He went out into the front room, leaving the Professor to drink his tea and listen to the growing chorus of dogs that barked and howled as the moon rose higher into the sky. A group of customers came into the front room and sat talking for an hour or so. When they had left, the caouadji put out the fire and stood in the doorway putting on his burnous. 'Come,' he said.

Outside in the street there was very little movement. The booths were all closed and the only light came from the moon. An occasional pedestrian passed, and grunted a brief greeting to the caouadji.

'Everyone knows you,' said the Professor, to cut the silence between them.

'Yes.'

'I wish everyone knew me,' said the Professor, before he realized how infantile such a remark must sound.

'*No* one knows you,' said his companion gruffly.

They had come to the other side of the town, on the promontory above the desert, and through a great rift in the wall the Professor saw the white endlessness, broken in the foreground by dark spots of oasis. They walked through the opening and followed a winding road between the rocks, downward toward the nearest small forest of palms. The Professor thought: 'He may cut my throat. But his café — he would surely be found out.'

'Is it far?' he asked, casually.

'Are you tired?' countered the caouadji.

'They are expecting me back at the Hotel Saharien,' he lied.

'You can't be there and here,' said the caouadji.

The Professor laughed. He wondered if it sounded uneasy to the other.

'Have you owned Ramani's café long?'

'I work there for a friend.' The reply made the Professor more unhappy than he had imagined it would.

'Oh! Will you work tomorrow?'

'That is impossible to say.'

The Professor stumbled on a stone, and fell, scraping his hand. The caouadji said: 'Be careful.'

The sweet black odor of rotten meat hung in the air suddenly.

'Agh!' said the Professor, choking. 'What is it?'

The caouadji had covered his face with his burnous and did not answer. Soon the stench had been left behind. They were on flat ground. Ahead the path was bordered on each side by a high mud wall. There was no breeze and the palms were quite still, but behind the walls was the sound of running water. Also, the odor of human excrement was almost constant as they walked between the walls.

The Professor waited until he thought it seemed logical for him to ask with a certain degree of annoyance: 'But where are we going?'

'Soon,' said his guide, pausing to gather some stones in the ditch. 'Pick up some stones,' he advised. 'Here are bad dogs.'

'Where?' asked the Professor, but he stooped and got three large ones with pointed edges.

They continued very quietly. The walls came to an end and the bright desert lay ahead. Nearby was a ruined marabout, with its tiny dome only half standing, and the front wall entirely destroyed. Behind it were clumps of stunted, useless palms. A dog came running crazily toward them on three legs. Not until it got quite close did the Professor hear its steady low growl. The caouadji let fly a large stone at it, striking it square in the muzzle. There was a strange snapping of jaws and the dog ran sideways in another direction, falling blindly against rocks and scrambling haphazardly about like an injured insect.

Turning off the road, they walked across the earth strewn with sharp stones, past the little ruin, through the trees, until they came to a place where the ground dropped abruptly away in front of them.

'It looks like a quarry,' said the Professor, resorting to French for the word 'quarry,' whose Arabic equivalent he could not call to mind at the moment. The caouadji did not answer. Instead he stood still and turned his head, as if listening. And indeed, from somewhere down below, but very far below, came the faint sound of a low flute. The caouadji nodded his head slowly several times. Then he said: 'The path begins here. You can see it well all the way. The rock is white and the moon is strong. So you can see well. I am going back now and sleep. It is late. You can give me what you like.'

Standing there at the edge of the abyss which at each moment looked deeper, with the dark face of the caouadji framed in its moonlit burnous close to his own face, the Professor asked himself exactly what he felt. Indignation, curiosity, fear, perhaps, but most of all relief and the hope that this was not a trick, the hope that the caouadji would really leave him alone and turn back without him.

He stepped away a little from the edge, and fumbled in his pocket for a loose note, because he did not want to show his wallet. Fortunately there was a fifty franc bill there, which he took out and handed to the man. He knew the caouadji was pleased, and so he paid no attention when he heard him saying: 'It is not enough. I have to walk a long way home and there are dogs. . . .'

'Thank you and good night,' said the Professor, sitting down with his legs drawn up under him, and lighting a cigarette. He felt almost happy.

'Give me only one cigarette,' pleaded the man.

'Of course,' he said, a bit curtly, and he held up the pack.

The caouadji squatted close beside him. His face was not pleasant to see. 'What is it,' thought the Professor, terrified again, as he held out his lighted cigarette toward him.

The man's eyes were almost closed. It was the most obvious registering of concentrated scheming the Professor had ever seen. When the second cigarette was burning, he ventured to say to the still squatting Arab: 'What are you thinking about?'

The other drew on his cigarette deliberately, and seemed about to speak. Then his expression changed to one of satisfaction, but he did not speak. A cool wind had risen in the air, and the Professor shivered. The sound of the flute came up from the depths below at intervals, sometimes mingled with the scraping of nearby palm fronds one against the other. 'These people are not primitives,' the Professor found himself saying in his mind.

'Good,' said the caouadji, rising slowly. 'Keep your money. Fifty francs is enough. It is an honor.' Then he went back into

French: *'Ti n'as qu'à discendre, to' droit.'* He spat, chuckled (or was the Professor hysterical?'), and strode away quickly.

The Professor was in a state of nerves. He lit another cigarette, and found his lips moving automatically. They were saying: 'Is this a situation or a predicament? This is ridiculous.' He sat very still for several minutes, waiting for a sense of reality to come to him. He stretched out on the hard, cold ground and looked up at the moon. It was almost like looking straight at the sun. If he shifted his gaze a little at a time, he could make a string of weaker moons across the sky. 'Incredible,' he whispered. Then he sat up quickly and looked about. There was no guarantee that the caouadji really had gone back to town. He got to his feet and looked over the edge of the precipice. In the moonlight the bottom seemed miles away. And there was nothing to give it scale; not a tree, not a house, not a person. . . . He listened for the flute, and heard only the wind going by his ears. A sudden violent desire to run back to the road seized him, and he turned and looked in the direction the caouadji had taken. At the same time he felt softly of his wallet in his breast pocket. Then he spat over the edge of the cliff. Then he made water over it, and listened intently, like a child. This gave him the impetus to start down the path into the abyss. Curiously enough, he was not dizzy. But prudently he kept from peering to his right, over the edge. It was a steady and steep downward climb. The monotony of it put him into a frame of mind not unlike that which had been induced by the bus ride. He was murmuring 'Hassan Ramani' again, repeatedly and in rhythm. He stopped, furious with himself for the sinister overtones the name now suggested to him. He decided he was exhausted from the trip. 'And the walk,' he added.

He was now well down the gigantic cliff, but the moon, being directly overhead, gave as much light as ever. Only the wind was left behind, above, to wander among the trees, to blow through the dusty streets of Aïn Tadouirt, into the hall of the Grand Hotel Saharien, and under the door of his little room.

It occurred to him that he ought to ask himself why he was doing this irrational thing, but he was intelligent enough to know that since he was doing it, it was not so important to probe for explanations at that moment.

Suddenly the earth was flat beneath his feet. He had reached the bottom sooner than he had expected. He stepped ahead distrustfully still, as if he expected another treacherous drop. It was so hard to know in this uniform, dim brightness. Before he knew what had happened the dog was upon him, a heavy mass of fur trying to push him backwards, a sharp nail rubbing down his chest, a straining of muscles against him to get the teeth into his neck. The Professor thought: 'I refuse to die this way.' The dog fell back; it looked like an Eskimo dog. As it sprang again, he called out, very loud: 'Ay!' It fell against him, there was a confusion of sensations and a pain somewhere. There was also the sound of voices very near to him, and he could not understand what they were saying. Something cold and metallic was pushed brutally against his spine as the dog still hung for a second by his teeth from a mass of clothing and perhaps flesh. The Professor knew it was a gun, and he raised his hands, shouting in Moghrebi: 'Take away the dog!' But the gun merely pushed him forward, and since the dog, once it was back on the ground, did not leap again, he took a step ahead. The gun kept pushing; he kept taking steps. Again he heard voices, but the person directly behind him said nothing. People seemed to be running about; it sounded that way, at least. For his eyes, he discovered, were still shut tight against the dog's attack. He opened them. A group of men was advancing toward him. They were dressed in the black clothes of the Reguibat. 'The Reguibat is a cloud across the face of the sun.' 'When the Reguibat appears the righteous man turns away.' In how many shops and market places he had heard these maxims uttered banteringly among friends. Never to a Reguibat, to be sure, for these men do not frequent towns. They send a representative in disguise, to arrange with shady elements there for the disposal of captured goods. 'An opportunity,' he thought quickly, 'of testing the accuracy of such statements.' He did not doubt for a moment that the adventure would prove to be a kind of warning against such foolishness on his part — a warning which in retrospect would be half sinister, half farcical.

Two snarling dogs came running from behind the oncoming men and threw themselves at his legs. He was scandalized to note that no one paid any attention to this breach of etiquette. The gun pushed him harder as he tried to sidestep the animals' noisy assault. Again he cried: 'The dogs! Take them away!' The gun shoved him forward with great force and he fell, almost at the feet of the crowd of men facing him. The dogs were wrenching at his hands and arms. A boot kicked them aside, yelping, and then with increased vigor it kicked the Professor in the hip. Then came a chorus of kicks from different sides, and he was rolled violently about on the earth for a while. During this time he was conscious of hands reaching into his pockets and removing everything from them. He tried to say: 'You have all my money; stop kicking me!' But his bruised facial muscles would not work; he felt himself pouting, and that was all. Someone dealt him a terrific blow on the head, and he thought: 'Now at least I shall lose consciousness, thank Heaven.' Still he went on being aware of the guttural voices he could not understand, and of being bound tightly about the ankles and chest. Then there was black silence that opened like a wound from time to time, to let in the soft, deep notes of the flute playing the same succession of notes again and again. Suddenly, he felt excruciating pain everywhere — pain and cold. 'So I have been unconscious, after all,' he thought. In spite of that, the present seemed only like a direct continuation of what had gone before.

It was growing faintly light. There were camels near where he was lying; he could hear their gurgling and their heavy breathing. He could not bring himself to attempt opening his eyes, just in case it should turn out to be impossible. However, when he heard someone approaching, he found that he had no difficulty in seeing.

The man looked at him dispassionately in the gray morning light. With one hand he pinched together the Professor's nostrils. When the Professor opened his mouth to breathe, the man swiftly seized his tongue and pulled on it with all his might. The Professor was gagging and catching his breath; he did not see what was happening. He could not distinguish the pain of the brutal yanking from that of the sharp knife. Then there was an endless choking and spitting that went on automatically, as though he were scarcely a part of it. The word "operation" kept going through his mind; it calmed his terror somewhat as he sank back into darkness.

The caravan left sometime toward midmorning. The Professor, not unconscious, but in a state of utter stupor, still gagging and drooling blood, was dumped doubled-up into a sack and tied at one side of a camel. The lower end of the enormous amphitheater contained a natural gate in the rocks. The camels, swift mehara, were lightly laden on this trip. They passed through single file, and slowly mounted the gentle slope that led up into the beginning of the desert.

That night, at a stop behind some low hills, the men took him out, still in a state which permitted no thought, and over the dusty rags that remained of his clothing they fastened a series of curious belts made of the bottoms of tin cans strung together. One after another of these bright girdles was wired about his torso, his arms and legs, even across his face, until he was entirely within a suit of armor that covered him with its circular metal scales. There was a good deal of merriment during this decking-out of the Professor. One man brought out a flute and a younger one did a not ungraceful caricature of an Ouled Naïl executing a cane dance. The Professor was no longer conscious; to be exact, he existed in the middle of the movements made by these other men. When they had finished dressing him the way they wished him to look, they stuffed some food under the tin bangles hanging over his face. Even though he chewed mechanically, most of it eventually fell out onto the ground. They put him back into the sack and left him there.

Two days later they arrived at one of their own encampments. There were women and children here in the tents, and the men had to drive away the snarling dogs they had left there to guard them. When they emptied the Professor out of his sack, there were screams of fright, and it took several hours to convince the last woman that he was harmless, although there had been no doubt from the start that he was a valuable possession. After a few days they began to move on again, taking everything with them, and traveling only at night as the terrain grew warmer.

Even when all his wounds had healed and he felt no more pain, the Professor did not begin to think again; he ate and defecated, and he danced when he was bidden, a senseless hopping up and down that delighted the children, principally because of the wonderful jangling racket it made. And he generally slept through the heat of the day, in among the camels.

Wending its way southeast, the caravan avoided all stationary civilization. In a few weeks they reached a new plateau, wholly wild and with a sparse vegetation. Here they pitched camp and remained, while the mehara were turned loose to graze. Everyone was happy here; the weather was cooler and there was a well only a few hours away on a seldom-frequented trail. It was here they conceived the idea of taking the Professor to Amedjel and selling him to the Touareg.

It was a full year before they carried out this project. By this time the Professor was much better trained. He could do a handspring, make a series of fearful growling noises which had, nevertheless, a certain element of humor; and when the Reguibat removed the tin from his face they discovered he could grimace admirably while he danced. They also taught him a few basic obscene gestures which never failed to elicit delighted shrieks from the women. He was now brought forth only after especially abundant meals, when there was music and festivity. He easily fell in with their sense of ritual, and evolved an elementary sort of "program" to present when he was called forth: dancing, rolling on the ground, imitating certain animals, and finally rushing toward the group in feigned anger, to see the resultant confusion and hilarity.

When three of the men set out for Amedjel with him, they took four mehara with them, and he rode astride his quite naturally. No precautions were taken to guard him, save that he was kept among them, one man always staying at the rear of the party. They came within sight of the walls at dawn, and they waited among the rocks all day. At dusk the youngest started out, and in three hours he returned with a friend who carried a stout cane. They tried to put the Professor through his routine then and there, but the man from Amedjel was in a hurry to get back to town, so they all set out on the mehara.

In the town they went directly to the villager's home, where they had coffee in the courtyard sitting among the camels. Here the Professor went into his act again, and this time there was prolonged merriment and much rubbing together of hands. An agreement was reached, a sum of money paid, and the Reguibat withdrew, leaving the Professor in the house of the man with the cane, who did not delay in locking him into a tiny enclosure off the courtyard.

The next day was an important one in the Professor's life, for it was then that pain began to stir again in his being. A group of men came to the house, among whom was a venerable gentleman, better clothed than those others who spent their time flattering him, setting fervent kisses upon his hands and the edges of his garments. This person made a point of going into classical Arabic from time to time, to impress the others, who had not learned a word of the Koran. Thus his conversation would run more or less as follows: 'Perhaps at In Salah. The French there are stupid. Celestial vengeance is approaching. Let us not hasten it. Praise the highest and cast thine anathema against idols. With paint on his face. In case the police wish to look close.' The others listened and agreed, nodding their heads slowly and solemnly. And the Professor in his stall beside them listened, too. That is, he was *conscious* of the sound of the old man's Arabic. The words penetrated for the first time in many months. Noises, then: 'Celestial vengeance is approaching.' Then: 'It is an honor. Fifty francs is enough. Keep your money. Good.' And the caouadji squatting near him at the edge of the precipice. Then 'anathema against idols' and more gibberish. He turned over panting on the sand and forgot about it. But the pain had begun. It operated in a kind of delirium, because he had begun to enter into consciousness again. When the man opened the door and prodded him with his cane, he cried out in a rage, and everyone laughed.

They got him onto his feet, but he would not dance. He stood before them, staring at the ground, stubbornly refusing to move. The owner was furious, and so annoyed by the laughter of the others that he felt obliged to send them away, saying that he would await a more propitious time for exhibiting his property, because he dared not show his anger before the elder. However, when they had left he dealt the Professor a violent blow on the shoulder with his cane, called him various obscene things, and went out into the street, slamming the gate behind him. He walked straight to the street of the Ouled Naïl, because he was sure of finding the Reguibat there among the girls, spending the money. And there in a tent he found one of them still abed, while an Ouled Naïl washed the tea glasses. He walked in and almost decapitated the man before the latter had even attempted to sit up. Then he threw his razor on the bed and ran out.

The Ouled Naïl saw the blood, screamed, ran out of her tent into the next, and soon emerged from that with four girls who rushed together into the coffee house and told the caouadji who had killed the Reguibat. It was only a matter of an hour before the French military police had caught him at a friend's house, and dragged him off to the barracks. That night the Professor had nothing to eat, and the next afternoon, in the slow sharpening of his consciousness caused by increasing hunger, he walked aimlessly about the courtyard and the rooms that gave onto it. There was no one. In one room a calendar hung on the wall. The Professor watched nervously, like a dog watching a fly in front of its nose. On the white paper were black objects that made sounds in his head. He heard them: *'Grande Epicerie du Sahel. Juin. Lundi, Mardi, Mercredi. . . .'*

The tiny inkmarks of which a symphony consists may have been made long ago, but when they are fulfilled in sound they become imminent and mighty. So a kind of music of feeling began to play in the Professor's head, increasing in volume as he looked at the mud wall, and he had the feeling that he was performing what had been written for him long ago. He felt like weeping; he felt like roaring through the little house, upsetting and smashing the few breakable objects. His emotion got no further than this one overwhelming desire. So, bellowing as loud as he could, he attacked the house and its belongings. Then he attacked the door into the street, which resisted for a while and finally broke. He climbed through the opening made by the boards he had ripped apart, and still bellowing and shaking his arms in the air to make as loud a jangling as possible, he began to gallop along the quiet street toward the gateway of the town. A few people looked at him with great curiosity. As he passed the garage, the last building before the high mud archway that framed the desert beyond, a French soldier saw him. *'Tiens,'* he said to himself, 'a holy maniac.'

Again it was sunset time. The Professor ran beneath the arched gate, turned his face toward the red sky, and began to trot along the Piste d'In Salah, straight into the setting sun. Behind him, from the garage, the soldier took a pot shot at him for good luck. The bullet whistled dangerously near the Professor's head, and his yelling rose into an indignant lament as he waved his arms more wildly, and hopped high into the air at every few steps, in an access of terror.

The soldier watched a while, smiling, as the cavorting figure grew smaller in the oncoming evening darkness, and the rattling of the tin became a part of the great silence out there beyond the gate. The wall of the garage as he leaned against it still gave forth heat, left there by the sun, but even then the lunar chill was growing in the air.

(*From The New Yorker*)

# I SEE YOU NEVER

BY RAY BRADBURY

*THE SOFT KNOCK* came at the kitchen door, and when Mrs. O'Brian opened it, there on the back porch were her best tenant, Mr. Ramirez, and two police officers, one on each side of him. Mr. Ramirez just stood there, walled in and small.

'Why, Mr. Ramirez!' said Mrs. O'Brian.

Mr. Ramirez was overcome. He did not seem to have words to explain.

He had arrived at Mrs. O'Brian's rooming house more than two years earlier and had lived there ever since. He had come by bus from Mexico City to San Diego and had then gone up to Los Angeles. There he had found the clean little room, with glossy blue linoleum, and pictures and calendars on the flowered walls, and Mrs. O'Brian as the strict but kindly landlady. During the war, he had worked at the airplane factory and made parts for the planes that flew off somewhere, and even now, after the war, he still held his job. From the first, he had made big money. He saved some of it, and he got drunk only once a week — a privilege that, to Mrs. O'Brian's way of thinking, every good workingman deserved, unquestioned and unreprimanded.

Inside Mrs. O'Brian's kitchen, pies were baking in the oven. Soon the pies would come out with complexions like Mr. Ramirez's, brown and shiny and crisp, with slits in them for the air almost like the slits of Mr. Ramirez's dark eyes. The kitchen smelled good. The policemen leaned forward, lured by the odor. Mr. Ramirez gazed at his feet, as if they had carried him into all this trouble.

'What happened, Mr. Ramirez?' asked Mrs. O'Brian.

Behind Mrs. O'Brian, as he lifted his eyes, Mr. Ramirez saw the long table, laid with clean white linen and set with a platter, cool, shining glasses, a water pitcher with ice cubes floating inside it, a bowl of fresh potato salad, and one of bananas and oranges, cubed and sugared. At this table sat Mrs. O'Brian's children — her three grown sons, eating and conversing, and her two younger daughters, who were staring at the policemen as they ate.

'I have been here thirty months,' said Mr. Ramirez quietly, looking at Mrs. O'Brian's plump hands.

'That's six months too long,' said one policeman. 'He only had a temporary visa. We've just got around to looking for him.'

Soon after Mr. Ramirez had arrived, he bought a radio for his little room; evenings, he turned it up very loud and enjoyed it. And he had bought a wrist-watch and enjoyed that, too. And on many nights he had walked silent streets and seen the bright clothes in the windows and bought some of them, and he had seen the jewels and bought some of them for his few lady friends. And he had gone to picture shows five nights a week for a while. Then, also, he had ridden the streetcars — all night some nights — smelling the electricity, his dark eyes moving over the advertisements, feeling the wheels rumble under him, watching the little sleeping houses and big hotels slip by. Besides that, he had gone to large restaurants, where he had eaten many-course dinners, and to the opera and the theatre. And he had bought a car, which later, when he forgot to pay for it, the dealer had driven off angrily from in front of the rooming house.

'So here I am,' said Mr. Ramirez now, 'to tell you that I must give up my room, Mrs. O'Brian. I come to get my baggage and clothes and go with these men.'

'Back to Mexico?'

'Yes. To Lagos. That is a little town north of Mexico City.'

'I'm sorry, Mr. Ramirez.'

'I'm packed,' said Mr. Ramirez hoarsely, blinking his dark eyes rapidly and moving his hands helplessly before him. The policemen did not touch him. There was no necessity for that. 'Here is the key, Mrs. O'Brian,' Mr. Ramirez said, 'I have my bag already.'

Mrs. O'Brian, for the first time, noticed a suitcase standing behind him on the porch.

Mr. Ramirez looked in again at the huge kitchen, at the bright silver cutlery and the young people eating and the shining waxed floor. He turned and looked for a long moment at the apartment house next door, rising up three stories, high and beautiful. He looked at the balconies and fire escapes and back-porch stairs, at the lines of laundry snapping in the wind.

'You've been a good tenant,' said Mrs. O'Brian.

'Thank you, thank you, Mrs. O'Brian,' he said softly. He closed his eyes.

Mrs. O'Brian stood holding the door half open. One of her sons, behind her, said that her dinner was getting cold, but she shook her head at him and turned back to Mr. Ramirez. She remembered a visit she had once made to some Mexican border towns — the hot days, the endless crickets leaping and falling or lying dead and brittle like the small cigars in the shop windows, and the canals taking river water out to the farms, the dirt roads, the scorched fields, the little adobe houses, the bleached clothes, the eroded landscape. She remembered the silent towns, the warm beer, the hot, thick foods each day. She remembered the slow, dragging horses and the parched jack rabbits on the road. She remembered the iron mountains and the dusty valleys and the ocean beaches that spread hundreds of miles with no sound but the waves — no cars, no buildings, nothing.

'I'm sure sorry, Mr. Ramirez,' she said.

'I don't want to go back, Mrs. O'Brian,' he said weakly. 'I like it here. I want to stay here. I've worked, I've got money. I look all right, don't I? And I don't want to go back!'

'I'm sorry, Mr. Ramirez,' she said. 'I wish there was something I could do.'

'Mrs. O'Brian!' he cried suddenly, tears rolling out from under his eyelids. He reached out his hands and took her hand fervently, shaking it, wringing it, holding to it. 'Mrs. O'Brian, I see you never, I see you never!'

The policemen smiled at this, but Mr. Ramirez did not notice it, and they stopped smiling very soon.

'Goodbye, Mrs. O'Brian. You have been good to me. Oh, goodbye, Mrs. O'Brian. I see you never!'

The policemen waited for Mr. Ramirez to turn, pick up his suitcase, and walk away. Then they followed him, tipping their caps to Mrs. O'Brian. She watched them go down the porch steps. Then she shut the door quietly and went slowly back to her chair at the table. She pulled the chair out and sat down. She picked up the shining knife and fork and started once more upon her steak.

'Hurry up, Mom,' said one of the sons. 'It'll be cold.'

Mrs. O'Brian took one bite and chewed on it for a long, slow time; then she stared at the closed door. She laid down her knife and fork.

'What's wrong, Ma?' asked her son.

'I just realized,' said Mrs. O'Brian — she put her hand to her face — 'I'll never see Mr. Ramirez again.'

(*From Ladies' Home Journal*)

# THE APPRENTICE

## BY DOROTHY CANFIELD

THE DAY had been one of the unbearable ones, when every sound had set her teeth on edge like chalk creaking on a blackboard, when every word her father or mother said to her or did not say to her seemed an intentional injustice. And of course it would happen, as the fitting end to such a day, that just as the sun went down back of the mountain and the long twilight began, she noticed that Rollie was not around.

Tense with exasperation at what her mother would say, she began to call him in a carefully casual tone — she would simply explode if mother got going: 'Here Rollie! He-ere boy! Want to go for a walk, Rollie?' Whistling to him cheerfully, her heart full of wrath at the way the world treated her, she made the rounds of his haunts: the corner of the woodshed, where he liked to curl up on the wool of father's discarded old sweater; the hay barn, the cow barn, the sunny spot on the side porch. No Rollie.

Perhaps he had sneaked upstairs to lie on her bed, where he was not supposed to go — not that *she* would have minded! That rule was a part of mother's fussiness, part, too, of mother's bossiness. It was *her* bed, wasn't it? But was she allowed the say-so about it? Not on your life. They *said* she could have things the way she wanted in her own room, now she was in her teens, but —— Her heart burned at unfairness as she took the stairs stormily, two steps at a time, her pigtails flopping up and down on her back. If Rollie was there, she was just going to let him stay there, and mother could say what she wanted to.

But he was not there. The bedspread and pillow were crumpled, but that was where she had flung herself down to cry that afternoon. Every nerve in her had been twanging discordantly, but she couldn't cry. She could only lie there, her hands doubled up hard, furious that she had nothing to cry about. Not really. She was too big to cry just over father's having said to her, severely, 'I told you if I let you take the chess set, you were to put it away when you got through with it. One of the pawns was on the floor of our bedroom this morning. I stepped on it. If I'd had my shoes on I'd have broken it.'

Well, he *had* told her that. And he hadn't said she mustn't ever take the set again. No, the instant she thought about that, she knew she couldn't cry about it. She could be, and was, in a rage about the way father kept on talking, long after she'd got his point: 'It's not that I care so much about the chess set. It's because if you don't learn how to take care of things, you yourself will suffer for it. You'll forget or neglect something that will be really important for *you.* We *have* to try to teach you to be responsible for what you've said you'll take care of. If we——' on and on.

She stood there, dry-eyed, by the bed that Rollie had not crumpled and thought, *I hope mother sees the spread and says something about Rollie—I just hope she does.* .. .. .. .. ..

She heard her mother coming down the hall, and hastily shut her door. She had a right to shut the door to her own room, hadn't she? She had *some* rights, she supposed, even if she was only thirteen and the youngest child. If her mother opened it to say, 'What are you doing in here that you don't want me to see?' she'd say—she'd just say——

But her mother did not open the door. Her feet went steadily on along the hall, and then, carefully, slowly, down the stairs. She probably had an armful of winter things she was bringing down from the attic. She was probably thinking that a tall, thirteen-year-old daughter was big enough to help with a chore like that. But she wouldn't *say* anything. She would just get out that insulting look of a grownup silently putting up with a crazy unreasonable kid. She had worn that expression all day; it was too much to be endured.

Up in her bedroom behind her closed door the thirteen-year-old stamped her foot in a gust of uncontrollable rage, none the less savage and heartshaking because it was mysterious to her.

But she had not located Rollie. She would be cut into little pieces before she would let her father and mother know she had lost sight of him, forgotten about him. They would not scold her, she knew. They would do worse; they would look at her. And in their silence she would hear, droning on reproachfully, what they had said when she had been begging to keep for her own the sweet, woolly collie puppy in her arms.

How warm he had felt! Astonishing how warm and alive a puppy was compared with a doll! She had never liked her dolls much after she had held Rollie, feeling him warm against her breast, warm and wriggling, bursting with life, reaching up to lick her face. He had loved her from that first instant. As he felt her arms around him his liquid, beautiful eyes had melted in trusting sweetness. And they did now, whenever he looked at her. Her dog was the only creature in the world who *really* loved her, she thought passionately.

And back then, at the very minute when, as a darling baby dog, he was beginning to love her, her father and mother were saying, so cold, so reasonable — gosh, how she *hated* reasonableness! — "Now, Peg, remember that, living where we do, with sheep on the farms around us, it is a serious responsibility to have a collie dog. If you keep him, you've got to be the one to take care of him. You'll have to be the one to train him to stay at home. We're too busy with you children to start bringing up a puppy too.'

Rollie, nestling in her arms, let one hind leg drop awkwardly. It must be uncomfortable. She looked down at him tenderly, tucked his leg up under him and gave him a hug. He laughed up in her face — he really did laugh, his mouth stretched wide in a cheerful grin. Now he was snug in a warm little ball.

Her parents were saying, 'If you want him, you can have him. But you must be responsible for him. If he gets to running sheep, he'll just have to be shot, you know that.'

They had not said, aloud, 'Like the Wilsons' collie.' They never mentioned that awfulness — her racing unsuspectingly down across the fields just at the horrible moment when Mr. Wilson shot their collie, caught in the very act of killing sheep. They probably thought that if they never spoke about it, she would forget it — *forget* the crack of that rifle, and the collapse of the great beautiful dog! Forget the red red blood spurting from the hole in his head. She hadn't forgotten. She never would. She knew as well as they did how important it was to train a collie puppy about sheep. They didn't have to rub it in like that. They always rubbed everything in. She had told them, fervently, indignantly, that of *course* she would take care of him, be responsible for him, teach him to stay at home. Of course. Of course. *She* understood!

And now, when he was six months old, tall, rangy, powerful, standing up far above her knee, nearly to her waist, she didn't know where he was. But of course he must be somewhere around. He always was. She composed her face to look natural and went downstairs to search the house. He was probably asleep somewhere. She looked every room over carefully. Her mother was nowhere visible. It was safe to call him again, to give the special piercing whistle which always brought him racing to her, the white-feathered plume of his tail waving in elation that she wanted him.

But he did not answer. She stood still on the front porch to think.

Could he have gone up to their special place in the edge of the field where the three young pines, their branches growing close to the ground, made a triangular, walled-in space, completely hidden from the world? Sometimes he went up there with her, and when she lay down on the dried grass to dream he, too, lay down quietly, his head on his paws, his beautiful eyes fixed adoringly on her. He entered into her every mood. If she wanted to be quiet, all right, he did too. It didn't seem as though he would have gone alone there. Still —— She loped up the steep slope of the field rather fast, beginning to be anxious.

No, he was not there. She stood irresolutely in the roofless, green-walled triangular hide-out, wondering what to do next.

Then, before she knew what thought had come into her mind, its emotional impact knocked her down. At least her knees crumpled under her. The Wilsons had, last Wednesday, brought their sheep down from the far upper pasture, to the home farm! They were — she herself had seen them on her way to school, and like an idiot had not thought of Rollie — on the river meadow.

She was off like a racer at the crack of the starting pistol, her long, strong legs stretched in great leaps, her pigtails flying. She took the short cut, regardless of the brambles. Their thorn-spiked, wiry stems tore at her flesh, but she did not care. She welcomed the pain. It was something she was doing for Rollie, for her Rollie.

She was in the pine woods now, rushing down the steep, stony path, tripping over roots, half falling, catching herself just in time, not slackening her speed. She burst out on the open knoll above the river meadow, calling wildly, 'Rollie, here, Rollie, here, boy! Here! Here!' She tried to whistle, but she was crying too hard to pucker her lips.

There was nobody to see or hear her. Twilight was falling over the bare, grassy knoll. The sunless evening wind slid down the mountain like an invisible river, engulfing her in cold. Her teeth began to chatter. 'Here, Rollie, here, boy, here!' She strained her eyes to look down into the meadow to see if the sheep were there. She could not be sure. She stopped calling him as she would a dog, and called out his name despairingly, as if he were her child, 'Rollie! Oh, *Rollie,* where are you?'

The tears ran down her cheeks in streams. She sobbed loudly, terribly; she did not try to control herself, since there was no one to hear. 'Hou! Hou! Hou!' she sobbed, her face contorted grotesquely. 'Oh, Rollie! Rollie! Rollie!' She had wanted something to cry about. Oh, how terribly now she had something to cry about.

She saw him as clearly as if he were there beside her, his muzzle and gaping mouth all smeared with the betraying blood (like the Wilsons' collie). 'But he didn't *know* it was wrong!' she screamed like a wild creature. 'Nobody *told* him it was wrong. It was my fault. I should have taken better care of him. I will now. I will!'

But no matter how she screamed, she could not make herself heard. In the cold gathering darkness, she saw him stand, poor, guiltless victim of his ignorance, who should have been protected from his own nature, his beautiful soft eyes looking at her with love, his splendid plumed tail waving gently. 'It was my fault. I promised I would bring him up. I should have *made* him stay at home. I was responsible for him. It was my fault.'

But she could not make his executioners hear her. The shot rang out. Rollie sank down, his beautiful liquid eyes glazed, the blood spurting from the hole in his head — like the Wilsons' collie. She gave a wild shriek, long, soul-satisfying, frantic. It was the scream at sudden, unendurable tragedy of a mature, full-blooded woman.

It drained dry the girl of thirteen. She came to herself. She was standing on the knoll, trembling and quaking with cold, the darkness closing in on her.

Her breath had given out. For once in her life she had wept all the tears there were in her body. Her hands were so stiff with cold she could scarcely close them. How her nose was running! Simply streaming down her upper lip. And she had no handkerchief. She lifted her skirt, fumbled for her slip, stooped, blew her nose on it, wiped her eyes, drew a long quavering breath — and heard something! Far off in the distance, a faint sound, like a dog's muffled bark.

She whirled on her heels and bent her head to listen. The sound did not come from the meadow below the knoll. It came from back of her, from the Wilsons' maple grove higher up. She held her breath. Yes, it came from there. She began to run again, but now she was not sobbing. She was silent, absorbed in her effort to cover ground. If she could only live to get there, to see if it really were Rollie. She ran steadily till she came to the fence, and went over this in a great plunge. Her skirt caught on a nail. She impatiently pulled at it, not hearing or not heeding the long sibilant tear as it came loose. She was in the dusky maple woods, stumbling over the rocks as she ran. As she tore on up the slope she knew it was Rollie's bark.

She stopped short and leaned weakly against a tree, sick with the breathlessness of her straining lungs, sick in the reaction of relief, sick with anger at Rollie, who had been here having a wonderful time while she had been dying, just dying in terror about him.

For she could now not only hear that it was Rollie's bark; she could hear, in the dog language she knew as well as he, what he was saying in those excited yips; that he had run a woodchuck into a hole in the tumbled stone wall, that he almost had him, that the intoxicating wild-animal smell was as close to him — almost — as if he had his jaws on his quarry. Yip! Woof! Yip! Yip!

The wild, joyful quality of the dog talk enraged the girl. She was trembling in exhaustion, in indignation. So that was where he had been, when she was killing herself trying to take care of him. Plenty near enough to hear her calling and whistling to him, if he had paid attention. Just so set on having his foolish good time, he never thought to listen for her call.

She stooped to pick up a stout stick. She would teach him! It was time he had something to make him remember to listen. She started forward.

But she stopped, stood thinking. One of the things to remember about collies — everybody knew that — was their sensitiveness. A collie who had been beaten was never 'right' again. His spirit was broken. 'Anything but a broken-spirited collie,' the farmers often said. They were no good after that.

She threw down her stick. Anyhow, she thought, he was too young to know, really, that he had done wrong. He was still only a puppy. Like all puppies, he got perfectly crazy over wild-animal smells. Probably he really and truly hadn't heard her calling and whistling.

All the same, all the same — she stared intently into the twilight — he couldn't be let to grow up just as he wanted to. She would have to make him understand that he mustn't go off this way by himself. He must be trained to know how to do what a good dog does — not because *she* wanted him to, but for his own sake.

She walked on now, steady, purposeful, gathering her inner strength together. Olympian in her understanding of the full meaning of the event.

When he heard his own special young god approaching, he turned delightedly and ran to meet her, panting, his tongue hanging out. His eyes shone. He jumped up on her in an ecstasy of welcome and licked her face.

But she pushed him away. Her face and voice were grave. 'No, Rollie, *no!*' she said severely. 'You're *bad*. You know you're not to go off in the woods without me! You are — a — *bad* — *dog*.'

He was horrified. Stricken into misery. He stood facing her, frozen, the gladness going out of his eyes, the erect waving plume of his tail slowly lowered to slinking, guilty dejection.

'I know you were all wrapped up in that woodchuck. But that's no excuse. You *could* have heard me, calling you, whistling for you, if you'd paid attention,' she went on. 'You've got to learn, and I've got to teach you.'

With a shudder of misery he lay down, his tail stretched out limp on the ground, his head flat on his paws, his ears drooping — ears ringing with doomsday awfulness of the voice he so loved and revered. He must have been utterly wicked. He trembled, and turned his head away from her august look of blame, groveling in remorse for whatever mysterious sin he had committed.

She sat down by him, as miserable as he. 'I don't *want* to scold you. But I have to! I have to bring you up right, or you'll get shot, Rollie. You *mustn't* go away from the house without me, do you hear, *never!*'

Catching, with his sharp ears yearning for her approval, a faint overtone of relenting affection in her voice, he lifted his eyes to her, humbly, soft in imploring fondness.

'Oh, Rollie!' she said, stooping low over him. 'I *do* love you. I do. But I *have* to bring you up. I'm responsible for you, don't you see?'

He did not see. Hearing sternness, or something else he did not recognize, in the beloved voice, he shut his eyes tight in sorrow, and made a little whimpering lament in his throat.

She had never heard him cry before. It was too much. She sat down by him and drew his head to her, rocking him in her arms, smoothing him with inarticulate small murmurs.

He leaped in her arms and wriggled happily as he had when he was a baby; he reached up to lick her face as he had then. But he was no baby now. He was half as big as she, a great, warm, pulsing, living armful of love. She clasped him closely. Her heart was brimming full, but calmed, quiet. The blood flowed in equable gentleness all over her body. She was deliciously warm. Her nose was still running a little. She sniffed and wiped it on her sleeve.

It was almost dark now. 'We'll be late to supper, Rollie,' she said responsibly. Pushing him gently off, she stood up. 'Home, Rollie, home!'

Here was a command he could understand. At once he trotted along the path toward home. His plumed tail, held high, waved cheerfully. His short dog memory had dropped into oblivion the suffering just back of him.

Her human memory was longer. His prancing gait was as carefree as a young child's. Plodding heavily like a serious adult, she trod behind him. Her very shoulders seemed bowed by what she had lived through. She felt, she thought like an old, old woman of thirty. But it was all right now. She knew she had made an impression on him.

When they came out into the open pasture, Rollie ran back to get her to play with him. He leaped around her in circles, barking in cheerful yawps, jumping up on her, inviting her to run a race with him, to throw him a stick, to come alive.

His high spirits were ridiculous. But infectious. She gave one little leap to match his. Rollie pretended that this was a threat to him, planted his forepaws low and barked loudly at her, laughing between yips. He was so funny, she thought, when he grinned that way. She laughed back, and gave another mock-threatening leap at him. Radiant that his sky was once more clear, he sprang high on his spring-steel muscles in an explosion of happiness, and bounded in circles around her.

Following him, not noting in the dusk where she was going, she felt the grassy slope drop steeply. Oh, yes, she knew where she was. They had come to the rolling-down hill just back of the house. All the kids rolled down there, even the little ones, because it was soft grass without a stone. She had rolled down that slope a million times — years and years ago, when she was a kid herself. It was fun. She remembered well the whirling dizziness of the descent, all the world turning over and over crazily. And the delicious giddy staggering when you first stood up, the earth still spinning under your feet.

'All right, Rollie, let's go,' she cried, and flung herself down in the rolling position, her arms straight up over her head.

Rollie had never seen this skylarking before. It threw him into almost hysterical amusement. He capered around the rapidly rolling figure, half scared, mystified, enchanted.

His wild frolicsome barking might have come from her own throat, so accurately did it sound the way she felt — crazy, foolish, like a little kid, no more than five years old, the age she had been when she had last rolled down that hill.

At the bottom she sprang up, on muscles as steel-strong as Rollie's. She staggered a little, and laughed aloud.

The living-room windows were just before them. How yellow lighted windows looked when you were in the darkness going home. How nice and yellow. Maybe mother had waffles for supper. She was a swell cook, mother was, and she certainly gave her family all the breaks, when it came to meals.

'Home, Rollie, home!' She burst open the door to the living room. 'Hi, mom, what you got for supper?'

From the kitchen her mother announced coolly, 'I hate to break the news to you, but it's waffles.'

'Oh, *mom!*' she shouted in ecstasy.

Her mother could not see her. She did not need to. 'For goodness sakes, go and wash,' she called.

In the long mirror across the room she saw herself, her hair hanging wild, her long bare legs scratched, her broadly smiling face dirt-streaked, her torn skirt dangling, her dog laughing up at her. Gosh, was it a relief to feel your own age, just exactly thirteen years old!

*(From The New Yorker)*

# THE ENORMOUS RADIO

## BY JOHN CHEEVER

JIM and Irene Westcott were the kind of people who seem to strike that satisfactory average of income, endeavor, and respectability that is reached by the statistical reports in college alumni bulletins. They were the parents of two young children, they had been married nine years, they lived on the twelfth floor of an apartment house in the East Seventies between Fifth and Madison Avenues, they went to the theatre on an average of 10.3 times a year, and they hoped someday to live in Westchester. Irene Westcott was a pleasant, rather plain girl with soft brown hair and a wide, fine forehead upon which nothing at all had been written, and in the cold weather she wore a coat of fitch skins dyed to resemble mink. You could not say that Jim Westcott, at thirty-seven, looked younger than he was, but you could at least say of him that he seemed to feel younger. He wore his graying hair cut very short, he dressed in the kind of clothes his class had worn at Andover, and his manner was earnest, vehement, and intentionally naïve. The Westcotts differed from their friends, their classmates, and their neighbors only in an interest they shared in serious music. They went to a great many concerts — although they seldom mentioned this to anyone — and they spent a good deal of time listening to music on the radio.

Their radio was an old instrument, sensitive, unpredictable, and beyond repair. Neither of them understood the mechanics of radio — or of any of the other appliances that surrounded them — and when the instrument faltered, Jim would strike the side of the cabinet with his hand. This sometimes helped. One Sunday afternoon, in the middle of a Schubert quartet, the music faded away altogether. Jim struck the cabinet repeatedly, but there was no response; the Schubert was lost to them forever. He promised to buy Irene a new radio, and on Monday when he came home from work he told her that he had got one. He refused to describe it, and said it would be a surprise for her when it came.

The radio was delivered at the kitchen door the following afternoon, and with the assistance of her maid and the handyman Irene uncrated it and brought it into the living room. She was struck at once with the physical ugliness of the large gumwood cabinet. Irene was proud of her living room, she had chosen its furnishings and colors as carefully as she chose her clothes, and now it seemed to her that the new radio stood among her intimate possessions like an aggressive intruder. She was confounded by the number of dials and switches on the instrument panel, and she studied them thoroughly before she put the plug into a wall socket and turned the radio on. The dials flooded with a malevolent green light, and in the distance she heard the music of a piano quintet. The quintet was in the distance for only an instant; it bore down upon her with a speed greater than light and filled the apartment with the noise of music amplified so mightily that it knocked a china ornament from a table to the floor. She rushed to the instrument and reduced the volume. The violent forces that were snared in the ugly gumwood cabinet made her uneasy. Her children came home from school then, and she took them to the Park. It was not until later in the afternoon that she was able to return to the radio.

The maid had given the children their suppers and was supervising their baths when Irene turned on the radio, reduced the volume, and sat down to listen to a Mozart quintet that she knew and enjoyed. The music came through clearly. The new instrument had much purer tone, she thought, than the old one. She decided that tone was most important and that she could conceal the cabinet behind a sofa. But as soon as she had made her peace with the radio, the interference began. A crackling sound like the noise of a burning powder fuse began to accompany the singing of the strings. Beyond the music, there was a rustling that reminded Irene unpleasantly of the sea, and as the quintet progressed, these noises were joined by many others. She tried all the dials and switches but nothing dimmed the interference, and she sat down, disappointed and bewildered, and tried to trace the flight of the melody. The elevator shaft in her building ran beside the living-room wall, and it was the noise of the elevator that gave her a clue to the character of the static. The rattling of the elevator cables and the opening and closing of the elevator doors were reproduced in her loudspeaker, and, realizing that the radio was sensitive to electrical currents of all sorts, she began to discern through the Mozart the ringing of telephone bells, the dialing of phones, and the lamentation of a vacuum cleaner. By listening more carefully, she was able to distinguish doorbells, elevator bells, electric razors, and Waring mixers, whose sounds had been picked up from the apartments that surrounded hers and transmitted through her loudspeaker. The powerful and ugly instrument, with its mistaken sensitivity to discord, was more than she could hope to master, so she turned the thing off and went into the nursery to see her children.

When Jim Westcott came home that night, he went to the radio confidently and worked the controls. He had the same sort of experience Irene had had. A man was speaking on the station Jim had chosen, and his voice swung instantly from the distance into a force so powerful that it shook the apartment. Jim turned the volume control and reduced the voice. Then, a minute or two later, the interference began. The ringing of telephones and doorbells set in, joined by the rasp of the elevator doors and the whir of cooking appliances. The character of the noise had changed since Irene had tried the radio earlier; the last of the electric razors was being unplugged, the vacuum cleaners had all been returned to their closets, and the static reflected that change in pace that overtakes the city after the sun goes down. He fiddled with the knobs but couldn't get rid of the noises, so he turned the radio off and told Irene that in the morning he'd call the people who had sold it to him and give them hell.

The following afternoon, when Irene returned to the apartment from a luncheon date, the maid told her that a man had come and fixed the radio. Irene went into the living room before she took off her hat or her furs and tried the instrument. From the loudspeaker came a recording of the 'Missouri Waltz.' It reminded her of the thin, scratchy music from an old-fashioned phonograph that she sometimes heard across the lake where she spent her summers.

She waited until the waltz had finished, expecting an explanation of the recording, but there was none. The music was followed by silence, and then the plaintive and scratchy record was repeated. She turned the dial and got a satisfactory burst of Caucasian music — the thump of bare feet in the dust and the rattle of coin jewelry — but in the background she could hear the ringing of bells and a confusion of voices. Her children came home from school then, and she turned off the radio and went to the nursery.

When Jim came home that night, he was tired, and he took a bath and changed his clothes. Then he joined Irene in the living room. He had just turned on the radio when the maid announced dinner, so he left it on, and he and Irene went to the table.

Jim was too tired to make even a pretense of sociability, and there was nothing about the dinner to hold Irene's interest, so her attention wandered from the food to the deposits of silver polish on the candlesticks and from there to the music in the other room. She listened for a few moments to a Chopin prelude and then was surprised to hear a man's voice break in. 'For Christ's sake, Kathy,' he said, 'do you always have to play the piano when I get home?' The music stopped abruptly. 'It's the only chance I have,' a woman said. 'I'm at the office all day.' 'So am I,' the man said. He added something obscene about an upright piano, and slammed a door. The passionate and melancholy music began again.

'Did you hear that?' Irene asked.

'What?' Jim was eating his dessert.

'The radio. A man said something while the music was still going on — something dirty.'

'It's probably a play.'

'I don't think it *is* a play,' Irene said.

They left the table and took their coffee into the living room. Irene asked Jim to try another station. He turned the knob. 'Have you seen my garters?' a man asked. 'Button me up,' a woman said. 'Have you seen my garters?' the man said again. 'Just button me up and I'll find your garters,' the woman said. Jim shifted to another station. 'I wish you wouldn't leave apple cores in the ashtrays,' a man said. 'I hate the smell.'

'This is strange,' Jim said.

'Isn't it?' Irene said.

Jim turned the knob again. '"On the coast of Coromandel where the early pumpkins blow,"' a woman with a pronounced English accent said, '"in the middle of the woods lived the Yonghy-Bonghy-Bò. Two old chairs, and half a candle, one old jug without a handle . . ."'

'My God!' Irene cried. 'That's the Sweeneys' nurse.'

'"These were all his worldly goods,"' the British voice continued.

'Turn that thing off,' Irene said. 'Maybe they can hear *us*.' Jim switched the radio off. 'That was Miss Armstrong, the Sweeneys' nurse,' Irene said. 'She must be reading to the little girl. They live in 17-B. I've talked with Miss Armstrong in the Park. I know her voice very well. We must be getting other people's apartments.'

'That's impossible,' Jim said.

'Well, that was the Sweeneys' nurse,' Irene said hotly. 'I know her voice. I know it very well. I'm wondering if they can hear us.'

Jim turned the switch. First from a distance and then nearer, nearer, as if borne on the wind, came the pure accents of the Sweeneys' nurse again: '"Lady Jingly! Lady Jingly!"' she said, '"Sitting where the pumpkins blow, will you come and be my wife,' said the Yonghy-Bonghy-Bò . . ."'

Jim went over to the radio and said 'Hello' loudly into the speaker.

'"I am tired of living singly,"' the nurse went on, '"on this coast so wild and shingly, I'm a-weary of my life; if you'll come and be my wife, quite serene would be my life . . ."'

'I guess she can't hear us,' Irene said. 'Try something else.'

Jim turned to another station, and the living room was filled with the uproar of a cocktail party that had overshot its mark. Someone was playing the piano and singing the Whiffenpoof Song, and the voices that surrounded the piano were vehement and happy. 'Eat some more sandwiches,' a woman shrieked. There were screams of laughter and a dish of some sort crashed to the floor.

'Those must be the Hutchinsons, in 15-B,' Irene said. 'I knew they were giving a party this afternoon. I saw her in the liquor store. Isn't this too divine? Try something else. See if you can get those people in 18-C.'

The Westcotts overheard that evening a monologue on salmon fishing in Canada, a bridge game, running comments on home movies of what had apparently been a fortnight at Sea Island, and a bitter family quarrel about an overdraft at the bank. They turned off the radio at midnight and went to bed, weak with laughter. Sometime in the night, their son began to call for a glass of water and Irene got one and took it to his room. It was very early. All the lights in the neighborhood were extinguished, and from the boy's window she could see the empty street. She went into the living room and tried the radio. There was some faint coughing, a moan, and then a man spoke. 'Are you all right, darling?' he asked. 'Yes,' a woman said wearily. 'Yes, I'm all right, I guess,' and then she added with great feeling, 'But, you know, Charlie, I don't feel like myself any more. Sometimes there are about fifteen or twenty minutes in the week when I feel like myself. I don't like to go to another doctor, because the doctor's bills are so awful already, but I just don't feel like myself, Charlie. I just never feel like myself.' They were not young, Irene thought. She guessed from the timbre of their voices that they were middle-aged. The restrained melancholy of the dialogue and the draft from the bedroom window made her shiver, and she went back to bed.

The following morning, Irene cooked breakfast for the family — the maid didn't come up from her room in the basement until ten — braided her daughter's hair, and waited at the door until her children and her husband had been carried away in the elevator. Then she went into the living room and tried the radio. 'I don't want to go to school,' a child screamed. 'I hate school. I won't go to school. I hate school.' 'You will go to school,' an enraged woman said. 'We paid eight hundred dollars to get you into that school and you'll go if it kills you.' The next number on the dial produced the worn record of the 'Missouri Waltz.' Irene shifted the control and invaded the privacy of several breakfast tables. She overheard demonstrations of indigestion, carnal love, abysmal vanity, faith, and despair. Irene's life was nearly as simple and sheltered as it appeared to be, and the forthright and sometimes brutal language that came from the loudspeaker that morning astonished and troubled her. She continued to listen until her maid came in. Then she turned off the radio quickly, since this insight, she realized, was a furtive one.

Irene had a luncheon date with a friend that day, and she left her apartment at a little after twelve. There were a number of women in the elevator when it stopped at her floor. She stared at their handsome and impassive faces, their furs, and the cloth flowers in their hats. Which one of them had been to Sea Island, she wondered. Which one had overdrawn her bank account? The elevator stopped at the tenth floor and a woman with a pair of Skye terriers joined them. Her hair was rigged high on her head and she wore a mink cape. She was humming the 'Missouri Waltz.'

Irene had two Martinis at lunch, and she looked searchingly at her friend and wondered what her secrets were. They had intended to go shopping after lunch, but Irene excused herself and went home. She told the maid that she was not to be disturbed; then she went into the living room, closed the doors, and switched on the radio. She heard, in the course of the afternoon, the halting conversation of a woman entertaining her aunt, the hysterical conclusion of a luncheon party, and a hostess briefing her maid about some cocktail guests. 'Don't give the best Scotch to anyone who hasn't white hair,' the hostess said. 'See if you can get rid of that liver paste before you pass those hot things, and could you lend me five dollars? I want to tip the elevator man.'

As the afternoon waned, the conversations increased in intensity. From where Irene sat, she could see the open sky above Central Park. There were hundreds of clouds in the sky, as though the south wind had broken the winter into pieces and were blowing it north, and on her radio she could hear the arrival of cocktail guests and the return of children and businessmen from their schools and offices. 'I found a good-sized diamond on the bathroom floor this morning,' a woman said. 'It must have fallen out of that bracelet Mrs. Dunston was wearing last night.' 'We'll sell it,' a man said. 'Take it down to the jeweller on Madison Avenue and sell it. Mrs. Dunston won't know the difference, and we could use a couple of hundred bucks...' '"Oranges and lemons, say the bells of St. Clement's,"' the Sweeneys' nurse sang. '"Half-pence and farthings, say the bells of St. Martin's. When will you pay me? say the bells at old Bailey..."' 'It's not a hat,' a woman cried, and at her back roared a cocktail party. 'It's not a hat, it's a love affair. That's what Walter Florell said. He said it's not a hat, it's a love affair,' and then, in a lower voice, the same woman added, 'Talk to somebody, for Christ's sake, honey, talk to somebody. If she catches you standing here not talking to anybody, she'll take us off her invitation list, and I love these parties.'

The Westcotts were going out for dinner that night, and when Jim came home, Irene was dressing. She seemed sad and vague, and he brought her a drink. They were dining with friends in the neighborhood, and they walked to where they were going. The sky was broad and filled with light. It was one of those splendid spring evenings that excite memory and desire, and the air that touched their hands and faces felt very soft. A Salvation Army band was on the corner playing 'Jesus Is Sweeter.' Irene drew on her husband's arm and held him there for a minute, to hear the music. 'They're really such nice people, aren't they?' she said. 'They have such nice faces. Actually, they're so much nicer than a lot of the people we know.' She took a bill from her purse and walked over and dropped it into the tambourine. There was in her face, when she returned to her husband, a look of radiant melancholy that he was not familiar with. And her conduct at the dinner party that night seemed strange to him, too. She interrupted her hostess rudely and stared at the people across the table from her with an intensity for which she would have punished her children.

It was still mild when they walked home from the party, and Irene looked up at the spring stars. '"How far that little candle throws its beams,"' she exclaimed. '"So shines a good deed in a naughty world."' She waited that night until Jim had fallen asleep, and then went into the living room and turned on the radio.

Jim came home at about six the next night. Emma, the maid, let him in, and he had taken off his hat and was taking off his coat when Irene ran into the hall. Her face was shining with tears and her hair was disordered. 'Go up to 16-C, Jim!' she screamed. 'Don't take off your coat. Go up to 16-C. Mr. Osborn's beating his wife. They've been quarrelling since four o'clock, and now he's hitting her. Go up there and stop him.'

From the radio in the living room, Jim heard screams, obscenities, and thuds. 'You know you don't have to listen to this sort of thing,' he said. He strode into the living room and turned the switch. 'It's indecent,' he said. 'It's like looking in windows. You know you don't have to listen to this sort of thing. You can turn it off.'

'Oh, it's so horrible, it's so dreadful,' Irene was sobbing. 'I've been listening all day, and it's so depressing.'

'Well, if it's so depressing, why do you listen to it? I bought this damned radio to give you some pleasure,' he said. 'I paid a great deal of money for it. I thought it might make you happy. I wanted to make you happy.'

'Don't, don't, don't, don't quarrel with me,' she moaned, and laid her head on his shoulder. 'All the others have been quarrelling all day. Everybody's been quarrelling. They're all worried about money. Mrs. Hutchinson's mother is dying of cancer in Florida and they don't have enough money to send her to the Mayo Clinic. At least, Mr. Hutchinson says they don't have enough money. And some woman in this building is having an affair with the superintendent — with that hideous superintendent. It's too disgusting. And Mrs. Melville has heart trouble and Mr. Hendricks is going to lose his job in April and Mrs. Hendricks is horrid about the whole thing and that girl who plays the 'Missouri Waltz' is a whore, a common whore, and the elevator man has tuberculosis and Mr. Osborn has been beating Mrs. Osborn.' She wailed, she trembled with grief and checked the stream of tears down her face with the heel of her palm.

'Well, why do you have to listen?' Jim asked again. 'Why do you have to listen to this stuff if it makes you so miserable?'

'Oh, don't don't don't,' she cried. 'Life is too terrible, too sordid and awful. But we've never been like that, have we, darling? Have we? I mean we've always been good and decent and loving to one another, haven't we? And we have two children, two beautiful children. Our lives aren't sordid, are they, darling? Are they?' She flung her arms around his neck and drew his face down to hers. 'We're happy, aren't we, darling? We are happy, aren't we?'

'Of course we're happy,' he said tiredly. He began to surrender his resentment. 'Of course we're happy. I'll have that damned radio fixed or taken away tomorrow.' He stroked her soft hair. 'My poor girl,' he said.

'You love me, don't you?' she asked. 'And we're not hypercritical or worried about money or dishonest, are we?'

'No, darling,' he said.

A man came in the morning and fixed the radio. Irene turned it on cautiously and was happy to hear a California-wine commercial and a recording of Beethoven's Ninth Symphony, including Schiller's 'Ode to Joy.' She kept the radio on all day and nothing untoward came from the speaker.

A Spanish suite was being played when Jim came home. 'Is everything all right?' he asked. His face was pale, she thought. They had some cocktails and went in to dinner to the 'Anvil Chorus' from 'Il Trovatore.' This was followed by Debussy's 'La Mer.'

'I paid the bill for the radio today,' Jim said. 'It cost four hundred dollars. I hope you'll get some enjoyment out of it.'

'Oh, I'm sure I will,' Irene said.

'Four hundred dollars is a good deal more than I can afford,' he went on. 'I wanted to get something that you'd enjoy. It's the last extravagance we'll be able to indulge in this year. I see that you haven't paid your clothing bills yet. I saw them on your dressing table.' He looked directly at her. 'Why did you tell me you'd paid them? Why did you lie to me?'

'I just didn't want you to worry, Jim,' she said. She drank some water. 'I'll be able to pay my bills out of this month's allowance. There were the slipcovers last month, and that party.'

'You've got to learn to handle the money I give you a little more intelligently, Irene,' he said. 'You've got to understand that we won't have as much money this year as we had last. I had a very sobering talk with Mitchell today. No one is buying anything. We're spending all our time promoting new issues, and you know how long that takes. I'm not getting any younger, you know. I'm thirty-seven. My hair will be gray next year. I haven't done as well as I'd hoped to do. And I don't suppose things will get any better.'

'Yes, dear,' she said.

'We've got to start cutting down,' Jim said. 'We've got to think of the children. To be perfectly frank with you, I worry about money a great deal. I'm not at all sure of the future. No one is. If anything should happen to me, there's the insurance, but that wouldn't go very far today. I've worked awfully hard to give you and the children a comfortable life,' he said bitterly. 'I don't like to see all of my energies, all of my youth, wasted in fur coats and radios and slipcovers and — '

'Please, Jim,' she said. 'Please. They'll hear us.'

'*Who'll* hear us? Emma can't hear us.'

'The radio.'

'Oh, I'm sick!' he shouted. 'I'm sick to death of your apprehensiveness. The radio can't hear us. Nobody can hear us. And what if they can hear us? Who cares?'

Irene got up from the table and went into the living room. Jim went to the door and shouted at her from there. 'Why are you so Christly all of a sudden? What's turned you overnight into a convent girl? You stole your mother's jewelry before they probated her will. You never gave your sister a cent of that money that was intended for her — not even when she needed it. You made Grace Howland's life miserable, and where was all your piety and your virtue when you went to that abortionist? I'll never forget how cool you were. You packed your bag and went off to have that child murdered as if you were going to Nassau. If you'd had any reasons, if you'd had any good reasons —— '

Irene stood for a minute before the hideous cabinet, disgraced and sickened, but she held her hand on the switch before she extinguished the music and the voices, hoping that the instrument might speak to her kindly, that she might hear the Sweeneys' nurse. Jim continued to shout at her from the door. The voice on the radio was suave and noncommittal. 'An early-morning railroad disaster in Tokyo,' the loudspeaker said, 'killed twenty-nine people. A fire in a Catholic hospital near Buffalo for the care of blind children was extinguished early this morning by nuns. The temperature is forty-seven. The humidity is eighty-nine.'

*(From Tomorrow)*

# THAT'S MY JOHNNY-BOY

## BY GEORGE R. CLAY

MY *MOTHER* and my father — for a number of years afterward I still referred to him as 'daddy,' but one day this seemed forced and I adopted 'father' — were divorced in 1928. I was almost eight years old at the time and I remember mother's telling Alan and me — John was twelve and knew pretty much what was happening — that my father had gone to New York on business and would probably not be back for a month. This was in August. When my father did not return for my birthday in October, mother said he had taken ill in New York and not to expect him, even for Christmas. During the months that followed I began to understand, through obtuse references made by a few of my school friends and from the way the subject was avoided by all grown-ups, especially mother, that something permanent had taken place.

The next summer my mother set up a dress shop, and the following winter she got a job selling bonds. She was an attractive woman in her early thirties: small, dark, very straightforward and energetic. Not long ago I met a lady named Mrs. Burke who had been a telephone operator where mother worked, and she said mother was one of the best bond sellers they had ever had there, even though she was competing with the brightest young men in Philadelphia. Mrs. Burke said a lot of the men were jealous of mother because she used all her woman's charm and all her social contacts to outsell them, and that mother was sometimes referred to as the Bond Queen of Philadelphia. I've often noticed how tradesmen and servants take to mother, and I think what they like most is the way she is sure of what she wants done and of how she wants it done. She goes to so much trouble to show them exactly what she means that they can't help but do it right; and when they do, she appreciates it, and it flatters them to know she appreciates it. I've seen it happen time and time again: with an antique dealer who was redoing an old Pennsylvania Dutch cupboard she had picked up from some farmer for two dollars; or the carpenters who built a new wing on our summer house; or the man who came to lay the cleaned rugs on our main staircase in Chestnut Hill. I've seen her get quite stern with them, and they always respect it.

Her single objective after she left my father — he did not officially leave her; it never would have happened that way — was to educate us three children. She had been awarded complete custody by the court, and my father was only allowed to visit us a certain number of times every year.

He came to see us first in the spring of 1929, on a Wednesday. John and Alan and I had just come from Miss Lockhood's afternoon dancing class. The orchestra had played 'Easter Parade' six times. I kept humming it, but I was sick of it. We were dressed in our blue serge suits, starched white open-collar blouses, short pants, and patent leather pumps. It was the last class of the year, the one at which prizes are given, and I remember Alan had won first prize for the greatest improvement throughout the past season. It was a long blue wooden racing car, and Alan was as proud of it as John and I were envious.

Miss Hughson, our English governess, called for us at four o'clock. She had difficulty trying to drive on the correct side of the road and, at the same time, break the news that daddy was coming to see us sometime before supper.

He must have been alone in the sitting room reading a magazine when we arrived, because before Miss Hughson could get the front door open, he rushed out into the hall, still holding the magazine in his hand. He threw it onto the hall table and, without any words at all, crouched down, bracing himself to receive us. Alan flew into his left arm, I into his right, while John went around and hung onto his neck from the back. Laughing and groaning, he lifted the three of us up and carried us into the sitting room and dumped us on the sofa. 'Good gravy,' he gasped, 'you kids aren't getting any lighter, are you?'

I am not very clear on what we talked about during that visit. He was naturally proud of Alan's racing car, but said he remembered my being the best dancer of the three and John's always being most popular in the cotillions — so we all felt gratified. Then — and this part I am sure of — I asked him whether he remembered the tinder box. He said of course he did, and did I still have it? It was unfair of him to ask the question that gave him away, and I felt so badly about it I couldn't clear my throat enough to explain.

The tinder box was one of those symbols that becomes so important in a child's life that he remembers it as long as he has a memory. Daddy had given it to me the year we were in France. It was the afternoon of allowance day. I ran and told him I had saved one franc, twelve centimes — more than either John or Alan had saved. 'Well,' he said, 'since you seem to be the banker in the family, how about opening a foreign department?' I looked puzzled, and he said, 'Come on upstairs. I have something you might like to see.' After rummaging around for a long time in his top bureau drawer, he finally brought it out and handed it to me — a small metal box, decorated with running ostriches on its rounded bronze lid and with orange felt material covering the bottom. 'It's a tinder box, Paul,' he said. 'Open it.' Inside was a pile of foreign coins he said he had collected during the war. I spread all the coins out on his bed and, for the next two hours, played with them — putting them in little piles according to color and feeling their metal faces and even smelling them to see if I could detect any difference between the silver and the brown ones. After that, every night before going to bed, I would pick the coins out at random and try to guess without looking or feeling whether they had a round hole, a square, a triangle, or no hole. When I got to know every coin just from the size and weight of it, I felt wealthy. It was something I had — a possession and an accomplishment — that neither John nor Alan could take away from me.

One night I boasted about this to John, and, seeing that I cared so much about them, he plotted to get them. John wasn't very conscientious in school — we went to a little English kindergarten on the outskirts of Jean les Pins, where we fed the chickens or played rugby at recess — but he was a demon at getting things if he suspected they had special value.

To thwart any attempt he might make on my tinder box, I took it down to the beach the next morning and hid it in the sand a short distance from our beach umbrella. I felt smart about my hiding place and became especially friendly to John all that morning as we played on the beach and watched the beach artists making colored sand pictures and talked in French to the Russian prince who sold the strawberry tarts his mother made. After that, John and I wandered far up the old stone breakwater and pretended we were pirates: that we had sailed over from North Africa and were the first white men to land on this rocky coast of France.

After a long time of playing, Jeanne, our French nurse—she didn't last long—came after us. She was distinctly annoyed that we had not told her where we were going, and Alan, who was five then, was crying because some little girl had taken his sand shovel. In her nervous but absolutely unbending fashion, Jeanne bustled the three of us home, gargling angry dialect the entire way.

It wasn't until just before bedtime that I remembered about the tinder box. Of course, I never found it. I cried myself to sleep that night, and went down every morning I could to hunt for it, but Jeanne told me I was a silly little boy when I pestered her to try and remember where she had placed the beach umbrella that day.

I told daddy in hopes that he might either find it or replace it, but he had just had another fight with mother and scolded me for being so selfish. He said it served me right, and it was a self-taught lesson I would never forget. For months after that I had a recurrent dream: that I was a pirate captain who came upon a secret cave in an island far out in the Mediterranean, and I discovered there the tinder box—only it had grown a thousand times in size and contained gold and rare jewels—and that I was the richest man in the world. I asked mother if it were possible for a box buried in the sand to sink down and down and eventually float out to sea, and she said, yes, she thought so.

What I wanted to tell my father during that first visit was that I had had this dream again, last night, after two years of not dreaming it—and to suggest that I might dream it every night before he came to see us. John, I think, knew what I meant, but he didn't say anything because he didn't want to embarrass daddy.

After a while we had tea—it was one of Miss Hughson's customs, exercised with absurd ritual whenever she thought there was a chance to show off what she considered our newly acquired manners — and daddy asked us how we were doing at school and whether we played baseball, and then it was time for him to go because mother was coming home. Alan asked the question that was in my mind: why mother's coming home made it time to go? We all thought he had really come to see mother and arrange about living with us again. But daddy laughed it off — he had the most contagious laugh I have ever heard; it was so wonderful it made people forget what they wanted to know, or that they had ever asked a question to provoke it — and got up and put on his hat. He hugged us each individually, pressing us with the cheek that didn't have the rash (it was a light strawberry rash he said he had picked up from eating raw horsemeat in Austria during the war; he had always had it, and it seemed to re-enforce his good looks rather than mar them); then he tipped his hat to Miss Hughson, promised us he would be back just as soon as he possibly could, and opened the door and walked out.

The three of us together never saw him again. My mother remarried in 1932. She left her job, of course — Augustus Ramsey, my stepfather, came from a family that is often mentioned in books for or against rich people — and sent Alan and me to boarding school in New England.

I liked school and I loved the vacations, but the best part of all was traveling to and from Boston. It meant changing at New York's Pennsylvania Station, taking a taxi to Grand Central, and catching a special school train from there. Alan and I used to have particular things we always did during the wait in Grand Central. First, we could buy all the comic magazines we could afford, then go down to the Oyster Bar and order two dozen cherrystone clams apiece, then go to the news theatre until train time.

John, by then, had finished, or rather quit, college and was working for an advertising firm in New York. Apparently, he knew my father better than I did, because he asked me if I wouldn't like to meet him at Grand Central — this was after Christmas vacation, my fourth-form year — so we could see each other for that hour or so. I hadn't thought much about my father for some years, with the established routine of boarding school and new friends and full vacations to occupy me, so it seemed sudden and exciting. We arranged to meet at the information booth at twelve-ten.

For some reason, Alan was not with me that day. I think he was visiting a school friend in New Hampshire. Anyway, I was there at the information booth, ten minutes early; and I waited until one o'clock before my father showed up — without John. Standing there waiting for him, I had wondered whether the arrangement was quite fair to mother, and what she might say if I wrote her from school about it. But when I saw him, I knew it couldn't be wrong; just as I knew, of all the people in Grand Central, that he was my father.

The first thing I had noticed was that he seemed much smaller than I had remembered him. He was wearing a shapeless chesterfield, and its left pocket was badly torn. I think he had on the same hat he had worn in 1929, and though it was quite a cold day, he didn't have any gloves. He was thin. I could tell from the way he walked that he was thin underneath the coat. His rash looked like sickness now, with a two-day growth of beard over it, but his eyes were the same mild blue and his smile seemed even kinder, because his face was sad.

He kissed me and said: 'You're looking awfully well, dear. John says you're getting good marks. Did you have a nice vacation? Did you get my Christmas card? I sent it a little late.' I knew he hadn't sent any Christmas card, by the way he said it and because I had never received one from him — and I knew the other statements were things he had planned to say — but I still could not block that strong affection that welled up whenever I saw a photograph of him or remembered the sound of his voice.

It was time for my train then. He carried one bag while I carried the other and a pair of skis mother had given me for Christmas. Walking across the waiting room, we didn't say anything, and it made me feel uncomfortable because I thought, with five minutes together in seven years, a father and son ought to have something to talk about. Then he laughed — he laughed nervously, a way I had never heard him laugh before — and said, 'Have you heard the one about the Roosevelts, Paul? . . .' I said, no, I hadn't, and then he mumbled a dirty joke. I was so startled at the fact of his telling it that I didn't listen, and I wasn't even able to affect a laugh. Then I tried desperately to remember one to tell him, but my mind went blank.

All the way up on the train I could think of nothing but dirty jokes, and by the time we pulled into Back Bay Station, I had remembered twenty-seven of them.

I finished school in 1939 and started college that fall — the September Great Britain went to war with Germany. It's hard to explain just how exciting it was to start college at that particular time. I think Archibald MacLeish had something to do with it: he made a speech to the new Freshmen the night we arrived, in which he stated with severe finality that one out of every five young men listening to him would be dead within ten years. That thought, combined with the natural ideals carried over from school and the intellectual curiosity charged by the new student's conception of Harvard University, catalyzed me into a sort of insatiable fervor that I had never felt before and have certainly never felt since. Every idea was worth arguing, every thought worth expressing, every person worth making an intimate friend of — every moment was priceless. The Goddesses we worshiped were Imagination, Spontaneity, Sincerity, and Verbosity. We had metaphysical arguments over scrambled eggs at five o'clock in the morning and usually worked off our inevitable hangovers by writing bad poetry.

For me, through some transformation which I don't fully understand, my father was an important influence in all this. Perhaps he achieved his exalted position through being, in my mind, the symbol of everything my mother rejected. She was the dispenser of a never-quite-adequate allowance; the surveyor of my marks; the one who insisted that I start now to prepare myself for some practical future. She was the arch example of energy focused on Victorian objectives. Her aims for her sons were staunch character and material success, and the first must necessarily precede the second. She worried a little if our friends were eccentric, and insisted that we answer our dinner-dance invitations on time. Once I gave her *Sons and Lovers* to read, and she said she couldn't force herself past the second chapter. She had never heard of Rivera or Engels.

My father, on the other hand — I had heard more about him now from John — seemed a bold, free, and expressive personality. He lived in Greenwich Village with a woman (John had never met her; her name was Christina) who was supposed to be his wife. He had had many kinds of jobs — from hard labor to selling first editions. I could understand, Freshman year, why my father had never been able to live with my mother happily. He wouldn't, I reasoned, allow himself to be tied down to the Philadelphia suburban existence: the five-fifteen, golf on Saturday, church on Sunday. If he wanted to tell me a dirty joke, he had a perfect right to tell me a dirty joke. His license was the license of impulse.

The summer of my Sophomore year, I worked as a runner in the bank that my grandfather had directed when he was alive. John had left the advertising job and was working in my grandfather's company, two blocks away. It was hot and uncomfortable in the city and there was little diversion, even on week-ends. One day at lunch — John and I met at Bookbinder's once or twice a week — we decided to drive over to New York and stay with Father, provided that he could put us up in his apartment.

We waited until my mother and stepfather were in the mountains (my stepfather usually took his vacation a week before and a week after Labor Day); meanwhile, John prepared the way for us in New York.

Willkie was campaigning for President at the time. I remember, going through the Holland Tunnel in the station wagon, the radio was cut off in the middle of his platform declaration.

When we finally arrived at the address — between Sixth and Seventh Streets on Seventh Avenue — it was after four. The building was a narrow, brownstone apartment house with a grocery store on the ground floor. I looked at John and he shrugged and cleared his throat and said, 'Well — what are you waiting for?'

There was a step-up and then a typical little dirty marble entryway — marble like the floors of men's rooms in movie theatres. Under the built-in mail boxes were name tags. It seemed incongruous to see 'Mr. & Mrs. John C. Boyd' on one of them: as if an impostor had picked himself the worst accommodations in the city and used our name out of spite. I'll have to admit there was an element of distaste, probably based on shame or snobbery, in my initial reaction; but it was mixed with wonder, with curiosity, and, most of all, with anticipation.

I pressed the button and got an immediate return buzz from inside. Pushing open the door, we were admitted to a narrow wooden stairway that made up for its lack of light by an almost forbidding odor. I have encountered the smell several times since, and each time, it has given me a sick feeling. You get it in twenty-five-cent rooming houses and in the back parts of poorly ventilated pool halls. You also get it in a telephone booth if the door is closed tight and you smoke a cigarette all the way through.

For a moment, I forgot John was with me, and began climbing toward the uncovered light bulbs at the top of the stairs, as if that held some inexplicable salvation — as if getting to the light bulb had been the purpose of my trip to New York. If I could get there, I was safe — from what, I could not have said.

We had not covered more than half the distance to the landing, however, before our presence was established as legitimate by the unexpected appearance of a woman from the door at the extreme front end of the second-floor hallway. My immediate impression was that she must be one of those lodgers who does not rise until late afternoon, thereby purposely exposing herself to the embarrassment of meeting early callers while still in a state of semi-undress.

By the sunlight, which cut through her opened door and sliced across the hallway bannister, I could see that her face was loose and wrinkled, both soft and unhealthy looking, so that one could not decide whether the effect achieved was her own fault or a trick of circumstance. Auburn-red hair, uncontrolled masses of it, struggled witch-like about her heavy shoulders. Her body was big and almost shapeless under a cheap, green kimono that burst open below the neck, revealing the upper portion of a tight, pink brassiere that was doing its inadequate best to restrain her spongy bosom.

When she first saw us (we were, after all, creeping up the stairs), I expected her to scream something derisive and duck back into her room. She didn't. Her movements were undeniably toward John and myself.

'Oh!' she uttered, in a parrot-like squawk, 'these must be my boys!' Rubbery pink arms, the color of flesh as it is usually painted rather than as it actually is, protruded from her short sleeves, and I saw that she was just now trying to fasten the top buttons of her kimono. 'Of course, they are, of course! That's my Johnny-boy, and you are

Paully. Oo, Johnny-boy, you're even better looking than your daddy! Come here, the two of you, come quickly and kiss Tina before she knocks your blocks off!'

John and I bounded to the landing two steps at a time, shouting, 'Hello!' and 'Tina!' and 'For gosh sakes, it's wonderful to see you!' as if we'd have been disappointed by any less energetic a reception from such an old and dear friend. Upon arriving at the top, we were swallowed in her fleshy smotherings: together — there was sufficient surface — then one at a time, so vigorously that I dropped the car keys, which I had neglected to pocket. As I stooped to pick them up, Tina held John at arm's length.

'Johnny-boy, you're so damn good-looking — Oop! I swore, didn't I? Tina swore. Tina swears too goddamn much. But,' she added, 'people should be allowed to swear in a world like this. Oh God! God! They should be *forced* to swear! I'd rather swear than drink. No, I wouldn't. Anyway,' she concluded, giving me a quick little pat on the cheek, 'I can do both today, can't I? Because you are both so good-looking — Oh, that Johnny-boy! — and you are both here . . . *and* — Tina loves you both.' With this she sucked in her breath and threw her arms around us once more. Then, without giving us the opportunity to do or say anything articulate — indeed, her motions from the outset had seemed but minor gyrations in the execution of one grand, swooping assignment — she ushered us into her apartment and slammed the door.

Tina inspected herself in the vestibule mirror: 'Good heavens,' she said, affecting a British accent, 'I look a positive mess! Your daddy brought me this from Paris,' she explained, fumbling again with her kimono. 'You can't *imagine* how old the miserable thing is. But I still look lovely in it, don't I?' She twirled clumsily into the center of the room, screwing up her face like some twentieth-century gargoyle and addressing us in an odd, scraped, coaxing voice. 'Don't I?' she repeated, pirouetting in the opposite direction.

She did not, however, wait for a reply. Her demonstration shifted rapidly to another object: a wire-haired terrier that, at this moment, pushed through the kitchenette door and began scampering about the square room in a dizzy, circular manner — from bed to window sill to card table to couch and back to the floor, barking as hard as he ran.

'Oh, youuuuuu!' shouted his mistress, lunging at the animal with a determination halfway between scorn and affection. When she got within reach, the terrier jumped onto the sill, sprang to the floor and began zig-zagging behind her on the rug. After these antics, accompanied by a great deal of noise from both participants, had been run through several times, the dog allowed himself to be caught on the bed — almost as if the bout had been fixed to end at this location. Tina, having gathered him up, pressed his wriggling form to her and presented him to us.

'Now Champ,' she said, addressing her captive between gasps, 'for Christ's sake, hold still while I introduce you to daddy's boys. This is John Channing Boyd, Junior. And this is Paul Phillips Boyd. And *this*' (she held the animal at arm's length and shook him gently) 'is Champagne Boyd, Vingt-whatever-it-is. Weet. He was nursed on a case of Pommery your daddy bought before he lost his, shall we say, money? Weren't you, baby! Weren't you! Yes, you were. Oh yes, yes, you were. Jesus, he smells — ' She relaxed her hold, and the dog pounced to the floor, prepared to continue the sport.

This ceremony completed, Tina repaired to her buttons — a piece of business she had never seemed to get through properly. John took off his coat, sat down on the day bed and quieted the dog by stroking him. I looked at him, sitting there on the bed with the dirty, mussed bedclothes under him and the panting terrier on his lap. Tina, grotesque, and I was beginning to think, enchanting, stood on the other side of the room, also looking at John. He *was* handsome: conventionally handsome, but something more than that. Mother's complexion and deep brown eyes were combined with my father's facial structure: his jaw and his cheekbones. The set of the face was strong, stubborn, manly in the most obvious ways. Like my father, he was just saved from being a collar ad by some indefinable softness, by a vulnerability about his eyes and mouth that always seemed to say, 'Tell me what to do. Tell me what *you* would do.' I had the uncanny feeling of seeing my brother for the first time. And then, as if quite by accident, apologetically, a stray breeze stumbled onto the window ledge, and fell exhausted against the mustard curtains, drawing my attention away from John.

It was a beautiful day, and the day came through the open windows. Mild and clear and suddenly quiet, so that each outside noise could be heard separately and each object inside seemed covered with its own share of sunlight, the aging New York summer filled the unfamiliar room. Without haste, I took in the furnishings and accoutrements — so complete in their disarray that they required no organization. Or perhaps, and I preferred to think this, they had a subtle organization of their own: the fake fireplace, its cheap tile hearth littered with old cigarette butts; the big brown couch covered with old newspapers, victrola records, and overflowing ashtrays; the warp-legged card table, staggering under the weight of a dusty typewriter, piles of detective novels, and more piles of yellow writing paper. The sun showed off each spectacle, and nothing seemed to need relation.

For a minute Tina said nothing. She appeared to be looking at a spot in front of John's shoes. Then the flow of hilarity resumed as if it had never been blocked.

'Paul!' she turned and almost screamed at me, 'Take off your coat! I know damn well you're hot and, if you're hot in your own real father's apartment, for God's sake say so, and then for God's sake *do* something about it! Oh, I love you, darling Paul. Tina loves you, but she honestly can't stand to have you sitting there looking so Christly hot. That's right — No, there isn't room in there; if you open that damn door any further, fifteen years of junk will pile onto the floor. Clear some of that stuff away. They're only my stinking literary efforts. I write, you know. Tina writes. Did you know there was talent in the family? Which reminds me: We've got to celebrate! But first, tell me: What do you think of Tina? What do you think of your daddy's wife?' With mock dignity, she sat down on the sofa, crossed her legs and reached for the cigarette box. 'She's been stewing all afternoon, planning to receive you with appropriate . . . Well, anyway, now she wants to know what the h-e-double-l you think of her.' She tapped the cigarette on the top of the box. 'Pleasantly surprised? Or unpleasantly unsurprised? Of course, our butler just joined the army, and our silverware was pawned last week, and we're fresh out of crumpets, so we can't possibly serve tea. . . .'

'We think,' I said, 'well, what the hell — we think just what you wanted us to. You're obviously terrific.'

'Ooosh,' she rushed at me, 'I'm mad about you! But that bastard brother of yours,' she squeezed me, 'that Johnny-boy. . . .'

'Wait a minute!' John protested. 'Paul just spoke before I did. Paul always speaks first. That doesn't mean anything. Golly —'

'Golly-golly-golly-golly-golly. I rate a golly from Johnny-boy. And sober, too. Tina must be good.' She propelled herself to the day bed, ballooned hesitantly over John and, bending down, kissed him facetiously — but none the less passionately — on the mouth, then swirled back to the middle of the room as if nothing had happened. 'Johnny-boy, throw Champ out the window, will you, — and get some glasses, darling, and ice and coca-cola,' she said. 'They're in the refrigerator. Other way. That's the bathroom — you can go there later. To the left of the door. Got it? Just yank the trays out. Sit down, Champ; you can go out in a minute.' John slammed the refrigerator shut and there was a noise of water splashing against metal.

'What kind of things do you write, Tina?' I sat on the window sill and looked down onto the pavement, then propped my right foot up on the sill and looked over at my stepmother.

'In the bath tub,' she sighed, sinking back and throwing her arms along the tops of the cushions, 'I fill the bottom of the tub with cold, cold water, then I put a board — that board there, by the fire-place — across the rims of the tub and the typewriter on the board. It's the only way to write, the *only* way. Don't take so long, Johnny-boy'; she jerked forward and shouted sideways — 'And bring the doo-dad, the — what the hell is it? — the opener, or a knife or something. Because we're going to open a new bottle.'

'New bottle of what?' John appeared in the doorway, holding a tray of ice and coca-cola and glasses.

'Rum. Behind the refrigerator.' She sank back again and beatifically regarded the ceiling. 'What do I write? I write,' she said, 'Tina writes detective stories.'

It was long after dark and we had almost finished the bottle of rum before my father arrived. There was a click, a key click in the door, and then he was standing there, just inside the apartment, holding a brown paper bag in his arms. His gentleness and the quiet, affectionate terms in which he greeted us were in such contrast to the past few hours that I sobered up almost immediately. He made no apologies, except for being late. 'Couldn't get away,' he said, and cleared his throat and began again: 'Couldn't — impossible . . .' He seemed about to go on, but decided against it and broke off with a helpless little shrug: 'You understan'?' Then he took John and me by the hand and suddenly — perhaps from the forced smile on Tina's face—it occurred to me that he was drunk and wanted us to keep him from losing his balance. He smiled—a charming, resigned smile—and said, 'I'm all right now,' and let go of our hands. It was as if he assumed our acceptance of these surroundings, of his wife, even of his condition, just as he had accepted them. And sensing this, we went further: we regarded them as something better than anything we had yet known.

He said very little, but whatever he said was in his kind, smoothing voice. When I was describing the military courses that had recently been added to Harvard's curriculum, he offered a conclusion of his own—added it almost parenthetically, as a casual fragment of perspective. 'Won't do much good,' he said, looking in Tina's direction, but not at her. 'War does worse things than killing,' he rocked forward on the sofa, turning his head, and smiled sheepishly at John and me. 'Lot worse.' Then—'But go on, Paul. I interrupted you.'

We cooked and ate the soup and spaghetti he had brought in the paper bag, and we kept drinking. Tina dominated every turn of conversation, alternating between magnificently strung oaths and soap-opera sentiment. Afterward we walked to Sheridan Square to a cellar night spot where Tina became very drunk and wept profusely over the performers, over us, over the war in Europe, and over a baby she had lost early in her first marriage. My father drank a lot—his capacity seemed inexhaustible—and hardly said anything, but now and then I would catch him observing John or myself and then he would smile. Once when I asked him whether he liked his job—representing a publishing company at the World's Fair, Tina had explained it; actually, he was in charge of a booth that sold encyclopedias—he ran a finger along the edge of his rash and said: 'Yes—very kind to me, Paul—know? Kine.' I felt like throttling all the encyclopedia publishers in the world.

When we returned to the apartment, it was early morning, somewhere between three-thirty and four. I remember pulling a bed down from the wall and undressing and falling into it. My father and Tina slept across the room, but when I lay down they were still up. A big alarm clock was ticking loudly on the mantelpiece and an all-night record program was playing on the radio behind the couch. My father was sitting on the couch, smoking a cigarette and looking straight ahead. I half expected him to lean forward, point at me and say: 'Have you heard the one about the Roosevelts, Paul? . . .'

He either didn't hear me or didn't understand me when I said good night. Tina was in the kitchenette. I felt John get in bed beside me. I moved over a little and turned on my side. He settled with his back to me and then I closed my eyes.

How long I dozed I do not know. I was awakened by a quick, repeated sound. My stepmother was slapping my father. He was still sitting on the couch, facing ahead, and she was kneeling in front of him, slapping him hard, back and forth across the face. 'Wake up — John. Wake up — for Christ's sake — wake up, John. Open your goddam mouth — say something, John.' She kept slapping him and slapping him. Then she dragged him to the other bed and set him down and placed his head on the pillow and his feet up and covered him with a sheet. After that I heard her moving around, undressing, and I think I dozed again.

The next time I awoke she was sitting on my brother's side of the bed, shaking him gently and whispering. She was in her slip and she was smoking a cigarette, whispering to John, shaking him between whispers. He turned over on his back and he must have opened his eyes, because she began carrying on a conversation. It took a little while before he answered her; I guess he had been asleep. 'Johnny-boy, are you sicky? Do you feel bad, Johnny-boy, see spots or anything? Here, let me rub your forehead.' The all-night record program was still going on and the clock was ticking loud and she would take deep puffs on her cigarette and then blow out, completely emptying her lungs. John answered her incoherently and she went on. 'Look at me, Johnny-boy,' she whispered, faster than at first. 'If you only knew, baby. You must know. Move over a little for Tina, honey — just a little?' She took a last puff and threw her cigarette away. I felt that side of the bed go down, and then her fingers accidentally touched my back as they went over John's stomach. Now John was saying, 'No, Tina — get out, Tina, there isn't room for you here. Please get out. I'm tired, Tina, please!' The radio was playing 'Easter Parade' and it ended and the announcer began talking tired humor and for a minute Tina didn't say anything or move, but I could smell her perfume. It smelled sweet, like cheap pastry; like strawberry tarts.

Then she said, 'Johnny-boy, Paul would be just as comfy on the couch, wouldn't he? You wake him and ask him to sleep on the couch, baby. Will you do that for Tina? Will you?' John whispered something to her that I could not hear, and Tina said, 'All right, baby, all right, Johnny-boy,' and I could tell she was excited.

There was a lot of shifting around while she got out of bed and went into the bathroom and closed the door. I tried then to be asleep. For a few seconds I concentrated hard on sleep. I thought of sand: of the bed sinking down and down and washing lazily out to sea. When the spigot turned on, John shook me.

'Have you been awake?' he asked. I sat up and rubbed my eyes and grunted. 'Have you been awake the last ten minutes?' he repeated. I nodded. 'Let's go,' he said. I nodded.

We both dressed quickly and quietly, putting on everything but our shoes. My father was still lying on his back, breathing deeply. His left arm stretched straight out beyond the edge of the bed. I thought how cramped he would feel in the morning and considered placing the arm back on the bed, and then I thought to hell with it. I could hear Champ growling to himself in the kitchenette as we opened the apartment door. We put our shoes on downstairs.

The unexpected brightness of the September night was refreshing. I looked up at the two open second story windows as we pulled away from the curb. Tina must still have been in the bathroom, because there was no commotion of any kind: the apartment was silent, except for the faint, late music of the radio.

*(From Harper's Magazine)*

# VISITOR FROM PHILADELPHIA

## BY JOHN BELL CLAYTON

THE BOY who was spending the summer at the Haywoods' and who asked all the questions and did not talk like us Churchfield boys came up the road bouncing the tennis ball and stopped at our gate.

'Come on in,' I called out.

The honeysuckle had grown so thick up the front of the porch that Grandma could not see the road very clearly from where she sat in the swing.

'Who is that?' Grandma asked.

I said, 'Willard.'

Grandma's tatting shuttle continued its unbroken darting stroke into the thread that had by now begun to trail its fashionable design like a kite's tail into her small lap. 'I knew a family of Willards in St. Louis,' Grandma said. 'They were fine aristocratic Southern people.'

'His first name is Willard,' I told her.

'That is a peculiar first name,' Grandma said.

Willard stepped over the low gate without breaking the bounce of his tennis ball, without looking in fact at either the gate or the ball but appraising the house with that distant and faintly sniffing expression with which he seemed to view each new thing, and came on up to the porch and said, 'Is this where you live?'

I said, 'Yes.'

Grandma said, 'How do you do, Willard?'

Without looking at Grandma, Willard said, 'Hi.'

He caught and held the tennis ball at the top of a bounce and gestured broadly toward Grandma with the closed hand and asked, 'Is she one of your relatives?'

Grandma said, 'Eh?'

I said, 'She's my grandmother.'

Willard started the ball again and said, 'What's she so grim about?'

I said, 'I don't know what that means.'

'Skip it,' Willard said.

Grandma looked up at Willard. 'Young man,' she asked sharply, 'where are you from?'

'Philadelphia,' Willard said. 'Why?'

Grandma's mouth clicked shut in its customary thin straight line and for the time being she said not another word.

Willard chucked the ball against the porch wall, parried it with a practiced flat palm, and then tattooed it between palm and concrete.

'Do you have a room?' he asked me.

I said, 'Sure.'

'Let's look at it.'

I said all right and arose from the steps and Willard came up the steps and started across the porch and into the house still bouncing the ball and Grandma said, 'Young man!'

Willard said, 'Yes?' Not 'ma'am'—just 'Yes?' leaving the question hanging there nonchalant and unanswerable.

And Grandma said, 'Do you do that in Philadelphia?'

Willard paused, puzzled, and said, 'Do what?'

Grandma said, 'Bounce tennis balls in the homes of your friends in Philadelphia?'

Willard gave me a peculiar patronizing sidelong look and pocketed the tennis ball and with the index finger of his right hand described four small quick circles on the side of his head, the side away from Grandma.

We went up to my room and I showed Willard the pennants Ray had sent back from the Military Academy and the big colored picture of Ray that Mother had ordered from the man who came that day and took away with him the snapshot and Mother's check for forty-nine dollars and and ninety-eight cents and then sent back the picture of Ray behind the thick convex glass and the big oval gilt frame and along with it, as the promised surprise bonus, behind the same thick glass and in the same kind of frame, the picture of General Pershing. And we were not certain at first who either picture was supposed to represent and then we figured it out and hung up the picture of Ray but not the picture of General Pershing because Grandma, actually and using profanity for the only time in my hearing, said, with her lips pursed in that tight and inexorable manner, 'Take that damn Yankee's picture out and put it in the woodshed!'

Willard looked at the picture of Ray and pulled the ball out of his pocket and began to bounce it idly on the floor and said, 'What's *he* so grim about?'

I said, 'I don't know what you mean. It's not a very good picture of Ray.'

Willard said, 'Skip it. What else do you have?'

We went downstairs and out the back and I showed Willard the cellar and then the stable and the Maxwell and the ice house and the acetylene lighting plant and then we came back into the living room and I showed him my tinfoil collection and then his eyes fastened on the big picture over the piano and the ball halted in midair and he pointed and said, 'Who is this one?'

I said, 'That's my great-uncle or somethin'.'

'What's the uniform — Western Union?'

'He fought in the war,' I said.

'What's he mad about?' Willard asked. 'Somebody steal his marbles?'

'Mad because we lost the war, I reckon,' I said.

'What war?' Willard said. 'We didn't lose the war. The Germans lost the war. Or hadn't you Virginians heard?'

'I'm not talkin' about that war,' I said. 'The other war.'

'He looks like a Western Union messenger to me,' Willard said, flopping into an armchair and beating the ball against the rug in short, rapid strokes. 'What kind of bush-league war did he fight in?'

Through the open window I heard Grandma clear her throat.

'The War Between the States,' I said.

'Never heard of it,' Willard said flatly. 'World War. And the Revolutionary War and the Civil War —'

Through the window I heard Grandma clear her throat again. She didn't have a cold. She never had colds in the summertime. It was not the sound of a throat being cleared. It was the sound of granite being chipped.

'Young man, that is a likeness of my brother, General John J. McCausland of the Army of the Confederacy!'

For just a moment we could hear only the renewed slight rocking of the swing and I knew that after the one single pause the tatting shuttle was now dipping in its sure undeviating stroke.

Willard gave me a slightly supercilious grin and said, 'How much does that make eggs sell for?'

'That Grant!' I heard Grandma say. 'That Grant!'

I knew she had started now and the remembered venom would have to spin out and trail away like the fashion of the thread spilling faintly into her thin lap.

I heard Grandma bite off the words: 'Less Sheridan than Grant! Less their deeds than their manners!'

Willard transferred the ball to his left hand and once more described the quick turns with his right index finger. 'Who's she talking about? What Grant?'

'The General,' I said. 'The one my great-uncle fought against.'

'I have seen him,' Grandma said, not to Willard or to me or to anyone, '— many times! Lying there in the gutters in St. Louis — *dead drunk!*'

Willard patted the ball against the surface of the rug while listening in curiously to Grandma's words.

'What's Grant being drunk have to do with it?' he asked.

'I don't know,' I said.

'Why don't she just forget it?' Willard asked.

'I don't know,' I said.

I knew that now the shuttle would be flashing back and forth as Grandma's remembered bitterness must have flashed and Grandma said, 'I never blamed John —not once. Not one single time did I ever blame him for burning Chambersburg — '

Willard glanced up at the picture in quick seriousness and with a faint tinge of alarm and pointed at it with the ball-contained hand.

'Did he burn down a town?' he asked incredulously.

I said, 'Sure.'

'Chambersburg. Where is that?'

'In Pennsylvania,' I said.

Willard got slowly out of the chair and looked at me with curious injury and hostility. 'That's my state.'

He took a sharp noticeable breath.

'—I would have done the same myself,' said Grandma, 'whether the orders came from Early or whether they never came at all. I have seen him not once but more times than I can count, stretched out there in the gutter—'

'You ought to be ashamed of yourselves,' Willard said angrily.

'What for?' I said.

'For keeping that picture in here!'

'He was my great-uncle,' I said.

'The dirty old barbarian!'

I gave his shoulder a shove. I could not help it. 'Don't you say that in this house,' I said.

Willard took one tentative step toward me and then halted and turned abruptly to the door. 'Don't shove me,' he said. 'I am going to leave.'

'I hope you don't come back,' I said.

I followed him to the porch and watched him start down the walk. Halfway to the gate he hauled the tennis ball from his pocket, slammed it once against the concrete, caught it, turned his head and said over his shoulder, 'Cuckoos!'

I started down the steps.

'Tucker!' said Grandma.

I said, 'Yes, ma'am.'

'That young man is still our guest.'

Willard bounced on out to the gate, flung a knee across it with strained casualness, and Grandma leaned forward in the swing and peered out toward the gate, holding the thin lips compressed, and sat there until the moment—the instant—Willard's right foot touched the ground on the other side and the left foot cleared the fence and after exactly one second of grace, for good measure and perhaps through some lost tradition, and she even now beginning again to ply the flashing shuttle with the nervous but undeviating fingers, the occupation that would absorb her complete attention so that she could not at the same time observe or deter my pursuit, settled back in the swing and said quietly, 'Tucker, that young man is no longer our guest.'

(*From Good Housekeeping*)

# A LETTER TO MR. PRIEST

## BY MARGARET COUSINS

*WHEN* Marshall Fannin returned from court that wintry afternoon, he saw the long, official-looking letter propped against the bowl of narcissus on the hall table. Josephine usually poked his mail into one of the pigeonholes of the desk, as if to postpone the possibility that the envelopes contained statements of accounts owed. But this was such a splendid, crackling document, rich in watermarks and bearing a New York cancellation, that she must have been convinced it could contain only good news.

Marshall shed his wet coat, then leaned down to dispose of his rubbers.

An arthritic pang, sharp as jealousy, rattled his knee joints. He grimaced, not so much from pain as from the realization that his bones seemed to creak these days, and straightened up, trying to deny the stoop in his tall body.

'Jo,' he bellowed up the stairs.

'All right, dear,' Jo murmured, as if she had a mouthful of hair-pins. 'I'll be down directly.'

There was a small rosy fire in the living-room fireplace, and he went toward it gratefully, sinking into the shabby armchair that reflected the indentations of his person and, to a degree, his personality. It was an old leather chair, the wings outlined in brass nailheads, the mahogany feet scuffed and scarred—no longer handsome but reliable. It had been menaced in Josephine's periodic grapplings with modern decoration, but he had managed to hang on to it. It seemed sturdy to him, a quality he had come to appreciate.

It had been a hard day. He had lost a case of a peculiarly trying nature. The plaintiff, Willard Moss, had not been present for the simple reason that he was lying inert in a plaster cast, where he might probably spend the rest of his days, since his back was broken. He had suffered this accident due to what Marshall considered criminal negligence on the part of the Remnick Construction Company. Though repeatedly warned about the state of their various scaffoldings, Remnick had not seen the light before young Willard plunged to his agony. It had been such an open-and-shut case that Marshall was still bewildered by the devices of the defendants' young and flashy attorney, who had managed to trip all the witnesses and obtain the verdict. Marshall saw himself outwitted, but it was not so much that as the failure of justice that bore him down, the blow to his continuing conviction that right must be done. He brooded over this unhappy situation, and his own responsibility, while he turned the letter in his hands. Then he slit the envelope and read:

Dear Mr. Fannin:

The class of 1917 of Franklin University will celebrate its thirtieth anniversary with a Grand Reunion on May 23, 1947, on the greatly enlarged campus of Franklin. On this occasion the new Law Building will be dedicated and we want to urge you warmly to attend, to renew old friendships and revisit the scenes of your undergraduate days.

Your committee is preparing a commemoration brochure of this noteworthy class, and in going over our records we observe that you were nominated in 1917 as 'The Man Most Likely To Succeed.' Due to the distance of your home from Franklin we have somewhat lost track of your activities, and we wondered if you would favor us with a report of your accomplishments to date to be included in our booklet. We feel that this material will be of great interest to your classmates and to all the friends of Franklin. Thanking you in advance, I am,

Very sincerely yours,
Adam Priest,
Grand Reunion Chairman

Marshall leaned his head against the back of his leather chair, and his mouth twisted in irony. Most likely to succeed, he thought. The most likely to succeed!

Well, thirty years is a long time. Time creeps so slowly, laying its invisible hand upon the bones, cooling the brow, slowing the heart, and always there is so much to do it is not possible to notice that the years are hurtling past and the promises of glory are being dispelled. He could scarcely remember that fledgling among the creeper-covered towers of Franklin, the beamish boy whose silver tongue swayed the rooting section and the Forensic Society alike. How callow he must have been — a skinny, lantern-jawed kid, in love with the sound of his own voice, in love with the law, in love with life. And ignorant — so ignorant except when it came to torts and theories and the things you read in books. Cocky, they called him, Cocky Fannin, The Man Most Likely To Succeed. He summoned up that long-ago class day, the plunging thrill of his accolade, his elaborate modesty, and the secret, wonderful notion he entertained that he might yet be President.

Marshall grinned a little at the ludicrous recollection. 'Fine bunch of Cassandras,' he grunted. 'Just goes to show what kind of judgment *they* had!'

Thirty years, he thought wryly, and what have you done — what have you done? Well, this was not the time to reconstruct the ordinary events of an ordinary life, but when he unfolded the evening paper, he found his mind wandering from the burden of confusion and dismay in the news and working its way backward over the little hillocks of a personal career.

He had had such plans. It was a time when you made plans, orderly, workable, based on the maxims of a young nation, just coming into its flower. If you worked hard and you did the right thing, then you succeeded. In the train of success came material security, the money-bags, the lands and the rooftree, the one woman and the children to carry on your name with honor, the respect of the community, the beneficent power aimed at the common good, the eternal triumph of justice in a democratic sphere, life, liberty, and the pursuit of happiness! Nobody has ever improved on that line about the best-laid plans.

From the beginning of their final year of schooling, Marshall Fannin and Oliver Benedict had sworn eternal friendship and decided to take the world over as a team. Neither Fort Mason nor Prestridge, from which they derived respectively, seemed to provide sufficient arena for their separate or combined talents. They were headed for New York, to quell jurisprudence and, when they got around to it, Wall Street. At the time they both had pretty girls with pretty names, Cynthia Wall and Muriel Folkstone, who lived in substantial country houses on Long Island — wonderful girls with great cloudy puffs of hair over their ears, high-heeled, sixteen-inch boots, and coats of gray squirrel fur.

Marshall and Oliver had wangled letters of introduction to James Garrett of the firm of Garrett & Grainger in Church Street, and already they saw upon the ground-glass doors of this successful establishment the legend, 'Garrett, Grainger, Fannin & Benedict.' It was unthinkable to them at the time that their destinies could be thwarted by a luxury steamship which they had never seen. But when the *Lusitania* went down, they were faced with postponement.

'It's not a question of wanting to go or not wanting to go,' Marshall said solemnly. 'We've got to make the world safe for democracy!' Everybody said that in those days.

'The dogs!' Oliver snorted, always more emotional. 'The butchers! Look what they've done to Belgium!'

The day after Commencement they enlisted, shivering with the excitement and the intimations of history and tentatively calling each other 'Buddy.' They had a few weeks in Camp Yaphank, groaning under the physical slugging of the training, pipe-stemmed in their wrapped puttees, lopsided in their ugly, bulky blouses, and owlish under their campaign hats. Then they were separated. They had a last decorous evening with the girls at the Biltmore, chaperoned by Mr. and Mrs. Wall. Marshall kissed Cynthia good-bye behind a bank of palm trees, and when she clung to him in tears, he whispered, carried away, 'I could not love thee, dear, so much, loved I not honor more!'

He never saw Cynthia again. A few months later she married a new-minted lieutenant in the new-minted air force. He never saw Oliver again either. Although he was slogging around in the mud of a foreign country three months before Oliver got there, he was still slogging around some months after Oliver had died, his lungs full of mustard gas. It was the bitterest event of the war to Marshall, who never before had been able to use the bayonet without revulsion.

He had got the Distinguished Service Medal and a little bronze Croix de Guerre, but that was such a long-ago and faraway war —

such a minor war, in a way — you could hardly call it accomplishment. No use saying it had been a just war to him, a war of deep personal conviction, worth dying for — it hadn't worked out.

When Marshall was discharged early in 1919, he spent his first free weekend in New York, but it seemed big and confusing to him without Oliver. He could not imagine himself going to see Mr. James Garrett and asking for a job. He couldn't remember anything about the law actually, it had been so long since he had thought about it, and the thought of Mr. Garrett, hidden behind polished doors, warded by receptionists and secretaries and assistants, cold and busy, dismayed him. He decided to lower his sights and get a little experience before he stormed this fortress — in a smaller town — Atlanta or Dallas or Memphis.

When he got off the train in Fort Mason, his mother was waiting for him.

'Where's Pop?' he asked, when he had kissed her.

'The Judge is poorly,' his mother said (she had that habit of referring to her husband by his title, even in his presence). 'He hasn't been well for several months. I didn't mention it — I just couldn't bear to worry you.'

'But he's not down, is he?'

'Yes, Marsh, he is.'

Old Judge Fannin, immobilized by a stroke, was propped in a rocking chair in the back sitting room. 'Thank the Lord you've come, boy. The office is going to pot,' he said, his face working.

'Why, that's nonsense,' Marshall shouted, to hide his shock and fear. 'You'll be back in a day or two.'

Judge Fannin shook his head. 'You better get down there tomorrow and straighten things out.'

It was impossible to say, 'But I don't want to practise in Fort Mason. I'm going to hang out my shingle in Atlanta or Dallas — some city place.'

'Okay,' he said. 'I'll show you how to run a law office!'

As he lay on his back that night, staring at the ceiling with that old moiré of rainwater circles on it, he told himself it would be only for a while — a year or two. In the melancholy night, trapped by his pity, he revised his plans. In the morning he walked down the somnolent streets to the I.O.O.F. Building and climbed the stairs to the rooms of Judge Preston Fannin, opened the rolltop desk, and began to sort the dusty papers.

In six months his father was dead, and he was a country lawyer. There are no prizes for accepting responsibility. Who can call that accomplishment? It's instinct — doing the right thing. Just as the needle of the compass leans to the north, so does a man's inconvenient conscience show him the way.

But it was a thwarting thing, the insignificant cases, the miserable little fees, which were the fees of a neglected practice; that and the inability of Fort Mason to think of him as anything but Judge Fannin's boy. His clients made a habit of wishing the Old Judge were still alive, shaking their heads and saying aloud, 'He'll never be the man his father was.'

He had time to brood, and in the throes of his irritation he tried to summon that resplendent hope of himself — the great trial lawyer, striding up and down before the jury, playing upon the twelve men as if they were an instrument and he the musician, wooing them with his voice and his wisdom, triumphant in the accomplishment of justice — going home to his complex social life, moving with Cynthia through the brilliant assemblages and hearing people say, 'There goes the next Attorney General! That beautiful woman is his wife.' Then he would lock the office and go home to supper, and later he might sit in the stuffy dark of the Fort Theatre, staring at Mabel Normand or Constance Talmadge. They were his girls.

He met Josephine Burns at a picnic, though he'd known her since she was ten. She was a wiry little scrap, thin and quick in all her movements, with olive skin and dark, inquisitive eyes. Her black hair was cut in a long Dutch bob, which was still so unusual that it made her look strange. He thought how homely she was, with her straight boy's figure and her squarish face. He had a taste for blondes with soft, indefinite smiles — girls like Cynthia, who, though now a Long Island matron, still inhabited his thoughts.

'Remember the time you picked me up when I fell off my bicycle?' Josephine asked in her husky voice.

'Was that you?'

She stared at him without subtlety. 'You were my first crush,' she said.

He felt embarrassed.

He didn't know how he happened to get paired off with Josephine, except that he was always running into her and people began to think of them as a couple. She was a funny, unpredictable girl, childish in some ways, who made him laugh and startled him with her quick, uprushing emotions and the wild fantasy of her moods.

But he couldn't take her seriously — not until the day he found out that the Mattewan Land Company case he had been fighting to get had gone to his competitors, Stephens & Smith. The Mattewan people had decided that he was too young to handle anything that had so much at stake. He was glooming in the office at ten o'clock at night when he heard a step on the wooden stair and Josephine opened the door.

He gave a guilty start. 'What are you doing here, Jo?'

'I saw your light,' she said. 'I thought you must be up here worrying about something.'

'I'm no good, Jody,' he said. 'I'll have to wait about forty years to be good enough for them. I can't get anywhere.'

'They're just fools,' Josephine broke out. 'They just don't know how wonderful —'

'I reckon they're right. I haven't made much progress in a year. Always the leavings of the business!'

She sat down beside him. 'It's just because life is still simple for people our age,' she said. 'Before long the people we know will be staggering under the burdens of the world and you'll be helping to lighten them, Marsh. You oughtn't to be discouraged because another generation doesn't take you on. Your day is tomorrow.'

It was her confidence that broke him. But who could tell where that kiss began or ended? They were flung together in swift, passionate embrace. Her compact body was pressed against his in painful recognition, and the dark silk of her hair fell around his neck. He was aware of her hands gripped together behind his collar and of the primeval beat of his blood. It was a kiss devoid of compassion or tenderness, the fierce effort to meld two spirits.

Marshall thought still with pity of languid lovers, requiring the moonlight, music, the fragrance of summer. Under the bald yellow lamp bulb, surrounded by the garnered examples of man's dissension bound up in cracked leather, among the ink-stained, shabby tools and the fusty air of jurisprudence, he claimed the wild heart. He had always intended to marry a city girl.

Those were exciting years, the years of beginning — the struggle and striving, the mammoth victories that now seemed so insignificant, the depressing failures that now seemed thoroughly unimportant, the children being conceived and born and growing into definite personalities and long legs; the enthralling microcosm of family life and the power and glory, the fear that goes with being the provider. He used to lie awake at night and marvel at it all.

Economically the times had been stringent. He needed clients. When the Myridon Oil Company sought him as counsel in a title case, he knew it was the opportunity of his lifetime. It was money, publicity, celebrity even.

'The documents are all on our side,' Jack Snell said. He was president of Myridon, a suave, expensive operator with shrewd instincts. 'It's just a matter of interpretation of the law.'

Marshall brooded over his decision, but it was a waste of time. He foresaw that he might persuade a jury to rationalize a fine point. He could not forget old man Bizbee, who had homesteaded the arid land, earned it with his toil, owned it actually. Poor old man Bizbee, he could scarcely read. That land was part of his body, after twenty years of scratching it with a plow, grubbing it with his muscles, watering it with his sweat.

'Looks like I can't take this case, Snell,' Marshall said.

'What do you mean?'

'My interpretation just won't jibe with yours,' Marshall said.

'Are you crazy? I thought you were ambitious. I'm going to win this case, you know that. I just asked you because I like you.'

'I'm grateful, Snell. I guess I'm a fool.'

'You're a hick,' Snell said. 'You're a high-grass Pollyanna, and I'm lucky. I found it out in time.'

'It's a good thing all around,' Marshall said. 'Don't forget your hat.'

Josephine was waiting for him that night with her eyes shining. When he told her, the sparkle seemed to go out of her for a minute. They needed money, might as well face it. 'I'm sorry, honey,' he said. 'I don't know what came over me.'

'You did right,' Jo said. 'I wouldn't have had it any other way.'

He had often thought about that incident. It was a fork in the road. You took one direction and maybe you wound up a senator, a citizen of the world. You took the other, and you were Marshall Fannin, LL.D., Fort Mason. He reconnoitered in his mind where he might be and what he might be doing now if he had represented Myridon — how different his life might have been. Snell was right. His stand hadn't mattered at all. Old man Bizbee lost his land.

'When the big chance turned up, I muffed it,' Marshall thought. 'Put that in your brochure, Mr. Priest!'

But it was after that he seemed to gain stature in the community. People tried to overlook the fact that he continued to be a Wilsonian advocate, putting it down to aberration.

'If you would just keep your big mouth shut,' said Finis Cooper, the party chairman, 'you could be elected to the legislature.'

'How can I keep quiet and run for office?' inquired Marshall.

'You don't have to go around yelling that the country is a pack of fools, do you? It makes people lose confidence in you.'

'If people don't have confidence in me, I couldn't represent them very well, could I?'

'You're just not cut out for politics, Marsh,' Finis said. 'You're not practical.'

He had wanted that nomination. It was one of the most hurtful things that ever happened to him, being rejected. He wondered why he could not conform, if the end justified the means. You could do more about the Ku Klux Klan inside a lawmaking body than outside it. You couldn't do anything outside it but fume and rage. All you needed for nomination and election was to keep your mouth shut, and it was just an adage that silence gives consent. The nature of his business was argument, so he argued with himself, but he didn't win. And he wasn't nominated, either.

'We don't care,' Josephine said staunchly. 'It's their loss.'

'I wish the party was as biased as you are.'

'They'll find out!'

It was all negative. There was nothing you could put your finger on and say, 'This is what I did!' It didn't mean anything to repeat, 'This is what I didn't do.' It sounded craven and weak, dredging up refusals, as if he were a balky horse.

He didn't run for office, but he began to have more than he could do. It was something to have people trust him. 'Mr. Fannin, save my boy, he didn't do nothing wrong . . .' or 'I came to you, Mr.

Fannin, because you done the right thing about that Lacey case,' or 'I reckon you know I'm guilty. We can go on from there,' or 'I need your help, Fannin, and you're honest.' The tide of human misery that washes over a lawyer washed over him. He wasn't brilliant, but he was sound and earnest and a good pleader. They paid him off in various ways, and there was money enough for the boys to get schooling and to keep the house up and buy Josephine a fur coat. 'In 1929 I bought my wife a beaver coat.' There was no way to explain what that meant in the way of pride. He had thought, 'Now we're on the way.' He had never lacked for clients from then on, but there were several years when the crops failed and there was a drought and something seemed to happen to all the money in the world.

His mind veered away from the most dramatic moments of his life when he thought about himself. It was not pleasant for a civilized man to remember, nor had he ever been able to discuss it with anybody. It sickened him a little to think of it now — that hideous, humid, suffocating Saturday afternoon, with the heat lightning flickering in the sullen sky, the low murmur of men in the streets of Fort Mason, the wretched boy who was cowering in a cell in the county jail. The prisoner's alleged offense had been inexcusable and brutal, but when times were hard, men seemed to have less perspective on law and order. There was in them some wish to hurt, a lust to break the tragic monotony with violence.

He had never seen a mob before, nor could he have imagined it. The streets were full of men, little knots of men, and their pestilential murmur.

He stood at the window of his office, looking down into the street, and he thought, 'I wish it would rain. Might clear the air.'

It was seven o'clock. The twilight had fallen, but the scorch of day lay on the air like a wool blanket. He was hardly aware of what that murmur portended, for it had never occurred to him that the horrible things you read about could happen before your eyes. He was about to put on his seersucker coat and go home when he stopped looking at the sky and looked down into the street and observed a group of men, hot and jostling, straggling up the street, augmenting itself as it came, murmurous with the angry sound of hysteria. There was such a sickness in the sight that he was immobilized for a minute, not able to take in its intent. When it broke over him, he hurtled down the stairs, running as he had not thought it possible to run, gasping and sweating in the breathless air.

The keeper of the flimsy jail was an old man, hard-of-hearing and tremulous.

'Where's the sheriff?' Marshall asked. Then, louder, 'The sheriff! Sheriff Gaines!'

'Gone. Gone to the city.'

'Then quick, get on the telephone. Call Bakersville and tell them to send help. We're in trouble!'

The clamor of voices beat in his ear, and he knew the aggregation had turned the corner.

'What's up?' the old man said.

'Listen,' said Marshall. 'They're coming after Gus Wood!'

'What?'

His frustration was so intense that he wanted to strike the old man. 'Give me the keys!' he shouted. 'And get out of here — out the back way — fast.'

He took up the bunch of heavy keys and put them in his pocket and gave the old man a shove. 'Hide!' he shouted. Then he forced himself to go out the door and stand there, waiting. He was terrified. His face turned gray and the water poured off him and his throat was dry. They struggled up to the door of the jail, making that inhuman sound. He looked into the massed faces, distorted and scarlet, and shut his eyes.

'Get out of the way, Fannin.'

'No,' he said.

'You know what we're after! Nothing's going to stop us.' There was a surge forward.

'He ain't going to need a lawyer, Fannin!'

This was the time for oratory, but he was mute.

'Come on, what are we waiting for? Rush him.'

Marshall stepped from the shadow of the door into the unprotected glare of the light over the worn granite steps that led to the prison. He didn't cut much of a figure — a thin, middle-aged man in a dank seersucker suit. His head was aching, but he stood rooted to the spot, a frail, dubious monument of resistance.

'This is my home,' Marshall said. 'This little cranny of the world where I was born. I live here, but wherever I live, I must first live with myself, as you must live with yourselves. If I cannot live with myself, I am better dead, for then I cannot live with anybody else. I have nothing to lose by standing here. My responsibility to the fool inside these walls is no more or less than my responsibility to you and to all men everywhere. I never saw his face, but if you are to be able to look into mine and I into yours, I cannot run away. If you take him, you must take me first!'

Marshall paused to swallow a sob. His instinct noted the dying away of the hideous clamor of their combined voices. His own voice fell strangely on his ears. He did not know where the words originated. Out of some fold of memory his thesis sprang to his lips in syllables he had no time to plan.

'Reason is the law of life. Without it we are clods, and law itself is nothing else but reason. I appeal to your reason, without which survival is not worth the candle. *The accused shall enjoy the rights to a speedy and public trial by an impartial jury.* This is the law of the nation to whose allegiance I am sworn. I will protect that law with my last breath, with my last drop of blood, for I am a soldier on a perennial field of battle, and the honor of my country is at stake as much as my own! How can you stand there and bear witness to the sabotage of the American ideal? Go home and hide your shame!'

He was panting for breath; he could hear his hoarse gasping in the stupefied quiet of the mob. On the outer edges it had begun to disintegrate, at first a few skulking figures and then little knots of the chastened moved off toward the town, slowly and then hurrying as if pursued. But the core stood transfixed, struck dumb, packed together in wavering silence. Then out of heaven poured the deluge, a curtain of cold, pelting rain, staved with lightning and the loud detonations of thunder. They broke like frightened children, scuttling for cover, wordless at their deliverance.

He stood in the rain and watched them go. The rain drowned his cotton clothes and ran in rivulets off his shoulders. When he staggered home at last the crisis was past. Sheriff Gaines had returned from the city where he had gone for help, spirited the tawdry prisoner away. Josephine was standing at the gate, crying. She had heard everything.

'How could you risk your life?' she cried. 'Doesn't your family mean anything to you?'

'Let me alone,' he said, and took his sickness upstairs.

It hadn't been courage. The taste of fear had turned his mouth to acid. It was impossible to take credit for a civilized instinct. It had been misery and horror from the beginning to the end, washed over by Josephine's anguished tears. That had been, in his lifetime, his sole oration.

In 1937 he was the leading lawyer in Mason County, summoned often to the capital tribunals. He was too busy to enjoy his modest prosperity. He was also too busy to think much about Hitler, and he didn't like to anyway, because it reminded him of that mob in front of the Mason County jail. When Chamberlain came home from Munich, Marshall Fannin looked at his sons, Burns and Cary, and his heart turned over. It was already too late.

This new war smote him far more personally than the one he had fought in. He had dwelt with reason a long time, and unreason deteriorated him. He kept seeking the answer, and of course he found it, in the files of his own office, in the books that lined his walls. The cause and the prevention, the lawlessness and the law, the necessity for every man to till his own acre, to mend his own fences, to insist that right be done and the responsibility of society to enforce it. This conclusion burst over him with a blaze of conviction and novelty, and he forgot that it had been true for two thousand years and more. But it got him through the perilous days when one of his sons was in prison camp in Bavaria and the other was lying in a hospital on the Hawaiian Islands. It gave him an Olympian patience with the false starts and the dire confusion of his country. It gave him faith that sacrifice wasn't wasted. He was glad that he had been able to spend his life stumbling in the vanguard of Justice, however limited his horizon.

It gave him hope for a new world.

'I found my philosophy,' he thought, 'but it wasn't new.'

Two years had passed, and the bright promise of global law was beginning to dull around the edges. The boys had come home, battered but ambitious. Cary had put out for New York to pursue a familiar dream. Burns, obviously aghast at Marshall's unbusinesslike methods, had entered his father's law office to revolutionize it. It looked now as if Marshall might eventually have time to become county judge, but Burns thought in no terms smaller than the Senate. How unoriginal life is, Marshall thought, and how impatient the individual man. He has only to look at the record and know how slowly we progress, with each generation adding its small accretion — two steps forward and one step back — and that every step has its inception in the mind and heart of some single human being. Progress is a personal thing, and no man is too small to have his stake in it, if he cares. Who could despair when he cherished such a secret?

'What are you doing here in the dark?' Josephine asked. She was standing in the doorway, with his youngest grandchild, Caroline, a sorceress of five.

'I must have dropped off,' Marshall said.

Josephine bent over and kissed him. She had got plump and her Indian tresses had turned a little, but her eyes had never changed. He caught her hand between his cheek and shoulder. 'Hello, old lady,' he said.

'If I called you 'old man,' you wouldn't like it,' she complained.

'It wouldn't be true,' Marshall said, though he looked much older than his years. 'When you come in a room, I'm just a boy again.'

Josephine snorted, but he knew that she was pleased.

'I found my love,' Marshall thought. 'What else is there?'

Marshall leaned over and picked up Adam Priest's letter. 'I've got to write a note,' he said.

'Well, hurry,' Josephine directed. 'It's time for dinner.'

'It won't take long.'

He went into the back sitting room, which had been fitted up as a home office, and sat down at the typewriter. Caroline trailed him and stood nudging his knee. Marshall wrote:

Dear Mr. Priest:

Thank you for your kind letter with its cordial invitation to return to Franklin for the reunion of the class of 1917. It would give me great pleasure to be there, but unfortunately I have an appeal coming up in district court in May — an accident suit in which I have a strong personal interest — so I shall have to decline. I would enjoy seeing the fine new Law Building, for any temple dedicated to the blind goddess has my earnest blessing. I hope you will offer my congratulations to the faculty and student body.

It is very good of you to wish to include my accomplishments in the commemoration brochure. When the old gentleman looks at his medals, he finds that they are so few and far between that they don't bear discussion. I fervently hope that the members of the class of 1917 have displayed more judgment in after-life than they did on that class day when they nominated me 'most likely to succeed.' I am just a country lawyer. There's honestly nothing to tell.

I wish you the most unqualified success in your undertaking, and please give my greeting to any who happen to remember me.

Sincerely yours,

MARSHALL FANNIN

He folded the letter into an envelope, and Caroline exercised her prerogative of licking the stamp.

'There,' she said.

He looked down at her. 'How would you like to be President?' he asked.

'Sure,' said Caroline. 'Okay!'

Marshall grinned. 'Well, you never know,' he said, and went in to dinner.

(*From '47 — The Magazine of the Year*)

# THE HOLLOW HEART

## BY M. F. K. FISHER

WHEN Martha went to the door and saw Bob standing there, her heart did not beat faster nor did her cool voice change, although it was the first time she had been with him since the final decree more than six months before. Oh you handsome smiling devil, she thought with a kind of affectionate stoniness.

'Hello,' she said, smiling back at him.

He came with ease into the familiar rooms, the way he walked into the Plaza or the Ritz, and they went to the little rear room that had always been the heart of the house, her mother's room with the desk and the ferns and the old magazines. Then he sat down neatly, with that same air of intimate warmth, like a sleek well-fed condescending tomcat. Martha watched him for a minute, full of amusement at feeling so calm and seeing him so unchanged.

'I was drinking sherry,' she said, holding up her glass.

'No thanks,' he said quickly.

'I know you hate it. But there's no Scotch.'

'No. I'm on the wagon. Really.'

'Since when?' He must be terribly in love, she thought, to do that. He looks it, very fit. Some girl's stronger than I was.

'Couple of months, anyway. It's not so bad. But tell me about yourself. You look marvelous, really marvelous.'

His shallow blue eyes smiled gaily at her, and she could see how easily he was breathing under his finely tailored gabardine with all the creases just so and the tie and the belt buckle, as if he still were in uniform. The fatness above his belly was gone. He looked marvelous, really marvelous. Martha grinned.

'There's not much to say,' she said, feeling stupid before his gay politeness. 'I'm fine, of course. And the children . . .'

'Oh God yes! How are they?'

'They're fine.' She watched coolly how he bit once at his lower lip, and puckered his light feathery brows a little, and let his eyes go tragic for an instant. Late, but good, she thought. She waited until he had straightened his shoulders, silent gallantry in a little cape over them, a cloud about him. That's over, she thought. All the stops are in good working order, ready to be flicked in and out. He plays them all. He's all right. 'They're fine. They love it here.'

'Do they miss me?'

'Well, darling . . . at that age . . . and then of course they didn't see much of you for so long . . . Of course you probably know Dodie is here too, with her three. She's getting a divorce.' He looked almost embarrassed at the amusement in her voice, as if it were vulgar.

'And Nan was here when I came, with Peter!' Martha kept on laughing, to tease him. Finally he laughed too.

'What does your father think?' he asked.

'He likes it. He calls this 'Ex-Marital Manor' in his worse moments, but he really loves having all the kids here, and they adore him. It's an odd set-up, of course . . . but fortunately we're three sisters who like each other.' She thought of the house full of women, their little, tired father, the wild mixture of children so lively and so hungry. . . .

'Too well. You like each other too well,' the man said, and Martha saw his full easy mouth whiten along the edges for a second, as if a bright eye flashed from a crack in a cave or a snake darted its tongue into the sunshine. Then he was gay again.

She drank at the sherry. 'But you,' she said urgently. She felt happy, in a cool way, that he had come at last. The months of letters from lawyers, the suavity, the too-easy lack of quarrels, and the way everyone complimented her on how civilized the whole process had been: They all dissolved before this happiness, which at the same time was impersonal. She watched him shrug, and waited for the familiar signs of his next act. She had given the cue, and she wondered whether he would imply wounded misunderstood manhood or something more debonair—a well-bred wolf new-running from the den. The signs came. She sighed with a kind of relief. He was the wolf.

He looked mischievously at her, and his mouth curved in a half-teasing smile, one from which she hid her secret eyes because her twin sons had it too. 'Me?' His smile flickered over her, taunting, daring. 'I'll be made a partner in the firm in ten days. And I'm behaving outrageously, Babe. I'm on the prowl.'

'I thought you would be.'

'I always have been, of course.'

She wanted to throw the rest of the sherry in his face, his smug, teasing face. But that would please him, who had so often asked for but never seen such a gesture from her. He was trying to make her angry . . . How angered he himself would be to learn that it was only boredom she felt! She stood up, still smiling, and said, 'I'm going to the pantry for some more. Are you sure you won't have any?'

He stood up too, as easily as always, well-oiled. 'Where's everybody?' He sniffed the air suddenly as if he scented something powerfully exciting.

Martha looked coolly at him. 'Dodie has the twins and Nan's kid in the park. Nan's marketing. We're between maids, as you may have guessed. And the children, or Peter anyway, won't be home until late . . . baseball. That leaves me alone with you.'

She burlesqued the last words fatuously, feeling like a high-school girl ready to make a remark about the villain's etchings. But the man was against her. She could feel his heart beating through the cloth, the flesh, the ribs. Her heart was pacing it.

'Mart, Mart,' he said softly, as softly as a ghost against her temple. 'Mart, we still do the same things to each other. Mart, you know that, don't you?' She was falling, dying, drowning, and she held on to the wine glass as another might hold to the idea of God.

There was the cracked voice of Peter in her ears. He stood in the doorway to the sunny little room. On the back of his head he had a beany cut from one of his grandfather's old hats. It was covered with autographs copied from magazines: Bob Hope, Lana Turner . . . His eyes were as blank as a cat's.

'Aunt Martha I came home early may I have a cookie?' he asked tonelessly, looking over her shoulder.

She left her free hand on Bob's arm. She had never run for a streetcar in her life, and she was not going to start ignominious leaping for the benefit of a twelve-year-old boy. She told herself so, sternly, trying not to feel sick.

'You remember your Uncle Bob, don't you, Peter?'

'How do you do sir may I take a couple of cookies?'

Martha felt helpless before his stern blank face. 'Of course,' she said, and he was gone. The air was stiff with shock and disapproval.

Bob puffed out his breath. 'God,' he said. 'Kids are awful. Will ours be like that?'

'They're young yet. But I suppose so. I was going to get some sherry.'

Everything was all right for a time. Martha put the cover back on the cookie jar on the sideboard, and in the pantry poured herself wine, noting abstractedly that the goblet she was using was bigger than necessary, while all the time she felt the man's eyes on her and knew that she was impervious again, covered with a kind of shell of chastity. The obvious fact that at least one crack in the shell had shown did not bother her: Peter's cold presence had sealed it. Of that she was sure.

Back in the little sitting room, Bob leaned against the soft cushions of the old fat couch, and she sat primly down beside him, as if he were the curate come for tea.

'I miss your mother, God rest her soul,' he said. 'I meant to write when I heard. This room . . .'

'Yes, we all do.' Martha tried not to smile, hearing him say God-rest-her-soul. He always said that, in such an oily voice, like a sleek priest, about people who had died: waiters, movie stars, politicians, his friends. Now her mother . . .

'I suppose the mess we got into didn't help,' he muttered, and his head sank into his raised fists. She watched him dispassionately. He was being tragic. She recognized the whole act again. She wanted to yell at him that probably the mess and her coming home with the twins and then the divorce had given her mother one of the few bits of happiness on her deathbed. But why should she ever speak the truth to him? He would not recognize it, never having felt it in his private self. She felt stronger than he, superior.

He looked at her, quickly, and she saw his lips rimmed flashingly with white. The adder's tongue . . . He was angry.

'You're laughing at me,' he said.

'No Bob . . . really.'

'Oh Mart!' His face crumpled. She looked at it, and saw that he was going to be charmingly, boyishly sorry for himself. She felt very tired. He leaned near her, and sure enough the gay smile in his flat blue eyes clouded, and his mouth pulled down heartbreakingly.

Then he knocked the goblet from her hand, and she could feel his heart beating hard again, just as hers, to her great surprise, was beating hard too. She heard his voice, a ghost's voice, close against her temple. 'We are alone, aren't we, darling? Didn't you say that? Mart, Mart, what you still do to me!'

She lay back against the soft fat cushions, her mother's cushions, willynilly. The man who had once been her love, her own true love at that, pressed heavily against her. She thought of the broken goblet: three that week . . . she was drinking too much, getting careless . . . it was almost time to make the twins' formula.

'Mart,' he murmured ferociously, and she knew that her arms were around him. A drab, she thought clearly. A broken-down servant in a cheap boardinghouse waiting for that cute Mr. Murgatroyd who travels in silks to make his annual visit. A two-bit drab, waiting for the prettyboy to drop in for free.

Bob was looking at her, his eyes cruel as mirrors, with herself reflected in them tiny and distinct.

'Stop it,' he said. 'Stop! What are you doing, damn you?'

She said nothing, but she could feel her heart slow hideously in her stone-like body.

'You look like a wife,' he said, and there was loathing in the way he said it so quietly. 'You lie there thinking. Don't think. Don't always be putting things into sentences, with the commas just so. That's what you do.' He sounded puzzled, as if he had at that instant bowed how-de-do to someone he had always known but never recognized as a social equal.

Martha lay silent against the cushions. She felt about an inch thick.

'I'm going.' Bob stood up and put all his clothes into line again, automatically, as if he were still a soldier. 'I'll send the twins something from town, something really nice. Do the payments come through all right?'

'Yes, thanks. Everything is in order.'

'I still think you're a damn fool not to ask alimony for yourself. Other women do.'

'I'm not other women,' Martha said, and her lips were stone.

'I'm going,' he said again.

'Thank you for coming,' she said politely, still sprawled on the couch. She knew that if Gandhi and John L. Lewis walked through the door arm in arm she would not be able to move this way or that. Suddenly she asked in a childish voice, 'Didn't you come on purpose, then?'

Bob stopped at the edge of the room. 'Hell no,' he said. 'My boss had a date near here. I asked to be dropped off . . . thought I'd kill an hour. I can't keep him waiting, of course.'

'Of course not. Good-by.'

'Good-by, Babe.'

She heard him stop at the cookie jar and then slide the lid back softly, the way Peter did when he was pretending to steal. The door slammed. She crawled into herself on the couch, bent in two with anguish, sick with desire and a dread of all the years ahead. She saw how her sons would smile at her, gay and urgent and teasing, and behind them would be the father, and there would be the times when she would twist in pain, knowing herself hollow with love, hateful and proud as stone.

(*From The Atlantic Monthly*)

# 'FLY, FLY, LITTLE DOVE'

BY PHILIP GARRIGAN

*IN THE DUSK* of the third day we were ordered out of the trucks beside a mass of tents, which bewilder the eye seeking analogies, for they resemble nothing but tents. Before it was altogether dark we marched off with heavy bags on our shoulders and took our assignments, six men to a tent. We sat on the bare cots and waited to be called for blankets.

At just that time, which with its dark and stars and strange tropical trees would otherwise have been romantic, the Mexican with the guitar began to sing and play, and another sang with him. This second Mexican I had not seen, but the first I remembered by the guitar. On the bag he carried (with difficulty because he had also to carry the guitar) was a large tag with the childish lettering of the name Francisco Llorado. I saw him as we came down between the tents, and I remembered that *llorado* is Spanish for weeping or sorrowful or something like that. And now this Francisco was singing, and someone with him, and playing the guitar.

The song itself was sad, and that brought his name again to mind, so that I said I must look tomorrow and see the name of the other. I should have known after riding all day in the same truck; but the recruit is stunned by the Army, and sometimes his reactions are not normal for weeks. That is how it was with me, sitting there on that sagging cot in a tent with the fly ripped, thinking not of that but of home and my wife, because we were separated for the first time.

Thinking of this I might have had tears in my eyes, but nobody would have noticed in the dark. Yet the guitar itself could not be sad, no matter how Francisco might sing to it. So I sat there and filled my mind with the silly resolve to find out the name of the second Mexican. Soon after, a sergeant ran up and down the line bellowing, to herd us out for our bedding. He made it look as if he had to drive us, but we were glad enough to go.

When we got back and had somehow arranged the blankets in the dark, we took off only our shoes and hats and belts, and crawled into what little warmth there was. For a long time the two Mexicans continued their singing—how long I don't know, because I fell asleep while they were still going on. That night and many others afterward their singing seemed like a lullaby, a little faint because it came from a distance of three tents to the left. But when I spoke to one in that tent, a Pennsylvania Dutchman called Uzzenfuss, he said it nearly drove them crazy and it kept them awake until two in the morning sometimes. They all cussed about it, but they understood that the Mexicans were lonesome. We were all lonesome.

The days that followed our arrival are painful to dwell upon. We were delivered over to drillmasters and instructors uniformly obscene and abusive, or humorous in a macabre way. Only the simplicity of the things they had to teach prevented us from absorbing their moronism along with their brutality. We became able to march in cadence, to carry a rifle and simulate the fierce rage of bayonet practice, to wear the ubiquitous gas mask. There were many other things, too, learned at great cost of standing or dog-trotting for hours in the sun, over the mud, or sitting until our legs went to sleep, or crawling on our faces through the thorny bushes. We learned them all and still know a little about them, some of us.

The Mexicans were not made happy by all this. I could sometimes hear their discussions in their own language; and now and then someone in a near-by tent would in the dark night call on Jesus Christ to witness what a trial they were to English-speaking people in need of rest. I passed them on my way to and from drill; and almost always they were sitting on their cots, with all the tent flaps rolled up, conversing loudly and at the same time sadly—for they often wept together, the sound of their voices choked by their sobbing. I wondered what they were saying, but I was already learning too much to take up Mexican. I had told my wife, before I left home, that I would surely learn Russian in the Army. There would be so much time.

Nevertheless, the sight of their devotion to one another, and the lonely melancholy of their life, were affecting. I am not myslf inclined to meddle with anyone's life, and very little with my own. But there were some who spoke of them with sympathy, feeling that these two were just a projection of all of us, a plaintive protest against the harshness of a climate supposed to be forever sunny, of pretty understripers and their outhouse rhetoric, or perhaps against the separations of war, which we all felt.

In time we grew accustomed to the serenades, and I came rather to expect them. I would lie in the blankets, thinking of my wife and of the weeks of last summer in that New England seaside town, wondering if our child would be a son to shiver in the tents of the war after this one. Oh, this was not bitterness — only the searching fingers of music in the mind, probing for thoughts to cancel the aches of the body.

But not everybody was thus probed and canceled. Four or five times, this or that group of drunken tentmates returned from town with the same conspiracy, hatched in some scuffed barroom booth. They would gather before Francisco's tent, as once I saw them do, and when all was quiet one of them would slip in to steal the guitar. Every time, they found the two friends awake, clutching it; and their clamor brought around the guard. One night, as I afterwards heard, the Mexicans made no noise — but the marauder came out swearing, with a six-inch scratch on his forearm. Because of the dark he only presumed this had been done with a knife. But that was the end of that idea.

We were in a training camp from which large numbers were shipped every day to far ports of the country, and some overseas. It was another matter, however, that accounted for many of the gaps in the lines and names crossed off the rolls. Partly from the climate, new to most of us, and partly from the wind whistling through the tents, and the gray Florida sand sifted into us at every pore, we all suffered a peculiar irritation of the nose and throat, in which we had a high fever, a dry racking cough that doubled us up in pain, and finally bronchitis.

Sick call was well attended, but heavy as it was, most of us stayed away from it as long as we could. It was not wise to tempt any Fate in this place. I nursed my troubles along for two whole weeks on remedies bought in town. When at last I had to report myself, it was not so bad as I had expected. It was strange that the stripers kicked us around sick or well; but the medical officers (except when they disliked a man's face or remarks) were as solicitous of us as if we had all been private patients at customary prices. From a straightforward interview with a major, I drew an assignment of a week in quarters, and some foul potion which seemed to be mostly menthol.

That week I spent in writing long letters to my wife and in lying on a cot in the tent of the Charge of Quarters, who had a small radio. At home I had more than two hundred records; but I had not heard any good music except on one afternoon when the officer in charge of the swimming pool tuned in a Mozart program and was too busy to change it. Nobody else dared. I lay there in the midst of the naked sunbathers, and listened so long I could not move without pain for the next three days.

The Charge of Quarters swept the dial for hill-billy music; and though opinion was divided as to whether it was better than no music at all, I listened hour after hour.

I was sitting there of a Friday in the late afternoon, when the second Mexican ran in, crying that Francisco was dying. His name was Juan Fernandez, and he spoke English on occasion. It was only that he and Francisco preferred to use their own language. It was for the same reason that I sometimes thought to myself in French — because nothing was farther from that life than French. But, as I said, this Juan Fernandez ran in saying that Francisco was dying.

All of us went to the tent; and there it seemed that he was indeed dying, so the Charge of Quarters ordered Lambroso to go for the ambulance. Now Lambroso was quartered with a bad knee, and it was twenty minutes before the ambulance arrived. Meanwhile there was nothing we could do but stand there while Juan addressed his friend urgently, grasping him by the shoulders and shaking him as if he were a small child who would not wake up. Francisco seemed to be in a stupor, breathing with difficulty and great noise. I usually cross the street to avoid the sight of a dead dog; but I could not leave there, so my mind put off its horror by speculating with all its strength on the appearance of these two beings.

The moving pictures had accustomed me to handsome Mexicans.

But these two were not so; they were ugly in the sense that they did not look like the rest of us. Short and squat, they had round heads, high cheekbones, and protruding lips. Their noses were flattened, their faces closer to black than to olive, and their hair coarse and unruly. On the back of Juan's neck it flowed over the collar in a jagged line of bristles. Francisco's mouth was open on a thick tongue and yellowed teeth, some of them broken. He lay there with his eyes shut, running with sweat, and struggled to breathe.

When the ambulance finally came, the driver and attendant brought in a litter and set it down. They pulled the blankets off the Mexican and rolled him expertly on the litter, throwing one of the blankets over him. Except for a hat, he was fully dressed. When they slid him in, Juan tried to go along. They took him by the arms and threw him out. Then he tried to put the guitar in with Francisco. The attendant pushed it back at him. I was surprised that he hadn't thought it simpler to throw the instrument on the ground and break it. He closed the doors at the back, went to his seat, and they drove off. We felt relieved to be able to go then, and only the Charge of Quarters remained. He told us later he had felt sorry for Juan, so he had taken him to the lieutenant.

Before this tribune it came out that Francisco had been sick for three weeks without medical attention. In the morning Juan would get him something to eat and they would slip out into the fields of Spanish Sword to hide until we had gone to drill. Then they would come back and Francisco would lie down. At the approach of anyone of official appearance, Juan would give warning and they would slip away again. At night in the dark Francisco still played the guitar, however poorly; and in the face of this, nobody knew there was anything wrong. Only, this particular day when Juan tried to rouse him he had not even waked. They were not afraid of the doctor, Juan insisted, only of the sergeant. The sergeant had said (*all* the sergeants said it as a matter of course) that if any relative of the dog as far as his eye could see was crazy enough to go on sick call, thus avoiding drill, he personally would double-time him from hell to breakfast or until his legs were worn off right up to the knees and beyond, whichever took longer.

The lieutenant was a humane man, but I have no report of his conversation with the sergeant. For infractions of discipline the lieutenant put Juan on the rock pile, but promised he would be told how Francisco was progressing. Twelve times in the first half hour he had to lead Juan back to the rocks and assure him that there was no change, that everything was all right. After retreat, in an unsatisfactory state of mind, the lieutenant left camp and stayed in town overnight.

Francisco died. He had been moribund when we saw him, and he did not regain consciousness. I never found out how they told Juan, or who it was who carried the word. Shortly after that I was shipped, and so far I haven't met anyone who was at that camp with me.

Only, as I was standing in the doorway of my tent that evening, Juan came down the street from the direction of the hospital. He was crying. He went into his tent, and I heard him trying to play the guitar and sing. His fingers, unlike Francisco's, were not apt; the music stumbled awkwardly. His voice, though passable in accompaniment, was broken and choked with sobs. I had not listened half a minute when I decided to go to the Post Exchange for a bottle of beer, which ordinarily I do not like. I had four.

Uzzenfuss told me about it afterward. He was shipped out with me, but went to a different place. Having nowhere to go, those in his tent had to sit and watch Juan as he tried to sing and play. Finally, Uzzenfuss said, the Mexican took the guitar outside and filled it with toilet paper (we all carried it — for we never found it where we might have expected to) and grass. Then he set it on fire; and while it burned he went into the tent and came out again with a heavy silver bracelet no one had ever seen before, and a large bandanna handkerchief. These were all he owned in the world. Everything else belonged to the Army.

Nobody could do anything, Uzzenfuss said. They just sat and watched him go; and behind him the guitar spat and crackled in the flames, and each string as its supports were burned out cried harshly once and for the last time. Juan did not say good-bye or look back. He went to the gate; and when the guards stopped him, he talked to them, gesturing toward the direction in which the sun had just gone down. Then there was a struggle as he tried to go by them; at first it was mild, but grew wilder as his efforts aggravated the guards. After all, as Uzzenfuss said, they have orders not to use any more force than they have to.

In the end they had to hit him over the head a few times. It wasn't a nice thing to see, Uzzenfuss said, and I knew he meant not just because of the clubbing. These details he told me as we sat on our barracks bags in the back of the truck, going away.

I was going to write my wife about it. But I decided not to. From her letters I think she worries about what is likely to happen to me so far away. At this station, when we arrived, I sent her three little bottles of wine to put in her shadow box on the dining-room wall. That brings her collection up to twenty-three, all different.

(*From The Atlantic Monthly*)

# MIAMI-NEW YORK

## BY MARTHA GELLHORN

*THERE* were five Air Force sergeants and they got in the plane and found seats and began to call to each other across the aisle or over the chair backs, saying, How about it, Joe, I guess this is the way to travel, or saying, Where do they keep the parachutes? or saying, Boy, I've got a pillow, what do you know! They were loud and good-natured for a moment, very young, and young in their new importance of being bomber crews, and they wanted the other people, the civilians, to know that they belonged in a different, fiercer world.

There were a half dozen of the men who seemed always to be going to or coming from Washington, the men with gray suits, hats, hair, skin, and with brown calf brief cases. These have no definite age and curiously similar faces, and are all equally tired and quiet. They always put their hats in the rack above the seat and sit down with their brief cases on their laps. Later they open their brief cases and look at sheets of typed or mimeographed paper, or they go to sleep.

The stewardess was young, with blonde hair hanging to her shoulders. She had a neat body of the right height and weight, and a professionally friendly voice. Fasten your seat belts, please, she said. Would you like some chewing gum? Fasten your seat belt, please, sir. Chewing gum?

A woman who had traveled a great deal in planes, and never trusted them because she understood nothing about them, sat in the double front seat behind the magazine rack. This was the best seat, as she knew, because there was enough room to stretch your legs. Also you could see well from here, if you wanted to see. Now, for a moment she looked out the window and saw that the few palm trees at the far edge of the field were blowing out in heavy plumes against the sky. There was something so wrong about Miami that even a beautiful night, sharp with stars, only seemed a real-estate advertisement. The woman pulled off her earrings and put them carelessly in her coat pocket. She ran her hands through her very short dark upcurling hair, deliberately making herself untidy for the night ahead. She hunched her shoulders to ease the tired stiffness in her neck and slouched down in the chair. She had just leaned her head against the chair back and was thinking of nothing when the man's voice said, Is this place taken? No, she said without looking at him. She moved nearer to the window. Anyhow, she said to herself, only eight or ten hours or whatever it is to New York; even if he snores, he can't snore all the time.

The plane taxied into position, turned, the propellers whirled until in the arc lights of the field they were great silver disks, the motor roared, and the plane started that run down the field that always, no matter how many times you had sat it out, no matter in how many countries, and no matter on how many fields, bad fields, dangerous fields, in whatever weather, always stopped your heart for one moment as you waited to see if this time it would work again; if this time, as all the other times, the enormous machine would rise smoothly into the air where no one really belonged except the birds.

'Made it,' the man said softly to himself.

She looked at him then. He had said it as she would have said it, with wonder, with a perpetual amazement that the trick worked.

He turned to her and she could see he wanted to talk. She would only to have to say yes, and smile, or say nice take-off, or say, what a lovely night; anything would do. But she was not going to say anything and he was not going to talk to her if she could help it. I have ten hours, she said in her mind to the man, and she said it threateningly, and they are mine and I don't have to talk to anyone and don't try. The man, finding her face closed against him, turned away, pulled a package of cigarettes from his pocket, and made a great distance between them, smoking and looking straight ahead.

She could not ignore him though he did nothing to force her attention. She had seen him without really looking; he was a Navy lieutenant and the braid on his cap, which he still held, was grayish black; his stripes and the active-duty star were tarnished; his uniform looked unpressed, and he had a dark weather-dried sunburn. His hair was a colorless blond, so short that it seemed he must have shaved his head and now the hair was just growing in, a month's growth probably.

With resentment, because she did not want to notice him, she studied him now, not caring if he turned his head and caught her. She looked at him with unfriendly professional eyes, the beady eye of the painter, her husband called it. The man's face, in repose, looked brooding and angry; the whole face was square. His eyebrows lay flat and black above his eyes, his mouth did not curve at all, and his chin seemed to make another straight line. There were three horizontal lines marked one after the other across his face, and blocked in by the hard bones of his jaw. But when he had turned to her, wanting to talk, he had been smiling and his face had been oval then, with all the lines flared gayly upwards. Perhaps the gayety came from his eyes, which were china blue, or was it his mouth, she thought, trying to remember. It was a very interesting face; it belonged to two different men. She wondered where he had picked up this dark, thinking, angry man, who showed on his face now.

Damn, she said to herself, what do I care? Let him have six faces. But it was a fine problem. How could you paint one face and make it at the same time square and oval, gay and longingly friendly, but also shut-in, angry and indifferent.

I wonder what she's sore about, the man thought mildly behind his complicated face. She doesn't look as if she was the type of woman who's sore all the time. Pretty women weren't usually sore all the time. He could place her, in a vague general way, as people of the same nationality can place each other. She had money and she had taste; her clothes were not only expensive and fashionable, which was frequent, they were the right clothes and she wore them without concern. He had not heard her voice but he imagined what it would be; Eastern, he thought, rather English. She would say things like, it's heaven, or he's madly energetic, or what a ghastly bore, saying it all without emphasis. She would be spoiled, as they all were, and at a loose end as they all were too. But her face was better than most. He did not think of women as stupid or not stupid. He simply thought her face was not like everyone's; it was small and pointed and even though she was sore, she could not make her face look dead. It was a lively face and her eyebrows grew in a feather line upwards over very bright, very dark eyes. Her hands were beautiful too, and he noticed, looking at them slantwise and secretly, that the nail varnish was cracking and she had broken or chewed off the nail of her right pointer finger. It was childish and careless to have such nails, and he liked that best about her. Sore as a goat, he thought mildly to himself. Then he forgot her.

He relaxed, behind the angry square of this second face that he had never seen and did not know about. He relaxed and enjoyed himself, thinking of nothing, but simply enjoying being alive and being home or almost home. He had been gone eighteen months, and without ever saying it to himself, because he made no poses, not even practical, realistic poses, he had often doubted that he would get back. Whenever he began almost to think about not ever getting back (and this was different from thinking about dying, there was something like self-pity about not getting back, whereas dying was just a thing that could happen) he would say to himself, grim and mocking, life on a destroyer is a big educational experience; you ought to be grateful.

He had worked briefly in his father's mills before he became an officer on a destroyer, but he did not want to be a businessman again. Or rather he could not remember what it was like, being a man in an office, so he had no interest in it. He did not want anything now except to be happy. He was happy. He rested behind his face and told himself how fine and comfortable the seat was and what a fine time he'd had last night in Miami with Bob Jamison and those two beauties and what a fine time he would have tomorrow and all the other days. Oh boy, he said to himself, and stretched all through his body without moving, and felt the fine time bathing him like soft water and sunlight.

No doubt he has a splendid little wife waiting for him, the woman thought. He is evidently going home and from the looks of him, his face and his clothes, he has been somewhere. He has ribbons sewn to his blue serge chest. Ribbons could mean something or nothing; every man in uniform that she knew had ribbons. They rode nobly and with growing boredom from their homes on the subway down to Church Street and presently they had ribbons.

They lived in expensive over-crowdedness in Washington and wandered around the Pentagon building and went to cocktail parties in Georgetown and had ribbons. There were, for instance, those two faintly aging glamour boys, with silver eagles on their shoulders and enough ribbons to trim hats, who had just returned from London. She had always known these two and she was prepared to believe that they knew as much about war as she did, and she was certain that they had never ventured much farther afield than, say, Piccadilly Circus, in case they worked in Grosvenor Square. So what real ribbons were or what they meant, she did not know. However, looking at this man, she thought that his ribbons would mean something. His wife would know about the ribbons at once, if she did not know already, and she would be very proud. Why shouldn't she be, the woman asked herself irritably, what have you got against wives?

Am I not in fact a service wife myself? she thought. Could I not wear a pin with one star on it, a little oblong pin made of enamel if you haven't much money, but you can get it in sapphires, diamonds, and rubies if you feel that way? Have I not just returned from seeing my husband off in Miami? Thomas, she said to herself, is so used to getting what he wants that he believes the emotions will also perform as he wishes. A man is leaving for service overseas; he has forty-eight hours leave; his wife flies to him to say goodbye; they have forty-eight lovely last hours together and the lovely last hours were like being buried alive, though still quite alive so you knew all about it, with a stranger whom you ought to love but there it is, he is a stranger. Fine wife, she told herself, everyone handles this perfectly; all women manage to run their hearts smoothly; patriotism, pride, tenderness, farewell, homesickness. I'm not such a bitch as all that, she thought, defending herself; Thomas is only going to Brazil. I wouldn't mind going to Brazil myself. I should think he'd be enchanted to go to Brazil. As long as you aren't doing your own work, it's far better to be in Brazil than in Miami or Pensacola or the Brooklyn Navy Yard.

Only, if I were a real wife, a good wife, a service wife, I'd have made more of a thing of his going. Why does he want to be fooled, she thought angrily, why does he want to fool himself? Why does he go on about loving me when I am everything he dislikes and distrusts? She could hear Thomas now, and her heart moved with pity despite the anger. I love you more than anything, Kate, you know that; I only want you to be happy. Thomas believed it while he said it, and she felt herself to be cold and hard and ungrateful and somehow hideous, because she did not believe it at all.

She groaned and moved her body as if it were in pain. The man beside her turned, and stared, but he could not see her face. All he saw was the stiff line of her right shoulder, hunched up away from him. The woman was saying to herself, desperately, forget it, forget it. There is nothing to do. It cannot be understood; leave it alone. You cannot know so much about yourself; you cannot know why you thought you loved a man, nor why you think you no longer love him. It is not necessary to know. It's an enormous world, she told herself, with millions of people in it; if you're not even interested in yourself why can't you stop thinking about your own dreary little life? Thomas will be gone months, a year, two years. *Stop thinking about it.*

Suddenly, and without any sort of plan or direction from her brain, she pulled the great square diamond engagement ring and the baguette diamond wedding ring from her left hand, pulling them off brutally as if they would not come unless she forced them, and she thrust the two rings into her coat pocket with her earrings. Then she rubbed her left hand, crushing the bones of the hand together and pulling at the fingers. The man beside her, who had seen all this, said to himself, 'Well, for God's sake what goes on here?' She's not sore, he thought, she's nuts. Then he amended that thought; nuts, or in some trouble of her own. He wanted no part of trouble; he did not understand it really. Living had become so simple for him that he understood nothing now except being or staying alive.

The stewardess turned off the overhead lights in the plane and one by one the small reading lights on the walls were turned off and presently the plane was dark. The bright grayish night gleamed in through the windows. Two of the men from Washington snored weakly and one of the Air Force sergeants snored very loudly as if he enjoyed snoring and was going to do as much of it as he wanted. Then the snoring became a part of the plane sounds, and everything was quiet. The woman with the short, upcurling hair slept in a twisted sideways heap. The lieutenant leaned his head quietly against the chair back and stretched out his legs and settled himself without haste to sleep until morning.

In sleep his face was even more square and brooding. He seemed to be dreaming something that made him cold with anger or despair. He was not dreaming; it could not be a dream because it was always the same when he slept. It was as if he went to a certain place to sleep. This place was an enormous darkness; it moved a little but it was not a darkness made up of air or water: it was a solid darkness like being blind. Only the dark something around him had weight and he was under it; he was all alone, lying or floating, at ease, in no pain, pursued by nothing, but simply lying in absolute aloneness in the weight of the dark. He could not see himself, he could only feel himself there. It was terrible because there seemed no way to get out, and yet he did not struggle. He lay there every night and every night he was trapped in it forever, and every morning when he woke he was grateful and astonished though he did not remember why, as he did not remember the place where he had been sleeping.

This sleeping in a complete empty heavy darkness had come on him, gradually, on the ship. He knew nothing about himself and considered himself an ordinary man, quite lucky, doing all right, with nothing on his mind. Nothing had happened to him that had not happened to hundreds of other men. Even talking, in the wardroom, with others of his kind he recognized himself and knew there was nothing special about him. They talked very badly, without thought and without even knowing how to manage their language. It was almost like sign language the way they talked. But surely he felt what they all did.

When the first destroyer was sunk by a bomb, and he jumped overboard (but not nearly so far as he always imagined it would be — it didn't seem any farther than jumping from the high dive at the country club) and swam around and found a raft, he had first been mindless with fury. He did not know what the fury came from: was it because they were hunted and hurled in the sea, was it rage against their own helplessness, was he furious to lose the ship for which he felt now a strong unexpected love, was it fury for himself alone, fury at this outrageous tampering with life? He was so angry that he could not see or think; he did not remember swimming and he did not know how he had gone to the raft. Then the fear came as he watched the Japanese planes, so close above the water, searching them out where they splashed like driven terrified water beetles or hung together like leeches on a log. The fear was as cold as the water and made him weak and nauseated; then it too went. They were picked up very quickly; nothing had happened to him.

There was another time when he stood behind the forward gun crew and seemed to have nothing to do himself. He watched the sailor firing the Oerlikon and saw his body bucking against the crutch-like supports of the gun, and he saw the faint bright stream of the bullets, but the man behind the Oerlikon seemed terribly slow, everything seemed slow, he himself had never had so much time and so little to do. This must have lasted a few seconds, but it was a large quiet piece of time and his mind said clearly: this is crazy, what are we all doing? Then his mind said it much louder: this is crazy. Finally he was not sure he had not shouted it out, because the thought was bursting in his mind. *This is crazy.*

Even that was not very remarkable; most of the other men thought everything was pretty screwy. You had to kill the Japs after they started it all, naturally you couldn't let them get away with it. You had to do it since that was how things were, but it was crazy all the same. If you began to think about it, about yourself and all the men you knew out here in this big god-awful ocean, to hell and gone from anywhere you ever wanted to be, and what you were doing and what everybody was doing everywhere, it was too crazy to think about. Then if you tried to think how it all started and what it was about and what difference it would make afterwards, you went crazy yourself. He had not actually talked this over with anyone but he knew the others felt as he did, Bob Jamison and Truby Bartlett and Joe Parks and the other men he knew well.

They all agreed in a simple easy way: they were the age that was in this war, if they'd been older or younger they wouldn't be, but this was what had happened and this was what they had to do. You made a lot of jokes and longed loudly for tangible things, liquor and a fine room at the Waldorf or the St. Francis, depending on taste, with a handy beauty. You played bridge or poker when you had a chance, for higher stakes than before. Time passed; you were the same man you always were. All you had to do was stay alive if you could.

Yet every night he went to this empty solid darkness and was forever buried in it, without hope or escape or anyone to call to.

The man, who had been asleep, woke suddenly and found his face ten inches from the woman's face. She had turned towards him in her sleep. Her eyes were closed and she looked very pale, tired, and a little ill. Her mouth was wonderfully soft. The man was not quite awake and he looked with surprise at this face he had not expected to see, and thought, she's lonely. He was thinking better than he would have done, had he been awake and protected by a long habit of not noticing and not thinking. She's sick lonely, he thought to himself. Without intending to, he leaned toward those soft lips. There was the face, waiting and needing to be kissed. Then he woke enough to remember where he was, and stopped himself, shocked, and thought, God, if I'd done it, she'd probably have called out and there'd have been a hell of a goings-on. He sighed and turned away from her and let his body relax, and slept again.

The plane skidded a little in the wind; it seemed to be forcing itself powerfully through air as heavy as water. The people in the plane slept or held themselves quietly. The plane began to smell close, smelling of bodies and night and old cigarette smoke.

Suddenly the woman felt a hand on her hair. The hand was not gentle; it pressed down the rumpled curly dark hair and stroked once from the forehead back to the nape of her neck. She woke completely but did not move, being too startled and confused to understand what had happened. The hand now left her hair and with harsh assurance rested on her breast; she could feel it through the thin tweed of her coat. She wondered whether she was dreaming this; it was so unlikely, that she must be dreaming it, and in the dark plane she could not see the hand. She looked over at the man and saw his face, dimly. He was asleep, with that troubled brooding look on his face. The hand was quiet, heavy and certain. The hand held and demanded her. What is he doing, she thought. My God, what is happening here? They certainly come back odd, she thought, with a kind of shaky laugh in her mind.

The hand insisted, and suddenly, to her amazement and to her shame, she knew that she wanted to lie against him, she wanted him to put his arms around her and hold her, with this silent unquestioning ownership. She wanted him to wake and hold her and kiss her. It did not matter who she was or who he was, and the other people in the plane did not matter. They were here together in the night and this incredible thing had happened and she did not want to stop it. She turned to him.

When she moved, the man sighed, still sleeping, and his hand fell from her, rested a moment in her lap, and then slowly dragged back, as if of its own will and apart from the man, and lay flat along his side. She waited, watching him, and presently her eyes woke him. He saw the woman's troubled, sad, somehow questioning face and the soft lips that asked to be kissed. He moved his right arm and pulled her as close to him as he could, but there was something between them though he was too sleepy to notice what it was, and he kissed her. He kissed her as if they had already made love, taking all that went before for granted. Having waked up in other places, and not known exactly what had happened, only knowing there was someone to kiss, he did not feel surprised now. Lovely lips, he thought happily. Then he noticed with real surprise that this thing digging into his side was the arm of the chair and then he knew where he was. The woman had pulled away from him and from his owning arm and his assured possessive mouth.

'I'm Kate Merlin,' she whispered idiotically. She sounded panic-stricken.

The man laughed softly. He did not see what anyone's name had to do with it. 'I'm John Hanley,' he said.

'How do you do?' she said and felt both ridiculous and mad, and suddenly laughed too.

'Let's get rid of this obstruction,' he said. The woman was frightened. He took everything so calmly; did he imagine that she always kissed the man sitting next to her on the night plane from Miami? The lieutenant worked at the arm of the chair until he discovered how to get it loose. He laid it on the floor in front of his feet. She was leaning forward and away from him, not knowing what to say in order to explain to him that she really wasn't a woman who could be kissed on planes, in case that happened to be a well-known category of woman.

He said nothing; that was evidently his specialty, she thought.

He got everywhere without opening his mouth. His body spoke for him. He collected her, as if she belonged to him and could not have any other idea herself. He brought her close, raised her head so that it was comfortable for him, and kissed her. The harsh and certain hand held her as before.

This is fine, the man thought. It was part of the fine time in Miami and part of the fine time that would follow. He seemed to have a lot of luck—but why not, sometimes you did have luck, and he had felt all along that this leave was going to be wonderful. He had waited for it with such confidence that it could not fail him. Now he would kiss this lovely strange soft woman, and then they would go to sleep. There was nothing else they could do on a plane, which was a pity, but it was foolish to worry about something you couldn't have. Just be very damn grateful, he thought, that it's as fine as it is. You might have been sitting next to the Air Force, he thought with amusement, and what would you have then? She smelled of gardenias and her hair was delicious and like feathers against his cheek. He leaned forward to kiss her again, feeling warm and melted and unhurried and happy.

'How did you know?' the woman said. She seemed to have trouble speaking.

'Know what?'

'That you could kiss me?'

Oh God, he thought, we're going to have to talk about it. Why in hell did she want to talk?

'I didn't know anything,' he said. 'I didn't plan anything.'

'Who are you?' She didn't mean that; she meant, how did it happen?

'Nobody,' he said with conviction. 'Absolutely nobody. Who are you?'

'I don't know,' she said.

'Don't let it worry you,' he said. He was beginning to feel impatient of this aimless talk. 'Aren't we having a fine time?'

She took in her breath, rigid with distaste. So that was what it was. Just like that; it might have happened with anyone. Come on, baby, give us a kiss, isn't this fun. Oh *Lord,* she thought, what have I got into now? She wanted to say to him, I have never done anything like this in my life, you must not think. She wanted him to appreciate that this was rare and therefore important; it could not have happened any night with any man. It had to be alone of its kind, or she could not accept it.

The man again used silence, which he handled far better than words, and again he simply allowed his body to make what explanations seemed necessary. She felt herself helpless and glad to be helpless. But she could not let him think her only a willing woman; how would she face him in the morning if that was all he understood?

'You see,' she began.

He kissed her so that she would not talk and he said, with his lips moving very lightly against hers, 'It's all right.'

She took that as she needed it, making it mean everything she wanted him to think. She was still amazed but she was full of delight. She felt there had been nothing in her life but talk and reasons, and the talk had been wrong and the reasons proved pointless: here was something that had happened at once, by itself, without a beginning, and it was right because it was like magic.

The man pressed her head against his shoulder, pulled her gently sideways to make her comfortable, leaned his head against the chair back, and prepared to sleep. He felt contented, but if he went on kissing her much longer, since there was nothing further he could do about her now, it might get to be tiresome and thwarted and wearing. It had been good and now it was time to sleep; he was very tired. He kissed the top of her head, remembering her, and said, 'Sleep well.'

Long ragged gray clouds disordered the sky. The moon was like an illuminated target in a shooting gallery, moving steadily ahead of them. The plane was colder now and one of the Air Force sergeants coughed himself awake, swore, blew his nose, sighed, shifted his position, and went back to sleep. The stewardess wondered whether she ought to make an inspection tour of her passengers and decided they were all right. She was reading a novel about society people in a country house in England, which fascinated her.

The woman lay easily against the lieutenant's shoulder and let her mind float in a smooth warm dream of pleasure. After the months of gnawing unlove, this man sat beside her in a plane in the night, and she no longer needed to dread herself as a creature who loved nothing. She did not love this man but she loved how she felt, she loved this warmth and aliveness and this hope. Now she made plans that were like those faultless daydreams in which one is always beautiful and the heroine and every day is more replete with miracles than the next. He would stay in New York, at her house even, since she was alone. Or would it be better if they went to a hotel so that there would be nothing to remind her of her ordinary life? They would treat New York as if it were a foreign city, Vienna in the spring, she thought. They would find new odd little places to eat, and funny places along Broadway to dance, they would walk in the Park and go to the Aquarium and the Bronx Zoo; they would sight-see and laugh and meet no one they knew and be alone in a strange, wonderful city. Someday he would have to go back where he came from, and she would go back to her work, but they would have this now and it was more than she had ever hoped for or imagined. And she would paint his strange face that was two faces, and he would be fresh and exciting every day and every night, with his silence and his fantastic assurance and his angry and happy look.

The plane circled the field at Washington and seemed to plunge onto the runway. The thump of the wheels striking the cement runway woke the man. He sat up and stared about him.

'Put the chair arm back,' the woman whispered. 'Good morning.' She did not want the stewardess to look at her with a smile or a question. Her hair must be very soft; she would like to touch it, but not now. She looked at him with loving intimate eyes and the man looked at her, quite stupidly, as if he had never seen her before.

'The chair arm,' she said again.

The man grinned suddenly and picked up the chair arm and fitted it back into its place. Then he turned to the woman and his face was merry, almost jovial.

'Sleep well?' he said.

'I didn't sleep.' She had not imagined his face so gay, as if he were laughing at them both.

'Too bad. Well,' he said, 'I think I'll go and stretch my legs. Coming?'

'No, thank you,' she said, terrified now.

The Air Force sergeants jostled each other getting out of the plane. One of them called to the stewardess, 'Don't leave without us, honey.' They all laughed and crossed the cement runway, to the airport building, tugging at their clothes, tightening their belts, as if they had just come out of a wrestling match.

The men with brief cases took their hats and coats from the stewardess and thanked her in gray voices for a pleasant journey, and walked away quickly as if they were afraid of being late to their offices.

In the front seat, Kate Merlin sat alone and listened to the stewardess talking with some of the ground crew; their voices were very bright and awake for this hour of the morning. Kate Merlin felt cold and a little sick and dismal, but she would not let herself think about it.

Then he was back beside her and the stewardess was moving down the aisle, like a trained nurse taking temperatures in a hospital ward, to see that they were all properly strapped in for the take-off.

They fastened their seat belts again and then the plane was high in the mauve-gray early morning sky.

'Do I remember you said your name was Kate Merlin?'

'Yes.'

'Think of that.'

How did he say it? she wondered. How? Complacently?

He was evidently not going to say anything more right now. She looked out the window and her hands were cold. The man was thinking, Well, that's funny. Funny how things happen. He had remembered the night, clearly, while he was walking up and down the cement pavement by the airport building in Washington. It had seemed strange to him, in the morning, but now it seemed less strange. Being an artist, he told himself, they're all a little queer. He had never met an artist before but he was ready to believe that they were not like other people. And being so rich too, he thought, that would make her even queerer. The extremely rich were known to be unlike other people. Her husband, but his name wasn't Merlin, was terrifically rich. He'd read about them: their names, like many other names, seemed to be a sort of tangible asset — like bonds, jewels, or real estate — of the New York columnists. Her husband had inherited millions and owned a famous stable and plane factories or some kind of factories. Thomas Sterling Hamilton, that was his name. It seemed peculiar, her being a successful painter, when her husband was so rich and she didn't need to.

'I've read about you,' he remarked.

I have read nothing about you, she thought. What am I supposed to say: you have the advantage of me, sir?

'I even remember one,' he said in a pleased voice. 'It said something about how your clients, or whatever you call them, were glad to pay thousands for your portraits because you always made them look dangerous. It said that was probably even more flattering than looking beautiful. The women, that is. I wonder where I read it.'

It was too awful; it was sickening. It must have been some revolting paragraph in a gossip column. She would surely have been called a society portrait painter and there would be a bit about Thomas and his money.

'What does a painter do during the war?' he asked.

'Paints,' she said. Then it seemed too selfish to her and though she was ashamed to be justifying herself to this man, she said quickly, 'I don't know how to do anything but paint. I give the money to the Russian Relief or the Chinese Relief or the Red Cross, things like that. It seems the most useful thing I can do, since I'm only trained as a painter.' She stopped, horrified at what she had done. What had made her go into a whining explanation, currying favor with this man so he would see what a splendid citizen she really was.

'That's fine.' The civilians were all busy as bird dogs for the war, as he knew, and it was very fine of them and all that but it embarrassed him to hear about it. He felt they expected him to be personally grateful and he was not grateful, he did not care what anybody did; he wasn't running this war. Then he thought, This isn't at all like last night. He looked at the woman and saw that she looked even better in the morning. It was amazing how a woman could sit up all night in a plane and look so clean and attractive. He felt his beard rough on his face and his eyes were sticky. She looked delicious and then he remembered how soft she had been in his arms and he wondered what to do about it now.

'I imagined Kate Merlin would be older,' he said, thinking aloud.

It was only then that she realized how young he was, twenty-four or perhaps even less. His silence and his assurance and his closed dark second face had made him seem older, or else she had not thought about it at all. She was appalled. What am I becoming, she wondered, am I going to be one of those women without husbands who hunt young men?

'I'm old enough,' she said curtly.

He turned and smiled at her. His eyes said, I know about you, don't tell me; I know how you are. It was the man of last night again, the certain one, the one whose body spoke for him. This talent he had when he was silent worked on her like a spell.

He seemed to understand this and very easily he reached his hand over and rested it on the back of her neck, where her hair grew up in soft duck feathers. Her body relaxed under this owning hand. 'Yes, I am,' she said dreamily, as if he had contradicted her, 'I'm thirty-five.'

'Are you?' he said. She could feel his hand change. It was quite different. It was a hand that had made a mistake and did not know where it was. It was a hand that would soon move away and become polite.

The man was thinking, thirty-five, well, that *is* old enough. That makes it something else again. And being an artist, he said to himself uneasily. It seemed to him that there was a trick somewhere; he had gotten into something he did not understand. She probably knew more than he did. She had perhaps been playing him along. Perhaps she was thinking he was pretty simple and inexperienced and was amused at how he came up for the bait.

The woman felt that something very bad, very painful, was happening but she could not name it and she held on to her plans of last night because they were happy and they were what she wanted. She said, in a tight voice, and mistrusting the words as she spoke them, 'Will you be staying in New York?'

'I don't think so,' he said. Speaking gave him a chance to take his hand away and light a cigarette. It might be fun in New York, he thought, meeting all those famous people she would know. He could go with her to El Morocco and the Colony and those places and see her kind of people. She would be something he hadn't had before, thirty-five and a celebrity and all. It might be fun. But he felt uneasy about it; this was not his familiar country. This was not how he saw a fine time, exactly. It was complicated, not safe, you would not know what you were doing. And how about her husband?

'Don't you know?' she said. He did not like that. That sounded like giving orders. That sounded as if she meant to take him over. He was suspicious of her at once.

'No,' he said. His face wore the shut-in, indifferent look.

'What might you be doing?' she insisted. Oh stop it, she told herself, for God's sake stop it. What are you doing now; do you want to prove it to yourself?

'I'll be going home first,' he said. Give it to her, he thought. He didn't like that bossy, demanding way she suddenly had. 'Springfield,' he added. She would be thinking now that he was a small-town boy from Massachusetts and that was all right with him.

Then he thought with sudden pleasure of Springfield; he would have a fine time there for a while, a fine time that he understood. He might go on to Boston, where he knew his way around, and have a different but still excellent sort of time. Later, at the end, he would go to New York for a few days but by himself, on his own terms. He did not want to get mixed up. He did not want anything that he could not manage. He just wanted to have a good easy time with nothing to worry about. She wasn't in his league; he didn't know about married rich, famous women of thirty-five.

The woman felt so cold that she had to hold herself carefully so that she would not shiver. A middle-aged woman, she told herself with horror, hounding a young man. That was what he thought. She had offered herself to him and he had rejected her. He did not want her. She was too old. If only the plane would move faster; if only they would get there so she could hide from him. If only she did not have to sit beside him, sick with the knowledge of what he thought, and sick with shame for herself. She did not know how to protect herself from the shock of this rejection.

The plane flew north along the East River and in the fresh greenish-blue light the city appeared below them. It looked like a great ancient ruin. The towers were vast pillars, planted in the mist, with sharp splintered tops. The squarish skyscrapers were old white temples or giant forts, and there was no life in the jagged quarry of buildings. It was beautiful enough to rock the heart, and suddenly the woman imagined it would look like this, thousands of years from now, enormous and dead.

The man leaned forward to look out the window. 'Pretty, isn't it?' he said.

He had really said that and he meant it. That was all he saw. But then it was all right. Whatever he thought of her did not matter; he was too stupid to care about. But she knew this was a lie; nothing had changed. There was the fact and there was no way to escape it; he could have had her and he simply did not want her.

They were the last people off the plane. The other passengers had seemed to block their way on purpose. The woman sent a porter to find a taxi. She would escape from his presence at least, as quickly as she could. When the man saw the taxi stopping before them he said, 'Not taking the airline car?'

'No.' She did not offer to give him a lift in town. Oh hurry, she thought. The man started to move her bags to the taxi. 'Don't bother,' she said, 'the porter will manage.'

He seemed a little puzzled by this flight. 'Good luck,' he said, shutting the door behind her, 'hope I'll see you again some place.' It was a thing to say, that was all.

'Good luck to you,' she said, and hoped her voice was light and friendly. She did not actually look at him.

'Where to, Miss?' the taxi driver asked. She gave her address and pretended not to see the man saluting good-bye from the curb.

It might have been fun, the man thought, as he watched the taxi turn and head towards the highway. Oh no, hell, he told himself, complications. It was better this way. He began to feel relieved and then he put the whole business out of his mind; he did not want to clutter up his mind with questions or problems and perhaps spoil some of his leave. He thought about Springfield and his face was oval now, smiling. He was in a hurry to get in town and get started. He would not let himself consider the good time ahead in numbered days; he was thinking, now, now, now. He had erased the woman entirely; she was finished and gone.

After the cab passed the gates of the airport, the woman leaned back and took a deep breath to steady herself and to ease the pain in her throat. She covered her eyes with her hand. It's just that I'm so tired, she told herself. This was what she would have to believe. It's nothing to feel desperate about. It's just that I'm so tired, she thought, forcing herself to believe it. It's only because I've been sitting up all night in a plane.

*(From Harper's Magazine)*

# SPARROW'S LAST JUMP

## BY ELLIOTT GRENNARD

WE HAD SEEN 'Specter of the Rose' and the talk got around to Nijinsky and somebody said, 'Imagine if they had a camera going when Nijinsky blew his top!'

I wanted to tell them I got Sparrow Jones down on acetate the night he was taken away, but they would have wanted me to play the record for them. They were the kind who would say, How can you compare a jazz musician with Nijinsky? They would have said, I want to own that platter, what a collector's item!

Telling me? I guess everyone who read the last *Jazz Year-Book* and saw how Sparrow rated would want a copy of the last record he made. I could probably sell 20,000 in a month, maybe 50,000, once word got around. And don't think I can't use that kind of sale. Hot jazz doesn't sell the way Freddy Martin or Sammy Kaye does, you know. You get a 10,000 copy sale and you think you're doing great.

I even played around with the idea of releasing the record and tossing the dough into the pot to pay for Sparrow's sanitarium. But when a thing like that happens right in front of your eyes! I don't want to see it again every time I hear the record.

I had just got back from New York that morning, and on the way over to my room I thought I might as well stop in at Jackson's Jazz Record Shop and see how my disks were going. I release only three records every two months and when you're a little guy in this business, you're smart if you give it that personal touch. That's all I'd been doing for six weeks; dropping in on record dealers between L. A. and New York, giving them a big, well hel-lo.

Jackson is my best customer in Hollywood. He can't afford to—

and doesn't want to—stock everything he'd have to if he held Victor, Columbia, and Decca franchises, so Jackson pushes the off-labels. Not a big business but not a bad one, when you figure there are eighty-nine off-labels on the market and most of them wax nothing but hot jazz.

I said, 'Hi ya, Jackson,' sneaking a quick look at the walls to see if my stickers were up.

'You ain't real, McNeil?' he said. Then he asked me what I heard from the mob and I told him the big news in the East was be-bop. I said, I was thinking of getting hold of Sparrow Jones and cutting me some of this be-bop.

Jackson bared his teeth in what he thought was a grin. 'You're clowning, Browning? There's a cat spinning your Basin Street album in the booth who'll run you out of town if I tell him you're going to wax be-bop.'

Jackson was kidding on the square. 'New Orleans' collectors are murder. They swear that jazz died in 1924 and anyone who didn't personally rock the cradle of jazz with his own two beats is strictly commercial. Benny Goodman? A bed-chamber music clarinetist who couldn't shine Jimmy Noone's shoes.

Me, I don't argue. I put my stuff out under three different labels: N'Orleans, Southside, and Hep. That way, nobody gets mad at anybody.

I went back to see this character in the booth, and not only because it's good business. The truth is, I like all kinds of jazz—Louis, Duke, Goodman. Even when I don't exactly like it, or understand it—like be-bop—I respect what the boys are trying to do. What the hell, how many guys collected the Duke before the middle thirties?

When I open the door of the booth what do I hear but some frantic trumpet that could only be Dizzy Gillespie. Before I can ask myself if I'm hearing things or what, I see it is no character playing the Gillespie record. It's big Hughie Hadliffe.

Hughie is one of my favorite people, and I hadn't seen him since I went East six weeks back. I yelled, 'Hughie!' and I pumped his arm.

Hughie always gives you a solid handshake because that's the way he is, solid and serious. With his glasses on, Hughie looks like an interne, which is what he would have been if he hadn't decided after three years of college that being a Negro doctor is pretty tough going. So instead of breaking his back, Hughie stuck to the trumpet that had been paying his way through school.

But he still looked like a medic. No little nanny-goat whiskers for Hughie, even if shaving under the lip was supposed to hurt your playing. And no dark glasses, either. The only thing screwy about Hughie was that he had gone on a be-bop kick and had chucked up a sweet job with Basie, plus a bookful of recording dates every month. That's the trouble with be-bop. Once you start hearing those screwy chords in your ear and get those offbeats in your system, you can't play any other way. The old way is too straight, too on-the-nose.

'How's my boy?' I asked.

Hughie shook his head. 'He's not doing so good.'

I said, 'Hugh?' and then I realized he thought I was asking about Sparrow.

Jazz musicians have single-track minds. They eat, drink, and sleep their music. They're so hipped, if somebody comes along with something new, they make him God. That's the way it was with Hughie and Sparrow. Hughie had heard Sparrow one night, and when Sparrow asked if he'd like to play with him, Hughie dropped everything. Sparrow was his boy, and the way he saw it, there could be only one boy.

'Doesn't he like it at the Club?' I said.

'He likes it all right, I guess.'

I saw he didn't feel like telling me, but I asked anyway. 'What's the matter?'

Hughie sort of shrugged. Not indifferently, but like he didn't know what to say.

Jazz musicians don't pop off a lot. Like when you ask them about jazz; they don't trust words to say what they feel, so they dummy up. If they don't like something and you ask them, they kind of turn away and say, 'Well. You know.' If they like something, they'll grin and say, 'That's all right.' When they're really gone on someone, they'll say, 'Man, he plays fine!'

So when Hughie didn't say anything, I knew this business about Sparrow was something big. That changed my plans.

'Too bad,' I said. 'I wanted you and Sparrow and the band to make some records for me.'

Hughie straightened up. 'Gee, that would be great, Harry. No kidding, great. Why don't we do that? We got some fine numbers. Real fine.'

I thought, what goes on here? This isn't the Hughie I know. 'Take it easy,' I said. 'You just told me different.'

Hughie's shoulders dropped. I knew he couldn't keep up that fast chatter.

'Sparrow's sick,' he said quietly. 'I don't know how long he's going to hold up. I thought it would be nice if he made some records while he could.'

It gave me a stab seeing Hughie like that, but I didn't want to let on. 'Forget it,' I said. 'I'll drop in at the Club one of these nights and we'll talk to Sparrow about a date.'

Hughie looked solemn. 'If you're going to record Sparrow,' he said, 'you better do it soon.'

Then I knew it was bad.

Jackson's got a loose lip, so I tried to duck him on my way cut. He popped up from behind the counter just as I was passing.

'I forgot to tell you about Sparrow,' he said. 'Man, his wig is really loose. Looks like he's blowing his top for good.'

I purposely misunderstood. 'Yeah, I hear he's playing fine.'

'When he can hold his instrument,' Jackson said. 'Man, he's got a tic that makes a Holy Roller look like she's holding still!'

That meant it was all over the street.

I couldn't put Sparrow out of my mind. He got this job at the Club about four weeks back, and it should have made him feel good. He'd been laying off for nearly eight months, and that's a long time for a guy who's worked steady since he was fourteeen. I decided to look in on him that same night.

The Club was a bottle joint on Central and 38th. Not much of a place for a guy who's played the best locations in the country, but be-bop was too new to have a following and no Los Angeles night club operator with a big overhead was going to take a chance. Especially a white night club.

I know these clubs. They don't get started till one, so I got there a little after two. I took a table next to the bandstand and ordered some setups. The boys were just going on, so while I unwrapped my bottle I watched. When Sparrow sat down in his chair and turned around I nearly caved. He wasn't the same Sparrow.

It was hard to believe this middle-aged man was only twenty-two years old. His dark skin used to be tight, with a shine to it; now it set on his bones like black putty. His eyes were big and round and empty, and the expression on his face was just about the saddest expression I've ever seen. It made you think he wanted to cry inside, only he had tried and found he couldn't.

I remember when his tight little body used to operate like a precision machine. When he used to get set to play, his eyes would narrow down and his body would get taut, as if a spring had been wound up. And then he went. Anybody who heard him those three years with Joe Pepper's Hot Five knows how Sparrow could go. He went so fast and so far that the last year he was with them, Joe and the others couldn't keep up. That's when they began calling him 'Sparrow.' He was playing just too frantic.

Sparrow never could play with a big band; his tone was too personal, his intonation too full of shadings to blend with other saxophones. That's why Joe Pepper's band was good for him. They played blues, and Sparrow kept them from dragging. Then the band played only jump tunes at a medium tempo, and Sparrow really began to jump.

That's when the trouble between him and Joe started. Joe wanted to keep the beat nice and relaxed, but they just couldn't hold Sparrow down. He kept pushing the beat harder and harder, driving it ahead. It didn't become faster, it just stopped being relaxed. And then Sparrow began playing notes that made Joe uneasy.

When Sparrow quit the band, he found he had no place to go. He was playing in another world. It wasn't until Hughie went with him, and they got Jimmy Brash on piano, Joe Miggs on drums, and Fat Stuff on bass, that Sparrow had someone he could play with. Sparrow would tear loose until Hughie caught it; then they were playing together. The other three just about hung on, but it didn't matter. That's the outfit I had planned to record. Looking at Sparrow sitting there, I didn't think there was a chance.

I didn't want to stare at him but I couldn't help myself. He was twitching and jerking like a machine gone crazy. It was the worst tic I'd ever seen. First his head would snap to the right, then to the left. Then maybe four times to the right. Meanwhile his legs would shoot out at cockeyed angles and a shoulder would jerk. Sometimes one part of him moved, sometimes two or three parts at the same time, but you couldn't anticipate any of it. It had no pattern, no rhythm. And all the time his face didn't show it knew what his body was doing. It just looked sad.

The band was supposed to be Sparrow's, but Hughie was taking care of things. He said what tunes they would play, who would take the solos, and they got ready. I looked to see what they were doing about Sparrow, but they acted like he wasn't there. Except that when I saw the way their expressionless eyes passed over him, I knew they were thinking plenty about him. It was just one of those things too big for words, or expressions.

Hughie beat off on 'Oh My, Oh My,' a crazy, hopped-up be-bopper, and Sparrow stopped twitching. Then his head jerked to the right about twenty times, fast, in time with the music. Suddenly his head stopped jerking, his body went rigid, and his legs performed a nightmarish buck-and-wing step. When he came out of the step, the snap swung his chair clean around while his saxophone flew to his lips — and he was blowing with the first beat of the second chorus, right on cue. Only his chair was facing the back of the bandstand and Sparrow was blowing to the empty wall. On the last beat of the phrase, his chair swung around again and Sparrow was blowing to the room. I mean, really blowing.

It was the old Sparrow again and the band knew it. They didn't look at him, or smile, but they knew it and the way they played proved it.

I must have been holding my breath for thirty seconds. When I let go and sat back in the chair, my body ached as though it had been caught in an ice-crusher. I poured myself a double and tried to relax by concentrating on the music. A lot that helped.

You know what be-bop's like? I don't mean in musical terms; the guys who play it don't even try to explain it. They don't even call it 'be-bop.' They just say it's 'frantic,' and maybe that's the best way of describing it when you consider that the dictionary says frantic means: 'violently mad or distracted; outrageous; transported by passion.' Personally, I don't go that far. I think of be-bop as: 'tense, agitated; controlled hysteria.'

Sparrow and Hughie had worked out some unison choruses your ear couldn't follow, and when they finished the set, the other three boys were smiling. I could just hear them saying, 'Man, that was fine. Real fine.'

Hughie joined me for a drink but Sparrow stayed in his chair. He didn't do anything or look at anything. He just sat there like he was asleep, only he had his eyes open. Hughie and I drank without talking. Our eyes didn't let go of Sparrow.

'What goes?' I asked finally.

Hughie shrugged.

'He been drinking too much?' I hesitated. 'Or taking anything?'

I could see Hughie making up his mind to tell me. 'He's been on morphine lately.'

I said, 'Oh.'

Hughie didn't want to leave it at that. 'Sparrow used to take a drink like anyone else, but that last year with Joe Pepper he was beginning to play frantic and he was afraid he couldn't keep up with it. He started drinking heavy, then he began on reefers. When it didn't give him what he was looking for, he tried morphine.' Hughie shook his head sadly. 'I've tried to tell him that stuff never helped anybody's music.'

The old story. I knew how most of the old-timers got started taking things. They'd play some cheap café from seven till unconscious, then have to be at a recording studio at nine in the morning. They'd smoke a weed and get a lift from it, then think that's what made them play good. They found out different, but the kids that followed had to learn it for themselves, the hard way. It made me sore.

'How good did he think he could get, for Christ sakes! He's only twenty-two, and there aren't three guys on his instrument who can touch him right now!'

'Sparrow's like that. He's always fussing about his playing, thinking up new ideas, new ways of using his horn.' Hughie looked at me, wondering if I'd understand. 'Sparrow worries. He meets strange people and they tell him he's a genius, and he feels like a fool not knowing what to say back to them. He never went past the eighth grade, and how much chance has a Neg—' Hughie changed it. 'How much chance has Sparrow had to mix and learn about things? He's got a feeling all he knows is how to play. That's why he works so hard on it; it's all he's got to give.'

I thought, And I'm shooting my mouth off. What do I know how it's like for a colored guy in a white world, even a guy with Sparrow's talent? He meets other musicians and that's all right; with them it's the way you play your instrument that counts. But the others. The ones who discover jazz and collect records and think that makes it all right for them to go scouting for Negro musicians like on a scavenger hunt. Or the magazine writers looking for stories they can sell, talking so palsy-walsy and making the guy they're interviewing feel like he's something that crawled out from the woodwork. Or the drunk at the bar who thinks it's okay to throw his arm around a colored musician and say, 'Why don't you and me go out tonight and get us some high yaller gals?'

And Sparrow felt it was up to him; that he had to justify their interest in him. For that he was playing his heart out.

I was thinking of something I could talk about when I saw somebody I hadn't noticed before, sitting at the drums behind Sparrow. He was swishing the wire brushes on the snare drum, and while he wasn't looking right at Sparrow, I got the feeling he was watching him all the time.

'Who's that?' I asked Hughie, pointing with my chin.

'That's Cappy. Sparrow's band boy.'

He looked about thirty-five, kind of old to be a band boy. I grinned. 'This job must pay better than I thought.'

'Cappy doesn't take anything from Sparrow,' Hughie said. 'He just wants to be around him.'

I know how jazz fans worship great musicians. 'Sparrow his boy?'

Hughie smiled. 'That's his boy.'

He watched Cappy for a while. He had a nice smile. He kept a soft rhythm going with the brushes, as if he were caressing Sparrow's back with it. It seemed to keep Sparrow quiet. I got to thinking about Sparrow making some records and the more I thought about it, the more I felt the way Hughie did.

'How about a recording date?' I said after a couple of minutes. 'Think Sparrow would be able to make it?'

Hughie got eager again. 'He was fine this last set.'

I thought, What the hell. 'Tomorrow? I'll get the Sunset Studio for seven, so we can eat first.'

'Tomorrow'd be fine.'

'Want me to talk to Sparrow?'

'I'll tell him,' Hughie said.

He stood up and the other boys got up from where they had been sitting. Cappy didn't stop swishing those brushes until Joe Miggs took over the drums. When Cappy passed Sparrow, he made it a point to run his hand accidentally across Sparrow's shoulders. He waited near Sparrow until the boys started the first number, then he stepped back. He smiled an apology when he saw he had almost bumped into my table.

I smiled back. 'Have a drink?' I asked.

He said all right, and he pulled out a chair so it faced the bandstand. He took his eyes off Sparrow when I reached for my bottle.

'Make mine plain coke,' he said in a nice easy way.

I said sure, and I signaled the waiter.

'You play drums?' I asked when we had both taken a drink.

'Uh-huh. I used to play tenor.'

'No more?'

'I ain't played in four years,' he said in that easy way of his.

I looked at him, wondering.

'Maybe you remember me,' he said. 'Cappy Graystone?'

Then I remembered. 'Sure. You were with Webster when he had his big band. And before that, the Rhythm Riders.'

Cappy smiled. 'You remember. That's nice.'

I started to say, 'Why'd you stop playing?' when I changed my mind.

Cappy caught it, but he didn't seem to mind. 'I was sick,' he said. 'Like Sparrow.'

I steered away from that. 'He sure plays that horn,' I said.

'Nobody plays like Sparrow,' Cappy said. Then he grinned, shyly. 'I started him.'

I said, 'No kidding.'

Cappy liked that. 'Yeah, I started him. I taught him his first piece. Thirteen years ago. He was nine, and I was playing my first big job. The old Paradise Ballroom.'

The band had finished the opening number of the set and was started on the next. Cappy's eyes opened wide.

'That's it! That's the piece I was telling you.'

I listened to Jimmy Brash playing a piano intro, and what surprised me was how slow he was playing it. Be-bop bands hardly ever play anything slow. Then I recognized the tune. It was 'Sweet Sue,' and that was another surprise. They hardly ever play standards. Sparrow came in on the up-beat and Cappy's smile reached from ear to ear.

'Can you beat that man?' he said. 'He's playing it for Cappy. He knew I was bragging on him.'

I peered at Sparrow but his face had the same dead-pan expression. He didn't know we were alive, let alone talking about him. Then, just when I decided it was all a coincidence, Sparrow's face twitched like he was winking and he honked five notes of the melody right at Cappy. Cappy went crazy.

'I hear you talkin'!' he yelled back. 'Play it for Cappy, boy! Play it for Cappy!'

Sparrow proceeded to do things to Sue she never would have believed possible.

The table couldn't hold Cappy after that. He had to get up close where he could almost touch the sad-looking boy with the saxophone.

The next number was a fast one again, and right in the middle of it Sparrow's sax shot up in front of him, over his head, like someone had pulled a string on it. I thought he was clowning for Cappy but I changed my mind fast. Sparrow couldn't bring the instrument down. He kept playing it in that position until Hughie brought the number to an abrupt end.

The boys on the stand shot Hughie a quick look and he motioned, That's all, to them. They walked off the stand and Cappy pried the instrument out of Sparrow's hands.

It was too much for me. I threw some bills on the table and beat it out of there.

At six, I gave up trying to fall asleep. I phoned Hughie, figuring he'd be home by then. Hughie answered the phone himself. 'How is he?' I asked.

'Cappy took him home right after you left.'

'Jesus,' I said. 'Is that the way he's been?'

'Last night was the worst.'

'Look,' I said. 'What about it? You think we ought to go through with that date? Put him through the wringer for a lousy couple of records?'

'It might be the last time for a while.'

I cursed. 'Shall I go get him tonight?' I asked.

'Cappy'll bring him.'

I said okay, and banged the phone down in its cradle.

I wondered how smart I was, letting myself in for this. Counting the band, the studio, engineers, and incidentals, my recording sessions set me back a thousand bucks apiece. An awful lot of dough. I cut four tunes on each date and I can generally figure on them selling enough to get me back my costs. But unless one of the four sides turns out to be a real seller, I'm in the hole. You can't stay in business just making back your costs. If Sparrow showed up in the condition I saw him last, I'd be lucky if I got back the price of a pack of cigarettes.

I bought a bottle on the way to the studio and by the time the boys arrived, the bottle was a little less than half full.

When I saw Sparrow I stopped worrying, he looked so much better. He still had that dead-pan look but he wasn't twitching. I said hello, but I guess he didn't hear me. I didn't know what else to say, so I handed him the bottle. He held it for a while without looking at it, then he took a swig. He made a mouth like it was Clorox. It didn't look like he wanted more, so I took the bottle from him and handed it around. Everybody but Cappy took a good slug. Then Hughie got busy laying out the tunes.

Sparrow sat quietly where Cappy put him, puffing a cigarette Cappy put in his mouth. I thought it was going to be all right, but I felt fidgety. I clomped around the big studio, avoiding the group around the piano and drums. Then I looked at Sparrow and saw his eyes weren't blank any more. They were staring, with the same sad expression I remembered from the night before. It began to get me.

I told Hughie we'd cut everything and I went back into the mixer's glass booth.

I watched them through the glass window. Cappy handed Sparrow his instrument and I saw the boys waiting for him to tune up. When Sparrow didn't make any motions, I looked at Hughie. He didn't look at me.

'Let's go,' I said to the mixer. 'It's a take.'

The mixer looked at me like I was crazy. 'Aren't they going to warm up?'

I didn't answer, so he switched into the engineer and told him it was a take. Then he switched into the studio and told the boys to watch the lights. The white light would go on first, then the red. The red meant play. That's so you can time the number and get your three minutes.

Hughie nudged Sparrow and pointed to the light bulbs on top of the window where I sat. Sparrow put his instrument in his mouth and stood up at the mike. They waited for the lights. The white light went on. That meant ten seconds more. It seemed like a year. Then the red light flashed on. Hughie beat off with a nod of his head and they swung into 'Wing Ding.'

It was no good. 'Wing Ding' has a tricky opening where the sax and trumpet play against each other, accenting different beats. It's got to be right or it sounds like a clambake. Sparrow came in a beat late, fouling it up.

The mixer switched into the studio and told them to try it again. Then he switched over to the engineer's room, telling him to smear it and get ready for another take.

The white light went on again, then the red. This time Sparrow came in a beat too soon.

The third time he was late again.

We tried it twice more but it was no use. Sparrow wasn't focusing. The boys looked embarrassed. Cappy came over to the booth and yelled through the glass window. We would have heard him anyway, the mike was on.

'It's those lights,' Cappy pleaded. 'They make him tight. He'll play good when he's relaxed. It's those lights.'

I pulled the switch and called in to Hughie that we'd try another tune without lights. 'Whenever you're ready, tell me.'

Cappy put Sparrow back on his chair and lit another cigarette for him. The others stood around for a while, not doing anything. Then Jimmy Brash started playing something on the piano, just anything. The bass and drums picked it up, and Hughie started noodling. After a minute, Sparrow joined in from his chair, nice and easy. Then Sparrow began to blow hard and the music jumped. They jammed choruses for five minutes before Hughie waved it to a close. He looked at Sparrow.

'How about "The Sparrow Jumps"?' he asked. He didn't wait for an answer. 'No lights this time, Sparrow. You start and we'll come in. Let's make this something, Sparrow. Okay?'

Sparrow blinked and it shocked me. I hadn't realized his eyes had been staring wide open all the time. He stood up, pushing the chair away with the back of his legs, and he stepped up to the mike. His body was tense the way it used to get years ago when he was ready to play. Nobody moved. Then I poked the mixer and he called in, 'Ready for a take,' to the engineer.

'The Sparrow Jumps' is a showcase piece; no arrangements, nothing. Just Sparrow soloing, with Hughie and the piano playing figures behind him. Sparrow tore off the opening cadenza at a tempo that brought the boys' heads up. They were used to playing the 'Jump' at a good clip, but this was, what I mean, fast.

I didn't know what might happen. I crossed my fingers. Then I uncrossed them. The band was playing like it never played before and Sparrow was going like a bat out of hell. But it was more than that, it had an excitement that gave me goose pimples; the kind of excitement that hallmarks all the really great records and still comes through long after the wax has worn thin and what you hear is only an inkling of what was. I thought, man oh man. The hell with whether I get my four sides. This one's enough. This is for the books. When this hits the record stores—

The music seemed to be getting faster and I looked to see what the hell Joe Miggs was thinking about on his drums. The time is always the same in jazz. If it starts slow, it stays slow. If it starts fast, it stays that way, it doesn't get faster. Only this was. Then I saw Jimmy Brash's face had a funny look. His fingers were flying but that wasn't bothering him. Then my ears caught it. It was the chords. They weren't jibing with what Sparrow was playing. Sparrow was changing keys, sometimes in the middle of a phrase. The bass player had the same worried look. They had been playing together long enough to follow any of Sparrow's changes, but he was getting away from them. Only Hughie couldn't be shaken off. He managed to hang on, and how he did it I'll never know. I guess only a guy who felt about Sparrow the way Hughie did, could. It was the most frantic, wonderful, exciting music I had ever heard.

Sparrow's tic had returned but I didn't catch it right away; I'd watched too many jazz musicians swing their shoulders and shimmy their knees while they played. Even when I knew the tic was there, I couldn't always follow it. Sparrow's head would jerk to one side and notes from his horn would catch the swing back, making the jerk part of the musical phrase. The same thing happened when his body twitched or his legs kicked out. Music caught the spasm at the point it broke off, completing it. It was as if the jerks and twitches were musical sounds Sparrow could hear. That's what made it different from the night before. This had pattern, rhythm; it was so all of a piece you couldn't tell whether you were seeing it or hearing it.

Then you couldn't miss it. His whole body began to twitch crazily, and what he played was crazy in exactly the same way. It had to be, if his jerks and twitches were notes Sparrow could hear. And that's the way he was hearing it.

The other boys kept playing, but they were watching him the way I was. I thought I was losing my mind. I don't know how long I watched it before I got hold of myself. I pressed down on the switch, yelling, 'Stop it! Stop it! Stop it! Stop it!'

The boys stopped, gradually, their music sort of trickling away, their eyes still on Sparrow. He was still going, his twisted music and his tortured body all mixed up in one long insane convulsion.

I stumbled out of the booth and grabbed him. I held him tight until the notes from his horn finally petered out. I could feel his tremors in my fingertips. I eased him onto a chair, still holding him.

The other boys were looking at me, like they were expecting me to do something. I didn't know what to do. I only knew we couldn't leave him in whatever crazy world he was inhabiting. We had to bring him back, give him something he could tie onto, something familiar, something rational. I looked for Cappy. He was standing right behind me, but I saw his face and I knew it was up to me.

'Jimmy! "Sweet Sue"!' I snapped my fingers at the piano player.

'Play it, for Christ sakes!' Jimmy began playing, good and slow, and distinctly. I held Sparrow's shoulders so they couldn't move. I spoke right into his face. 'I want you to play this for Cappy! You hear?' I thought, I've got to get through to him, I've got to. 'Play this for Cappy. *For Cappy.*'

I felt Sparrow shiver. Then he looked up slowly. I saw meaning come into his empty eyes. His mouth opened, closed, then opened again, and he whispered, 'Cappy?'

I was screaming inside but I kept my voice quiet. 'Yes, Sparrow. Cappy.' I bent closer. 'He wants to hear you play. Will you play this for him, Sparrow? For Cappy?'

I could see him struggling with the idea, then he nodded solemnly, like a little boy saying, 'Yes, sir.' He wet his lips, fixed his mouth around his instrument, and his toe tapped out a careful 1-2-3-4. Then Sparrow played 'Sweet Sue' for Cappy. You know how the neighbor's kid sounds when he's practicing his new lesson, squeaky and screechy but earnest — so damned earnest? That's how Sparrow sounded when he played 'Sweet Sue.' Exactly as it must have sounded that first time, thirteen years ago.

I left Cappy crying like a baby, and I headed for the nearest bar.

Yeah, Sparrow's last recording would sure make a collector's item. One buck, plus tax, is cheap enough for a record of a guy going nuts.

(*From The Atlantic Monthly*)

# THE HUMAN FLY

## BY RALPH GUSTAFSON

*THE MORNING* proved hot and cloudless and the crowd which had assembled in front of Boulanger's Hardware Store was becoming impatient. The handbills had promised that the climb would start at eleven sharp. For two weeks householders in the town had been inundated with pink notices announcing the death-defying climb in bold-faced type, superlatives, and exclamation points. The handbills had come in the mail, had been slipped under front doors, shoved into the hands of people in the streets.

The advertising had become irritating, but it had been effective. Spectators began to arrive as early as nine-thirty; an hour later the street was blocked. Policemen, posted at the nearest intersections, waved the traffic away from the clogged thoroughfare. Groups of late-comers kept attaching themselves to the mass of people until the crowd gave under the pressure and tossed up fractions onto window sills and lampposts, where they sat and clung, astoundingly individual. Despite the crush, a clear space, half the width of the street, remained before the entrance to the Boulanger building. A dozen cops lined its arc, leaning their backs against the crowd. But the core of the crowd was stationary. The people around the space made no move to enter it and even answered any pressure behind them with their own weight. The space was before that part of the building which, as advertised, the Human Fly was to climb.

The crowd was restive. The clock tower of the post office on the corner struck the half hour harshly. From a lamppost someone yelled, 'Where's the Fly?' and was promptly answered, 'He's got cold feet.'

Nicholas looked around at the voice, which came from his left. The humorist, a little man holding a pipe out of his mouth, was looking about with a smirk on his face.

'Why don't they begin?' Louise asked. Nicholas turned back to her and again wondered why she had insisted upon coming. She hated crowds. He knew that she disliked being touched, that submission to her own elaborate terms was the almost impossible fee. He examined the rich waves of hair escaping the pert skullcap she wore. His fingers instinctively wanted the feel of the blackness of her hair at the neckline crushed between the pads of his thumb and forefinger.

They were standing at the edge of the space before the entrance of the building. Nicholas had argued against the whole idea of lending oneself to a cheap and morbid advertising stunt, let alone making a pleasure out of pushing and being shoved in a crowd for two hours. Louise had only smiled and said that Mr. Boulanger had to sell his pots and pans, didn't he? If she wanted to go, she did, that was all. But he wouldn't pretend to understand or make a virtue of it. Nicholas had been prepared to call for Louise early enough so that at least they would be spared shoving into the jam. But Louise was less comfortable. She had not started for the street until a quarter of an hour before the event was scheduled to start. She drove Nicholas into the alleyway behind the block of buildings in which the hardware store stood, left the car there, and led him up the back steps into the passageway between two buildings. She had arranged for the janitor to let them in at the side door. They walked through the offices, out of the front door, and across the space in front of the crowd.

Nicholas had felt his cheeks redden at their performance. The policemen merely gaped at their appearance from the wrong direction. Louise told them, 'This will do very nicely, thank you,' and they let her and Nicholas through their line at the exact center of the semicircle as though she had a right to it from the simple fact of demanding it. There had been nothing else for the police to do. But Nicholas had seen the hostility of the people near-by and agreed within himself that it was a shabby trick. He whispered to Louise that they shouldn't have come that way, and she replied without any attempt to modulate her voice that he needn't be a fool if others were. He shut up before her intensity. He looked at her and for a moment dislike passed slowly through his mind—leaving him startled at the course his emotion had taken.

A murmur arose in the crowd. Two heads appeared in a raised window in the sixth story. They were apparently examining the lower sash. Nicholas looked up the line of windows to the roof. The sashes of each had been fixed with wooden inserts so that steady openings were made available from the base to the top of the building eight stories above.

Nicholas felt cheated. 'All he needs now is a ladder.' It was as if the discovery that the windows had been fixed left their maneuver to get ahead of the crowd even shabbier.

'He can still fall, can't he?' Louise might just as well have told him not to be a logical bore. And it was true. The face of the building presented opportunities enough for a distorted conclusion on the pavement below. Between each window and the one above it was a four-foot stretch of wall sheer of any handhold except the inch provided by an ornamental line of jutting bricks. Above the top window, seventy-seven feet above the street level, the six-foot stretch of brick to the flat roof was folly.

The two heads in the window withdrew and presently three people appeared from the main entrance of the building. A couple came first, the woman in spangles and braid, the man in the faded sweater and trunks of an acrobat. Their costumes were tawdry in the daylight. They were followed by Mr. Lacroix, vice-president of Boulanger's. Importantly extending both arms above his head, he commanded attention from various sectors of the crowd, and after two or three minutes of doubt whether his gestures would have any effect whatever, he began speaking. It was the great pride and honor of Boulanger's Hardware Store — departments for everything needed in the kitchen and the home — it was with the greatest pleasure that Boulanger's could present the Human Fly.

With all the persistent preparation, Boulanger's had omitted to supply its vice-president with a microphone. His voice could hardly have been heard across the street. The crowd shoved closer. The people in front were jostled forward. Nicholas edged himself behind Louise and tried to take the pressure of the crowd from her. He put his arms around her waist.

As he held her closely, Nicholas shifted his forearms upward until he could feel the small weight of her breasts on them. The sensation familiarly excited him. She had never allowed him any physical intimacy until they had become engaged—after he had been invalided home just before the end of the war in Europe. He had silenced a machine-gun nest by bayonet and had been sent home with a burst of shrapnel in his back and with the D.S.O. It had been vaguely understood before he had left for overseas that they would marry, but he had never felt sure until after his return. His exploit at Nijmegen seemed to make a difference to Louise. She had made him tell it in detail, and it was only then, in the hospital, that he knew she wanted him to touch her. But as he now stood protecting and holding Louise he found himself questioning her. He sensed that she was unaware of him, that she was not sharing his feeling that the crowd, the whole morning had taken meaning when he put his arms around her. Nicholas relaxed the tension of his arms. Perhaps his need for expressed affection, his uncertainty of himself, made him too demanding.

The vice-president had finished his declaration. He made a condescending gesture to the Human Fly to carry on and then re-entered the building with the woman wearing the sadly pretentious costume, whom he had introduced as the daring wife of the Human Fly. The Fly turned to the building.

He was a slight little man who immediately engaged the sympathy of Nicholas and struck him with pathos. The forlorn expression of his features was ludicrously contrasted by a resentful fuzz of reddish hair which covered to an exact line the back half of his head. The combination of such a comical circumstance with the daring of what he did no doubt ensured the Human Fly his success. His appearance on the first window sill restored at once the good humor of the crowd and was the signal for hand clapping and a few shouts. But the reception jarred Nicholas as obtuse. The preliminary bows, flexings of muscle, and testings of support which the man had gone through had been empty of any attempt to establish the fiction that the theatrical flourish was important to the success of the climb. It was plain to Nicholas that the man had gone through his act by rote, and it made him depressed. He resented the lettering, BOULANGER'S BUYS ARE BEST, attached across the back of the man's sweater.

Nicholas began to sentimentalize. The man was capable of better things than such futile sensation mongering. His appealing attention toward his wife and her ignobling indifference during the vice-president's oration hinted at a drama greater than that which the man was now providing. Nicholas decided the man was foolishly and hopelessly entangled in an unworthy love. It would be as if the teasing habit which Louise had of drawing attention to his own diffidence in company were really meant as ridicule, as if Louise forced him into irrational demonstrations to prove that his love was at the same time independent yet worthy of return. The Human Fly clinging to the second-story sill of Boulanger's was deliberately placing the responsibility for a human life on the love of the woman in shabby braid. It was a threat and an appeal.

Nicholas laughed. The man was probably a shoddy exhibitionist who beat his wife.

'Do you find this funny?'

The focus of Nicholas's mind sharpened on the present. 'No — no, I was only laughing to myself.' He had irritated Louise. 'I was only thinking of this man climbing the building and an elevator inside.'

'Well, *you* can still use it.' There was no amusement in Louise's voice and Nicholas turned the remark against himself. Louise knew heights made him giddy. His lame improvisation aggravated Nicholas's resentment. He constantly felt a necessity to switch his thoughts into something which he felt Louise might prefer him to say. It was a habit of mind of which Nicholas was only half aware — but he was conscious of following it often enough to be left uncertain. Alternately he measured himself as dull and inadequate or unwillingly suspected that Louise in some inexplicable way was making him appear so. As he often did, Nicholas now avoided bringing himself to a conclusion. He said nothing more to Louise and let his attention be taken up outside himself.

The Human Fly had reached the fourth story. He was climbing cautiously but steadily. From each sill he drew himself upright by using the opening made at the top of each window; then taking his weight on his left forearm and transversely on his right foot raised against the side of the window aperture, he inched his body upward until the fingers of his right arm made the ornamental projection of bricks in the middle of the space of wall between the windows. To those watching below, the man seemed for a moment to be clinging to sheer wall. Then his left foot found the top of the slightly open sash as his left hand grasped the sill above.

Nicholas quickly admitted that the challenge of the building, despite the fixed windows, was being more than fairly met. The promise that the climb would be 'death-defying' was not mere publicity jargon. An error in the rhythm of the man's muscles between the windows would pitch him to the street below. Every nine feet, the man consigned his life, for a fraction of a minute, to the traction of the rubber on his running shoes, then to the contraction of his fingertips on an inch of brick.

Nicholas's indignation against flamboyant advertisement sharpened to anger against whatever had committed the courageous pinch of life to the monstrous fortuity of its position. As he watched the Human Fly, a slowly struggling thorax of green liquid hoisted on its waving pairs of viscous legs at the direction of the grotesque multiplex eyes, Nicholas felt sick with humiliation. He looked away, lowered his eyes to Louise. She was tense, staring at the gamble above her. Nicholas searched the assurance of her eyes, her cheek, the tangible assurance of the curve of her lips. The familiar impulse surged through him to negate his passion with them. To possess and in the possession free himself of them.

Louise suddenly was aware of his attention. For a fraction of a second her eyes diverted. Their command and scorn struck him. The curt gesture of her body to free itself from contact with him was redundant. In his imagination, Nicholas saw the flat of his hand strike her cheek so that her head jerked. But he stood there, his hands at his sides, his breath moving heavily. Then he hated himself, the constant preoccupation with his own insides, the romanticism which he allowed his passion. He stood, trying to detach the pulsing drive of his thought and emotion. But the truth behind his imagination again gripped him: it was as if he saw Louise's eyes fill with horror, follow the hurtling body, fascinated, the drop from the building to the street at her feet, her absorption away from him smashed obscenely and finally on the pavement.

Nicholas looked up. 'He's going to make it,' he said.

Louise did not reply, and as he looked up, Nicholas himself

became absorbed by what he saw. The Fly had reached the space between the top window and the roof where the stretch of brick was greater. It seemed impossibly higher than the height of the climber. He saw the small clutching figure above him pause. For a minute the Fly made no movement as he clung to the last window, then one of his arms groped awkwardly behind him. The crowd in the street below watched without sound or movement, caught between an assured excitement and possible horror. Again the arm of the Fly gestured. He was in difficulty. Then Nicholas made out what it was. The man had taken a handkerchief and was drying each of his hands. The speck on the building was stationary for a moment more, then began to grope upwards.

It was over quickly. With a studied smoothness the Fly, balancing on his toes on the window's top aperture, slid his body upright, reached for the width of an ornamental beam-end, and in the impetus provided simultaneously by a foothold on the projecting line of brick and repulsion from the beam-end leaped for the edge. For an instant his body seemed poised in space, then his arm went over and he was on the roof.

The crowd burst into applause. Nicholas had hardly had time to follow the agile grace of the feat. Shouts were added to the clapping as the Human Fly, a diminutive silhouette against the light sky, reappeared at the edge of the roof. Another figure joined him. It was his wife. They bowed to each other and to the street below. Then as the Fly withdrew from sight, the woman began gesticulating toward the crowd. At first Nicholas couldn't make out her meaning, then he saw little colored leaves of paper floating down toward the spectators below. Really, the other had been enough without Boulanger's advertising more of his bargains.

Nicholas moved impatiently. 'Let's go.' At least they needn't go through the anticlimax.

But Louise still stared upward. 'It isn't over yet.'

Nicholas looked back. The Fly was again in sight. As his wife finished distributing her pile of leaflets to the air, he placed first a table at the edge of the roof, then a rocking chair on it. The spangles of the woman's costume glinted tinily in the sun as she turned to steady the table. The Fly, stepping up on it, struck a posture with his arms spread toward the sky, then sat down in the chair, lighted a cigarette, and began rocking. At the same time a voice burst forth with startling raucousness in front of Nicholas. A loud-speaker began belching words at the crowd. It was the vice-president again, from the interior of the store.

'For godsake let's go!' Nicholas said.

Without taking her eyes from the top of the building, Louise said, 'Well go, then.' Then Nicholas remembered how she had said, 'It isn't over yet.' In the same way. Tense, with anger and fascination, yet coldly objective. The tone behind the words somehow implicated Nicholas. Instinctively he felt humiliated and mocked. He gave way to the anger and frustration which flooded up within him. 'I will,' he said.

But he found it impossible to get through the crowd behind him. It was still intent on the scene above. Nicholas surrendered before the resentment of the people he was disturbing and stopped a few feet away from Louise. He could see little of her except the round of her tiny skullcap bent back toward him as she gazed upward. Nicholas again checked himself as an exaggerating fool. And she would need his help when the crowd broke up. He stood a moment looking at the tiny skullcap, wondering, then looked to the top of the building.

The Fly was in the midst of a handstand on the seat of the rocking chair, his body a short parenthesis against the sky. His wife was steadying the table which held the chair. Nicholas's mind returned to what he had imagined was between them. The man whose daring was a plea and a warning to her love, a proof to subvert the injustice of the image in her eyes — a saddened, comical, hapless figure who by florid acrobatics only could express his love.

Then it happened. The woman had straightened away from the table into a melodramatic pose indicating her inverted husband and Nicholas later could remember nothing about the apparently perfect poise of the Fly to demand her movement. Suddenly she made a quick grab for the table. The rocking chair lurched and in a graceful arc the man came over the side of the building. He fell with ridiculous ease. A tiny apostrophe in slow-motion, upright, in control, that enlarged into the hurtling twisting figure of the Human

Fly. The sound of the impact filled Nicholas's belly with nausea. He had heard such a cry as the Fly's before — under bombardment.

Nicholas found himself beside Louise. 'Don't look, Louise! Don't look!' He pulled her round against him.

'Get away from me!'

In his astonishment at her command, he did as he was told. He looked blankly at her. She was staring at the motionless figure huddled on the pavement. Something white stuck grotesquely up through the lettering on its back. Then the edge of the crowd disintegrated and, as he still looked at Louise, Nicholas's mind came alive. Turning against the surge of people, he viciously fought a path away from her.

(*From The Atlantic Monthly*)

# WHY WERE YOU SENT OUT HERE?

## BY JOHN HERSEY

WITH abrupt acceleration, the heavy revolving front door of the Wagons-Lits Hotel started to swing around. After the door flaps had thudded twice, Colonel Potter Watson emerged on the outer side. He was about thirty-five years old, florid and strong-looking. He had on his lapels the brass vial-and-flame of Chemical Warfare, and he displayed, above his left breast pocket, only one overseas ribbon — a brand-new Asiatic Theater stripe. When he had stepped clear, the door slowed down a lot and let out Colonel William de Angelis, who wore the insignia of an infantryman and several decorations from the First World War. The second officer's face, that of a man about sixty, was a pattern of meaningless lines on contours that had apparently been interesting once, like an action map in a rear echelon headquarters after the fighting is over. Everything about the older man looked slightly dilapidated, except for a beautiful, flexible, braided swagger stick tucked under his left arm.

Colonel Watson stepped out to the front of the marble platform of the entranceway and greeted the heavy Chinese doorman by name, 'Good morning, Sung.'

The doorman tipped his visored khaki hat and said, 'Good morning, master,' and bowed slightly.

The older colonel, coming along behind, said dully, 'Good day.'

'Good morning, sir,' Sung replied, and did not bow to the older man. He told the officers that the eight o'clock shuttle bus to Peking Union Medical College, their headquarters, had just left.

Colonel Watson, the younger officer, said, 'Nice spring morning like this, why don't we take a ricksha?' Colonel de Angelis acquiesced. Sung lifted a fat hand as a signal to the coolies lounging on the footboards of a row of fancy Legation Quarter rickshas across the street. Several grabbed up the shafts of their vehicles and ran, pulling the rickshas, across to the entranceway and shouted competitively for the Americans' favor. Colonel Watson, recognizing a puller he had engaged once before, said, 'I'll take Number Thirty-Four here.' Colonel de Angelis, who did not know one coolie from another, accepted the most insistent puller. This man had run up the steps and was actually trying to push the elderly colonel toward his own ricksha. 'All right,' Colonel de Angelis said, 'take your hands off me.'

Instead of giving instructions in English to Sung for translation, Colonel Watson spoke directly to his coolie in fairly well pronounced Chinese: 'To Executive Headquarters. How are you today?'

The coolie mumbled a reply and pulled out ahead. The older colonel's puller followed.

Colonel Watson turned and said over his shoulder to his companion in the other ricksha, 'No dust today. Look at that sky.'

The two rickshas turned into Legation Street. Along the sidewalks, the horse chestnuts and acacias, whose leaves had suddenly fanned out from buds after a rain the week before, were still and fragrant. Policemen in black uniforms argued noisily in front of a large building on the left, which they were apparently appropriating as a station; their hubbub seemed to be all about how to unload some furniture they were moving. A couple of Chinese college girls rode up the street on bicycles, careless of the way their slit dresses exposed their thighs; Colonel Watson watched them, but the older man did not. He was looking, as he had been bid to do, at the sky. How sharply the roof tiles of the buildings they passed were edged against the blue! And what blue! Pure, a color one could see only over Peiping, with the lucency of porcelain, he thought. He saw Colonel Watson turn again and heard him shout cheerfully, 'Spring moves along a lot faster here than it does in Hartford.'

Colonel de Angelis found the younger man's exuberance annoying. He realized all at once that he had nothing specific and absolute with which to compare the North China weather, for he had nothing to remember as home — just the series of camps through which a regular Army man passes: was there ever spring at Fort Bragg or Camp Mills or Fort Sam Houston? how fast did all those seasons move along? Colonel Watson's remarks, whether he intended it or not, were irritating, the older man reflected. He remembered, in sudden focus — as, for some reason, he had quite a few times in recent days, while he had been rooming with Colonel Watson — several scenes at Fort Sam Houston: a parade there, the barbershop on the post, his desk at C Company headquarters.

As the rickshas swung into Rue Marco Polo and passed a couple of curio shops, Colonel Watson leaned around again and called out, 'Don't get sucked into those places. Terrible gyp joints. Have you been down to Embroidery Street?'

'No.'

'I'll take you down there some day. Chinese city. Same stuff as up here, only you can bargain. I'll take you down.'

Colonel de Angelis decided at once that he did not want to go to Embroidery Street with Colonel Watson, who surely would bully the merchants and boast later of his triumphs. Colonel de Angelis was rather surprised at the vehemence of his feeling about the younger colonel. Ever since they had been put in the same room at the hotel, he had been annoyed by little things Watson did — the young man's long throat-clearing sessions in the bathroom in the mornings, his frequent and positive contradictions of what people said, his excellent appetite, his constant good spirits, his knowing everything and wanting to be so helpful — but Colonel de Angelis had not realized so clearly before how much he really disliked his roommate. Colonel de Angelis thought again of Fort Sam Houston; something about that place that had been trying to crowd into his memory ever since he had spent his first day with Watson. Maybe, he decided, it was because he had been about Watson's age when he was there. That was in 1921 and 1922; twenty-four and -five years ago. Yes, he thought, that must be it.

Colonel Watson had turned around again. 'I got a honey of a Shantung table set down there,' he said, 'a breakfast set, I think you call it. Only seven bucks. I knocked 'em down from twelve.' Then Watson snapped his fingers at Colonel de Angelis' ricksha puller and said to him in English, 'Say, boy, hubba-hubba a bit. Come alongside here.' He beckoned and flagged the coolie up. 'The Colonel and I want to talk to each other. That's better.'

The rickshas ran parallel. 'Seems funny,' Watson said, 'the way they sent so many of us over here at once — colonels and lieutenant colonels. Like it, so far?'

'Well,' Colonel de Angelis said, 'the food in the hotel is certainly punk. If they offer me another of those cold rice pancakes after breakfast —'

'I don't know,' Colonel Watson said, as he always did in preface to a disagreement. 'They have a darn good steak in the grille. I don't think the food is bad.' He paused, then said, 'How did they happen to send you out here? Did you ever hear?'

Colonel de Angelis wondered: Why did they send a hundred colonels and lieutenant colonels over to North China in one batch? How did they happen to choose one man or another from the tremendous replacement pool? How did they happen to pick so many men who had been passed over for promotion, and so many who had already been bumped back from brigadier? Why *did* they send me over here? The older colonel shrugged. 'You know the Army,' he said.

'I put in for this duty,' Watson said. 'The way I figured was, with the war over and me not getting overseas while it was on, China seemed like the best possible chance for advancement — for a younger man, that is,' he added.

Colonel de Angelis thought again of Fort Sam. What was it he was trying to recall? At Fort Sam Houston he had been a captain. Those were dismal barracks. He had had the fourth bunk from the end on the right side in G. His sergeant major — what was his name? Benny something or other — that was great the time Benny pretended to trip and butted into Rassmussen. What a pathetic old character Captain Rassmussen was! Pathetic old — wait! wait!

A silver C-54 roared low over the city and for a moment it seemed to be framed, from where the colonels rode, within the pailou, the high, skeletal ceremonial gate near the top of Rue Marco Polo. 'Look at that!' Colonel Watson shouted, and at once he launched into what was certain, if past recitals meant anything, to be a long account of his uneventful flight across the Pacific. Colonel de Angelis only half listened. The rasping, effusive voice went on and on; '. . . hit the runway right on the nose, and we hadn't been out of the overcast since Kwajalein . . .'; the story touched on all the commonplaces. Colonel de Angelis tried to distract himself by looking at the market, already crowded and obstreperous, spread out on the old glacis of the Legation Quarter, to their right as they rode—at the too colorful Japanese obis hung like wash on a line; booths where cloth shoes, old bottles, peanuts, suitcases, sweet potatoes, Chinese fiddles were for sale; men hawking, arguing in shouts, and talking loudly simply to be heard; and, at some distance on the curb, a bicycle tire repairer waiting patiently a few yards beyond a pool of broken glass he had scattered in the street. Colonel de Angelis remembered that he had had a bicycle at Fort Sam Houston. Fort Sam after the first war hadn't seemed such a bad place; there was not much to do except avoid mistakes. On the whole, looking back, it was pretty good duty. A captaincy is a satisfying rank, when you're young. It couldn't have been so much fun for Captain Rassmussen, at his age. ('. . . I never saw so many wrecked ships,' Colonel Watson was saying, 'as we did going in over Buckner Bay. My God, that must have been some typhoon . . .') Colonel de Angelis, called back by the younger man's voice when it seemed all at once to get louder, wondered what it was he so disliked about Colonel Watson. The other newcomers seemed to like him all right; they considered him cheerful, a good drinker, marvelous at liars' dice, skillful at bargaining with the Chinks—a great fellow, they said. One man had even congratulated de Angelis on the luck of his draw for roommate. Anyone could room with Watson who wanted to. Perhaps, Colonel de Angelis thought, he could speak to the Chinese WASC representative at the hotel that afternoon and get himself shifted to a single room. Let's see, he thought: Get a haircut, go over to the PX for nail scissors—what was the other thing he had to do in the afternoon? ('. . . absolutely clear over Shanghai . . .') What *was* it Watson brought to his mind—or to the very edge of his mind? Was it, he wondered for a moment, something about Captain Rassmussen?

On the way into Morrison Street, Watson directed the ricksha coolies in Chinese to turn in towards Executive Headquarters at the third hutung, rather than the second, so that they could go in the side entrance. 'You taking up Chinese?' he asked Colonel de Angelis. 'Or,' he went on in an affectionately teasing tone, 'are you one of these old dogs that refuse to learn new tricks? Helps a lot, I can tell you. I got a start on it back in the States. You see, I got wind of this assignment —' and he paused, as if waiting to be told that he would always land on *his* feet, and then went on, as if taking the compliment for granted, 'It doesn't hurt to keep some wires out. So when I heard about this, I lined myself up to have a couple of months in the language school up at New Haven. I still work on it pretty hard. It makes a difference, specially on bargaining. These merchants dope it out that they can't fool around: anybody that speaks even a few words must be an old China hand, that's the way they figure it. You meet a different type of people, too, with the language. You take down in Shanghai, while we were waiting to be shipped up here, I darn near got myself lined up with a sleeping dictionary. She was a honey. Belonged to a second lieutenant who got shipped home —'

The insults this bastard devises, Colonel de Angelis thought. The rickshas turned off Morrison Street into the third alley on the right. The older man looked at the headquarters compound, which now came into sight at the dead end ahead — the massive, handsome, pseudo-Oriental buildings that had once comprised a hospital and medical school, endowed by the Rockefellers, he had heard; now a house divided three ways — two kinds of Chinese and some Americans, all ostensibly trying to bring an end to civil war. What could he do there? He knew nothing about China. Every day he grew more confused as he watched the opposing Chinese and the Americans addressing one another with elaborate but artificial gestures, like those of marionettes, as if they were trying by sheer energy to make convincing the things they were saying — things that nobody could possibly believe. He had been in Peiping two weeks, and still there had been no decision as to whether he would be in the operations section here in Peiping or would be sent out with a field team. He was somehow afraid of the buildings, with the kind of vague fear he would have felt if the compound were still a hospital, with ether heavy in the corridors.

Colonel Watson, who had also been looking at the buildings,

turned and asked, 'No, really, aside from the food, do you think you're going to like it here?'

Like it? Like it? 'I guess it'll be all right.'

And then, unmistakably, in the sound of that 'Like it?' he recognized the one of whom Colonel Watson reminded him: it was of himself.

The Crescent, though by no means the finest speak-easy in San Antonio in 1921, nor that with the safest liquor, seemed to attract more soldiers and officers than any other. Its mirrors, cheap smoked wood wainscoting, and brass chandeliers were like those of an old saloon; the place was ironically decorated, Colonel de Angelis remembered, with cartoons of John Barleycorn, photographs of Volstead and Miss Frances Willard and a convention of Band of Hope children, framed clippings of prohibitionist news, and a cross-stitched motto: 'The voters do not have the courage to vote as they drink—Dr. N. M. Butler.'

Colonel de Angelis remembered that he and Captain Rassmussen had sat that night—a winter night, late in 1921, it must have been—at a table against the wall opposite the bar. The place was crowded with all sorts: fairly well dressed couples, workmen in denim, girls looking for pickups. Captain de Angelis' uniform was crisp and his buttons bright. Captain Rassmussen seemed very tired. He was nearly sixty and would never be anything but a captain. He had blond hair with some gray in it, and a ruddy, finely wrinkled face. He had been at Fort Sam Houston only about a month, and de Angelis had asked him, a few days before, to take a seventy-two with him to San Antonio.

When he had invited Rassmussen, de Angelis had believed he did it because he liked the older man, who had been cheerful enough around the post, and full of stories of the old-time Army; on the way into San Antonio, he had decided it had been because he pitied Rassmussen; and after a few hours in the town, when he had found that the older man had no appetite for food, hadn't the faintest desire to work up a date with a girl, wanted only two drinks, was satisfied with a captaincy, did not dislike his superiors, laughed about everything but never as if he meant it, wanted nothing, had nothing, was nothing—then de Angelis realized that he resented

Rassmussen. He began to tease him. At first he was fairly subtle, and stuck so close to the truth, alternately praising and criticizing the elderly captain, that Rassmussen could not, at first, be anything but gratified, if slightly puzzled, by his young friend's interest in him.

Later, however, when de Angelis found that his anger at the older man only grew with his own elation, he began to be comparatively obvious. He made more and more references to age. He talked about the Army's retirement and pension systems. He remarked that he had noticed how exhausted Rassmussen had looked out on parade a couple of days before. And he asked over and over whether Rassmussen liked being a captain at his age. Eventually this had become a half-drunken refrain: 'Do you like it? Do you like it?' At last the older officer said, without particular anger, but looking quite defeated, 'Say, I believe you're being darned unkind.' De Angelis apologized and protested — quite convincingly, he felt — that he hadn't meant a thing by his remarks. He had, of course; he knew he had. He had meant that he was young and had the best of his career ahead of him, and Rassmussen was getting old.

The rickshas pulled up at the side gate of the headquarters compound. Colonel Watson asked in Chinese how much his coolie wanted, and after several sentences of conversation, in which mock outrage was displayed on both sides, he gave the coolie some bills and turned away laughing.

'How much do you give these jokers?' Colonel de Angelis asked.

'Let him have five hundred,' Watson said. 'It's too much, but he'll give you a better ride next time.'

Colonel de Angelis handed his puller some bills. At once the coolie began protesting in noisy Chinese. 'What's he saying?' the older Colonel asked Watson.

'Just the usual stink. Come on.'

Colonel de Angelis stepped over the shafts and started toward the entranceway. The coolie followed with hands outstretched, sneering at the bill he held, talking louder and louder, higher and higher, and — it seemed to Colonel de Angelis — more and more abusively. The older colonel turned and said with as much authority and contempt as he could convey in a language that would not be understood, 'That's enough. Now hang up.' He wheeled and walked on. But the coolie only shouted more, and he ran and caught up with the Colonel and put a dirty hand on the officer's sleeve and then grabbed the sleeve and waved the bills in front of the American's face.

'Come on!' Colonel Watson shouted. He was about ten paces ahead. His voice was cheerful, and it was young.

The coolie tugged hard at Colonel de Angelis' sleeve. The elderly colonel turned abruptly and, reaching across with his right hand, pulled out his swagger stick and aimed and flashed it backhand.

Colonel de Angelis knew at once what he had done. He glanced around and saw that Watson had started walking springily — perhaps tactfully? had he seen? — up the steps into the entrance court. Colonel de Angelis looked out to see if there had been any American officers coming along the street; there had not. The coolie stood with his right hand partly hiding the red stripe the swagger stick had printed on his cheek, his left hand still stretched out waving the paper money; he was silent now.

With a slow, awkward, exaggerated movement, like that of a drunken man, Colonel de Angelis groped in his breast pocket for his wallet, took it out, opened it, got out a bill for a thousand Chinese dollars — twice the original fare — and offered it to the coolie, who took it and turned away without speaking. Colonel de Angelis stepped rather erratically toward the entrance. The two Chinese sentries standing at the gate saluted him with mechanical eagerness. He transferred the swagger stick from his right hand back under his left arm, and returned their greeting. As the old colonel started up the steps, he saw that the younger man was already indoors. There didn't seem to be any faces in the windows around the wide entrance court.

*(From Mainstream)*

# THE DAWN SWINGS IN

BY LANCE JEFFERS

*IT WAS* as if fists had been clamped down on his eyes and his brain, for he woke drugged. With effort, Willie held his eyes open. Slowly he raised himself to a sitting position, muttering in wonder at the phenomenon of deep sleep: 'Ah shore slep hard . . . ah shore slep hard.'

And it seemed there was something to remember, he didn't know what, but there was something to remember — it tried to force itself into his mind. Suddenly, without prior thought, he said to himself — Today ah vote — and he felt drugged no longer, he was wide awake, and fear was a rod that pressed against the wall of his belly and chest. It jerked down into the groin with every beat of his heart. The area behind his eyes felt filled with tears and he wanted to stretch out on the bed and cry in despair.

He had a vision of red-faced men sprawled on the sun-gashed, paint-peeling court-house steps. Without warning as he began to mount the steps, one of the men casually rose and blocked his way. Then all of them were a circle around him on the steps, regarding him with clinical eyes. . . . He wondered if it would be that way, what he would do next if it were . . . He tried to cut off the thought, destroy it, but it wouldn't go away.

A great sadness and self-pity flooded him. There must be some other way. . . . Maybe he shouldn't go. . . . Naw, he thought with angry shame; ah got to! He tried desperately to convince himself — hell, won't nothin' happen; ahm a vetrun. He became aware of sweat hanging on his forehead.

Mechanically he rose from the sheetless bed to dress, the threadbare O. D. shorts slipping far down on the bony hips and exposing in the front a gaping patch of black hair and burnt-brown skin. The top of his head nearly touched the festering paperboard ceiling. He was slightly stooped and carried his head down and a little on one side as if the neck were malformed. Tall as he was, it seemed as if he were always looking up at people. This, with his brown deer-eyes, and quiet mien, gave him the appearance of being very shy.

Stretching every minute, every movement, dreading the morning that lay before him, Willie poked feet through the legs of the old Army-issue sun-tans, arms into the faded sun-tan shirt.

His mother, black and small and crinkled, bent with age, appeared at the door, hands spread like transparent claws on a ragged, white apron.

'Mawnin', son.' Her creaking voice was weighted with dignity and forbearance.

'Mawnin',' he said shortly.

Though his head was averted, he could see her, feel her in the doorway, studying him. He wished she would leave him alone, get out and leave him alone. It was almost as if she were sucking his heart for pity, *trying* to make him feel bad. Get out!

He could feel her dejection and pain. He knew these were for him. He knew the words she would say before the sun stood astride the sky, knew that then he would feel bottomlessly sorry for her and for himself.

Jerkily, he pulled his belt to, and with unnecessary motions, straightened the cuffs of his shirt, as he waited for her to speak again. Then, with great relief, he heard the whip-cracking of grease on the stove. His mother half-turned her body to the noise. He could feel her relax wearily, and allow something other than him into her mind as she plodded back toward the kitchen.

Steam swirled above the plate that waited for him on the rickety kitchen table, heavy white plate laid with grits and black meat-strained gravy. Head down, he lapped up the hot food, cursing as it seared his mouth, but hurrying on, avoiding the sorrow-moulded eyes of his mother, sitting opposite him with folded arms, her food growing cold on her plate.

God damn it, he thought, why does she have to sit there like that!

Finished, he wiped his mouth with the back of his hand, roughly rose and pushed the chair away. He started hurriedly from the room.

'Son?'

He stopped in his tracks. He wanted to overthrow the table in her face, stalk from the room. It was bad enough, without her making it worse!

'Whatchawant?'

She was silent for a moment, as if reproving his tone of voice. Then, unable to restrain her grief, she cried, 'Son, why do you have to go down there? Why do you do this to your poor old Maw?'

Ancient hate fisted up within him — poor old Maw! Me in the schoolhouse, and her lyin' in a peckerwood's bed, tryin' to hustle a filthy dollar. You whore, le'me outa here!

As if divining what he felt, she began to rock slightly to and fro in the chair, and her jagged face shriveled. She made no sound, but tears zig-zagged down the seams of her face like water running down over cracked and dusty glass. He could be angry with her no longer; he loved her. And the hate of a second ago made what he felt for her now, a fist inside him to pull his guts — to make him want to kiss the tears from her face, to ask for forgiveness for his long bitterness toward her, and for what he was going to do now.

'Maw,' he cried, voice breaking.

She cried out as if run through with a sword, and sobbed uncontrollably, throwing her arms into the air. He knelt and drew her rocking, rigid body to him, feeling deep compassion, deep shame, for her.

'Maw,' he soothed her, 'ain no need to be skeered. It ain like it was when you was comin' up. Ain no need to be skeered atall . . .'

Gradually she quieted.

He was sure that now she would try to prevail upon him again, and he could take no more. Gently he pulled himself from her, stretched to his feet.

But she sat as if mummified.

'See ya tonight, Maw,' he said. He waited a second for her to answer, then quietly left the house, feeling selfish and all knotted-up inside, knowing he should stay longer with her, but tried and unwilling.

He walked down the dusty, dew-matted street, sun hanging red and wet above the unpainted clapboard houses which sat on either side of the street like rotted mushrooms. From the porch of one sailed clear and lyric into the morning a woman's loud laughter, sounding like a dawn-cock crowing. A middle-aged man, hard-muscled and drawn-faced, dressed in a pair of greasy overalls, stepped from his shanty. He threw down a cigarette-butt with a quick and bitter gesture. He looked up and down the street, then started away, head down, walking as if he were bucking a high wind.

Willie tried to sort things out in his mind. His mother had jumbled him up and he didn't know where he was. He had to know why he was going to the courthouse, why he didn't do what she wanted him to, that which almost surely would be better for him. The question was jangling threatening inside him that had to be silenced. It was all her fault — if she hadn't asked him not to go, he wouldn't feel like this — Christ! he hated her, she made a man wanta die!

All the old hate for her that had grown like a weed from poisoned earth blossomed within him again, the hate that had grown from sing-song taunts — 'Whose hands is in your mammy's drawers, whose hands is in your mammy's drawers?' — and the triumphant shouts of laughter that followed, as, insane with rage, blinded with tears, he chased his tormenters.

But the question clanged on, demanding to be heard — why did he have to go down there? . . .

He thought of the two horsemen, white-mantled from head to foot, peak-capped, who yesterday in the early evening had filed through the Negro section of the town, bearing between them a broad white banner, rudely patched with red paint: 'NIGGER VOTE AT RISK OF YOUR LIFE.' Of the silence that like a suffocating blanket fell over the streets as the horsemen passed; of the Negroes who stared long after them, fascinated, like a bird by a snake's eyes. He thought of his own sharp, stifled anger, and of the fear which yawned and held tight within his belly, held him fast where he stood until the plodding horsemen had passed from sight. Of last night and the fifteen-odd young faces, heavy with gravity in the dimly-lighted, ornament-littered parlor.

When they first came together last night, they had asked each other, a kind of terror in their eyes, 'See the Klan out tonight?' Then as they sat, apprehensive, each waiting for the other to speak, one brown, razor-faced man hysterically slashed the silence, frightened them all: 'If yall crazy nuff to get yaselves killed, go haid!' Without another word, he slammed out of the house. Soon — hesitant, shame-faced, mumbling excuses and apologies — three more followed, leaving the room cold and shrunken.

It was Willie who spoke first, his voice large and fierce in the little room.

'Any more chicken-bastards lef' in here?'

When he had said that, there was a solid warmth in the room, and the men drew nearer each other, feeling the warmth and knowing their strength.

Then he spoke again, feeling himself a leader, wanting to draw the men even closer together.

'Got to tough-it-out sometime!'

But it had fallen flat. He realized that as soon as he had said it. It had the effect of making the men sad.

He knew that anguish ate inside each of them, as in him, when, a few minutes later, they decided to go through with it. . . . Most of them were poor workingmen like himself; before they went to the Army, none of them worried about voting. . . . Now it was different. Why?

He thought with resignation: ain no need to ask mahself why — ah know why. Ahm jus scared, that's all. Tryin' to find some way of backin' out at the last minute.

And he remembered the ride home on the train from separation center, the day after he had been discharged. He would always come back to the ride on the train — that was the beginning of the reason why. . . .

On the ride home he had sat in the first car of the train; the train was a well-ventilated streamliner, with large, clean windows, reclining seats, soft neon lights overhead, and a porter in a white coat. Willie had a feeling of tired happiness, a soft-flowing happiness jumbled with a contented disbelief about really being out of the Army. He didn't feel like getting drunk and raising hell, or doing anything out of the way. He was content just to sit here, watch the swampland and the grey earth flee by, listen to the muted, smooth churning of the train-wheels, and now and then tell himself that he was out — for good.

Next to him sat a quiet, friendly white boy from Tuscaloosa. They had been discharged together and had met again on the train. That in itself was wonderful — that he and the three Negroes sitting opposite him, across the aisle, had not been asked to move to the forward, partitioned section of the car reserved for Negroes — that when the conductor, an extremely tall, sallow-faced man with a false-toothed smile, came through the car, he merely beamed at them and called them 'boys' in a friendly way, as if he weren't even aware of the law which stated that Negroes and whites were to be segregated.

One of the Negroes sitting across the aisle from Willie was a 1st Lieutenant, with a pair of crutches at his side. He was on leave, on his way to Atlanta. Beside the Lieutenant sat a white soldier, opposite him two Negro soldiers in a turned-around seat, and above him, sitting on the arms of the chairs, two white soldiers. All of them still in the Army, and Willie felt vaguely sympathetic and a little superior to them. The Lieutenant was telling stories of his experiences. The men were intent, listening. Every once in a while they would shake their heads, or break into crashing laughter and then gradually resume the intent silence. The only people in the car who appeared to object to the little gathering were the scattered few civilians, who looked on with stiff faces. Occasionally, however, their faces relaxed as they listened.

The Lieutenant was a small, dark-brown young man with a quick smile. A natural story-teller, he had a biting wit, and he talked in jerks with a hard, rasping voice. He seemed to be a fine fellow, for he talked as though he were an enlisted man too. Willie felt very warm toward him. And very proud of him too. Proud because he was an officer, but prouder still because of the purple heart and the combat infantryman's badge.

Willie would have joined the little group around the Lieutenant, but for some reason he couldn't bring himself to — as a matter of fact, didn't want to. It would have seemed too familiar. It was enough to sit here and think that this was a good way to be going home.

A big, plump M.P. with a fat-jowled face and Corporal's stripes on his shirt, worked his way down the aisle, hands on the seats to balance himself as he passed. He walked into the group of men opposite Willie. Without prelude he broke through the Lieutenant's voice. His own was heavy and plodding.

'All you colored fellas,' he said peremptorily, 'are going to have to move to the colored section.'

He nodded toward the partitioned-off section of the car, visible through the open door in the center of the partition.

The Lieutenant threw words into the air like torches.

'Where a man sits on this train don't have a *god* damn thing to do with you! Get out of here and go knock some drunks over the head!' There was laughter.

The M.P.'s head bobbed back as if he had been slapped. He recovered quickly. He stepped forward and snarled at the two Negro soldiers sitting opposite the officer: 'You fellas move up front before I get back or I'll arrest all of ya at the next stop!' He pointedly dropped his glance on the Lieutenant, and then turned around to Willie. He contemptuously flicked the discharge emblem on Willie's chest with his eyes.

'The same goes for you if ya know what's good fer ya!'

Fear struck like a knife into Willie's heart.

The M.P. started down the aisle.

The Lieutenant's hard voice ordered him back: 'Say, Corporal!'

He kept on going.

'CORPORAL!'

The M.P. opened the door to the vestibule between the cars. The train-wheel's rushing-roaring-grating flooded the car.

Willie began to rise slowly from his seat, regretting what he was doing as he did it, but unable to help himself. He felt a dim, distant anger toward the M.P., but stronger than that, he felt weary and afraid — the fear that struck him was paralyzing; he didn't have what it took to fight back — Christ, he was just out of the Army . . . four years . . . on his way home . . . if anything happened now . . . he had to get home at least . . . he was in the South; hell, anything could happen. . . .

As he took his duffle bag from the overhead rack, he felt the eyes of the white soldiers on him, sympathetic and wondering and contemptuous, and the eyes of the Lieutenant upon him, sad and bitter and contemptuous. Willie felt desperately ashamed, as if he were urinating in public, but he couldn't help what he was doing — it was as though his body were moving, and his mind were of no use at all. From the corner of his eye, he saw the Negro soldier nearest the window cross his legs, fold his arms and dig his buttocks into his seat as if it would take a team of horses to move him. Willie wondered if he were going to be the only one to move. With a feeling of sharp relief and justification, he saw the Negro soldier sitting nearest him suddenly get up, and start to take his bag from the rack. . . .

When Willie reached his seat in the Jim-Crow section, he slumped far down into it, sure that everyone's eyes were upon him. He wanted to leap through the window in his shame. He had no reason to move . . . M.P. had no power over him . . . he had let the Lieutenant down . . . he was a coward, less than a man. . . .

He called upon himself to go back to his old seat and get back the respect of the Lieutenant, the respect of the friendly white boy from Tuscaloosa. But he couldn't do it. His will had melted.

And as he sat, hating himself, he heard the laughter of the Lieutenant's group ringing loud and free again.

The M.P. didn't return. There was no one to arrest the two defiant Negroes at the next stop, nor the next.

When the train arrived at his station, Willie had to pass down the aisle past the Lieutenant's group. He knew their veiled eyes were upon him again as he passed, and he felt wretched and remorseful as he never had. . . .

In England and France and Germany he had learned — and it had been sewn into the fabric of his being — that not everywhere did men think and act as men did at home. Overseas, he had gotten a new respect for himself. But still, he rationalized about home, heatedly defended his home before the men in his company from the North who reviled the South — he rationalized about home, and sometimes convinced himself that it was not nearly so bad as some Negroes pictured it.

But the train incident struck to the core of his life — the way he had acted could not get the respect of the new Willie McHenry that had grown and developed in the Army. He had acted as if he had never left home — he had been stricken with fear that had sprung from the old days; he had failed to rise above a man who could not possibly have harmed him, even in the South.

He could fool himself no longer about home, nor about himself. The shame and self-contempt that ravaged him on the train grew quickly into shame and contempt for his whole life — for having lived so long without protest, without effort.

Willie found pavement beneath his feet. Trees stretched into the air along the street, green and their foliage heavy. They cast a damp early-morning shade over the ground. Brown and white houses, prim and tidy, nestled far back behind smooth-clipped lawns. Across the street a stone-hewn church reared into the morning, half-hidden behind tall shrubs and low-hanging trees.

He realized that he had been unconsciously directing himself to the store. For the first time he remembered that he should go there first and get Jim's permission for a half-hour off to go to the courthouse. Maybe he shouldn't ask. Maybe he ought to go right on to the courthouse — he didn't feel like fightin' with Jim. Naw, he'd go on to work. If he had to fight Jim, it might as well be now, before he went, and not after.

He turned into Denman Street, walking fast, anxious to seize the morning in his arms and call it his.

As he walked down the main street of the little business section, he was sure the eyes of the whites were upon him. They looked at him strangely, their eyes were darts into his back. His spine was a chain of ice at the thought: maybe they know what ahm goin' to do, maybe they know what's goin' to happen to me.

He walked faster and glanced behind him — with a crunch that ripped his breath out, he collided with someone. Instinctively he backed away, half-bent over in apology. Bill Ed Dickson, the hulking town cop, moved toward him, eyes slitted and bright with malice, thick wrinkled mouth pulled down.

'Hey nigger, you think you goin' somewhere?'

Desperate, afraid he'd spend the day in jail and not even get his chance to vote, he bowed and bowed to the white man, trembling, trying to force out the words. But they wouldn't come, and a voice miles down within him echoed up: Who the hell is you?

Dickson must have seen it in his eyes, for he half-raised his club, growling, 'What's your trouble, boy?'

But the voice down inside him wouldn't let him speak, and he suddenly didn't care, no matter what happened. He couldn't bring himself to apologize. He backed away from Dickson, turned, and almost at a run, fled down the street.

When he walked panting into the store, he found Jim the only one there, sitting on the front counter, his elbow resting on a pile of crisp blue jeans. He was reading the morning paper from New Orleans, crossing and recrossing his legs and angrily talking to himself. This was an old picture, one that Willie had come to know well, long before he went to the Army, and, walking into the store each morning he would feel a wrench of affection for the little old white man so brusque and peppery and good-hearted. He would silently laugh at Jim's funny ways: his unending petulant chatter to himself, full of curses for anything in the world that didn't suit his taste — his vehement, spittle-stained, hour-long advice to anyone who wasn't careful to avoid him — his ordering white people and black about as if he owned them. And with it all, he had a heart as big as a house — he'd give you the shirt off his back if he thought you needed it. Only thing was he'd never let you forget it. Funny little old man.

But this morning Jim wasn't funny; he was a threat. This morning was Willie's own, and no one with threats or orders would take it away from him. Walking into the store he felt hostile toward the white man, hostility a hard steel sheet within him.

'Mawnin', Mistuh Jim.'

Annoyance jabbed him, the thorn-pointed annoyance that always jabbed when he said 'sir' to a white man, called one 'mister.'

Jim's water-slicked, thinning grey head bobbed up, haggard thin little face frowning and resembling a wrinkled old peach.

'Mawnin'. Who you been runnin' from?'

'Nobody. Mistuh Jim. . . .'

The white man's eyes narrowed as he waited for Willie to continue.

'Mistuh Jim, ahd like to take an hour off now so ah kin go ovah to the cotehouse an cast mah vote.'

The words out, he placed his feet firm and flat on the floor, leaned forward, and held the steel sheet before him, ready for anything that might come—a perfunctory order to clean up the store before he thought about doin' *any* goddamn thing . . . a scalding flurry of words denouncing his stupidity and hardheadedness in wanting to vote. . . .

Instead, Jim seemed to shrink inside himself. He became a very old man, beaten and waiting for death. He bit his needle-thin lips and looked at the floor. Then he raised his head, and his eyes were wet and luminous. He looked at Willie as if trying to see far inside him.

Willie sensed the victory, and it leaped in him like a fresh flame.

Jim whispered; it was the sound of wonder and sorrow: 'Determined, are ya, boy?'

Willie said nothing. Let him do the talkin'.

'Yeah, I've seen it comin' for some time now . . . you can't he'p yaself . . . ah doan know . . . ahd give anything. . . .'

He was silent, looking at Willie. With sudden spirit he burst out: 'Boy, don't you know what your chances are of turnin' up for work tomorra if you go through with this? Why don't you come to your senses, go nawth, steada buttin' your head against a stone wall—ya kin get a good job up there, pay ya moren ah do—why do ya have to stay down here?' As he sputtered on, Willie drew what the man was saying close to him and examined it, and he had a feeling almost like a sexual yearning. . . .

Then he lashed the feeling from him. He cut the white man off: 'Mistuh Jim, steada tryin' to get me to go nawth, why don't you he'p me down here?'

'Why, whaddya mean?'

'Ah mean, why don't you go ovah to the cotehouse and vote same time ah do.'

Jim was stupefied. He drew deep within himself again.

Finally, after a minute, voice tired, he said: 'You know as well as ah do ah can't do that, Willie. Ah wouldn't do a nickel's wuth a business . . . ah wish—'

'Ah'll be back right soon, Mistuh Jim.'

Erect and scornful, proud of his victory, Willie walked from the store.

And outside the sun seethed upon the pavement, and stunned the air, sucked up the air, and scorched the vacuum that remained. There was no laughter on the streets, no laughter, only the whine of conversation beneath the awning of the general store, the occasional sound of rubber tires grasping the cement. People walked wet and heavy through the street, slowly, trying to compromise the heat.

As he neared the courthouse, fear began to ride his belly, pushing it down into the groin. There was a frenzied thrashing in his chest, and his throat felt as if it were overlaid with dead flesh. He felt as if his legs would give way at any moment.

There were no waiting men on the courthouse steps — the steps were empty, the steps and the streets and the grizzled green lawn; there was no noise, no one to be seen. The only way a man would know anyone was around was by the door's being open and the windows. A feeling of tremendous relief and jubilance surged up in him like a geyser.

Wasn't no need to be afraid, he thought, they wouldn't mess with a vetrun!

'Oh, Willie!'

The call was soft, almost like a purr. Pain like an electric shock flung itself through his body, and his intestines evaporated.

Where had the voice come from? But he must go on, no stopping now.

'Willie!' The voice was more urgent this time. And there was no mistaking it — it was a white man's voice. If he didn't answer it. . . .

He was rigid for a moment, not moving forward. Then he turned around stiffly to see where the voice had come from.

'Over here, Willie.'

It came from a brown '42 Oldsmobile sedan parked across the street and a few yards down. He wondered how he could have missed it. Completely numb, he walked toward the automobile, feeling almost as if he were floating. As he drew near, his mind automatically registered the fact: It was Rack Taylor who had called. He was sitting at the wheel, his handsome, deeply-tanned young face genial, his broad big shoulders limp. There was a man beside him in the front seat — it was Howard Johnson — and three in the back — Zore Kimball and Jack Griffin. The third looked like a stranger.

'Willie, what you doin' in the cotehouse today? Nigguhs don't usually have no business in the cotehouse, lessn it's stoolscrubbin'.' It was a pleasant statement of fact.

Through Willie's mind tumbled the rumors that had gone around about Reginald Henderson, the colored dentist's son. The Negroes had long known that one or two white girls had a habit of driving their cars into the Henderson garage late at night. Then one night Reginald had to be taken to Jackson for an emergency operation, old Mr. Henderson said an appendectomy. But soon after, talk began to get around that the operation had been to patch the damage Rack Taylor had done . . . they say Rack Taylor liked to get a colored woman in his big white house in the country and use a razor strop on her before . . .

A deep terror began to dig deep into Willie's body in slowly undulating waves.

The pleasant voice alerted him. 'Come ta the cotehouse ta vote?'

The terror dug deeper, deeper. But he was damned if he'd answer. He had a right to be here just like anybody else. He was damned if he'd answer.

'Watcha say, Willie?' He knew this was his last chance.

He was silent.

'Get inta the car, boy.' Now the voice was clipped, though still agreeable.

Willie stood unmoving, stubbornness and fright seared into his face. He said forcefully: 'Nosuh.'

Taylor's deep blue eyes, incongruous in the dark skin, fastened upon him — queer blue eyes that seemed to grab yours like pincers and hold them. Looking at Willie, he spoke to the other man in the front seat. 'Glove compartment, Howie.'

There was the slight click of a spring. Then the sound of metal scraping on glass, as Taylor slowly moved the muzzle of an automatic back and forth on the lowered glass of the car window.

His voice was no longer pleasant. It was flat and softly emphatic. 'Nigguh-boy, jump in this car if you don't wanna get your ass broke!'

Willie slowly reached for the door-knob, frantically searching his mind for something to do, something to do. . . .

Rack said: 'Zore and Josh?'

The two men piled lazily out of the back seat on Willie's side, pushing him roughly out of the way. Josh, the stranger, was a gangling, loose-boned man with an absurdly boyish, sun-reddened face. Josh. Why, Willie thought, that's Josh McLauren. Ah haven't seen him since ah went to the Army—he's shore got big! In his surprise at remembering McLauren, he forgot everything else, and for a split-second almost turned to speak to him.

From a great distance he heard the guarded growl of the motor. Involuntarily he looked over to the courthouse. In the windows where no one had been, young women in print dresses and men in shirt-sleeves had appeared. They were looking down at the car with set faces, as if they were bidding an enemy a grim and final good-bye. Willie longed passionately for the time of a minute ago to return, time when he could have made another decision—and it seemed that if he willed hard enough, it would return. This wasn't happening to him. He was looking in upon another man's destiny.

They were riding through town, and people were stopping in the streets to look after Rack Taylor's car with a nigger in the back of it. Only one thing was going to happen to him.

Rack's voice was pleasant again.

'You know, Willie, that was a ba-a-ad thing you did . . . wasn't it?'

It seemed to Willie that he was moving upward, forward, trying to grasp something elusive—he didn't know what—something that was just beyond his reach.

'Black sombitch don't know what's good fer 'im,' muttered Howie.

'Ya, see,' Taylor resumed, 'ah know you been layin' with white women and raisin' all kinda hell overseas. An' ah doan hold that against ya . . . but when you came home,' he concluded earnestly, 'ya shoulda been a good little nigguh-boy . . . shouldn't ya?

'. . . Now, if ya had used your head, you wouldn't be here now. You'ld be lyin' on top of some good black stuff, jus' grindin' away. Or, you'ld be thinkin' about it. But you ain thinkin' about it now . . . are ya?'

He paused again. 'What are ya thinkin' about, Willie-boy? . . . Tell me—what are ya thinkin' about?'

The blue eyes were upon Willie again in the rear-view mirror: 'Ya thinkin' about how you're gonna get that big thing of yours cut off? Maybe after all you are thinkin' about some good black stuff. Come on now, think about it—you're ridin', ridin'—'

As the voice purred on, hate rocked and pounded in Willie like a piston — he could have exploded with it. If there were only something he could do! To sit here and take it! He wouldn't go down like a dog, God damn if he would! He clenched his fists and stiffened his body for the attack, then relaxed. No, he'd wait. He'd make a plan. Fast, now, it had to be fast —

His eyes fell on a lube wrench lying on the floor near his foot, half-covered with a blanket, and a feeling of triumph boiled up hot and bitter inside him. You peckerwood son-of-a-bitches, sittin-there-thinkin' ahm gonna go down like a dog — you wrong, *you wrong!*

They turned off the macadam highway, and the purring voice stopped. The car elbowed its way over the ragged, deserted road. Dust pillared high into the air behind them. Beside the road rambled hay-colored bushes; beyond lay barren, parched fields.

Suddenly Willie broke into a wail: 'Mistuh Rack, please don't, suh; ahm sorry; please, good white folks, *please,* ah know ah did wrong, ah'll never do it again ——'

Sobbing piteously, he bent over and put his face in his hands. Howie snickered. There was a surprised grunt from Griffin at Willie's side, and he knew that Griffin was watching. But impatient, eager, unwilling to wait longer, he grabbed up the wrench and raised it to swing and there was a wild bull-cry from Griffin:

'RACK, LOOK OUT!'

(*From Cosmopolitan*)

# MORNING, A WEEK BEFORE THE CRIME

## BY VICTORIA LINCOLN

*THE DAY* that Mark Gurney died of enteric fever in China, the heavy buds of the peonies in his mother's Rhode Island garden were swelling, and the delicate black twigs of the Judas tree in the southern corner showed their first veil of soft green-yellow leaf under the dropping of its strange rosy flower.

Dolly Gurney stood at her bedroom window, looking down. It's mighty pretty, she thought dully. Well, it ought to be, the time she spends on it.

Old Lizzie, sitting in the chair behind her, had finished her sewing, and now she rose and laid it away. She was Dolly's maid, and had been her nurse. She turned toward the window, watching the tall, idle figure before it with anxious tenderness. She's been too quiet, lately, she thought. She's fixing for one of her days.

Dolly Gurney was a young woman of startling appearance. She had the tall and sweetly ample body of a Praxitelean goddess, the waist a little thick, the breasts a little small, but all rich, magnificent womanhood; and above it, set strangely on the slender, smooth, sweetly modeled column of the throat, was the head of a Dresden doll, a small woman's head of infantile prettiness, the eyes large, pure blue, with a trick of opening very wide, like the eyes of a young child. Her colour was clear and high, and her short fair hair fell naturally into its deep, bright waves.

Her beauty of face — which was exactly the kind she herself understood and admired — she regarded with a careless confidence, but her body, until she met Mark, had been to her a source of regret.

'I certainly have got a pretty face and pretty hair,' she would say to Lizzie. 'It's a mean old shame I have such an awful figure.'

'You ain't fat, honey. You're just right. It wouldn't become you to be skinny.'

It was what she wanted to hear, although she did not believe it.

Without Lizzie's love she would have had an empty childhood. Her mother had died in childbirth. Her father was a large but inconsiderable man, fond of cards and usually mildly tipsy from four o'clock in the afternoon on; her relationship with him, from babyhood, had been a protracted, stale flirtation. He was the prototype of 'the gentlemen,' and the dolls and frilly dresses that he brought back to her from his business trips were not, in her mind or in fact, so much the gifts of a loving father as *attentions,* like the flowers and the boxes of candy with lace paper and tiny gilded tongs which he had given her stepmother, Sally Anne.

Sally Anne herself had died at thirty, a gentle, vapid little woman without attachments. Dolly, thinking back, could remember only two bits of motherly advice that she had ever been given.

'You shouldn't laugh so hard,' Sally Anne had once said. 'It makes wrinkles. Look, Dolly, just smile gentle, like this.'

And once, when a gentleman had asked Dolly for a kiss, and she had complied, Sally Anne said, later, 'Always remember, dear, never give the gentlemen quite all they want. That's our right way to keep them happy, Dolly. Just you be sweet and let them think they know it all, but, Dolly, you always leave them something to hope for tomorrow—hear?'

She remembered that. But she remembered, too, what Lizzie had said about it.

'Did you do like that with Sam, Lizzie?'

And Lizzie had answered, 'You don't do a man that way when you love him, honey. I didn't do Sam no different than what he done me.'

'And did he love you, Lizzie? Up till he died, did he love you like he did when you got married?'

'More and more,' said Lizzie. And then, with a poetic quaintness which fixed the words in the child's mind, 'He was my heart. And I was his heart. If he'd lived old, we couldn't have changed to each other.'

'Maybe white gentlemen are different.'

Lizzie took a small white hand and laid it open upon her own, closing her long black fingers above it, firmly, with love. 'You and me different?' she asked softly. 'We different how we feel 'bout lovin' each other?'

'Course not. Not you and me.'

'No more our menfolks is different, honey.' She looked at the soft brown hair, the anxious little face. Suddenly a belated caution swept through her. 'How we're talkin'!' she said. 'Don't you tell Miss Sally Anne on me, now, hear? She'd yank me baldheaded.'

'Oh, I won't,' the child cried. 'I won't tell on you, Lizzie.' Then, tactlessly, as Lizzie's grateful arms hugged her close, 'You *know* I love to keep a secret on Mama.'

She forgot it all, then, but the words came back, coupled with the strong impulse of her superior body, to save, in a limited but fundamental way, her marriage with Mark Gurney.

Her father had taken her to New Orleans for Mardi Gras, and there she met him, at the home of her father's banker.

He stared at her, almost without speaking, through half the evening, and she thought that he was attractive, but queer.

'I thought Yankees were supposed to be real brainy,' she whispered to another girl. 'But this one certainly acts like he's been dropped on the head.'

Late in the evening he asked her to come out with him on the veranda. When she returned to the dancing the smug coquetry of her little face had been carefully rearranged, but behind it she was profoundly shaken. The passion of the New England Puritan, once it is liberated, has an intensity, a richness unequaled in happier natures. The strength of her response left her in no doubt as to how she should act, but in that headlong leap she would have found it hard to say whether she felt triumphant or helpless.

Shortly after they were married her father died. The big, inconsiderable man caught pneumonia in the mild Southern winter and accepted it, as he had accepted Sally Anne, his card games and his tippling, with a mannerly apathy.

Dolly wept by his deathbed. Her brief life with Mark had given her a curious feeling that she had treated her father ill, that there was something, some deep wrong in their relationship for which she should make amends, but she did not know how to go about it.

'Papa,' she said. 'Papa. You remember that doll-baby you brought me from Savannah, once? The one with the lovely, pink silk dress? That one?'

Did he remember? Did he hear? His suffused, staring eyes, his ugly breathing — which raised in her, in spite of herself, a trembling of anger — were unchanged, but she persisted, bowing her fine body above him, bringing her tired, pretty face close to his.

'I just loved it,' she persisted. 'I always just loved that doll-baby, Papa. I never thanked you for it enough. I just loved you for bringing it to me.'

But it was too late. The lids dropped over the unseeing eyes, the ugly breathing filled the room.

'Papa,' she said, 'this is Dolly. You hear me, Papa? I do love you, Papa. I would have loved you just the same if you didn't ever bring me any old doll-baby. You do hear me, don't you, Papa? It's Dolly talkin' to you. You know it, don't you, Papa? . . . I do love you.'

She began to cry terribly, like a child, with all the force of her strong body. Mark took her arm and led her out into the corridor. She sat down, her face in her hands, sobbing with total abandonment.

'I can't help being mad at him when he breathes like that,' she cried. 'I can't help it. Oh, Mark, he wouldn't answer me.'

Seeing that her tears in no sense resolved the extreme and mysterious anguish of her spirit, Mark forbore, with an effort, to touch her. And as it was only by touch that they ever achieved any sort of understanding, his impotence and confusion in the moment of her defeat equaled her own.

The next day she was calm, self-possessed, taking him with her to shop for a black dress. When she came out of the fitting room to show herself to him, her grief was quite real and in her face, but it was overlaid with a sort of demure pleasure. She looked, thought Mark, watching her curiously, anxiously, lovingly, like a child allowed to pour the coffee, to assume some small position of adult dignity in a mother's absence.

They had been married for a little more than a year when the war came, and Mark went into the Navy.

The year of marriage had been, for him, a year of extraordinary release and delight. If Dolly's passion was not equal to his own, she was at least docile and tender, all soft receptivity. His amazement at the possession of her rich beauty had increased rather than diminished. And she, for her part, was not at all frightened by the continuing intensity of his desire, but, rather, proud of it and of her own ability to content him. And still, he would wake sometimes, in the night, conscious of something wrong, very wrong and lacking, and he would withdraw from his own feeling with a sort of horror, as if it were perverse, abnormal; as if—he thought once, lying still and straight on the far side of their wide bed, not touching her as she lay beside him, heavy and still and infinitely womanly in her sleep—as if he had ravished a child.

And there were other things. A tinsel-embroidered evening scarf, not new, which he saw folded in a drawer that she had left open.

'Did Mrs. Wyatt give you this?' he asked.

'Why, no,' she replied. 'I bought it. Ages ago!'

Had she really owned it before? It was very pretty. Lucia Wyatt had worn one like it over her head to the country-club dance. Had she been wearing it when she left? He could not be sure, but it seemed to him that Lucia's head, then, had been bare.

And the lovely old Chelsea figurine that was thrown down from its table and broken in the Howlands' house. Dolly caught her foot in a rug and tripped and the figurine fell. It was irreplaceable, of course, and she felt very badly, so badly that the Howlands were sorry for her, sorrier than they were for themselves, and sorry, too—you could see it—that they had hurt her feelings earlier in the evening with that careless remark about Louisiana. She was clearly a defenseless child.

She was indeed a child—but defenseless? Caught her foot in the rug? Tall, graceful Dolly, who moved so wonderfully, whose walking, whose standing up and lying down, were lovely to see?

The instances, the little things multiplied; not fast, but enough, one here and one there. In a year there had been time for a good many of them.

And when the time came that Mark must leave her, he remembered them all. While he held her to him, his love, his dear woman, his wife—he remembered them.

'Of course,' said Imogene, his mother, who had known Dolly only for a day or two before the wedding, 'the poor child will come to us at Mount Leda.'

Dolly, at Mount Leda, with Imogene and his brother Brooks?

It was not the right solution, but apparently there was no right solution.

'Lizzie,' he said. 'I want to talk to you.'

'Yes, sir, Mr. Mark.'

He looked at the little woman standing before him. Lizzie had a low forehead, flat lips, the complexion of a plum, and her face, so uncompromisingly Negroid, was sensitive and wise, full of dignity.

'About Miss Dolly . . .'

He could not go on, of course; he could not put it into words, any of it, the deepest or the most trivial. But it was not necessary.

'Yes, sir. I'll look out for her, some way. Best's I can.'

'You know her, Lizzie, don't you?' he asked.

'Yes, sir. I know her right well. And I love her.'

He paused. 'My mother and my brother aren't the sort of people she's used to, Lizzie. They are very — well — individual.' He had no gift for translation, no real way of communicating with people of background dissimilar to his. But he felt that he was understood. 'I love them, Lizzie, and I am sure that you will. And that Miss Dolly will. But if there is — well — friction from time to time, Lizzie, do what you can.'

'Yes, sir.' Suddenly she took both of his hands in hers, and there were tears in her eyes. 'You had to go off away too soon,' she said. 'I kep' thinking, if she had a baby of her own, then maybe she'd be able to leave off being a baby herself. You know, she tries to sometimes, Mr. Mark. Like that day when her poor papa died, she was tryin' to then. That day she was tryin'."

'You know her in and out, don't you, Lizzie? Well, take care of her for me, will you?'

'As much as I can, Mr. Mark. Always have, always will. Lizzie'll do what she can.'

And with that Mark had to be content.

And now Lizzie looked at Dolly, standing so easily and nobly in the long white dressing gown that had been part of her trousseau, her childish face turned away as she looked down into the garden.

It was Isobel's garden, extraordinarily and completely hers. From the first wide massings of snowdrops and aconites to the final ruddy embers of the hardy chrysanthemums burning along the box walks and in the pleasant, secret recesses of the maze, it passed from winter sleep to sleep in a magnificence of vital and well tended being, a strong and princely garden, a garden rejoicing like a happily embodied soul in full realization of life. One who did not know Isobel well could hardly have imagined the intensity of jealous love that she expended upon it. It was absurd; it was disproportionate; but it was none the less true that now, in her middle age, Isobel knew only one passion more urgent.

Dolly was aware of them both.

'Lizzie,' she said abruptly, 'skin down and get me some flowers for this room. Don't you go pokin' around, askin' Miss Isobel what you can take, hear?'

The silence behind her was marked. Dolly Gurney's voice changed its pitch. It had been childishly imperious; now it was a dove's voice, so coaxing, so gentle.

'Go on, now, Lizzie, don't be hateful. I'm not askin' you to yank up her old garden, just fix me a nice, big, pretty bouquet. You know how she'll do, just a snip of this and a snip of that, sort of scrawny and mean. She never comes in here, Lizzie. You just go on and do like I say.'

She turned as she spoke, holding out her hand like a child to the tiny, black-skinned, gray-haired woman before her, but she saw no sign of relenting. Lizzie had a low forehead, a flat nose and wide lips, and in her face, so uncompromisingly negroid, was the clear dignity of the Ethiopian princesses who mated with the dynasty of Egypt.

'You just takin' one of your bad days,' said Lizzie. She spoke slowly and gently, like a calm mother with a difficult child. 'Now listen to me, you just get dressed and fixed up and quit lollin' round think' mischief and meanness. I don't know what you got against Mrs. Gurney, sweet and lovely like she is to you, but I ain't going to touch one of her flowers unless she tell me — hear?'

Her face, as she brushed Dolly's hair, as she helped her into her clothes, was somber, like the face of a mother who recognized some grave, permanent handicap in her child, who makes herself say, 'He will never run and jump like the others.' Or, 'He will never be able to keep up with his own class.'

Lizzie's eyes under the withered eyelids were sad; her thick, sensitive lips were calm. 'You just run downstairs now and be sweet and good,' she said.

Brooks, in the wide garret under the skylight, was at the clavichord. The room was unfinished, shaped like an enormous field tent. The rafters had been white-washed, and the floor was painted with a green deck paint, darkened with age.

'The handsomest room in the house,' Brooks had remarked years ago. 'The proportions, of course, not the detail.'

The sentence had tickled Mark, who never forgot it. Faced with any pretentiousness, any instance of affected delicacy, he would murmur, 'The proportions, not the detail.' And yet he sincerely loved and admired Brooks and would have been shocked to hear him spoken of as an incompetent, a sponge or a dilettante.

Brooks, for his own part, had very little opinion of himself, less than was justified, for he had missed genius by a very narrow margin. The sense of beauty by which both Imogene and Mark were plagued and justified appeared in him with a degree of pathological sensibility in which both pleasure and displeasure were felt with a torment of intensity. This painful over-refinement of life showed itself in the soft, dark, almost womanish eyes; in the smooth, transparent lids in which the veins showed oddly distinct; in the narrow hands with their nervous trick of thumb-hugging.

'I look,' he once remarked unhappily, 'like one of the saints on a religious calendar.' The comment had an unforgettable comic justice.

Brooks Gurney was a professional musician. He played the piano in concert with a limited but respectable success, and he composed music. As a composer he was witty, intellectual, highly formalized and fundamentally uninteresting. He was at the moment at work upon a symphonic suite, based upon Gogol's story, 'The Cloak.' It was the vitality of the narrative, the broad and handsome figuring of human emotion, which had tempted him into the undertaking; he was normally uninterested in program music. But in his hands Gogol had withered, and the satirical cacophonies which now ran out from his long, disciplined fingers had a static fragility, a lack of genuine importance approaching the macabre.

From time to time he lifted his hands from the keyboard, observing the color of his palms. They had taken of late to an odd trick by which one flushed and the other turned pale. After each examination he took his pulse by pressing his finger tips to the sides of his throat. About ninety-eight. No extra systoles today. He played again.

You could hardly have called him a hypochondriac, for he had been from his boyhood dismally aware of the psychogenic origin of his discomforts and had remarked, upon trying to enlist at the outset of the war, 'However, it's only fair to tell you I'm psychoneurotic. I mean, I don't mind if you don't.'

They had, to his real disappointment, minded a great deal.

And still he was never quite ridiculous, still he had a quality of life. Imogene's possessive greed had crippled him, invalided him, but it had not made him a fool.

He bent his head above the keyboard, and the accurate, unresonant, courteous voice of the clavichord filled the garret.

A faint light whispering of his music came down through the air like a wavering breeze and touched the ears of Imogene, where she sat on a low marble bench in the heart of the box maze, telling her that Brooks, her love, her dear one, was safe at home, near to her and safe.

She had come into the maze to enjoy her bed of auricula primroses. There were no flowers that did not please her. She rejoiced in them all, even the magenta phlox and petunias in the neglected farm dooryard that she passed upon her incessant country walks. 'Like a shipwrecked sailor,' she said coarsely, 'who'd rather have any woman than none.' But in the whole calendar there were none in which she took a delight approaching her delight in her auriculas, so small, so varied, each one exquisite and singular. And brief, so brief in their flowering time.

They lifted their small, fresh faces, charming and strange in subtle gradations of mauve, of brown, or rose-washed yellow. And Imogene stared at them in a passion of identification, taking them into herself in a greed of love that was deliciously enhanced by the sound of the clavichord, the quiet voice, the quiet welcome voice, telling her again and again that Brooks was near her, and alone.

This overweening sensibility, this wayward intensity of displaced affection, was wholly alien to her appearance. She was a tough old gypsy of a woman, thick in the waist, with straight, sturdy back and shoulders. Under the gray-brown curls, piled in a careless approximation of her girlhood pompadour, her dark, sun-weathered face had a queer, not unpleasant look of outlawry, like a pirate or a healthy witch.

She wore a shabby dress of faded blue seersucker, a brown cardigan with a button missing, old white sneakers. On her left hand, brown and strong, not very clean, an old gypsy's hand, was a magnificent sapphire centered by four large diamonds. It had been her mother's ring; she always wore it, and it was always dull with soap and gardening. To Mark and Brooks, as children, it had been part of her hand, like the square fingers, the short and broken nails.

The music, so faint and still so clear, now broke off in the middle of a phrase, and the moment of concentration broke with it. It was as if the auriculas had looked away, assumed their own identity again, refused her stare.

He has finished his work, she thought. He'll be coming out here.

She moved a little along the bench as if he had come already and she were making room for him. The blunt, dark face, relieved of its greedy preoccupation, softened.

Several times she lifted her head toward the central window under the roof of the old white house on the terrace above her. Once her eyes turned towards the windows of Dolly's room, and quickly turned away again, as if she rejected as quickly as it came the thought behind the glance. She waited for a long time, but Brooks did not come.

At length she stood up. 'I'll just go for a little walk,' she said. Her voice was matter of fact, her face composed, the bright blue eyes only a little set. 'I'll go down the lane,' she said to herself aloud. 'He'll know where I've gone. He'll come.'

A barberry bush at the head of the carriage drive was in blossom. She broke off a spray of it, turning it in her fingers, a spray of tiny yellow flowers with minuscule yellow centers. She walked down the long drive through the open fields, turning and turning the spray of barberry in her hands, mindless that the small thorns were lacerating her finger tips and making them bleed.

Dolly, mild as cream, came down the stairs. She looked in the long drawing room, the music room, the library.

'Well, my stars,' she said, 'where is everybody? Never knew such a crowd for pokin' off by themselves all the time.'

She glanced in the long mirror near the door. She was wearing a white dress with a deep soft ruffle at the neck. She smoothed it down, passing her hands over the beautiful body that Mark had taught her to admire. She smiled at the pretty, small face, the short fair curls, the little blue bow.

'Matter of fact,' she told herself, 'more'n half the time I'd rather have their room than their company.'

She wandered out into the garden and the maze, where she found and picked herself a bouquet of little pink and yellow flowers, breaking the stems too short, like a child. She sat down upon the bench, holding them in her large hands. Upon her face there was a curious, infantile look, partly of triumph, partly of fear.

'Lizzie's just an old fuss,' she whispered to herself. But in spite of the words, the triumph in her eyes faded. The odd, sly apprehension deepened.

'I guess,' she said aloud, 'I'll just go upstairs and put them on my dresser . . . No, I guess I'll fetch them up to Brooks. He must get lonesome, stuck off up there workin', all alone. I won't stay and hinder him long.'

Walking with her straight, easy stride, smiling delightfully at the thought of her own considerate amiability, she went into the house and once more up the stairs.

But on the second floor she hesitated. She glanced toward her own room, where she had left Lizzie, and saw that the door was safely closed.

Suddenly she ran into an empty guest room, opened the door to the bath, dropped the primroses into the toilet bowl and flushed them away.

Wrong, thought Brooks. It's all wrong. He pushed the manuscript aside and began to play again, from the beginning, quickly and nervously, hoping that the momentum would carry him past the bad interval and into the B-minor passage, the ghost in the dark square. Come up to it quickly, and it would develop its own necessary internal logic with none of this maundering. He felt himself nearing the difficulty like someone riding out of control at a deep gully. He felt his breath shallow and dry; his fingers remembered mechanically; his mind did not take over.

There was a quick step on the stair.

'That sure sounds right pretty, Brooks. You never let the ladies come up in your old hide-out?'

The small brown head appeared above the level of the floor, the curls bound in blue ribbon, dark eyes opened wide. 'You makin' up music, Brooks, or just playin'? Can I come up?'

The innocent, doll-like head lifted higher; step by step the superb and opulent body disclosed itself.

Brooks rose and came forward, his courteous smile only a little rigid with irritation. 'It's all right. It was going badly anyway.'

If only she didn't always have her head on, he thought unexpectedly, she'd be charming. Like the Victory of Samothrace. Couldn't talk, then, either.

'My, oh my,' she said. 'This is nice. Brooks, don't you tell Imogene, now, I came up here and bothered you. She'd skin me alive. You don't mind, do you, Brooks? That little old piano sounded so pretty, and I was feeling so awful lonesome.'

She walked with her slow, swinging step around the room.

'Goodness, you've got a huge big place up here. You could go roller skatin'.' She paused by a bookcase. Freud, Jung, Brill, the 'Summa Theologica,' numerous works of the Anglo-yoga persuasion. The varied history of Brooks's endless tinkering with his psyche. 'My what high-brow stuff! All belong to you?'

'Yes.'

'Goodness, you must be smart as Mark. I always thought you didn't go in for that kind of stuff. I thought you just played on the piano. I guess little old Dolly's just sort of dumb.'

No, it would be a mistake to take her head off. She would be less amusing. But why had she come? What did she want? She moved around the room as if she were looking for something that she had lost. Under the artful, artless prattle he could hear an urgency in her; his hypersensitive body responded uncomfortably to an inquietude that was moving somewhere below the bright shallows of her mind.

She sauntered back to him, eyeing the cot.

'I don't know if it's even proper for me to be calling on you like this, Brooks. Is this your den or your bedroom?'

'That's a nice distinction,' he said. 'But I'm sure, Dolly, it's quite chaste. Do sit down.'

She sat on the edge of the cot. She smoothed her ruffles. 'I know it's naughty for me, bargin' in on you like this, Brooks. But I get so lonesome. And Lizzie got out of the wrong side of the bed this mornin'. She was scoldin' me for every little thing.'

'I suppose you must get lonesome.'

'Brooks, why does Imogene hate me?'

'You imagine it, Dolly.'

'No, I don't, Brooks. She hates me so I can feel it coming right out of her and hitting against me. And you, Brooks. You make me feel like you thought I wasn't really there. Like maybe if you were to count ten with your eyes shut you could open them, and I'd be gone.'

'You imagine it. We don't feel like that. I don't.'

She looked at him quickly, her large brown eyes seizing on his face with a strange, unchildlike avidity.

'That's true,' she said quietly. 'Mostly you do. But you don't right now.'

She was a remarkable person, he thought. The quality of the outburst excited him; it was so obviously sincere, and at the same time so obviously spurious, done for effect. Her loneliness, her clear desire for some human contact frightened him. But over and above it her patent vulgarity and dishonesty lay like a cloak, infinitely reassuring. Looking at her, Brooks experienced a queer, half-painful, half-exultant leap of feeling.

Dolly Gurney was beautiful; she was Mark's wife; and she was wholly worthy of contempt. Freed by her very inferiority, her contemptibility, as she sat there now, Mark's wife, feeling her way blindly towards a momentary flirtation with Mark's brother, Brooks Gurney looked at Dolly. He did not know that Imogene's love had made him afraid of love and love's guilt, and love's open vulnerability and inevitable pain. He only looked at Dolly and realized with a shock of amazement, with a naïve and quivering stab of pride, with a delicate immediacy of renunciation as helpless and as prompt as his own inevitable good manners, that he lusted after her in his heart.

And Dolly knew it and responded. Her eyes, avid and yet promising nothing, were like souls driven by thirst. They fastened upon his face as if it were a cup that they would drain dry.

Dolly spoke first. 'I just know I shouldn't be up here,' she said.

Her eyes, drinking their satisfaction, were still upon his own; but she spoke with automatic archness, showing her dimples; and the falsity, the ludicrous bad taste of the words were a joy to him. He wrapped them about his vulnerable life like a sheltering garment.

'Of course you should have come,' he said. 'I was getting nothing done, and you were lonely. Come when you like.'

'Play me something, Brooks, will you?'

'I'd like to.' He looked at her, sitting on the edge of the cot, the large hands lying open in her lap. 'Lie down,' he said, 'and close your eyes and listen.'

What would she like? Something easy, something melodious and gay. His fingers, overcoming a little momentary tremor, ran into Purcell's 'Ayres for the Theayter.' After a few moments he heard her move restively.

'I'm not so strong for that high-brow stuff, Brooks. Don't you know something that's classical and still, you know, sort of nice and sweet?'

Smiling, his fingers at once steady and strong, he went into the 'Valse Bluette.' The saccharin nullities ran out oddly on the clear, literal voice of the instrument.

'Better?'

'Oh, that's lovely.'

But when it was done, she stood up. 'I'd better go now, Brooks. I'd sure hate for Imogene to catch me up here.'

'It wouldn't matter.'

But he knew that it would matter, and he saw that she knew he knew.

'I sure feel whole lots better. Thank you, Brooks. You've been real sweet. I feel as if we were just getting acquainted, don't you?'

'Yes.'

'You're tall, Brooks. Mark and I are just the same height. I'm not used to looking up at people.'

He looked down at the young, uplifted face, the child's face, the avid, unchildish eyes. The big white room was quiet, the May sunlight flooding down from the skylight in a quiet brilliance as absolute as dark. He felt himself leaning towards her with a compulsive, dreamlike deliberation. She did not move or draw back.

'If no one knows,' her eyes said, 'it will be the same as if it never happened, won't it? Won't it?'

He put his arms around her with clumsy stiffness, covering her lips with dry, unaccustomed lips. He dreamed about women, sometimes, but his dreams were violent and terrible, dreams of rape. He held her stiffly, in an agony of ineptitude. He had no idea, he realized, in sharp, hopeless misery, how much or how little one could do, what he could do.

Her soft body taught him, leaning upon him in the quiet brightness. Her moist lips taught him. She taught him by an utter, absolute compliance, so that he felt his strength greater than hers, his kiss deeper, his hands wiser and more aware. He set upon her like a woman in a dream, and through the somnambulistic exultation short, ugly words sounded over and over in his mind, as if he would destroy her with them even while he delighted in her fullness.

Suddenly, there was a little tearing of cloth, her hand went to the white ruffles at her breast, and she broke away from him, shaking.

'Brooks! For goodness' sake, Brooks!' she cried.

Her face was childish and frightened; she backed away from him as if she thought that he had only released her for a moment, as if she were too frightened to run away. And she was frightened.

He's queer, she thought. He isn't like Mark. He's queer.

She stared at him as if he were a stranger. The familiar, handsome face was quite composed now; only the eyes a little confused still, but gentle, apologetic, almost smiling.

'I tore your dress,' he said. 'I'm very sorry.'

She did not know what to say.

'Goodness, Brooks,' she said, 'people don't know anything about anyone, do they?' Her voice was shaky.

'Didn't you like it?' he asked. 'I thought you did.'

'I don't know. I wanted you to kiss me, and then it was like Mark, and I miss him so. And then I thought that you hated me. Brooks, do you hate me?'

'You're lovely, Dolly. You're lovely. Everything's all right, dear.'

She began to smile, pushing back her hair. 'I guess I was naughty. We were both naughty. We'll be good, now, won't we, Brooks?'

'As you say.'

She had started down the stairs when she turned again. 'Do you think I'd better not come back up here again?'

He held himself forcibly from laying hands upon her, from pulling her back to him once more. His voice had an unfamiliar roughness. 'What do you think?' he said. 'You'll be back, and you know it. We can't help ourselves now.'

He watched her go down the stairs, very quiet, and he thought that she was still frightened, but in a moment or two he heard her voice, strong and clear, singing in the lower hall. She was singing a spiritual, and her high, untaught voice came up to him clearly, so that he could hear her words.

'Sometimes,' she sang, 'sometimes I feel like an eagle in the air.'

'Good Lord,' Brooks whispered. 'Good Lord in heaven!'

He walked restlessly about the room. After a little time he returned to the clavichord, but as he sat down he was taken with a fit of shuddering, like the onset of a chill. He got up and ran down the stairs and out of the house.

He walked rapidly along the lane towards the main road. There was no objective in his mind, but he went at a jerky trot as if he were hurrying to an appointment.

At the end of the lane he saw Imogene coming towards him. She was turning a spray of barberry in her hands — small leaves, small flowers, small, fierce thorns — turning and turning it; and as he came closer he saw with a shock that the slow, mindless finger tips were torn, and the spray freaked with their blood.

Dolly was in the lower hall and still singing when she heard the cry from the maze. It was loud and strange, hardly recognizable, although she knew it was Imogene's voice.

'Look! Look! They're gone! Brooks, they're gone!'

Dolly became abruptly silent, and after a moment she went very quickly to her own room.

'Lizzie,' she said. Her voice was small and good, like the voice of a sick child. 'Lizzie, dear.'

The dark old face lifted, anxious and quick.

Trouble, Lizzie thought. More trouble. When she takes a streak like this, ain't nothing you can do, seems like, but just let it run out.

'What you want now?'

'My head aches, Lizzie. It aches perfectly awful. Can you sort of pull the shades down and bring me my lunch up here on a tray? Just tell 'em I don't feel so good, will you, Lizzie dear?'

No good askin' her questions. Just stir her up, frighten her into talkin' mean and tellin' lies. Just make us both feel bad.

She took the soft, pliant hand as she had taken it when Dolly was a little girl in Louisiana, sick from too much romping in the hot sun. She led her to the bed. 'Just lie down,' she said. 'Lie down and shut your eyes. Here, let Lizzie pull your shoes off.'

'Don't let anyone come in here botherin' me, will you, Lizzie?'

Must be something bad, this time.

'How'd you tear your dress?'

'I caught it on something.'

Her voice was cautious, secretive, but the question, oddly enough, restored a sort of composure to her face. She stretched her fine body and lay easier on the bed. She yawned. 'I'm sleepy.'

But Lizzie had gone to the window to pull down the shades. She looked down into the garden and saw Imogene coming into the house. She was staring straight ahead as she walked, and Brooks, following close behind her, had his eyes upon her, and his face was disorganized with nervous pity.

So that's it, thought Lizzie. So she did go and pull up Mrs. Gurney's best flowers after all. So that's her trouble.

Her heart, heavy with shame and love, filled with the tears that she was unwilling to shed. She stood with her back to the bed, pressing her thick, clear-edged lips together, holding her wrinkled eyelids open so that no tears could fall, staring at the drawn shade before her, her face sorrowful and shamed, her eyes quiet and wide.

Under her grief, her slow mind stirred again.

Never did say how she tore her dress, she thought. The blind, angry stare of Imogene's face rose before her again. Suddenly her old body was stabbed with a strange thrill of unrecognized, of unallowable fear.

'Mr. Mark's bound to come home soon,' she told herself. 'They're bound to let him come home soon. War's been over now, most a year. Praise the Lord, he'll be home soon! If he wasn't coming home soon, things might get bad around here. They might get right bad.'

(*From Mademoiselle*)

# THE TERROR IN THE STREETS

## BY ROBERT LOWRY

SHE CAME there because in all of Greenwich Village only that one street invited her. She had been living with Alma, cooped up in that tiny room of Alma's off Washington Square, and by her second week of searching for a place of her own she was willing to consider anything. The Village had been most attractive to her because she'd lived there for five years before the war. But just when she was ready to reconsider, to start searching in Brooklyn or far uptown, she came on the sign, a scarred, battered piece of tin swinging in the wind from its single twist of rusty wire: APARTMENT FOR RENT, Inquire within.

She went toward it without hope, wondering if at last there could really be a place for her in this city. The street did not discourage her, nothing could discourage her now, not even the foul sweet air that came from the open doors of the junk shop as she passed. Two mammoth trailer trucks unloading their merchandise at the warehouse down in the middle of the block cut the street in half, and from somewhere close by came the dull roar of a factory. But she didn't care; she stopped beneath the sign, read it again to make sure, then went up the five worn stone steps and through the dirty scrolled arch that was the front door of the tenement.

The names on the hall mailboxes were a strange assortment of unreadable lettering—some in Old World handwriting, others in typewriting torn from letters. Italian names, most of them. When she found *T. Bolini, Supt.,* she pushed the button, waited for the answering buzz, then started down the gloomy tile corridor toward Apartment 3.

Yes, there was a vacancy, Mr. T. Bolini told her. He stood there in his doorway like a mammoth Dopey from *Snow White* — dressed in a gray work shirt open at the collar, and black pants which draped down strangely from his enormous waist over his skinny legs. An idiotic look, half a grin, half a wide-eyed stare of fright, froze his unshaven face, and he stood bending back, looking down his bulbous red nose at her through the thick glasses.

She followed him up four flights of stairs and waited while he worked with the padlock. 'We put better lock on door,' he said. 'This nice place.'

It seemed fairly clean; no other virtues were apparent. A kitchen and two other rooms, none of them square, the windows looking out on a solid wall of factory. 'Print books over there,' T. Bolini told her. 'Toilet in the hall, you share it with other family. Are you all alone?'

'Yes,' she said, somehow unable to glance up into the wide simple eyes. 'I'm a painter.' Why was she always impelled, when someone asked her if she were all alone, to explain, 'but I *was* married for five years, my husband was killed in Italy.' Or killed in Japan, or in Germany. Perhaps that would have been a sweeter truth than the fact that he had come back alive, but not to her.

'Sixteen dollar a month,' T. Bolini was saying. 'You like?'

'Yes,' she said. 'I'll take it. When can I move in?'

Of course Alma came and approved. She puttered about nervously in her birdlike way, for some reason opening and closing all the doors between the rooms. 'But it's *clean,* Margaret,' she said. 'And there's lots of room. You can use this back one to paint in. A little furniture and some draperies.' It was a relief to move away from Alma, anyhow.

She found furniture: a new bed, two secondhand chairs, two unpainted bookcases, an oilstove and a small table. Draperies over the windows helped to shut out some of the factory noise. She made the back room her studio and she painted the fireplace, which had long ago been walled up, a dark green. Then she hung several of her own paintings around the center room and tried to think of the place as home.

Yet from the first day she was uneasy there. She worked on the large canvas she'd begun at Alma's, but the booming of the printing presses distracted her, and she felt continually the urge to flee, to get down out of this shoddy building, out of the street which reminded her at night of a gangster set in a movie. To flee for her life.

She examined all the reasons for her uneasiness and rejected them. It was a miserable, suspicious-looking street, but after all its inhabitants were hard-working Italian families. She could get ear stoppers to keep out the noise. 'It's only because I'm used to a smaller town,' she decided finally, thinking of the two years she'd spent in Arizona. She had originally gone down there to be with Ric, but they had had only two months together, living in a furnished room, before he'd left with his unit for San Francisco and embarkation. Why had she stayed on there? Not to remember their happiness, surely—there was almost nothing poignant to remember in the torrid nights when he came into town from camp and stayed with her. She had sensed even then that a separation of two or three years would only leave them farther apart. But she'd felt that if she waited in the place where he had last seen her, perhaps he would find it easier to come back to her, to begin their life again. As it turned out, that had been foolish. Long before he was ever due back he had told her. Yet she had waited on. She had waited till the war had ended, till a time she knew he must be back. One letter came from New York, in which he said the only thing for them was a divorce. He never wrote again.

'And now my life,' she thought, 'is mostly fear.' Fear of this terrible noisy apartment, the gangster street of warehouses and tough Italian boys and drab bars, and of the rest of the Village too. For it had changed from the sunny leisurely place she'd come to out of college—living here and working in an art store on Eighth Street before she'd met Ric, slender, uneasy Ric who had wanted so badly to be a writer. Yes, it had most certainly changed since those days.

It was the age of the groups on the streets late at night that made her most uneasy. The boys who stood by the all-night hamburger shop at the subway entrance on Sixth Avenue could not be more than sixteen or seventeen, and some seemed even younger. They were standing there at twelve noon and they were still there at midnight. These were faces that had never seen the war, but which came from some more terrible evil. One boy especially terrified her. He was dressed in a herringbone zoot suit, from the pegged bottoms of which showed pointed-toed light tan shoes. A collar pin clutched his striped shirt collar in tight, and out of the white scarf tucked about his throat rose a skinny neck with a thick vein throbbing in it, topped by a face bony, loose-lipped, with tiny light blue eyes and sandy hair slicked back from his knobby forehead with vaseline. A frightening, large-nosed face, the distance from the nose to the upper lip unusually long, and wrinkles everywhere on it: across the forehead, around the eyes, down each side of the mouth, creasing each cheek. His shorter companions were also types — square-faced boys with pimply foreheads, dressed in dark striped suits; skeleton-headed youths, like dwarfs, not boys, who nurtured the few hairs of a moustache on their upper lips. But all of these seemed only props around him. Or perhaps the real reason he stood out so was because of his color: he was light green. 'The bile of the world has backed up in him,' she thought.

They seemed to do nothing but wait, morning, noon and night. What they were waiting for was not obvious. Their eyes followed her when she went into the subway station to go uptown to see an art show, and their eyes were still there waiting for her return. She felt that of all the people she knew, this small crew of nervous chain-swinging idlers were the only ones who could have given an accurate account of her coming and going.

She tried to take up again the only life she could believe in now. The book factory shut down at 1 A.M., so she often worked at night. She wore an eye mask when she went to bed at three or four to keep out the morning light and she seldom got up before one in the afternoon. Then she ate and went out into the bitter street for a look at Washington Square, or a cup of coffee at the Waldorf cafeteria, or to visit a friend.

So few of the people she'd known before were still here, and the lives of these were changed completely. Carl Borens, the painter, was just out of the Army and practically bald. His wife, who'd written a much-publicized novel, was in an insane asylum, and he spent most of his time sitting around the Waldorf or in the Minetta Tavern talking about going to Paris to study on the GI Bill of Rights. Nan French was a tall slender girl with glasses who lived on an allowance and talked of painting some day (she was thirty-five, though, and she sketched only when she was in a roomful of people, her talent connecting up with some form of exhibitionism in herself). Nan was being analyzed and had taken to confessing to all of her friends as glibly as she did to her doctor. Plump little Alice Burgess had made money working in a defense plant during the war and had opened a costume-jewelry shop off Sheridan Square with her savings. Margaret saw them now and then and went to their parties or had them over to see her work and talk. But really she knew that her feeling for the Village, for her friends and even for painting was not the same. It no longer seemed to be a part of reality. Reality, the spirit alive in the world that she sensed most strongly, was something else now, no longer artistic activity, no longer friendship, but a kind of frenzy, a tension . . . .

She could not have said definitely what it was that distracted her so. But she knew it connected in some way with the crude lettering, WORLD OF SLOBS, splashed in white paint, on the apartment house up at the corner, with the teen-agers spending their days and nights on the street not for fun, not to shout and scream and tease girls as teen-agers before the war had done, but to watch with intense hateful eyes, to plot and to pose as plotters. The terror of the streets got into her paintings—they became wilder, more undisciplined. To get rid of him, she tried painting the face of the green hawk-nosed boy. But it only added to her terror, for she could not seem to capture what he really was, what he really represented in the world, what he and his companions would come to.

She was afraid at night, and she felt she could not trust the bolt on the door. But Mr. T. Bolini, whom she brought up to look at it, wouldn't listen to her. 'Why that a good bolt,' he said. 'You no be afraid with that bolt, I fix it myself.' She was afraid of the fire escape which ran down past her bedroom and she kept the window leading out onto it locked. What would she do, she wondered, if somebody did break into her miserable apartment—one of those youths who watched her so closely day and night? Surely no one would ever hear her with the rumbling of those printing presses for background. No one would hear, no one would find her for days.

She could have a lover, she thought. But she knew no one she wanted, no man she cared about. She had known Carl Borens too long, there could be no love with him. She had, she thought, known everyone too long — and under different circumstances — so that these old acquaintances seemed only friends of another self. As for living with a girl, she had had enough of that the months she'd spent with Alma. She lived a special kind of life, a life built around her painting, and it was foolish to think that she could change now. She was too old. She was thirty.

When precisely was it that the terrible boy began to speak to her? Certainly he had picked her out of all the people going in and out that subway entrance from the first day she'd moved here. But it must have been some time later, the second week anyhow, that she began to hear his squeaky voice call after her, often not until she'd reached the bottom of the subway stairs almost out of his sight. And it was always the same word — she'd misunderstood it at first.

'Hey, Lucy.'

She'd made that out finally. Her first idea was that he'd said 'juicy,' which had confused her even more. But Lucy was just as cryptic.

At home she would stop painting in the afternoon and lie on the bed, thinking of him, of the sinister little gang always grouped around him. 'Could there be,' she wondered, 'some connection between us I'm not conscious of? Could he know me from somewhere — from Arizona or from Ohio?' No, she was certain she'd never seen him before. And she was certain too that he'd never been anywhere but here. She felt almost that he'd been born there in the doorway — that he'd been the result of an assault somewhere on the street near by and deposited there by the subway entrance to spend his life as some sort of awful reminder. . . . What was she thinking? It was really all too ridiculous. She'd have to work harder and forget such foolishness. 'It comes from living alone,' she thought. 'And yet there is no other way of life for me. I've had my love, there's nothing important left now but work.'

But she could not work. When she tried to paint, something in her became excited, a delicious terror made her hands tremble, her face in the cold apartment grew warm. 'Is he there now?' she wondered. 'Is he *always* there? Does he have no home?' And then the idea came to her: 'He is thinking of me this moment too, he is waiting only for me.'

She had to sit down then, to smoke, to get herself under control. She tried to repulse the rush of ideas she had about the green-faced boy, but now they came faster than ever, she gave in completely to her terror. *Why was he waiting for her?*

She would have to go out on the street finally, not with the intention of venturing near the subway entrance but really only to flee from herself and her thoughts. She went over to Washington Square and watched the pigeons or talked to friends around the fountain. But always, before she came home, she found herself making some excuse to go near the hamburger shop. She passed by on the other side of Sixth Avenue, warmed with a cup of coffee at the Waldorf, trying to keep her eyes straight forward but not able to avoid glancing over there. And he seldom failed her, he was there, leaning against one of the buildings with his friends around him, the smirk that seemed to be for her alone on that repulsive face.

'Hey, Lucy.'

'I don't know him,' she kept telling herself. 'And he can't possibly know me. . . .' Then what was it?

She had eaten dinner at Alma's that Saturday night. Around nine, several people, among them Carl Borens, had come in (it was always amazing how many people Alma dared cram into that little room), and they had all sat around drinking highballs and talking. Alma was unimaginative enough to see that only painters were invited, so that most of the conversation was predictable: the current shows, the possibility of getting to Paris, Picasso, who had sold what for how much, the apartment shortage in the Village. . . . Margaret had already had six highballs and she was telling herself how senseless it was to remain here among people she did not really care to be with, when, during a lull in the little hubbub of talk in the room, she heard her own voice say:

'I wonder if the rest of you feel as I do about the streets these days?'

She realized immediately that she'd had too much to drink, but she could not help trying to excuse her original statement by adding: 'I mean the terror in the streets. . . . Aren't any of you afraid to go out?' Her heart began pounding. Though she realized that everyone in the room was looking at her in amazement, she did not try to hold back. 'I really can't see how you can talk so gaily about life when life is like it is.'

'Well, how *is* life?' It was a small dark girl with an unfortunate nose who was trying to be flip.

'I'm sure that Margaret means a good deal more than she's saying,' Carl Borens began.

She got up. She'd said almost nothing all evening and now she was talking like this. 'I think I'd better go.' She went to the closet and found her coat. 'I've had a lovely time, Alma.'

She must have amazed them all by walking out like that. Well, she really didn't care. She was drunk and she had talked about what was in her mind. It had certainly sounded foolish enough in words.

She was just opening the door to the street when she heard Carl call to her.

'I'm glad you gave me an excuse to leave,' he said. 'Shall we get something to eat?'

'I'm not hungry.' They walked on in silence before she said: 'I simply can't bear myself when I'm drunk. I always begin to say such ridiculous things.' But she was waiting for his answer, to see whether he'd understood something of what she meant.

'Oh, we all say ridiculous things.'

She felt utterly alone. She clenched her hands to try to keep from crying, but the tears came anyway. He wasn't looking at her, he was very tall above her and his eyes were far out ahead.

They were walking on Sixth Avenue. It must be two o'clock; almost no one around. But in a moment they'd pass the hamburger shop, she could see the crowd of boys from here. She managed to blow her nose and get the tears wiped away without his noticing.

'Do you see them?' she asked. 'That's what I mean . . . the gangs hanging around in the streets at all hours . . . the reports in the newspapers of terrible things happening to people. Rapes, girls cut in two. All the terror that the world seems to be now. When I lived here before the war it didn't seem to be like this at all.'

They were almost there. . . .

'I guess it's all in the way you look at life,' Carl said. 'Far as I'm concerned, life has just been a big bore since I've come out of the Army. It seems to me there's not enough violence.'

Yes, he was there . . . he was looking at her. He wouldn't dare say anything now, with Carl here. But he was twirling the chain, and she thought she saw a smile on that wide, loose mouth.

When Carl and she had got to her street she stopped. 'Please don't go out of your way. I can get home all right now.'

'It's no trouble . . .'

'No. It's just a few steps. Good night.'

She watched him disappear down Bleecker Street and when she was sure he wouldn't look around, she turned and walked quickly back along Sixth Avenue. She did not even glance at the boys as she passed them, she simply turned into the hamburger shop and took one of the stools nearest the door.

'A cup of coffee.' She put down the money and had just lifted the cup to her mouth when the boys from outside came in. Her heart almost stopped — there were empty seats around her and they were taking them. On her left a stubby youth with an enormous jaw was sitting himself down, and on her right . . .

She put the cup down with a clatter. It was he, he was looking at her. They undoubtedly knew where she lived, the floor, the apartment number. They knew about the fire escape running past her window, the weak bolt on the door. And he was looking at her, the green hawk-nosed boy. But he wouldn't speak. They'd been waiting for a night like this . . . when she was drunk . . . so drunk she'd been mad enough to come here to make sure of her suspicions. . . . She noticed that the hair pomade he wore had run down on his forehead, making the pimples there glisten.

She got up, hurried out on the street.

'Hey!'

She glanced back over her shoulder to see him framed in the bright doorway and she began to run . . . footsteps behind her . . . coming faster. No one in her path, the avenue deserted. She turned down her street, ran up the worn steps, into the dim hall. She had the momentary idea of banging on the first door she came to, but she did not, she kept running, up the four flights of stairs, down the hall to her own door.

Fumbling with the lock she heard him coming. She got it opened and ran in and threw the bolt. The she went back into the bedroom and made sure that the window lock was fastened.

She had just returned to the kitchen to turn off the light when the rap came. She began to tremble, each hair on her head pricked into her scalp.

Tap-tap-tap.

She waited in terrible agitation. Even when she heard his footsteps going away, she found herself physically unable to move. At last she sat down on a chair. She felt that she had come within an inch of dying and had escaped.

She would have to get away, yes. Tomorrow she'd get a second-hand dealer up here and sell the furniture, then she'd buy a train ticket back to Arizona. She had had her fill of what the world had become, she'd go back there and live her life out alone, work as a waitress or a salesgirl if she couldn't sell her pictures . . . anything would be better. . . .

After an hour she found the courage to fix herself a drink. But the drink had no effect on her. It was as if the terror she'd been experiencing these past weeks had made her incapable of reacting normally to anything.

When the morning light began filtering through her windows, she went exhausted to bed. She did not wear the mask. The last thought in her head was surprise at being able to sleep after all she'd been through. . . .

She awoke with the sun shining in her eyes. For a long while she did not attempt to move, but lay there letting the events of last night tumble haphazardly through her mind. Her running through the streets and coming back here, to this place—which she herself considered unsafe—seemed completely mad. Why hadn't she turned screaming into a café?

'It is almost as if I went there to tempt him to follow me,' she thought, 'then led him back here to make sure he'd have a secluded spot to do his crime.'

The idea seemed so close to the truth it frightened her. She got up and went out into the kitchen. The light was still burning and she turned it off. The chair she'd sat down on was where she'd left it near the door.

'My bag!' She went into the other room to look, but even while she did so she knew she had left it on the counter when she'd fled from the hamburger shop.

Well, it didn't matter. It could stay there. There was only some change in it, she would certainly never subject herself to going back for that. No, she must hurry, it was late in the afternoon already. She'd eat out and then find the secondhand man.

She dressed, found the five dollars she'd hidden in her dresser drawer and went back into the kitchen. She had trouble withdrawing the bolt—it must be rusty—but finally it worked. She opened the door and stood there unbelievingly.

Swinging, swinging by its strap from the outside doorknob, the cheap leather bag appeared before her, as real as her most awful fears. She grabbed it up in both hands, slammed the door shut again. A hysterical laughter broke from her throat, but when she sat down on the chair, still clutching the bag tightly, her eyes were blurred with the tears of an emotion she'd never known before. She could not take her gaze from it—this single concrete key to herself that the world had left as a token at her door.

(*From The Atlantic Monthly*)

# THE BURDEN

## BY JOHN A. LYNCH

I *DO NOT BELIEVE* the moon has anything to do with it. The moon affects the tide perhaps, but I do not believe it twists men's lives as some say. I do not believe it makes one man thrash on the ground and babble to his friends, and another man date his letter Monday when it is really Wednesday. Because that was what was being done and there was no moon on the nights that came immediately before or after these things. But there has been a moon since, and sometimes it has shone when one man would walk past his dying friend and offer no help, and another man would get up from his hole and go away in the night, and not be heard from again. But I do not believe the moon has anything to do with these things.

For the men would do these things themselves, and only themselves, and I could not help wondering about them. And sometimes I myself would do these things, and later on, when not doing them, would wonder again about those who did. Because when you are putting on your letter that it is Monday, you believe it is Monday, and even when a friend says it is Wednesday you put Monday. When you know you are right, you are going to do it that way. And when your friend goes on with his letter dated Wednesday, you know he is wrong, and you wonder about him.

Mike said it was because one thing and another add up until the little things have become a big thing. It is like the straws and the camel, he said. It is like the water dribbling through the dike until it is no longer a dribble but a flood. And when the days of the week come as fast as they sometimes do, you are apt to lose one or more of them.

When the days of the week lose themselves one after the other, the men are apt to lose themselves also, and Carl will shoot at a man who is the enemy and give away your position, which is a good one for the time, when what he knew was a man is really a turkey, and there is no likeness in the two. But it causes you to get out of your hole and go across the saddle of the hill to the other side where the cover is not so good, and you have to spend part of the night digging another hole. And Mike says that Carl should be sent back, that he is good no more; but all they do is put you on the post Carl had and the fear grows that you yourself will soon be shooting at a turkey instead of a man who is the enemy. And when you take off the safety every time you hear a rustle in the bushes, you do this a great number of times, and they are little times, little things, and soon you do shoot at the turkey, only this time it is a goat.

If you do this yourself you do not feel ashamed, but you say it *was* a man, and you were doing your duty, which is outpost. But if it is another man doing this, you wonder about him, and say to yourself that he has been tired too long and should be getting a rest, that he is not a good soldier any more, though he could be if he were to get a rest.

But how can there be rest when you begin at four in the morning of Monday or Tuesday or Wednesday to go out on the hillside, then over the crest of the hill and into the small valley which only yesterday was spaced with other men, who heard Carl's shot and your shot when everything else was still, and wondered if it was a signal that an attack was beginning. And if they thought it was a signal, then it is well that you did fire a shot, because they are not around now and maybe you yourself frightened them away. At least you can think that, and they cannot stop you from thinking it.

Nor can they stop you from wanting a home in Connecticut, all on one floor, and two bars in the house, one for ice cream and one for good liquor. Because you are now two days of fighting beyond the hill where Carl shot the turkey and you the goat, and you have not had water for twenty-four hours. Nor do you crave water now, for the thirst has gone beyond that stage and it is such that only ice cream and liquor will do. And there will be four flavors of ice cream, all in deep, cold holds because it is what you would need now to stop the dryness.

Mike said that he and George, who is dead now, once tasted water from a pool in which two of the dead enemy lay, and the water was good and it stopped their thirst. And when I asked him why they did not remove the dead bodies first, he said they were too tired, and anyway it wouldn't have improved the water a bit just to have the bodies laid to the side. And I wondered about that, because Mike and George had been there longer than I, and I wondered about them too. But I don't any more, because I have been thirsty, and if it was ice cream I would eat it with dead enemy flesh running all through it, because it would be ice cream and not the flesh that I would be eating.

The liquor is a different thing, however. That is for the hour after the thirst has been eased, and it must be pure. It is for the hour when the jaws have begun to function again and they can move up and down as if in eating a good steak. It is for the hour after the roof of the mouth has become softened again after so much dryness, and the tongue is again sensitive to taste. Because liquor must be tasted, and it must be poured through the teeth and in and out between the lips and the gums and around and around, so that you can forget the day of twenty-four hours just passed that you held a pebble in your mouth and rolled it and rolled it on your tongue, but there was no freshness left.

I first thought of the Connecticut home the night we stumbled down the rocks of a mountainside, and the word came down the column to 'hold it up,' and thirsty and tired I fell to the ground, and lying there wished for ice cream and liquor. 'Hold it up' was meant for one thing, and to me it was that I should now let myself fall on the ground. I remembered that a coin put in a machine brought forth a bar of candy, or one could get cigarettes that way, and soft drinks, and in other places a compartment for luggage, or a parking place for a car, or a postage stamp, or even a meal in some places.

Just so, the way to get a place of rest is to hear the words 'hold it up' come back through the column, and as each man hears the words he gets a place of rest, which is the place where he happens to be at the moment. And ahead you can see the men falling to the ground as each one hears the words, and when it comes your turn you fall too, but only after you have given the words to the man behind, because he is tired also and is looking for a place to rest, and a reason for it. And if you fall so that your back lies across an uncomfortable stone, you do not move it away you are that tired, but only lie there and are glad for what little rest there is. And rest can be had in all positions, except when spliced on a tree limb.

Because that is what happened to Paul when he fell to the ground that night, but kept falling for another twenty feet as he had rolled off the shelf of rock that we were crossing. And he called three times as he fell, but no more, and that was only because he was unconscious, and they found him hung in a low tree with a branch caught up in his crotch. That is rest also, I suppose, of another kind, more complete than most, but I do not prefer it, because though I have had it, I cannot remember what it was all about. Just that the pain of the mind and body becomes so great that all pain leaves, that is, it is no longer felt. Of course it is still there, but it has passed into an unfeeling stage and that is the equivalent of unconsciousness.

And having come down the mountain with only one casualty, who was Paul and had to be carried to the rear because we were making an advance, we stepped out into a valley at dawn.

There was a town farther on that I remember for one or two important things, and some of little import, of which there are always many, such as seeing a man cross the road holding a dripping, bloody chunk of meat, and the first impression that such a sight will make. I was alone, returning from the headquarters of the battalion to the headquarters of the company, which was lodged in a fine house with a large kitchen, with a stove and a table already set with meat and wine, which of course had been left by the men who were retreating before our advance, and which we didn't touch, at least we didn't the meat. The *vino* is something else again.

The sight of the man and the meat was a shock of a sort, probably anything as bloody as that would be, so I had to call and stop the man. He was a farmer, or so he appeared, and holding the chunk of bloody stuff out in his hand he said over and over, *'Cavallo, cavallo,'* keeping an eye on the rifle I held leveled at his body, because you could never afford to take a man's word in that time. Furthermore, his other hand clutched one of our blankets, and this was a shock in itself, seeing the blanket — perhaps once belonging to a friend whose death I did not yet know of, or at least he was or had been one of us — and the meat in such relationship that a man should emerge from a yard carrying only a blanket and a piece of fresh meat.

*'Tedeschi?'* I forced at him, prodding the meat with the muzzle of my rifle, forcing him to step backwards till he was against the wall of the house and could move no further. *'Tedeschi?'* I asked, hoping he would answer *'Si, si,'* not because I desired to know he had butchered one of the enemy, but because I feared it was one of our own, the blanket being there and all. But he only uttered *'Cavallo'* again, pointing to the yard from which he had just come, and I didn't go any further. There was no stains on the blanket, and I let him go. But the little thing that it was, lodged with me, and went with me into the town and beyond.

We were not the first to try to drive the enemy from the town, and the blanket must have belonged to one of those captured the night before or perhaps killed in the yard. At that time we were still a good distance away, and were moving forward to dig in on the hill below the town. Having arrived at that position early in the morning, we learned that the town was still in enemy hands and the first attacking force had suffered many casualties, and now it was our turn. Digging in, we waited for the dawn and the time we should split up our forces, one platoon to the south. But even before that, another company was to attack in the low hills on the right flank and attempt to force a withdrawal from the town.

It was while we were leaving our holes on the hillside and gathering our equipment, moving silently into our loose formation, that the shells began to fall. There was a scramble, as there always is at such a time, men running to the holes they have just left, or diving into other men's holes, or throwing themselves to the ground, behind a stone or two, no matter how small. But there were men wounded anyway, and above their cries there was Carl's screaming. He was not in a hole, but rolling on the ground, his face tortured, his eyes mad, and there was not a mark on him. He had tried to go forward one extra hour, he had tried to carry one extra straw, and now he no longer felt the pain in his mind. There was no need to say good-bye to him, because he could not hear us at all, but we took his carbine and his belt and the two grenades he was carrying inside his shirt.

Louis was lost also, but with him it was different, and perhaps better. He was ahead of me when the shells began to fall again, and I did not see him get hit, nor did I ever see him after that. But I was told, when I went back after our engagement to find his body, that he had been alive as they carried him down the hill below the town, and he had died there at the bottom, a hole as big as a silver dollar in the back of his skull. I asked had he been unconscious all the time and they said he had, and that made it easier for him. It would make it easier also when I had to tell Scotty, who had been Louie's close friend, but was now in the hospital from a wound of the last campaign.

So Carl and Louis were gone before we went into the town, which by this time — and it was mid-morning — had been fairly well evacuated by the enemy because of the action on the right flank. There were only a few shots, which hit no one, but we kept ready for anything, and until the men found the *vino* and the kitchen with the fine stove, it had been an orderly affair, no one taking chances, everyone on the alert. But wine is not to be reckoned with. Even in this town three of the men stood drinking in the front room of one house while one of the enemy stood in the well of the stairs, beckoning to them that he wished to surrender, waving a handkerchief, afraid to move forward, yet not even being able to surrender at that time. It was good wine, each house well stocked, so we had our choice of the bottles, and this time it was in real bottles and not in the straw-jacketed *fiasci* that served in the lower towns through which we had already passed, and at every house through the many hills.

One man who had been in the night attack I particularly remember because he lay on the road to the south of the town, and the one on which we marched, in rather orderly fashion, to make contact with the platoons coming in from the west and the east. He was lying with two others, and of the three he had got closest to the town, but he was actually only in the outskirts and only a few feet closer than his comrades. He was an Indian whom we called The Chief, and he was, of the three, the only one yet alive, and already he had lain there a matter of ten hours or so.

We filed by, the platoon of us, each man moving wearily along with his personal burden, and a few of us spoke to him, and one man gave him water from his canteen, and each man left him to the man behind, until they were all gone and I was the last man. Going down on one knee I pulled a blanket up on his chest, for he had already been partly covered with it, and he asked me what day it was. I answered, stumbling a little with the words, 'I don't know, but maybe it is Thursday.' He seemed satisfied with that, because he didn't say anything more, but just continued to look at me in a way I didn't understand just then, but which is the way death looks at you when it is in a man who is being dragged relentlessly and helplessly into the grave.

So we had our wine and we found potatoes in a house and these we cut and sliced into a frying pan in the kitchen, and chucking the stove full of wood, soon had a healthy fire and over it our pan of potatoes, which are good most any way, but best fried when you have not had potatoes for a long time. Our lard had a questionable source, specked with flakes of wood and earth as it was, but such a thing is not noticeable when it is in a pan with fried potatoes. No one spoke of Carl or Louis, but we laughed and sang a song or two. Nor did anyone speak of the Indian still lying on the road. For these things you do not speak of, nor hardly think of, when you have wine and potatoes, even if all you have is wine and potatoes, and nothing else, even though they are not a tasty combination, but only what is on hand. And the men were coming in with their souvenirs from time to time to show them around, a dress sword, a scarlet cap, a picture post-card album, a set of delicately carved goblets unearthed in some corner of a basement, a silver-headed cane, all of which they knew they would have to throw down again when we moved out of the town. All except the silver-headed cane perhaps.

Mike said the captain wanted me, which was Mike's way of saying that the captain wanted a man and I was the man, and that is how I happened to be returning later on from the battalion headquarters to which I had carried the captain's message, and where I learned how Louis had died. The headquarters was for the time in a shallow cave on the hillside below the town, a perfectly safe place, and an ideal one, for it had space enough for a dozen men. It lay halfway down a path that branched from the road that ran across the top of the hill, one end of which lost itself among the hills to the west and the other wound into the town that was now ours. It was the same road we had come in on, where we had passed The Chief, and where the others lay quietly beneath their blankets in the warm sun.

Going back to headquarters then, I passed the Indian for the second time. But this time he did not speak, but only turned his head slowly and looked at me again in that tired, deathly way. Nor did I speak, because I had not found out what day it was, and that was what he had asked me before. So I went on and delivered my message, which was that the town had been secured and outposts were in effect, and we would set up a road-block before nightfall. The colonel said there was no message in return, except that he would be there himself as soon as matters with the weapons company had been detailed. He asked in which building company headquarters was, and after I had told him that, I started up the path.

Fifteen minutes can be a quarter of an hour, and again it can be hundreds of seconds. It is a quarter of an hour when you are having wine and potatoes and showing souvenirs with a roof over your head, but it is hundreds of seconds when you are waiting in your hole during the shelling, and counting every one that comes in or goes over or plops with a lifeless sound, a dud. It is hundreds of seconds when you are going up a road into something you cannot see. I imagine it is always hundreds of seconds when you are dying.

The Chief had died in the fifteen minutes it took me to go down and back up the hill path. His blanket was still to the point where I had pulled it the first time I came by, but his eyes were staring madly and his mouth was open, showing his stained teeth, and a dozen blue flies were crawling on his tongue. More were buzzing and darting at his face, and I waved my hand to chase them off, then pulled the blanket over his face.

It was only a little further along that stretch of road that I met the farmer with the chunk of meat, and then I was back in the town, had made my report to the captain, and had gone in search of more wine because someone had taken the bottle that was mine behind a bucket in the corner. We started on the road-block as the evening began, and we dug our holes methodically, but with care because we would stay there all night. Mike and I dug together and he had brought a light machine gun up to the position, which we set up to face down the left fork of the road, another gun being trained to fire on the right fork, and a bazooka ready to fire either way. We camouflaged our work, drank again of what wine we had brought with us, and having been assigned our watches in one-hour shifts, lay down to sleep. The enemy did not try to come back into the town, and it was a good thing. Mike was on first watch and he fell asleep, and tired and drugged with wine we all slept the night through.

I had meant to ask Mike what day it was. There always seemed to be the question of the days in the week and no one could keep track of them. I remembered that once it had been Friday and the word was passed around that Father Whalen was coming up the next day. So he came up and it was Sunday, and what became of Saturday we asked among ourselves. No one could say about Saturday. Even Father Whalen said he didn't know, but he would ask someone when he got back, because it had seemed a short week. So Saturday was gone in that week, and in another week it was Tuesday and that was missing, and in another both Tuesday and Wednesday. But the days were not the only things missing.

When you speak to a man who is dying, and you perhaps smile at him and cover his chest with a blanket, then go into a house with a roof on it and there drink wine and eat potatoes, something is also missing. In every man this thing is missing, for stumbling along they have all, nearly a hundred during the day, gone past a man who is alive, and going past have thought no more about it, until he lay on the road long enough to die. Any one of you could have saved the life of The Chief, but not being on the road for that purpose you push on to the town, for the coin has been inserted and the handle turned and what comes out is your getting to the town and making it secure. Nothing else comes out and only a bullet or a shell can break the machine and prevent it from securing the town. If a man dies because you have secured a town and the wine and potatoes that go with it, is it your fault? The coin in the cigarette machine will not also secure a candy bar to be eaten after the cigarette has been smoked.

And for your defense you make this excuse, that with a town to be secured and a house to be occupied and a message to be delivered, you cannot be everywhere at once, cannot be doing everything. You can tell this to yourself and, when you find it gets weaker with each telling, you can bolster yourself by telling it to others. But they will only say, 'So what,' as if they do not know what you are talking about, because they have been fed on wine and potatoes and have gone beyond the town and are now looking up another hillside.

Lying along the paths and the road, and once in a while in the brush where they had fallen, were the others of the night attack, each one with a blanket drawn over him. And there were yet others, in green uniforms, ones without blankets, and fewer of them also, and they would be buried by our men later with *Karl* or *Ludwig* or *Josef* over them. For them we could not spare blankets, but would rather look into their stiff and sallow faces and curse them because they were who they were. But you do not like to look into the face of a friend who cannot look in return, so you must cover his face, and also his body, and make him comfortable until the burial detail comes with sacks and trucks to carry your friends away. And if they are a few days in coming, you do not want them to find your friends looking ugly and green, with their arms rigid, their lips drawn back over their gums, and their sad eyes gone back into their heads, and covered up they do not look this way. So finding them, the men of the detail will say that here was fought another battle, and here lie the brave men who fought it, resting beneath their blankets.

But let them find the enemy, and if he is staring purple and green all at once, you do not care, for it is only when the stench of him has become unbearable that he is worth covering. And sometimes then it is easier to move to another position, where you cannot see and smell him, but from which you may return to his side and see that he gets greener, and you say it is good for him, the dirty Kraut.

There were three days of hill fighting that followed before we took a holding position below the river. The attack had slowed down all along the front, and we were now to wait until some higher echelon would decide for us what was best to do, and feeling the coin register, we would do it.

Each night we crossed the hilltop and went to our positions of defense, carrying with us two machine guns, and every man his rifle or carbine or pistol, and each morning just before daybreak we left those positions and returned to the holes we had dug on the near slope of the hill. We slept in the daytime, sometimes in the holes and sometimes beside a haystack in the shade, and we had time to write letters again, and it was decided that the first day should be Monday, and the following be Tuesday, and so on until we had had seven days, and then we would start over again.

A road ran near us where we were in the daytime, and the cooks found us on the second morning, and there were two wheatcakes for each man and one strip of bacon. There was always water, and not far to go for it, and the wine had been found in the usual places because there were a few simple hillside houses nearby. It was beginning to be more of living, and as the body began to get its rest and the old ways came back to it, the mind also freshened, and we talked of Louis for the first time, because now we could remember him without it interrupting the occupation of a town or the clearance of the enemy from a hill. Also remembered were Paul and Carl, and guesses were made as to when we would see them again. But no one remembered The Chief, except me.

The talk was small, but it was what belonged to us, and it died down only when we became tired again and lay down by the haystack or in our holes to sleep, and when we went out on the forward side of the hill after dark. Out there we didn't talk, but two in a hole, slept and watched one at a time. And if we were both awake the time was passed one watching and the other digging the hole a little deeper, so that after four nights it was a very good and deep hole, and very safe.

But another thing we did at night was think. We didn't want to, but it was that we had to, and we arranged the events just passed, put them in order, one after the other as best we could, reasoned with some, and digested them. Putting them in sequence, we found they were the taking of a number of hills, and a mountain then, and the crossing of a valley at dawn. Beyond that it was a series of hills again, our town with the wine and potatoes, then more hills until we were now below the river and wondering when we would cross it and start up the hills on the far side, where already we could see our shells landing and the fires they left burning at night. These were the major things, then, the names and numbers that would go into the histories and be charted as advances of the campaign. And through them were interwoven, sometimes tangled, the death of Louis, Paul hung by his crotch in the tree, Carl screaming on the ground, the Indian by the roadside, the other bodies on the paths we took, the thirst and the hunger and the fear. But these things would not go into the histories, nor can they be charted.

It was on the fifth night that Mike left the hole and walked away. There were fires burning in three sections of the enemy ground, making rings of light on the far hills, and the moon was up, and it was not a night made for fighting. Except for the occasional rumble of artillery in the hills, and now and then a shot along the river, there was only the sound of men digging deeper into the ground, a little at a time, for the night is long and it passes slowly. I was asleep when Mike left our hole, and only when another man woke me to ask where Mike was, did I know he was gone. But I remembered that he had often spoken quietly of how close we were to the enemy, at least how close it seemed at night when we could see the fires, and occasionally the flash of their artillery, and once we heard the rumble of their trucks. And he spoke also of how tired he was, when would it all be over, and must there always be another objective ahead. And so he went out in the night and we saw him no more. The next day, in the afternoon, we were relieved at our positions and the fighting was over for a while, and we began to move out slowly to the rear.

If it was a straw upon a straw upon a straw that crippled the camel, just so numerous little things coming to you in the night, little things returning, will cripple you. No one can say just what moment of what day you begin to wonder more about yourself than about the others, the time that you are not sure of anything. The time that you are about to date a letter Monday and a friend says it is Wednesday and you put down Wednesday, because, though you are not sure if it is Wednesday, you are less sure that it is Monday. The crack in the dike widens and through it tumble the little things one after the other until they break loose. And when they begin to overflow, when you can no longer hold them in check, you are apt to get up from your hole and go away and not be seen again. Or suddenly you may scream and remember nothing. And later, when you are rested, they will tell you that you thrashed about so, it was necessary for six men to carry you to the aid station, and you were babbling when they left you there. But you do not remember that it hurt any, for the weariness and the horror and the stagnation of the mind had suddenly turned to unconsciousness.

This will go on, it will follow you and sometimes possess you so at night that you must get up from your bed and walk by yourself, and fight this thing by yourself, and keep the straws from burdening the camel, the flood from crumbling the dike. And because others cannot understand, they wonder about you, and you must go on alone. Because the days of fighting are over, the days of man killing man, the days of hunting—because those days are over, the extraordinary love of friends has passed also and you are alone. Because the days of staring at the dead faces, of waiting in the wet holes of the earth, the days of thirst and hunger, the days of fear—because those days are ended, they would expect that it is all ended.

But it cannot end for you, nor can you make it clear to them why it cannot end, and the burden is yours alone, and you must only hope that it does not grow too great. That the men walking out into the night do not call to you, that the man writhing on the ground does not stare with mad eyes, that the bodies beneath the blankets do not entrust themselves to you, that the days do not once again lose themselves, and falling, stumbling, wearing away into nothingness, carry you with them into insanity, or, withering slowly yet absolutely, lead you over the brink, into the deep abyss of escape, into the final flight from torture that is death.

(*From '47—The Magazine of the Year*)

# THE SEARCH

## BY VINCENT McHUGH

LATER I remembered the dull banging that night, somewhere over on the starboard side, as if some heavy object had come adrift in the rising swell. We were taking a little water amidships. It washed under the big tires of the dump trucks in the starlight. The Cap'n had no weather reports, but he believed there must be a disturbance to the northward. It could not be much, he said. They never got more than one or two storms a year in that area.

The ship walked through it at eighty-four shaft revolutions. We were going to a war and we did not intend to be detained by the weather. Her roll was slow and able; but as I lay reading in my berth that night I could hear Louis, over my head, grumbling about falling out.

I crawled out and looked at him. 'Are you really worried?'

'Yes, Mac,' he said, aggrieved.

I got him up and passed one of the light lines we had been using that day under his mattress. When he had crawled down again I rigged the line loosely over the bedclothes and put a reef knot in it. I showed him how to clear it in a hurry.

'There you are, son. Now don't bother Daddy any more tonight. Daddy's tired.'

A long time afterwards, when I had got back into my bunk and put the light out, he said: 'Thanks, Mac,' in the darkness. I lay there smiling until I fell asleep.

Next morning the sea was running fairly high and broken in a misty aluminum glare like the winter sun on ice. Louis finished loading the second Eyemo and laid it in my berth behind him. I was going over the shots I had down for the day. Gregg, the Gunnery Officer, was yarning about an evangelist called Jumping Jesus in Chapultepec, Tennessee, his home town on the Mississippi, and Earl stood grinning down at him.

Gregg stopped in the middle of a word and his gray eyes opened. There was a noise of confused shouting on the starboard side. It sounded like a fight. The Cap'n went through the passage bawling: 'Mr. Lovegrove! Mr. Lovegrove!' We could hear him running up the outside ladder. When he was halfway up he yelled something to the bridge. The alarm gongs went.

Gregg was up and through the door, running low like a sprinter out of the crouch. The ship hitched and faltered, as if we had scraped over a reef, and began to lose way. Earl shouted: 'What the God damn——' and went banging down the inside ladder. I pulled Louis's life jacket out of the rack and tossed it to him. People were yelling all over the ship now and I could make out the words: 'Man overboard!'

I said: 'Grab the camera, Louis,' and started for the door. Just as I got to it the *Hopi Victory* went full astern, throwing me against the jamb. Then I was out on deck, in the rolling glare of sun on the water, and climbing to the port bridge wing. The ship was vibrating, grinding against her own momentum. I saw the life rings somebody had tossed bob away from the side, then float forward, dragging like the traces of a runaway horse as the ship gathered sternway. The men were manning the No. 2 motor-boat.

Louis came up the ladder.

'Shoot the stern, Louis. The wake. Then the life rings along-side. Look. Then get the faces in the No. 2 boat as they swing it out. I'll be back.'

I went up to the flying bridge. I could see the whole ship: the gun crews at their stations, the men at the boats. Every head on deck was staring astern.

The Cap'n's voice rang like a bell. 'Mr. Grandjean,' he shouted to the Third Mate, who came running. 'Get a man into the mizzenmast with glasses. Here. Take these. And get somebody in the nearest guntub to watch him for signals and pass the word on the battle phone.'

Walt ran down the ladder.

'And Mr.—ah—Lovegrove,' the Cap'n barked through the megaphone. The Mate, at the tiller of the No. 2 boat, looked up. The rest of the boat crew gazed up anxiously at the same moment. 'Be sure you're all ready to lower quickly when you get the order.'

'Yes, sir,' the Mate called.

The Cap'n whirled. 'Anybody see anything yet, Lieutenant Huckaby?'

Gregg was at the No. 1 Battle Phone on the after rail of the flying bridge, his eyes narrow and intent. He shook his head.

'No, sir,' he said.

'God damn it,' the Cap'n said as if he were talking to himself. 'We'll get him if we have to comb this sea with a harrer.'

The helmsman, Lawrie, faced forward as usual, steering by the gyro. We had good sternway on now, eating back into the disappearing wake.

'Steady as you go there,' the Cap'n said.

'Steady as you go,' Lawrie repeated.

I walked over to Gregg. 'Who is it?'

He looked at me for an instant as if he had not heard me. 'Chicky,' he said, low.

I went back to Louis on the bridge wing. 'Did you get the boat crew when they looked up?'

'Yes, Mac,' he said. 'I like this light.' He sounded pleased.

'Good boy.'

We took the camera a little aft on the bridge deck and shot the Cap'n and the staring gun crew, Gregg pressing the earphone against his head, the Second Mate at the ship's phone, the two Deck Cadets near him, Lawrie at the wheel, and Crockett and Johnson, the Signal Men, talking quietly together. The Cap'n was pacing. I could see the shrewd knot between his eyes. He would be calculating the formulae: time, the known headway of the ship, her revolutions astern. He glanced at his watch.

The ship ran full astern for what seemed to me five minutes or more; and we had time to imagine the awful abandonment of a boy who saw the wake fade around him and the dark bulk of the *Hopi Victory,* loved as no one of us had yet loved her, diminishing in the glare of the inescapable sea. The propeller paused and we slid astern a moment longer in the weltering gleam of the swell.

Then we came ahead again, half speed, and when we got way on I could have shouted as I saw that we were turning on a half-left rudder to port. The Cap'n was right. That man was always right: a seaman born and made by the sweat of his hands and the active operation of his head. We should be somewhere abreast of Chicky now. The wind and sea on our starboard beam would have carried him off the course to leeward; and maneuvering the ship to port, with a little luck, could not help but bring him somewhere within the orbit of our circle.

That was how it happened. The man in the mizzen crosstrees saw him first, a black dot on the heaving metal skin of the water. We heard afterwards that it had been Swede, up there, who sighted him. He stood up and waved his arms, gripping the glasses in one hand; and we shouted, the first time we had ever shouted together. Louis got the camera on him as he pointed, far out and broad on the port bow.

Next moment the deep voice of the *Hopi Victory* spoke half a dozen times. This was no signal we knew. We looked at each other, wondering, and stared at the bridge.

'Just wanted to cheer him up,' the Cap'n said later. 'Let him know we were comin' for him.'

Then the watch in the crow's nest reported.

'Tell those people not to take their eyes off him no matter what happens,' the Cap'n barked. 'And Mr. Hannigan.'

'Yes, sir,' the Second Mate said clearly at the bridge phone.

'Full ahead. And ask the Chief to stand by for a little maneuverin'.'

The new surge of the ship came smoothly and almost at once. My God, I thought, remembering Emil and his boys suddenly with a sense of ridiculous guilt. What do they think's going on up here?

'The port side of the bridge, Louis. We'll see what we can get.'

'How do you know, Mac?'

He was folding up the legs of the tripod.

'We'll make a lee for him.'

He gave me one of those glances of surprised respect I found more disconcerting than his usual patient disapproval. We got the camera set up out of the way on the flying bridge. Lawrie had the wheel hard down and we were battering into the glare that made our hull look black in the molten swash rolling away from the bows. But it seemed to me the wind was softening.

Now the reports began to come in. The Cap'n was standing beside the helmsman, conning the ship with glasses.

'See him yet?' I said to Cowden, the quiet Gunner's Mate in the guntub at my elbow. He was Gregg's second-in-command: a fine boy, sensitive and intelligent.

'Yes, sir,' he said in that tone of submissive deference the Navy men were taught, and handed me his glasses.

I glanced at him in half-humorous dismay. When one of the ship's crew said *sir* to the Mate, it was no more than the seamanlike observance of a convention. The Navy made it a piece of calculated and enforced servility.

I said with rueful gentleness: 'I ain't *sir,* Mr. Cowden. I ain't sir to *no*body.'

Our eyes met. He smiled slightly and I grinned at him. 'Fifteen hundred yards,' he said. 'Maybe a little more. About two points on the port bow.'

It took me two or three minutes to find it. Then it might have been anything: a small keg, a tree trunk, or any drift of flotsam rising and vanishing behind the crests. Louis gazed at it and shook his head. We made one more shot, a slow pan across the watching faces, and went below to the bridge deck. We caught the men under us talking at the No. 4 boat, the restless pattern of their movements breaking and re-forming.

I said: 'How much film have you got?'

'About 15 feet.'

'Oh Christ.'

But he had sixty or seventy in the other Eyemo. I went in and brought it out. We could see Chicky plainly now. The ship was making a long turn to starboard of him. Below us, Lieutenant Shanahan, who had a pair of glasses, said that he was not trying to swim. Just keeping himself afloat.

'How does he look,' Osterlind said.

'Cold,' said Lieutenant Shanahan.

I took the camera we had been using inside and laid it in my berth. When I came out again Louis was winding the key on the other Eyemo and the ship was turning hard left. I could see it would be good. We would fetch him very close aboard in a beam sea.

'Louis, I want to pick him up over the heads of the men in the No. 2 boat. A long flat angle.'

He looked, 'You're crazy, Mac.'

We went down the after ladder to the boat deck. I found what I wanted at the corner of the house, moved two men a little and had it: the bodies of the men at No. 4, like a frame; beyond them, at the second perspective, the slant of the No. 2 boat and the heads in it; and beyond these, the lost sailor in the glaring infinity of water.

There was some feeling in it I had not hoped for: in the overwhelming loom of the ship, the intentness of her people, the small body detached from us in the vast wavering reflection of the sun. It was like a legend of our society: the society of the ship and the whole community of the world. We had seen, with the shock of instant vision, how one man could be lost and how he might be any or all of us. We understood that we could not have abandoned him, because in abandoning even one of our company we would have been deserting a part of each man and all of us. But we had come to take him back from the waters, we would save him alive; and for the first time we were whole and understood that we were whole.

Then he had moved out of the angle of the lens. Louis nodded. The propeller stopped and the great ship, silent in the noisy water, drove down on the small head in the sun. We were less than a hundred yards off. I touched Louis on the shoulder. We ran forward in the boat-deck passage and down the companion. The ship shuddered in reverse gear and stopped.

As we came out on the main deck, the Cap'n was bawling:

'Bosun! Bosun! Get that ladder out. 'Midships there. Pass the word.'

Cole, the Bosun and two or three of the others were securing the ladder. We began shooting at once, along the rail. They pushed the rolled-up ladder over the side. It went down with a rattle and splash.

The ship lay dead in the sea and any Jap could have her while the towhead boy swam like a tuckered dog in the crests. He was hardly fifty yards off now.

'You're all right,' the Cap'n shouted strongly. 'Just keep on swimmin'.'

We took the faces along the rail. No one paid any attention to us. Their expressions were easy, curious, almost indifferent. Chicky's face looked earnest and self-conscious. He was swimming hard. When he was still 15 yards off a life ring flapped just upwind of him. Seattle had swung it round his head and heaved it from the deck above. Chicky hooked both arms into it and they began to haul him in.

I looked up. The crew of the No. 2 boat were hanging over the gunwales. I talked to Louis. He gave me a bitter glance, climbed up and lay on his back on the rail. Little Red held him while I laid the camera on his chest. He caught the vivid mottling of reflected light from the water on the hull of the boat and the staring faces around its rim. It was the best shot we made that day. Then I took the camera and Louis slid down looking outraged.

Chicky was close aboard now. He let go of the life ring and swam the seven or eight strokes to the ladder. The swell rolled him against the rungs. He lost his hold and looked up with a quick panic in his eyes. Cole the Lascar saw it. He was over the rail and thrashing down. Wet to the thighs in the first swell, he caught the boy by the back of the shirt, picked him up like a puppy and hung him safe on the ladder. Then he ran up grinning and swung down on deck. There was a warm-hearted rough tenderness and gaiety about it that made everyone smile.

'Got him down there?' the Cap'n bawled.

'Yes, sir,' the Mate shouted from the boat over our heads. 'All clear.' The *Hopi Victory* shuddered. We were in motion again before Chicky's head came over the rail. The Bosun and two or three of the others grabbed him. The sodden belt was twisted at his waist and his hair looked like wet thatch.

'Y'all right, son?' the Bosun said.

Chicky jumped down on deck. He stood there an instant with his teeth chattering.

'Jesus,' he said mildly.

Louis glanced at me. 'It'll register, Mac.'

'Okeh. Change the angle. Back here.'

They were shouting for the Purser. The ladder came over the rail with a clatter. The ship was alive again, full ahead, and moving back on her course.

'He's got his shoes on,' Little Red cried in surprise.

'Why the hell didn't you take your shoes off?' Cole said.

Chicky looked at him gloomily. 'I p-paid ten bucks for those shoes in Frisco.'

We were smiling.

'Hold it,' I said. 'Do that again. Talk to him, Cole. You answer him, Chicky. Stand in that patch of sun. It'll only take a minute.'

'M-m-make it fast,' Chicky said.

We shot the talk and the listening faces. The camera panned down to Chicky's shoes, and the patch of sun wavered back and forth across them in the roll of the ship.

Then the others closed in around him and Arthur the Purser came pushing through, calling: 'Where is he? Where is he?' They wrapped him in the big blue ship's blanket, like a football player being helped off the field, and the crowd of faces milled close up to our lens as they took him in. Then we could hear the fluttering of the camera at the empty silence of the doorway.

'One more, Louis,' I said, and yelled up to ask the Mate to hold the boat.

'Hurry it up, Mac,' he called.

We climbed three sets of ladders to the bridge deck and faced the camera down at a sharp angle. They were talking and laughing in the boat: the Mate, the Junior Third, Earl, Jimmy Ferguson, Dybdahl, the third assistant engineer, and half a dozen others. Big Red started the winch and the boat groaned up on the davits to the cabin deck.

Then they came aboard, tumbling and whooping, jumping from the gunwale to the deckrail, leaping straight at the camera with palms outstretched to bring them up against the bulkhead as they came down. The Mate looked to see that the boat was clear and vaulted sedately over the rail.

(*From Harper's Magazine*)

# THE PROFESSOR AND THE PULI

## BY ROBERT MORSE

*THE PROFESSOR* and his wife made their way across a field scattered with young cedars. At their feet opened the wide gorge of the Delaware River. Beyond the river all of Bucks County, like a huge map, tilted upward into the late spring haze.

Mrs. Wood stopped for a moment to look more thoroughly at the far farmlands, the glittering silos, the high, terraced bluffs of the river. 'Oh darling, aren't you glad we came after all!'

'Always yield to an impulse,' he said firmly.

She thought: 'But *I* am the impulsive one. He means—doesn't he *always* mean—*choosing?* Choosing for eternity.'

They surmounted a little rise and saw their hostess waiting for them to come up to her. Martha Dodge had been Paula Wood's classmate at Bryn Mawr. In spite of successful years as an executive in a New York firm she still wore a certain perennial Bryn Mawr 'look.' Paula was fond of her, and an invitation to visit her friend's new farm had pleased her very much, although she was surprised when her husband volunteered an acceptance. 'Why not, my dear? A day in the country will do us no harm. . . .' This was his yielding to an impulse.

The three of them moved together toward a little clot of sheds and wire runways in the field beyond. Only Paula appeared to belong in this wide scene. It was not just that her golden, brown, and freckled colorings matched the colors of her surroundings. She was herself a fieldling, while her husband, for all his tweeds, looked pasted on, like a montage scissored from some other picture.

As for Martha, she strode ahead of them, unmistakably a career woman, educated at Bryn Mawr, who had bought a new farm. Her executive energies had already transformed the property. Her freshly painted barns contained the best cows, the finest horses. She was proud of these and of her white turkeys and Muscovy ducks. But the dogs were the great rarity and the apple of her hazel eye.

They exploded now into the bland springtime. Aroused by the sound of human voices and maddened by the prospect of human society, they came bounding from the shelter of the kennels or sprang upward from sleep among the grass of the runways to race noisily back and forth along the wire barrier. They were all alike, huge shapeless bundles of black wool, so agitated in every part one might have supposed there were three dogs under each matted coat.

'Oh Martha!' Paula cried. 'What *are* they? Where are their *faces?*'

'These are my *pulik,*' Martha said proudly. 'Hungarian sheep dogs, you know.'

They did *not* know, but they were enchanted by the frantic creatures, each struggling to place himself more favorably than his fellows to receive the attention of the visiting bipeds. As soon as one dog managed to stand on his hind legs and press belly and paws to the wire, the others would tumble him over, barking and snapping. At first the Woods were not sure whether the immense onrush was friendly or purely savage. But they soon made out it was all love, love, love, and they poked fearless fingers through to waiting tongues and ears.

Professor Wood noticed one *puli* that remained quiet in all the flop and tumble. He was perhaps the largest of all, and yet he allowed the others to tread him down with their careless paws. No joy touched him. He did not even try to avoid the jostling.

'Martha, is that big fellow over there sick?' asked the professor.

Feeling their attention on him, the dog began to tremble. His silver-rimmed eye rolled mournfully to them, then hid itself in the shaggy hairs of his face.

'Poor old Bundash, poor old Bundash,' said Martha in a harassed tone. 'No, he's not sick, he's like that. That's the way he is.'

'There must be *something* wrong with him. He looks so unhappy,' the professor said.

'I don't honestly know what's the matter with him. He had the same chance all the others had. But even as a puppy he acted just like that, scared and sort of neurotic—as if he'd had a nervous breakdown in the womb. He makes me uncomfortable. . . .'

'Uncomfortable,' said the professor to himself. 'Her efficiency must have met with one of its few failures. She only understands what "works." What does she know of the individual and his soul, the unlighted motives, the lethargies? Even a dog . . .'

As if partly aware, as if partly in defense, Martha went on: 'Everybody has always been specially good to him. I praise him and pet him but it doesn't seem to help. Sometimes I think if he could be separated from the others and live in the house—but I only get down a day or two a week, and the cook would have to take care of him.' She lifted her shoulders sadly. 'She hates dogs.'

The professor's heart, a very tender heart, went out to the woolly heap of misery. As if telepathically aware, the dog lifted his head for the first time and looked at the professor with both eyes, like an old Florentine shade sitting up in his tomb of fire to look at Dante. For a moment the two were alone in the world together. Then the other *pulik* all came barking and jumping, and Bundash's head was forced down under their paws.

It was too much. 'Paula . . .' began the professor.

'Always obey an impulse you know, dear,' Paula said, herself not untouched. 'But I don't think Flora would like it a bit.' Flora was a slim but aging dachshund, the tyrannical queen of the Woods' New York apartment.

Martha, who understood many things quickly, said: 'Oh if you would only take him. Being with you and the children would be the best thing in the world for him. I would *give* him to you. He's a really good dog, pure bred and all. . . . The truth is he makes me feel *guilty* somehow.'

When the Woods started for home that afternoon Bundash lay inert and uncomplaining in the back seat of their car.

Professor Wood steered them through the darkening New Jersey farmlands. He felt tender and aware in spirit, and a little tired, as if just returning from a minor but successful skirmish with the ever-present legions of Evil. There came to him images of a reconstructed, a saved Bundash. He saw him responding, gradually, to the happiness of home, the arms of the children about his neck, a dish of good food all his own, comfort, care, and above all an affectionate master to take him on long walks, to talk to him, to make much of him. He saw Bundash bounding and barking. Again and again he visualized a hairy black head laid on a certain tweed-covered knee. Surely love was the power, love was the key.

The fields were giving way to factories. Soon they must go through the Holland Tunnel. Suddenly Professor Wood thought of the Holland Tunnel with a new and rather frightening clarity. Years ago he had found his first passage through the tile-lined tube an intense experience. How would Bundash, who had never left the cedared acres of his birth, feel about the Holland Tunnel? What would he feel about the city beyond?

They came to the long plunge under the river. Their ears and eyes were assailed, as for the first time, by gleamings, clicks, and roars, and strangeness. There seemed to be an unusual number of cars and trucks. Many of them backfired in the echoing confinement. There was a smell of gasoline and hot machinery. 'Dogs have such marvelous noses,' he thought. Aloud then: 'Paula see how he's taking it.'

She stretched out her hand. 'He's shaking a little, that's all.' Paula was thinking apprehensively of Flora. Also there came to her an old vision of the Hudson rolling above them, the bottoms of ocean liners passing overhead. She was always prepared for a great rush of water, and only a second's time to say good-by to her husband. 'Good-by. I love you,' was the phrase she had rehearsed — and then the Hudson closing their mouths forever.

The tunnel remained, for this one more time, watertight — and they emerged in the paved spaces of lower Manhattan, so like a place where the dungeon of one tyranny has been cleared away to make room for the guillotine of its successor. But there were no mobs here, only thousands and thousands of metal vehicles streaming in curious patterns across the emptiness. These conflicting lines were not without their courtesies for their own metallic kind: one formation would halt to let another flow on, then would go ahead, then again stop. But there was no place in the pattern for flesh not cased in steel. Once Professor Wood had seen a pedestrian go under the wheels as if in a gesture of defiance. Tonight no one questioned the tide of machines finding their way home through the various openings in the buildings.

The Woods' Buick ('38) chose the raised uptown highway, and swept Bundash and the others past funneled ships on one hand ('Now I am above *them* . . .' thought Paula) and high, stepped towers on the other.

The three red-haired children were waiting for them in the comfortable, shabby apartment on 78th Street.

So was Flora.

The children were enraptured with their new playmate and wrapped arms of varying chubbiness about his patient neck. Flora, aghast, indignant for but a moment, sniffed Failure and leapt without a further glance to the comforts of the best sofa. There, after many imperial yawns, she affected to doze. But that was the end of Bundash for *her*. It was not the end of Bundash for the professor.

Food and water first. These were essential to the plan for the dog's reconstruction. He must be made to feel this was his home, and wasn't home to any dog the place where he was fed? But Bundash showed no wish to prolong his life. Again and again they coaxed his nose to a dish of meat, and he turned away as from some meaningless substance. Water he snuffled up in large quantities, but that was the extent of his co-operation in the plan.

However, the professor was encouraged to see that the dog stayed close to him, and he fancied that Bundash was grateful for the touch of his hand. The rest of the family made their overtures in vain. Their caresses seemed meaningless as the offerings of meat. Only the professor's voice reached him, but reached him slowly, as if the way to his far-off brain wound through muffling thickets of hair. He responded to commands only after painful minutes of immobility. And yet he responded. The long look man and dog had shared in the kennels *had* amounted to a sort of vow after all. But whatever bond Bundash might feel linking his fate to the professor's did not express itself in wags of the tail, friendly butts of the head, barks and prancing — only an oppressive propinquity. Of course it is too soon, the professor thought. Later we will see.

Presently Flora yapped a signal that it was time for her nightly visit to the curb. Confident and svelte, she jingled down the three flights of stairs. But tonight she had to wait a long time at the street door. Professor Wood did not find it easy to persuade Bundash to follow him to the sidewalk, and once there Bundash did not understand why — even with Flora's example. Or did he think the whole city was one enormous house? After half an hour the professor conceded failure, and they climbed the stairs again.

Long after the other Woods had gone to bed the professor sat up with his unsleeping protégé. He felt that his presence might be reassuring. Bundash, who showed a marked fear of open places, of the center with its dread limelight, had tried all corners, crawled behind all barriers, and settled at last in the kneehole of the professor's desk. This was to be *his* place. This was the cave from which he sent out his dark emanations of agony.

The professor found himself painfully receptive at some animal level long unused. It was more than a sympathetic intuition. The agony was within his own skin. 'How much of this am I getting from the dog, and how much is my own anxiety for a new responsibility — or just simply my own anxiety?' he asked himself. An experience of his youth returned to him: his first night at boarding school. The recollection pleased him. It seemed to him now that he had been just like Bundash, that what he had wanted then, more than anything, was a cave out of the light. But in two or three days he had made the proper adjustments, the first of the adjustments that led in a long line to the present day and to a reasonable invulnerability.

His brief boyish distress was a long time ago. Since then he had mastered all the major schools of thought. Aristotle, Kant, Bergson, Buddha, Marx, Pareto, Toynbee, Thomas Aquinas were familiar to him as his own pockets (which they had done so little to fill). There was scarcely an argument that he could not answer with the most effective response man's brain had been able to devise — as a trained wrestler knows the break for any hold. He gave courses in philosophy and ethics. His lectures in aesthetics had modified many of his students' lives because of the fervor of his belief in the seriousness of art and his rejection of niggling formulas. During the war he taught mathematics.

But he was not just a teacher. He had avoided and gone beyond the confinement of the academic world with its burning, spiteful rivalries and narrow scholarship. Completeness had been his deliberate goal, so that he had learned to play the easier Bach Preludes, and had made himself an expert in the structure of labor unions, both foreign and domestic. He knew more about Russia and her policies than ninety-nine per cent of the Russians. He could distinguish the 'periods' of Rubens, and was a deft hand with the income tax.

The professor brought the same ideal of completeness to personal relations, so that his friends were very various, ranging from an alcoholic medium, through bankers, golfers, society women, painters, to mechanics and a Greek bartender with a shoe fetish. These types he valued as nearly as possible in their own terms, and would have been acutely shamed if he had detected in himself any prejudice or want of fairness. When with his friends he drank rather a lot, but never got drunk — at least not in the way that forgets itself — merely sleepy.

In short he was a remarkable man, and reasonably invulnerable.

The rosary of his accomplishments slid dimly through the professor's mind, but brought no gratification. A swift thought darted out and away. Have I acquired all these things for my enrichment or for my defense? If defenses, which way are they faced — outward or inward? Have I been rolling stones against the mouth of a cave?

Bundash looked at him from his place under the desk. Nothing of the dog was visible but a single very clear, very round, beautiful eye shining out of a hairy darkness. Professor Wood made his weary way to bed, but he could not sleep. He could feel a steady pressure from the adjoining room. He knew there was no rest in the dark kneehole.

The eye was still there in the morning, a smoky jelly. Had it ever closed? Little Paula went on all fours to coax the dog to his food. '*Darling* Bundash, come out, come out!' she shrilled in tones that should have persuaded a Lazarus. Fat Jimson, the baby, exhorted: 'Hawo bub bosh.' But Bundash could not be moved. He needed a more difficult magic than the voices of children.

The professor marched in from his tumbled bed. Miss Feitelbaum, who secretly adored him from the third row of Ethics 404, would have been much dismayed by the ravages a sleepless night had worked in his orderly face. 'Oh *Daddy,* how funny you look!' cried candid Miss Paula. Bundash indicated by the merest lifting of his bulk that he recognized authority. A word of command at last penetrated the woolly forests that lay between him and the world. He rose to his feet with painful halts, like the first clay of life separating itself from the earth. He consented to be led to the street, but again he had no understanding of what was expected of him. The gates of his body remained sealed.

Block after block the professor walked him, and brought him home again at last, baffled. 'He undoubtedly needs the sight of trees and grass. I'll take him to the park after breakfast.' Professor Wood sighed; he had planned to give his morning to a great pile of students' papers, neglected over the weekend. He thought about reflexes. If you had never known anything but the country — if you were conditioned to green. . . . He had never quite noticed how little vegetation there was in New York. The only green they had seen on their morning walk was a tuft of crabgrass that had sown itself in an iron urn, sole ornament of a paved courtyard.

Again Bundash would not touch his breakfast. Again he drank a quantity of water. 'Surely with all that water in him . . .' thought the professor, and it was in a mood of new hope he started out for the park, the dog huddled at his heels. He had never been so aware of the traffic before — the roaring, the shriek of brakes, the sharp musketry of exhaust pipes, the hugeness of the busses, and their terrible whooshing sighs. By the time he had got them both safe across the perilous stream of Fifth Avenue the professor was in a sweat of empathy. It was at *him* the taxis had hooted, the trucks charged, the ten thousand strangers stared.

They were in the park at last. 'Now!' said Professor Wood.

Perhaps Bundash was still numbed by the horrid novelties he had just come through, at any rate he responded to the lawns and bushes as he had to everything else — he trembled faintly and maintained the forlorn dignity of despair. Pigeons whirled and strutted about him. Children raced and rolled. Bundash remained a black silence against the sunlight and green and motion — a silence without a face.

After some hours they started home, still unsuccessful. Between Madison and Park, Professor Wood, with his new animal awareness, sensed a change in the dog, a *willingness*. He was invaded at the same time by an unexpected knowledge, the knowledge of agoraphobia. They must find some protection against the exposed street. Instructed from within, he lifted the dog over a low privet hedge into a little stony enclosure. There was no doubt about Bundash's intention, but just at that moment an ambulance came howling from one direction, a fire engine bore down on them from another. Lesser fire cars with screams and clanging followed, like infernal chariots in attendance on the red terror of their Lord. The air was solid with sound. Windows jumped and chattered in their casements. The stones underfoot shuddered. And so did Bundash.

It was useless for the professor to command or coax, the *puli* refused to leave his frail shelter. After fifteen minutes his master was obliged to climb the hedge himself and lift the big, trembling dog in his arms. Some boys behind him laughed as he scrambled back to the street. No doubt he and his burden made a laughable picture, but he was too fiercely identified with Bundash's sensibilities to care.

Paula, when they got home, looked at her husband for a moment, then said: 'Dearest, I think you had better take one of your luminals. You know Dr. Spencer said to take one whenever you got jumpy again.'

This was only the first day. The second, following another sleepless night, was the same. Papers piled up on the desk. Bundash would not make water. Although he continued to drink greedily, he would not eat. He was taken for long walks, love was lavished on him where the subtlest insight failed, but he returned always to the kneehole in the desk.

'He just has no sense of joy at all,' mourned the professor, swallowing another luminal with an early highball. 'That's what is most terrible.'

'Now, now, Duncan. Just give him time,' said Paula. Much of Paula's tranquility came from her friendly confidence in Time. For this reason she rarely fretted about the children. When her husband read in their youthful backslidings a permanent corruption of character she was like to say: 'It's just a phase, dear.' And she was of course right.

But utter joylessness *was* the most terrible aspect of the dog. It amounted to not caring, not wanting to be saved. People who went to psychoanalysts surely had some undefeated quality in them that wanted to be saved from sickness of soul. They could talk. The analysts could draw words out of them. But weren't there others, so without the capacity to love, so joyless, so uninterested, that nothing could reach them in their cold secrecy? For them, all approaches, all bribes and lures and threats were alike meaningless. 'If only he could talk to me,' thought the professor, scarcely aware of his absurdity. 'But nothing can be done with him until he clears his body.'

The Woods' friends had learned of their experiment, and with the softheartedness of New Yorkers, phoned frequently for the latest bulletin. The phone stood on the desk just above the dog's cave, and each thrill of the bell pierced the professor to the brain. He or Paula would snatch up the receiver to say, 'No, not yet.'

A number of these friends dropped in at intervals for a cocktail and a look at Bundash. Each secretly felt he had an infallible way with dogs, but Bundash responded no more than a lump. Rather than being cheered by his well-wishers he depressed *them,* as if a black drop of the midnight marsh within him had found its way into the cocktail shaker. They began to drink like people keeping off the cold, defiantly. Mary Maple, who for decades had considered all males her province without bothering to count their feet, returned again and again to the seduction of Bundash. After four martinis she was the rough and ready Pal, after six she had shifted to the mysterious, all-understanding woman. Two more cocktails saw her on her knees screaming murder and obscenity into the cave under the desk. Suddenly she was sobbing. 'Not even a —— dog. Not even a black —— —— of a dog wants anything of me. What does any of *you* know?' They knew that her husband always seemed to find a job abroad.

Rosalie Reagen, who had progressed from unexamined Protestant, to Atheist, to Communist, to War Widow, to Catholic, had meanwhile struggled to draw attention from the dog to herself, launching to provocative word here, seizing an elbow there. Now, giving up, she said: 'Really, Mary dear, so like the twenties.' But Paula had already led Mary to a back bedroom with kindly murmurs.

The editor of the *Spartan Review* lifted the company to a purer air by drawing a comparison between Bundash and certain concepts and passages in Kafka. 'Now if you take K's insoluble problem of incommensurables . . .' he continued. The other visitors spoke less and less. They stared in awe at the shaggy reservoir of mounting urine.

Another day passed as before. The professor's mind was aching with his responsibility and failure. He introduced Bundash's case in his new lecture on Existentialism. It seemed a pertinent and illuminating example. But his strong instinct to externalize the trouble the *puli* had stirred up in him would have made the case seem pertinent to a discussion of any theme. Accordingly, after a long look at the rows of respectful faces turned to him, he began: 'Since the direction of thought I wish to take up this morning does not permit, logically, any vantage-point outside of life for logical examination, I think we can best begin with a story from life itself: Once there was a dog . . .'

Miss Feitelbaum's pencil slid over the page of her notebook. 'Once there was a dog . . .' she set down in her useful shorthand, then waited receptive and ecstatic for the next words. *This* was the stuff. Her pencil moved on, not missing a syllable.

The professor had reached his classroom by subway, so wrapped in familiar custom and last-minute ideas for his forthcoming lecture he had scarcely noticed how he traveled. But now, as he boarded the subway for his return trip, he found himself trembling. Ears, eyes, nose, skin, suddenly blared his surroundings at him. Had he ever been in this place before? There had never been so many people, people so angry or so indifferent, people slyly touching or crushing brutally against him. There had never been this train with its awful racket, reduplicated by the underground vaults. It was as if the spirit of Bundash, the whole dog, had crept into his skin and dispossessed his old self. Why else did he tremble? Why else did he ask himself: Has it always been like this?

At the next express stop he made a bolt for the street level, determined to walk home. Here there was another unending crush of people, anonymous as insects. The busses whooshed. The traffic attacked him. Smells and sounds came to his senses without the human censorship of disinterest. He was a dog for keenness, but Duncan Wood interpreted the evidence. 'What do any of *you* know,' he said almost aloud to the strangers, echoing poor Mary Maple. 'Do you know how you are suffering, each of you?'

It was the paving that offended him most. His feet could feel the grain and harshness of it, as if they had become shoeless paws. Was there really *earth* underneath the stone and the asphalt — or just more stone and a network of steam pipes and drains. All fertility seemed shut away under mineral slabs. Minerals rose around him to vast heights. Yet over and under these hard surfaces, he observed children playing hardily in the thick of the traffic, for want of a better place. He imagined that presently the nameless strangers would carry their young underground, clasping them in their forearms like ant eggs when the hill has been disturbed, to cells hollowed among the steam pipes.

He made his way up Lexington Avenue, buffeted by novel impressions. It was as if his senses were suspended just two feet above the sidewalk. He might have traveled on all fours, he was so aware of filth and gum trodden into the concrete, of wheels and hydrants, of human odors breathing over doorsteps.

He reached home at last, footsore, or padsore, his mind filled with dingy and ominous visions. The street sounds followed him into his apartment. He closed the windows against them, but, scarcely dimmed, they found their way to his dog-tender ear drums. Even his own children rasped his nerves — and for the first time. There seemed to be so many of them crowded into the narrow rooms, as if there were not air enough to go around. He even questioned his love for them. What is love? Does one really love anyone? He tried to summon up the shape of his love for these housemates, to probe and test the quality of its connective tissues. Nothing came to him but outside sounds and smells. There was still the desk to cling to, with its clear rectangular lines, with its piles of lecture notes, and papers, and well-known books. He would force himself to correct an examination. He seated himself in the usual chair, put on his glasses, and began to read, but the words meant little to him in his fatigue. He drummed on the desktop, his nails tapping desperately among the signs and symbols of his life work, among the paper proofs of long, ordered, intellectual endeavor.

He was drumming on the roof of darkness. Under this wooden planking his legs extended down into the kneehole, into Bundash's cave. There was no need for him to ask about Bundash's condition. He *was* Bundash.

In short the husk of custom had been stripped from him, and with it the tough tolerance required by city life. The little box of luminal was emptying rapidly.

Some time before daybreak he said to himself in his bed: Why — what hell have I been living in without knowing it? The picture of an alternative life formed in his half-dreaming mind. He could still escape the trap. He saw himself leaving Paula and the children, his work, everything he had been accustomed to love, and taking to the wilderness with Bundash. He saw a hermit's cave — no, that was *too* silly — he saw a shack by a pond, a pond curiously like his first imagining of Walden. He must find rebirth in those waters, wash away the old, contrived, weary, death-appeasing self like an accumulation of stale sweat. The pool was around him, fresh and gray in the dawn. A black form dived in after him — yes, Bundash was there all right. Presently that dripping head would be laid on his knee again, begging for a trout.

A thick, miserable coughing in the next room interrupted this revery. He and Paula stumbled through the door together. There stood poor Bundash vomiting into a viscous green and black puddle.

'No, no! It's too much. The dog is really sick,' and they bundled their *puli* off to a veterinary as soon as his office was open. Martha Dodge had recommended him in case of trouble.

Later, Professor Wood called Martha. 'I'm sorry, Martha. I'm afraid that dog is hopeless. We just can't keep him. Yes, I think he's really sick this time. I've left him at your vet's.'

He replaced the receiver with a sense of defeat and of relief as well. Paula's kind, charming eyes were on him. 'You know, Paula, I'm not sure it was just because Bundash got sick. I *had* to get rid of him. I think he was beginning to mean something to me, something quite awful.' For a moment the professor glimpsed Bundash as the enemy, persuading him ever nearer to the edge of danger, drawing him into his own deathlike world where all endeavor, all love, all planning for time to come, were reduced to futilities. Bundash was Death, he thought.

'But that is unfair,' he thought. 'How can a *dog* be blamed?' Meanwhile fat Jimson had pushed his untidy, resilient little person past the barrier of the professor's legs, and now regarded him from the twilight of the kneehole with an upward glance of unmixed geniality. 'If there was an enemy, he was in myself, and will always be there. I should bless Bundash for giving me this fresh glimpse of him. I have been given a chance to choose again, the only choice.' He looked fondly on Paula, and leaned to prod his young son in the stomach till the toothless chuckles rewarded him.

'Let's just have a martini before lunch,' said Paula.

'No, dear. My papers.'

Some days later the professor received a note:

Dear Duncan:

I picked up the puli at the vet's today. I'm sorry you had a bad time. The vet says there is nothing in the world wrong with him. He did everything he was supposed to, and seems in quite good spirits, better at least than I have ever seen him. I don't know how you did it in such a short time, but Bundash is now perfectly trained for the city. He heels perfectly and seems to know all about traffic.

I have given him to Brenda Arden — the actress, you know — and she is utterly enchanted with him.

By the way, what on earth did you say to the vet? You made a great impression on him. He was quite worried about you. He says he never saw a more nervous man. Have you been working too hard? It isn't fair to Paula. Why don't you both come down this weekend? I have a new litter of puppies. Perhaps you'd like one.

As ever,

MARTHA

(From Good Housekeeping)

# THE STUPENDOUS FORTUNE

## BY RUTH PORTUGAL

*BLACK SHEEP* — that was the only name the three sisters knew him by — had died a long time before they were born. He had died before their father was born, and even their grandmother never had seen him. He was not only the sisters' uncle, but their father's uncle as well, and it turned out that he was their grandmother's uncle and possibly their grandmother's mother's (or father's) uncle — but there the avuncular thread became lost in long-darkened generations.

Were they to ask their father just exactly what kind of uncle Black Sheep was, so they could be sure he was their great-great-uncle, let's say, or their great-great-great-uncle — or was he their great-great-great-great-? — their father would say something like: 'Children, I don't know. I'm reading. Please. For the Lord heaven sakes, it's the fourth time that I've tried to get through this one page!'

So they did not know what kind of uncle he was. They knew this, though: Black Sheep had gone to Africa. He had discovered diamond mines, and he had died, leaving an enormous, dazzling fortune, which really belonged to them.

The fortune would be theirs right now if Black Sheep had not changed his name. From what name to what name they could not find out, because their father just could not remember names; he got even their names mixed up, calling Hortense Ruth and Marjorie Hortense, and so forth. They did not know why Black Sheep was called that, but it was what they had heard him called. Marjorie's world particularly was peopled with three bears, who sat at a table to eat their porridge and slept in beds and talked; and there was the wolf who looked like Little Red Riding Hood's grandmother — and probably Marjorie's grandmother — and spoke like her and wore her clothes. So Marjorie was not surprised that someone in her own family had been a sheep. If he was called Black Sheep, he must have been a black sheep. ('Baa, baa, Black Sheep, have you any diamonds?' she sometimes would sing.)

Black Sheep had changed his name, and the records had burned in a fire, and until the sisters could prove that he was really their uncle, they could not get the fortune. It was being kept from them far away, in the Bank of England, in a place called Escrow.

Once some men called solicitors had come over from England to see their father and 'collect documentary evidence' — whatever that was. 'And of course there wasn't any. I could've saved them the trip,' their father would say, laughing. 'The newspapers got all excited. Even published a picture of Hortense; called her "Infant heiress to diamond fortune." I can remember, when I was a boy, some solicitors, smelling a nice fat fee, rushed over to see my mother; but their excitement went out like a light as soon as they found out we had no proof.'

'A hundred years after his death it becomes the property of the Crown,' was another thing they had heard their father say, as calmly as you please. He hardly ever spoke of the fortune, except when there was company.

'Daddy, show me where it says I'm the heiress to the fortune. I want to see my picture in the paper.' Hortense felt as famous as Mary Pickford. 'Show me!'

'Oh, I guess I have the clipping somewhere,' their father would say, with a lack of interest that was incomprehensible, as if it were no more important than yesterday's rainstorm.

'Just because your picture was in the newspaper, it doesn't mean I'm not an heiress, too. I wasn't born yet, that's all. I'm just as much of an heiress as you are,' Ruth would say to Hortense. 'Amn't I?' she would ask her father. 'Amn't I an heiress?'

'Me, too!' would come from Marjorie.

'You're all heiresses. Mrs. Astorbilt, Mrs. Rockefeller, and Mrs. Morgan. Now let me read.' And he would be back trying to get through whatever page he was trying to get through, as if maybe this time the words would turn into a sound proof wall.

Neither their mother nor their father ever had said, 'Children, would you like me to tell you the story of Black Sheep and the Fortune?' But the fragments had pieced themselves together imperceptibly, and it would not have occurred to them that there might have been a time when they did not know the story. Do you suppose a child can tell you when it was he first knew that milk is milk? Or that those two large presences were his mother and his father? Or when he listened to his first fairy tale? The story of Black Sheep and the Fortune always had been there, part of the state of things that had formed foreground and background from dim infancy.

It was like the pages of *My Heart at Thy Sweet Voice,* which they could not remember seeing on the music rack of the piano, the dark notes going up like broad stairs to a platform and going down again — up again, down again, just like the sounds they made when Mother played them on the piano. It was like the huge stuffed white bear on wheels that growled when you pulled the ring in its back; that, too, had been there always.

Well, then, they always had known about the Fortune.

'He was the black sheep of the family.' When had they first heard their father say that, his voice drifting toward them, like tobacco smoke, from the distant conversation of the grownups? 'Diamond mines. . . . An estate worth several million pounds. . . . Not a chance in the world of getting it.' And then there would be the rich, strong sound of adult laughter. 'Oh, well, it makes a good story, anyway.'

Or it had been their mother's voice reaching them when they were playing in the living room after supper. Perhaps she and their father were going over some bills, or discussing the furniture they wanted to buy and saying prices were high because it was after the war; and she would say: 'A villain to the end, not leaving a will. Think of what we could do with a few extra thousand, let alone all those millions.' And then their mother and father would laugh, and the sisters would stop their playing and take up the laughter, screaming, 'Millions!'

'Millions!' Marjorie would scream delightedly, not knowing why, just screaming 'Millions! Millions!' as she turned somersaults in her final great excitement of the day.

It would have happened just before the sisters' bedtime — the dimmed lamplight and the sound of Mother's voice and the image of Mother inextricably blended, become one memory picture. Already Mother in the living room was memory. It was hard to remember when Mother had stopped coming downstairs.

People no longer said to them, 'Where is your mother?' They said, 'How is your mother?' Because the facts that their mother was always in her bedroom and had a nurse named Mrs. Miller were part of the way things were now. They had not known Mrs. Miller was coming. She must have come when they were asleep. One morning the starched uniform was moving in large white sweeps around their mother's room.

Little by little, as they came to think: 'This is *my* doll, *my* book, *my* dress, *our* house, *our* car, *our* bear'—and no one else had a bear like it—'*our* mother is sick and has a nurse, and if we happen to like you, maybe we'll take you up to see our mother,' as this, and this and this became 'mine,' 'ours,' the Fortune emerged from the indistinct, formless acceptance that was older than memory and asserted itself as Our Fortune. It was their fabulous possession.

It was their favorite, real-life fairy tale—the three little sisters of the story were themselves. They—Hortense, Ruth, and Marjorie, 14 Spruce Street, Cedarhurst, Long Island—were really princesses. Did not royalty and wealth go hand in hand?

All three sisters slept in the room that had been Ruth's and Marjorie's, because Hortense's room now was Aunt Dot's (who was Mother's sister and so beautiful) and Uncle Billy's (her husband). They had come to live with them because of Mother's being sick.

'When we go to England and get it,' was the way the talk began, as the sisters lay in the dark security of their beds, with the safe sounds of family coming to them dimly from their mother's lighted bedroom just down the hall.

'We'll have to have at least one castle,' Hortense decided.

And before each of them stood her castle, every turret substantial in the darkness. They shivered a little with happiness and pulled their blankets high around their necks in the cold, airy room.

'And there'll be water around the castle, and knights and ladies-in-waiting,' Ruth singsonged, 'and we can ride in a wagon with horses, like the king and queen.'

'I'm gonta have my own wagon,' Marjorie shouted.

'Shhh,' Hortense said, because they were supposed to be going to sleep.

'Of course I'll have at least two personal maids,' she went on, her reverie climbing like a luminous cloud around her, 'to take care of all my evening gowns and my ermine wrap and my diamonds, and bring me breakfast on a tray — chicken livers.' That was what Daddy had with his eggs on Sunday morning.

'Jelly omelets.'

'Whipped cream.'

'And run the water in the bathtub, and pour in a lot of bath salts and junk,' Hortense concluded.

'I *won't* let 'm give me a bath!' Marjorie screamed.

'Shut up,' said Ruth. The darkness gave her courage to say that. There were certain words they were not supposed to say. Sometimes behind the closed door of the bathroom Ruth would mutter, 'Shut up shut up shut up shut up. Dirty slob dirty sap dirty bum dirty fool dirty dumbbell. Shut up shut up shut up shut up SHUT UP.' And then she would feel better.

'Shut up, yourself,' Marjorie had lowered her voice somewhat. 'I'm gonta have a chewing-gum factory in my castle,' she said thoughtfully.

'And a soda fountain.'

'And a different dress every day. I'll never wear the same one more than once.'

'Every single one of my dresses is gonta be new.' And Marjorie's voice rose again, shrill, defiant. Often her clothes had been Hortense's first, and then Ruth's. 'And they're all gonta be yellow.'

Night after night this was what they talked about, never growing tired of the repetition, as they never grew tired of the storybook stories; however often they listened to them, the stories unfolded anew. Each time the girls marveled at the miracle of the pumpkin coach, felt Cinderella's misery or Snow White's danger, held their breaths at the frightening parts with their giants and ogres and witches and wicked stepmothers and villains (Black Sheep was a villain; had not Mother called him that?); and yet, they weren't really frightened, because they knew the stories ended happily, as their own story was bound to. In the end, the three little princesses would get Their Fortune and live happily ever after.

Happily ever after. They would fall asleep on those words of blessed omen, as if they were the magic squares of wedding cake that maidens put under their pillows to dream on.

During the day, they streaked around the corners of neighboring houses in violent games of hide-and-seek, collected and traded 'samples,' stared at the pictures in the *Book of Knowledge,* treated the diseases of their dolls, had cookies and milk at three o'clock, saved pennies in piggy banks. In their chambray bloomer dresses — or if it were wintertime, in their chinchilla coats and tam-o'shanters — they appeared no different from other little girls on any Spruce Street or Maple Avenue of any American village.

But their princessness was with them always, like the small gold lockets little girls wear around their necks, neither the thin gold chains nor the heart-shaped pendants showing outside their dresses, but their fingers telling them the precious lockets are safe and close to them.

Other kids thought they were making believe about Black Sheep and Their Fortune, so they almost never talked about it, even to their best friends, with whom they went off, arms over shoulders, to whisper secrets and to feud on others. No matter how loudly the sisters squabbled, they were happiest together; then their princessness was not like the modest little lockets, but resplendent as a crown made of Black Sheep's diamonds.

On rainy days, when they were by themselves in their room, they would put a nursery chair on top of a big square chair borrowed from the kitchen, and drape the dais with bedspreads, and then cover themselves with Christmas-tree tinsel, which gave off a sparkle like diamonds; and with pomp and solemnity they in turn would mount the throne. 'I am a princess,' each announced to the castellated world that waited for them beyond the rain-covered windows of their bedroom on Spruce Street, rehearsing for the day when they would come out of exile and into their inheritance. It was hard to believe that the hundred years since Black Sheep's death could pass before they would be able to go to England and claim Their Fortune.

Only, when would they go to England?

'When? When?' had been running uneasily through their minds all the morning, under the excitement about their new pencil boxes, which Aunt Dot had helped them pick out at the store, and about who would be in their classes and the names of their teachers and the new school shoes and new plaid skirts they would put on for the first time tomorrow. Tomorrow would be the first day of school, when Hortense and Ruth would walk past the rooms they had been in last year, and Marjorie would walk into the first schoolroom of her life. Time, which seemed hardly to move, had just jumped suddenly; and now another whole, long, endless summer was ended. One night it would be December thirty-first, and when they awakened the next morning, it would be a completely new year. This was their first consciousness of finality, and it was a flaw struck in their solid faith.

They had left their new pencil boxes in a row on the piano, and now they were using the cement walk that led to their house for a game of 'One-two-three-a-lary, I spied Mrs. Sary, Sitting on a bumble-lary, Just like a chocolate fairy.'

'This is the last weekday morning we'll be playing A-lary,' Hortense said.

Hortense was up to stampsie-clapsie, Ruth was on clapsie, and Marjorie was still on plainsie. The ball had just bounced away from Marjorie again. It rolled under the privet hedge. Whoever let the ball get away had to chase it. So Marjorie was somewhere under the hedge.

'We've got to find out his name before it's too late,' said Hortense. 'He changed it just to keep us from getting Our Fortune. The filthy, rotten villain.'

Marjorie came back with the ball. 'I'm gonta kill'm.'

'He's dead, you idiot.'

'I don't care.' After a moment Marjorie asked, 'Who's dead?'

'Who-who-who what-what-what. Why don't you ever listen?' Hortense took the ball from her; it was her turn.

'Black Sheep, that's who. And we don't have to tell you everything,' Ruth said.

'You do so. Maybe *somebody* killed'm,' Marjorie said hopefully. 'He was just a dumb sheep.'

Hortense was doing stampsie-clapsie, but without much interest. When she missed the ball and it rolled onto the grass, she let it stay there and went over and sat on the stoop with the other two. 'Daddy doesn't even know how many years he's been dead. Maybe it's almost a hundred years already!' She stared at them in sudden alarm. 'Let's go ask Mother when we're going to England. We've got to get there.'

They let the screen door bang behind them and raced upstairs to their mother's room.

'Mother!' Hortense said. 'Maybe he's dead almost a hundred years already! Oh, Mother, we've got to hurry!'

'Who, darling?' Their mother did not lift her head from the back of the rose-colored chair she was sitting in. An open book was on her lap; her hands held the sides of it, as if the book were too heavy for them to lift.

'Black Sheep,' Ruth said.

'What are you talking about, darling?'

They tried to tell her, the three talking at once. 'The Fortune!' 'Maybe it's a hundred years already!' 'We've got to get to England!' 'When will you be better, so we can go? Next week?'

'Soon,' Mother said, as if it were hard to get the word out. She was looking at them. At this one's face and then that one's and that one's, and back again. 'Soon,' they saw her lips repeat, but no sound came, and tears were running down Mother's face.

'Mommy, what's the matter?'

Marjorie started to cry.

'Don't cry, baby. Don't cry, don't cry,' Mother said in a whisper, and all the while the tears were running out Mother's eyes.

And then Aunt Dot was in the room. 'It's all right, Ann,' she said to Mother.

And Mrs. Miller, the nurse, had her white-sleeved arms around them and was leading them to the door. 'Your mother's feeling a little tired this morning.'

As they went out of the room, Aunt Dot was saying: 'It's all right, children. I'll be with you in a moment,' and they saw her holding Mother's hand.

The fall ended, more quickly than had the summer, and the long winter ended, and the spring when Mother 'passed away'; and it was summer-fall-winter-spring-summer again.

It was two whole years later; another long summer was coming to its end, and Hortense, Ruth, and Marjorie had not got to England yet.

But England was coming to them. Today the Prince of Wales

was coming to the Rockaway Hunting Club, which was in Cedarhurst, to play polo. He would go along Spruce Street on his way to the club from the railroad station. The station was straight down the street, two blocks away.

The newspapers had not said anything about the train he was taking, so since breakfast they had been sitting on the curbstone in front of their house, waiting for the Prince of Wales.

Aunt Dot and Uncle Billy were away on a trip. Daddy had left for the city before they were dressed. There was no one, except Clara, the maid, to ask them why they were wearing their party dresses on a Tuesday morning, and she did not ask them.

Before sitting down, they carefully had brushed from the curbstone any fallen leaves and bird droppings.

'Sit on your bloomers, not on your dresses,' Hortense had told them. They sat, in their pink, blue, and yellow dresses, as stiff as the skirts that puffed out around them, their faces tense under the large black Milan straw hats with the streamers down the backs. The low curbstone thrust their knees almost up to their faces.

'There's the whistle!' one of them would say when a train was coming. They would sit up very straight, the circles of the three large straw hats turned in the direction of the station.

'Now, Marjorie,' Hortense would say, quickly giving her last-minute instructions, 'when you curtsy, don't pull your dress up so high your bloomers show. You always do that.'

'I don't.'

'You do so,' Ruth said.

'And don't you giggle.' That was meant for Ruth.

But the cars went past them from the station without the Prince of Wales.

'Maybe he'll be on the next train.'

And so they waited, straightening up each time they heard the whistle of a train.

They knew just what they were going to say to him. 'The Fortune is ours. And nobody knows his name,' they would tell him, 'but he really was our uncle, and that's Our Fortune.' 'Of course it is,' the Prince would say.

*'Maybe he's even got Our Fortune with him to give us.'*

('Daddy!' they would shout when he came home this evening. 'Surprise! We've got Our Fortune! Look at all the diamonds! He knew it belonged to us!')

'Now, *I'll* do the talking when he stops,' Hortense said.

It was noon, and the sun was making them hot and thirsty, but they did not move. They did not answer when some fresh boys on the other side of the street called taunts.

'Maybe we won't go to England at all,' Ruth said.

'Won't we have our castle?' Marjorie asked.

They had not thought of that.

'I'd rather go to Egypt, anyway,' Hortense said. 'But if you want a castle, you can have one.'

'Sure. We can have anything.'

At any moment Their Fortune would really be theirs.

'Lunch is ready,' Clara called.

They looked at one another.

'We can't have any,' Hortense yelled.

'Can't we have just a speck?' Marjorie asked.

'Well — ' Hortense was hungry, too. 'I know what. We'll take turns. But we've got to hurry. If he comes, we can yell to whoever's eating.'

So one at a time rushed in and gobbled some lunch and raced past the bewildered Clara and out again, to resume her place on the curbstone.

'I guess he decided to come after lunch,' Hortense said.

The afternoon grew late. The trains arrived and departed, but the Prince of Wales did not come.

'I think it's going to rain,' Ruth said.

'Then we'll get umbrellas,' Hortense said furiously.

Once they were sure he must be in a shining limousine coming down the street from the station. They stood up, their hearts banging, their mouths dry. But it was only an old man in solitude behind the chauffeur.

And then it was really late. It was the end of the day.

Finally Hortense said, 'It's time to go meet Daddy,' and they knew the Prince of Wales would not be coming.

The sisters, in their party dresses and straw hats, walked slowly down the street, so troubled they could not speak. They could see their father's train pulling into the station. They stood at the corner where they always met their father, and stared in final, desperate hope at the line of cars that sped past them.

Their father came, and they kissed him dumbly. He noticed that they were all dressed up. 'Who had a birthday party?' he asked as they were walking home.

'Nobody,' Hortense said in a very small voice.

'Who practised the longest today?'

No answer.

'And is the fiddle still in one piece?' he asked Marjorie. She had begun lessons the previous winter, and it already had cost their father three violins, because Marjorie left her violin anywhere, especially on chairs people sat in.

She nodded, not speaking.

As they came to the curbstone in front of their house, where they had kept their vigil, they all started crying.

'He didn't come,' they sobbed. 'He didn't come. He didn't come. We waited, and he didn't come.'

They fell on the couch in the living room, with their hats still on and their tears spilling down the wilted party dresses.

'Who didn't come?' Their father looked hot after the day in the city.

'The Prince of Wales. We were going to get The Fortune, and he didn't come.' The sobs were as loud as the words.

All the way home in the hot, dusty train he had seen the cool shower that would be waiting for him, the fresh clothes, the iced drink on the porch before dinner. He sighed and loosened his tie and faced the unfathomable distress of these children for whom he was responsible. And he did not know what to do. 'Try to tell me,' he said.

How does a man comfort three weeping daughters? If they fall down and bruise themselves, you pick them up and bandage the bruises — not as their mother could have done it, but you can do it somehow. But what of pain that makes them sob like this, as if the world were lost? What do you do? You don't have enough arms to put around the three of them.

'Try to tell me,' he said, and took Marjorie on his lap because she was the youngest.

At last it began to come out. Between sobs, the whole years-long expectation that had led them to sit on the curb all day in the sun, in their party dresses and Milan straw hats, played itself out to him, like a music box exhausting itself.

It was so absurd that he wanted to laugh.

'We were going to surprise you. When you came home, we were going to show you The Fortune. And the papers *said* he was coming to Cedarhurst today,' they cried heartbrokenly. 'You read it, too.'

'Oh, but, children — ' Yes, last night they had poked the news item under his nose. He should have said something then. But how was he to know what crazy notion they had taken? 'How do you ever know what is going on inside their minds?' he thought in despair. That story of the fortune — it was just a silly bit of family lore; every family has something like it that's good for a laugh. The children had asked him about it now and then, but he had not thought anything of it, had not dreamed they were taking it to heart. 'This time it's the fortune,' he thought, 'and next time it'll be something else, and how can I know what I'm supposed to do?'

He had to say something now. 'Children,' he said, trying to go as gently as he could, 'maybe he drove down by car. Anyway, I don't think the Prince of Wales could have done much about the fortune. Really. You see, children — ' wishing he were a teacher, someone who knew about children; afraid every moment of setting off another round of sobs — 'it's like this. If everybody who claimed to be the niece of a rich man got his money when he died, without having to prove she was entitled to it, why, then everybody would be doing nothing but taking money that didn't belong to them,' he finished weakly.

'But we really are his nieces.'

'But we haven't any way of proving it.'

He took out a handkerchief and helped Marjorie blow her nose.

'How would you like to go for a ride after dinner? I *think,*' he said, looking around at them, 'we might even drive to Hempstead for some ice cream.'

Oh, once in a while after that the sisters spoke of The Fortune. Like saying, 'He stole our money,' when they saw a newspaper picture of Sir Montague Norman, head of the Bank of England.

And there was the time years later when their father was going through old papers and came across one he handed to them. Hortense's baby picture had faded almost to daguerreotype dimness. Yes, it really did say, 'Infant heiress to diamond fortune.' But it was followed by a question mark. And it said, 'No documentary evidence can be furnished.'

Long after it had any meaning, they read Black Sheep's name, the one he had given himself when he changed it. It was the same as their butcher's. It was Meyer. The yellowed clipping said that he had been disowned by his family because they did not approve of his marriage; that he had refused to bear his father's name. (But what was his father's name? That was the door Black Sheep had slammed for all time), and had gone to Bavaria as Joseph Meyer and made a fortune as a brewer, and from there had migrated to the Transvaal, where he had amassed a greater fortune in the ivory trade and diamond mines; and that he had died intestate.

'He made *beer,*' Hortense wailed.

'The Black Sheep—' ignoring the Meyer—'must have loved that girl an awful lot.' Ruth sighed with delicious melancholy. 'Like Héloise and Abelard.'

Their fathers' name was mentioned as a supposed heir, but the list of supposed heirs included many other names.

'I thought we were the only heirs.'

'Lord knows how many there are. Hundreds, probably,' their father said. And he laughed. The girls laughed, too, a little hollowly.

'It's a gyp,' Marjorie said.

That was the end of it. Anyway, The Fortune had ceased to be part of their lives. When Ruth entered high school, she could not associate with Marjorie, and Hortense was making dates with boys and had little to do with Ruth.

In time they have come to tell it, as their father and mother told it, long ago, to company. 'Not a chance! Oh, well, it's a good story, anyway.' And everyone laughs.

*(From Today's Woman)*

# THAT'S THE MAN!

## BY MARY BRINKER POST

THEY had stayed later than they'd planned at the Boltons' party. Russell made one or two overtures toward leaving earlier in the evening, but Evelyn was having such a good time she only waved him away, pleading, 'I haven't been to such a nice party in months. Don't be stuffy and remind me how early we have to get up tomorrow.'

So he'd let her stay till she was ready to go, though he couldn't help thinking how hard it was going to be to catch the seven-fifty-five in the morning. He toyed with the idea of taking the eight-thirty-one instead, but that would make him late to the office and he'd only done that once, the time Terry was sick in the night and he'd had to get the druggist out of bed for a prescription.

Russell didn't like being late for work or appointments. He didn't like anything that interfered with the carefully planned, orderly pattern of his life. It wasn't that he was stuffy, as Evelyn sometimes kidded him. It wasn't that at all. He had a sort of, well, ideal, you might call it, of how he wanted to be.

A good, hard-working, orderly life was his goal and he thought he'd accomplished it. He paid his bills promptly, never overdrew his bank account, was in his pew every Sunday, never took more than two cocktails at parties, was a faithful husband and a kind, if firm, father. He and Evelyn belonged to two good clubs and their circle of friends, while not wide, was select and pleasant. Their children were charming and well-brought-up. The Kents were looked up to in the community and certainly that was well worth the effort.

'It's nearly two o'clock, Evelyn,' he said a shade reproachfully as they drove into their driveway.

'What if it is?' sighed Evelyn happily. 'I had a wonderful time, didn't you?'

'Well, yes I did. But it's going to be tough getting up at six-thirty.' He put on the brake, left the motor running, reached over and opened the door for his wife. 'Send Betty out right away, will you, dear?'

Betty was the fifteen-year-old sitter who lived on the next lane. Russell was always punctilious about taking the girls who stayed with the children home at night. Some of their friends let them walk up the lane alone, but Russell disapproved of that. The lane was perfectly safe, of course. In fact, the whole community was safe. There hadn't been a crime, outside of schoolboys breaking into summer homes or stealing a car occasionally, since the Kents had moved there. But still, Russell wouldn't want his daughter walking home in the dark and he didn't feel right about letting other people's daughters go home alone, either.

Betty got into the car, yawning.

'I'm sorry we kept you up so late, Betty,' he said.

She giggled. 'Oh, that's all right, Mr. Kent. I listened to the radio and then I took a nap on the sofa. Last week when I stayed with the Middletons' kids I didn't get home till three.'

'I'll pay you now, Betty. Fifty cents an hour up to midnight and sixty cents for the rest of the time.'

'Gee, thanks, Mr. Kent.'

Russell was always very fair about paying their sitters overtime after twelve. As a result of that and his care in taking them home, the Kents never had any trouble getting girls to stay with the children.

He saw Betty up to the door, waited till she was safely inside, then got into the car and started home.

It was a warm, August night and the moon was full. He drove with the window down, breathing the soft, fragrant air that smelled marvelously of meadow grass, honeysuckle and the Sound. The sky was very light and the moon shining through the trees cast a network of black, lacey shadows upon the lane. It reminded him of the night he proposed to Evelyn. There had been that white moon and the smell of honeysuckle and Evelyn's pretty, slender face, pale in the moonlight. Just before he came to their road he had a glimpse of the Sound, breathless and shimmering. His heart leaped at its unearthly beauty.

Afterward he couldn't explain why to anyone else, though it may have been because he was thinking about Evelyn and the days of their courtship, or because the party had overstimulated him, or because he'd been working too hard at the office and he needed to get alone for a few minutes, but he didn't go right home. Instead of turning off onto their road, he drove straight down the lane to the beach, and snapped off the engine and lights and sat in the car, gazing at the water under the spell of the great white moon. The tide was out and the beach was pure silver. Far out, ripples caught the moonlight in a glittering net that dazzled the eyes. The night was utterly still. The softly moving water made no sound as it pushed gently at the sand.

Russell had the curious feeling that he had stumbled upon a secret and mysterious scene, a hidden life that went on when human beings were safely in their beds. There was something compelling and haunting in the moon-washed beach, the dancing ripples, the dark waiting trees along the shore. It was almost as if there were a Presence there, something powerful and unknown, that held all the earth by shimmering, silver strings.

He didn't know how long he stayed, mesmerized by the scene, but at last he turned on the ignition and swung the car back up the lane. He was conscious of a vague feeling of unrest and longing as he drove into the garage and went into the house.

Evelyn was already in bed when he came up and she lifted her head from the pillow and stared at him. 'For heaven's sakes, where have you been? What took you so long? You've been gone nearly an hour.'

He was still under the spell of the moonlight and he didn't answer right away. He took the change out of his pockets and laid it on the dresser, along with his watch and keys, then began slowly to undress.

'Oh, well, if you don't want to tell me,' she said sulkily.

'I wasn't anywhere,' he answered. 'I mean — I just drove down to the beach to look at the moon on the water.' He turned and smiled at her oddly. 'It was the most glorious sight.'

She laughed. 'What are you doing, going romantic in your old age? I thought you couldn't wait to get home and go to bed. Were you alone?'

He frowned. 'Of course I was alone. I took Betty home and as I was about to turn off onto our lane I saw the Sound. I don't know what made me drive down to the beach. But it was a sight worth seeing.'

He hadn't gone to sleep yet, he was still thinking about the moonlit beach, but he must have been in a sort of doze, because at first he didn't pay any attention to the knocking on the door. Then the knocker thudded again and the pounding began. Evelyn stirred beside him, got up on one elbow and whispered sharply, 'Russell, what was that?'

'Someone seems to be knocking on the door,' he replied, still not moving.

'Knocking? Goodness, they're pounding the house down. Who on earth can it be?' Her voice sounded frightened.

He threw off the covers, groped for his slippers. 'I'd better go down and see.'

'Be careful, Russell. Ask who it is before you open the door,' she cautioned.

He switched on the hall light, pulled on his bathrobe and went downstairs. 'Who is it?' he called, his hand on the doorknob.

'The police,' said a harsh voice outside. 'Sorry to trouble you, Mr. Kent,' apologized Sergeant Henderson, after Russell had opened the door and stood staring in amazement at the uniformed officer on the porch.

'But what is it? What do you want at this hour of the night, Henderson?' cried Russell.

'Just want to ask you a few questions. Can I come in?'

'Very well.' The Sergeant stepped into the hall and Russell closed the door. He turned on the bridge lamp in the living room and the officer followed him.

'Have a chair,' said Russell and Henderson sat down on the sofa. Russell took the armchair by the lamp and not until Henderson began firing questions at him did he realize it had been a mistake to sit there with the light full on his face.

'Now, what's it all about?' he demanded, offering the policeman a cigarette. Henderson declined and Russell lit one for himself.

As he glanced up over the match flame he noticed that the officer was staring at his hands. A vague disquietude began to filter slowly into his mind. 'Has there been an accident or something?' he asked.

'Well, not exactly an accident,' said Henderson slowly. 'I'll tell you all about it after you've answered a few questions. You don't object, do you?'

'To answering your questions?' snapped Russell irritably, wondering why the fellow was being so indirect. 'Certainly not, if I can. But I don't mind telling you I'm anxious to get back to bed. I have to catch an early train in the morning.'

'I'll be as brief as I can.' Henderson leaned forward in his chair and his eyes were fixed on Russell's face. 'When did you retire tonight?'

'About half an hour ago, I should say. Though I can't see what business it is — '

'You will. Please just answer my questions, Mr. Kent. I realize what a nuisance this is and it's really only a matter of routine. But we have to check all the angles. I'm sure you have nothing to worry about,' replied the officer calmly, still in an apologetic voice.

Russell stared at him and something queer and cold caught at his throat. Why should there be anything for him to worry about?

'Were you out tonight?'

Russell nodded. 'My wife and I were at a party at Vincent Bolton's. We returned home a little after two.' Instinctively a guarded note had crept into his voice.

'Did you go right home after returning from the party?'

'Certainly,' retorted Russell brusquely. He was annoyed at the uneasiness he was beginning to feel.

'H'm.' The officer studied his face for a moment. 'Then I wonder why, if you returned from the party a little after two, that the engine of your car should still be warm at three-thirty.'

'My car?' Russell shot him a startled glance.

'Yes, sir. We took the liberty of examining your car before getting you up.' Henderson was still regarding him with a keen, thoughtful look.

Russell felt his face flushing. A wave of indignation went over him. What right did the police think they had, going around at this hour, examining the cars of respectable taxpayers? He burst out in an offended voice, 'What's the idea, going into my garage and examining my car? What were you looking for?'

'Just checking on your license and finding out whether your car had been used recently tonight,' replied the officer deliberately. 'You say you came right home from the party and went to bed?'

Russell flushed, stammered. 'Well, I — I didn't go right to bed when I brought my wife home. As a matter of fact, I took Betty, the sitter, home after that.'

'Then exactly what time would you say you put the car in the garage?'

'Around quarter to three, I suppose.'

Henderson looked worried and puzzled. 'How far away does this girl, Betty, live?'

'Oh, just up the next lane.'

'Then it would take you not more than five to eight minutes to take her home and return?'

Russell snubbed out his cigarette, lit another. This time his hand shook slightly, though he willed it not to. Lord, he thought, what's the matter with me? I don't know what this bird is after, but I've done nothing to be afraid of. 'That's about right,' he mumbled.

'Then what were you doing between a few minutes after two when you took Betty home and a quarter to three when you admit you returned to your house and put away the car?' There was a curious triumphant note in the policeman's voice and his eyes probed Russell's face.

'Well, I — I drove down to the beach to look at the moonlight on the water. It's — it's magnificent tonight.' His throat was dry and constricted and the airy gesture he tried to make to put himself at ease didn't quite come off.

'I see,' said Henderson and got up.

'Look here,' cried Russell sharply, his nerves tingling. 'What *is* all this? Why are you shooting these questions at me?'

'I'll tell you, Mr. Kent,' said the officer in a grave voice. 'A girl was raped tonight over in the Eastwood section of town on her way home from a late party, and the man drove away in a Chrysler sedan. The girl got the license number and when we called Motor Vehicle headquarters it tallied with yours.'

'Good lord!' gasped Russell, sinking back into his chair.

'You certainly don't believe that my husband had anything to do with such a horrible thing, do you?' Evelyn had come downstairs in her dressing gown and stood white-faced and blazing-eyed in the doorway.

Both men turned to look at her as she swept into the room. Russell suddenly felt warm and confident again. 'It's ridiculous, of course, my dear. There must be some mistake.' He turned and smiled easily at the officer. 'Sergeant, you haven't answered my wife. Do you think I had anything to do with it?'

Henderson looked embarrassed. Obviously he disliked discussing such a case before a lady. He cleared his throat, said apologetically, 'Of course, I don't, Mr. Kent. I'm sorry to have bothered you, but I've got a job to do. Have to check all the angles. And what else could I do when the girl was so positive about the license?'

'She was probably hysterical,' said Evelyn firmly, 'and got the numbers wrong. At a time like that I don't see how she could possibly remember a license as long as ours.'

'It's possible,' said Henderson respectfully but equally firmly. 'Some people have remarkable memories for numbers.'

'Well,' said Russell, having got to his feet when Evelyn appeared, 'I hope I've answered all your questions to your satisfaction. And now if that's all, my wife and I really would like to retire.'

'I-I'm awfully sorry, sir, but there's one more thing.' The officer hesitated, looked at Russell.

'Well, what is it?' The fear that had been creeping over him had vanished when Evelyn came down. Her indignation and the patronizing way she'd put Henderson in his place had restored his confidence and brought back all his irritation at the intrusion.

'The girl is outside in the police car with Burke. Would you come out and let her take a look at you?'

Evelyn drew in a sharp breath. 'You mean that Mr. Kent should subject himself to an identification? This is most insulting. My husband is a respected citizen of this town. He is a family man, a taxpayer. I've never heard of anything so insolent.'

Russell saw Henderson's lips tighten. His voice when he spoke was edged, no longer humble. 'I'm sorry, ma'am, but the girl has been more than insulted. I wouldn't ask Mr. Kent to do this if I weren't sure he is innocent. I could simply take him down to the station and book him on suspicion.'

Evelyn gasped, gave Russell a frightened look. He laughed, put his hand on her arm. 'My dear, there's nothing to worry about. Of course, I'll go outside with you, Henderson, and let the poor girl take a good look.'

'Thank you, sir,' murmured the officer and he and Russell went out the door.

The prowl car was in the driveway and Russell waited on the porch while Henderson went over and spoke to the policeman in the driver's seat.

'Will you step over here, sir?' he called and Russell walked down and stood in the driveway. The car lights went on and he blinked as the full glare was focused on him.

The car door opened and a disheveled young woman in a torn white dress got out and came toward him. His heart began to pound and he realized he was holding his breath. The palms of his hands were wet with sweat as the girl stared up into his face with wide, tear-stained eyes.

'Well?' asked Henderson quietly. 'Is this the man?'

The girl hesitated, stepped closer, pushing the dark, tangled hair off her forehead with a trembling hand. 'I — I — ' she began. 'He was about that tall and blond — sort of good-looking like him. . . ."

'You've got to be positive, miss,' cautioned Henderson patiently. 'This is a serious charge to bring against a man.'

'Let me — smell his hair,' she whispered. 'He used a funny smelling hair lotion.'

Russell bent stiffly while the girl's face came close to his. Suddenly she shuddered and drew back, sobbing. 'Yes!' she cried, bursting into tears. 'He's the one. Oh, I'm sure he's the one.'

Henderson took her back to the car and then he walked over to Russell who stood frozen to the driveway, his heart suffocating him.

'I'll have to take you with me, Kent,' said the officer brusquely.

'But it's utterly ridiculous. I swear to you I never saw that girl in my life. I wasn't in Eastwood tonight. Everything I told you in the house is true,' burst out Russell.

'If it weren't for the license—' began Henderson, wavering. 'And the fact that your car had been out—'

'I explained all that and she's simply made a mistake about the license, got the numbers wrong,' cried Russell.

'Maybe. But she's positive you're the man. Tall, blond, good-looking. And then the hair lotion. I noticed it myself. It's got a very distinctive odor.'

'Other men use it. It comes from the men's shop at Saks. Any-body can buy it!' He knew he was babbling, losing control. He felt trapped, hemmed-in. His eyes darted instinctively for a place to run to. Henderson's hand was on his arm.

'You'd better go inside and dress. I'll wait downstairs.'

Evelyn jumped up from the sofa when they came in. Her eyes searched Russell's face in a questioning look. He couldn't meet her gaze. Suddenly he felt guilty, as if he really were the man. He started upstairs and she ran to him, grabbed his hand.

'Russell, where are you going? Why did Henderson come back in with you?' she cried.

'I have to take him to the station, Mrs. Kent. The girl has positively identified him as the man,' said Henderson.

'Oh!' moaned Evelyn and dropped Russell's hand as if it were a snake. Russell gave her a queer look and when she tried to take his hand again, he pulled it away. Now he felt completely alone. For one moment, at least, though she probably would never admit it, his wife had believed him guilty.

He went upstairs heavily, shut the door behind him and sat down on the bed with his head in his hands, trying to think what he should do. The feeling of being trapped began to suffocate him again and he jumped up, looking wildly about the room. There must be something he could do. Some way to escape. He went to the window and saw the police car in the driveway.

I'm acting like a fool, he thought. I've got plenty of friends in this town. They won't let a thing like this happen to me. Quentin Lewis—he's the one. I'll call him. Good old Quent. I did a favor for him once—put up his name at the Beach Club. He's got influence, he's in politics or something.

Russell grabbed the telephone directory, thumbed through it feverishly. It took a long time to get the number. The phone rang and rang and at last a sleepy voice answered.

'Quent? This is Russell Kent.'

The voice muttered something and Russell went on in a rush of words. 'I'm in trouble, Quent. There's been a fool mistake. I'm being arrested for something I didn't do. Isn't there something you can do to help me? You've got influence around here.'

'Are you drunk, Russ?' asked the voice irritably. 'Because if you are, go back to bed and stop ringing up people in the middle of the night.'

'I'm not drunk, Quent. You've got to listen to me. The police are downstairs and they're taking me to the station. A girl got my license number mixed with another guy's — the fellow who did it, and they're holding me. But I didn't do it, Quent. Anybody who knows me would know that.'

'What're they holding you for, Russell?'

'Rape. But, good lord, Quent, you know I didn't do that.'

There was a long pause and finally Russell said, 'Quent? Are you still there?'

'Russ, I'm sorry as the devil, but there's not a thing I can do on a charge like that. I couldn't monkey with it. But if it's a false arrest, why don't you call a good lawyer?'

'You won't help me,' said Russell bitterly.

'I don't see how I can. Awfully sorry, old man.'

Russell put down the phone while Quentin Lewis was still explaining how sorry he was.

As he dressed mechanically, with stiff fingers, he could hear Evelyn downstairs, weeping and pleading. And when he came down, ready to go, she flung herself on him, sobbing. He put her away from him gently. 'Call Vincent Bolton, he'll know what to do. He's not a criminal lawyer, but he's good.'

Russell spent the rest of the night in the town jail. When Henderson brought him into the station, the Chief, who belonged to the Gun Club and had often shot clay pigeons with Russell, looked at him as if he'd never seen him before. Russell had intended appealing to him on the strength of their acquaintance at the Club, but he was so stunned by the blank coldness in the Chief's eyes that he couldn't think of anything to say.

Henderson locked him into the narrow, bare cell that smelled of strong antiseptics and left him. There was a drunk in the next cell who kept yelling obscene songs and cursing. Russell didn't try to sleep and since they'd let him keep his cigarettes, he smoked endlessly, pacing up and down, trying to figure out what had happened to him and why. Just before dawn it turned cold, or at least it seemed so to him. He began to shiver and his hands were like ice, so he wrapped the one thin blanket around his shoulders and sat on the edge of the cot.

He couldn't figure it out at all and the harder he tried the more confused he got. It was one of those hideous mistakes, those gross miscarriages of justice that you read about — innocent men being executed and the real criminal going scot-free. 'But that it should happen to *me,*' he groaned.

No one had tried harder to be a good citizen, to live respectably and decently. For years he'd been building up something that he thought impregnable and beyond reproach — a good name, a solid position in the community. Now it had all crumbled through a fluke, a bit of circumstantial evidence and the word of a hysterical girl.

If he hadn't had the impulse to go down to the beach to look at the moon, the car motor wouldn't have been still warm and Henderson would have realized that the girl had made a mistake.

What does respectability mean? he asked the narrow walls. How much good is it, if at one false move it can fall to pieces like a house of cards?

He got up and began to pace again, trailing the blanket after him. He stared out the barred window at the shell-pink dawn, mumbling to himself, 'People are wolves, that's what they are, all ready to tear each other to pieces. How secure are we? Do we live in a jungle?' He gripped the bars until his knuckles were white and suddenly he began to weep helplessly.

Vincent Bolton came to see him shortly after seven that morning. He looked sleek, rested, well groomed. He shook Russell's hand warmly, but his pink, closely-shaven face was embarrassed and his eyes avoided Russell's.

'This is a terrible thing, Russ,' he boomed. 'I couldn't believe it when Evelyn called me. Sorry I didn't get down sooner, but there wasn't anything I could do till morning.'

So you went back to sleep, rolled over on your fat back, while I was sweating it out here alone, thought Russell, but he only nodded.

'I'll have you out of here before noon, old man. Just give me time to raise bail.'

Russell caught his eye at last, fixed him with a direct, steady gaze. 'Just tell me one thing, Vincent,' he said. 'You don't think I did it, do you?'

The lawyer cleared his throat, ran his tongue over his moist lips. There was just a fraction of a moment before he laughed heartily and cried, 'Of course not, Russ. Of course not. It's definitely a case of mistaken identity. Now don't you worry about a thing. I'll get you out of this.'

Russell nodded and turned toward the window. Vincent followed him and patted his shoulder.

It was afternoon when Vincent came back and took Russell home, released on bail. He got into the front seat of Bolton's car, pulling his hat down over his eyes and his coat collar up and staring straight ahead all the way.

Evelyn met them at the door and when she saw Russell she burst into tears and threw her arms around him. He patted her arm and murmured something, but he didn't return her embrace or kiss her. He went into the house, hung his hat in the closet and went upstairs to the bathroom to brush his teeth. He'd been longing to do it all day.

When he glanced at himself in the mirror, he got a shock. He needed a shave, his face looked pale and dirty and his hair was wildly rumpled. The eyes that looked back at him from the mirror were bloodshot, with purplish-like shadows under them and his mouth quivered nervously. I look like a criminal, he thought.

Evelyn fussed over him nervously, trying to make him eat, assuring him over and over again that everything would be all right, that Vincent would get him out of it.

'For heaven's sake, Evelyn,' he cried at last, 'stop fussing over me. And do you have to keep laughing?'

She went white and tears came into her eyes and he stamped upstairs and went to bed. Even there she wouldn't let him alone. She came and sat on the bed, talking to him in a low, conspiratorial voice. 'I phoned the office this morning, Russell. I just told them you were ill and might have to stay home for several days. Was that all right? I thought I'd better tell them something.'

He grunted assent and turned toward the wall. 'I want you to know, darling, that I believe in you. I never for a moment thought any differently,' she said. He wanted to laugh or to slap her. What about that moment last night when you dropped my hand as if it were a toad? But he only turned his head and gave her a long look until her eyes wavered and she got up and went out of the room. Then he pulled the sheet over his head to shut out the afternoon light and went to sleep.

He slept deeply and heavily and what wakened him was the telephone. He waited for Evelyn to answer it and when it went on ringing, he got up and answered it himself. It was Bolton and his voice was triumphant.

I told you I'd break this case, Russ. The girl admitted under prolonged questioning that she wasn't positive you were the right man. She even said she wasn't exactly sure she'd got the license numbers right. The police just picked up a fellow in a Chrysler sedan with a license the same as yours except for two numbers. He hasn't got an alibi for last night and Henderson is pretty sure he's the guy. He'd been drinking and he doesn't remember where he was or what he did last night. He admitted having stopped for a drink at the Eastwood Tavern, near where the girl said she was attacked. They're bringing the girl in to identify him now. I'll call you back after she's seen him.'

'Okay, Vincent,' said Russell, then added wearily, 'Thanks,' and hung up the receiver. He sat at the telephone, staring at the wall. He supposed he should feel gratitude and relief. No doubt Vincent wondered why he hadn't said more, praised him for his good work. The fact was, he didn't feel anything at all, just a complete and desolate emptiness.

When Evelyn came back from picking up the children at school, he told her and she broke into a wild torrent of weeping. She grabbed his hand and kissed it, crying, 'Oh, darling, I'm so glad, so glad. If you only knew what I've been through!'

He smiled wanly and pulled his hand away, pretending he wanted to light a cigarette. 'I can imagine,' he said.

The fellow the police picked up confessed after the girl had positively identified him and Vincent wanted to sue for false arrest. But Russell just wanted to forget the whole thing.

But you can't forget a thing just because you want to. The morning paper had carried the story of his arrest on a 'statutory charge' as the press so delicately puts it, and while his boss accepted his explanation, expressed sympathy for his ordeal and said forget it, Russell didn't get the promotion he'd been promised on the first of the year.

The week end after his arrest there was a big affair at the Beach Club, dinner and dancing afterward. The Kents had already been invited to make up a party at one of the tables.

'I think we should go, dear,' said Evelyn in the serious, rather gentle voice she used now. 'I mean, it wouldn't look well for us to stay away because of what happened. Then people *would* have something to talk about.'

He couldn't explain to her how he felt about people now — their friends, all the people they knew — the way he'd felt ever since that ghastly ride back from the jail when he'd felt everyone was staring at him.

'All right, Evelyn, if you feel we should,' he said.

'Well, Jane Brody phoned today to remind us we were sitting at their table, but I suppose it was really to find out if we were going. I had to say yes, of course.'

'Okay. Since it's all settled.' He didn't want to talk about it. He didn't want to think about it and sometimes for a short while he managed not to, but then something would bring it back into his mind and his palms would begin to sweat.

He dressed very carefully and deliberately the night of the party, as if by being impeccably groomed he could escape the stigma that seemed to him must surround him. For the first time in his life he wanted a drink badly. But he didn't take one at home. He felt the need to be clear-headed.

Evelyn seemed to sense the mounting tension in him, though he said nothing. 'After all, dear,' she whispered, as they walked into the Club, 'they're our friends, you know.'

He thought of how he'd asked Quentin Lewis to help him and been turned down. He thought of the embarrassed way Vincent Bolton had patted his shoulder that morning in jail. 'Yes,' he said, 'they're our friends.'

Evelyn went into the powder room to leave her wraps and put on another dab of make-up. Russell left his coat and hat in the men's room. A couple of men were there washing their hands and laughing at some joke. When they saw Russell they stopped laughing and glanced at each other. He didn't know them very well, but on other occasions they'd always spoken. He hung up his coat and hat and went out quickly.

Evelyn hadn't appeared yet when he came out into the club lounge. He saw out of the corner of his eye, Jane Brody glance toward him and then turn quickly and begin to talk animatedly to the woman beside her.

There were several men grouped around the fireplace and since it was a cool, foggy night, the fire felt good in the big drafty room. Russell went over toward them. He wondered if it was just his imagination, but by the time he got there, they had left their chairs and were moving into the dining room. Only Peter Knowles, a wispy little man who'd always fawned on Russell for some reason, was left sitting by himself, smoking a cigarette. Russell went up to him, carefully arranging a smile on his face. 'Hello, Peter,' he cried heartily, holding out his hand.

Peter looked up in surprise, not used to being sought out. 'Why — uh — hullo, Russell,' he said, smiling and blinking his eyes. Then, as if he'd made a social blunder, a painful blush spread over his face. 'How — how are you?' He looked everywhere but at Russell and when Russell sat down in the chair beside him, he suddenly glanced at his watch, tossed his cigarette into the fire and got up with a jerk. 'Excuse me, will you, Russ? I've got to make a phone call.' He had been too flustered to notice Russell's outstretched hand and, as if it were offensive, Russell instinctively put it in his pocket.

He sat alone, smoking, until Evelyn came looking for him. 'Come on, dear. Everyone's going into the bar.'

For a minute he didn't answer because he was thinking, I could walk out now, while they're all in the bar, and no one would notice. But then he saw how anxiously Evelyn was looking at him and he thought, No, it wouldn't be fair to embarrass Evelyn that way. So he went with her into the bar, taking her arm, not so much out of politeness as for the need to feel someone close to him.

Jane's party had taken one of the small tables and there was just room for them to squeeze in. Jane said brightly, 'Hurry up, we're already one up on you,' and the others smiled vaguely and went on talking to each other. Evelyn, with a woman's social aplomb, began to chat with the woman next to her, but the man beside Russell was Quentin Lewis and he only nodded to Russell and went on telling a story to the rest of the men. Russell sat sipping his cocktail and when the men laughed at Quentin's story, he laughed too, though he hadn't been listening. Since he wasn't talking much, he had several cocktails.

It was like that all through dinner, although now and then someone would say something to Russell, as if suddenly aware that he was at the party too. The food at the Club was always excellent, but he didn't know what he was eating and it was hard to get it down. When the dancing started, as soon as the tables were cleared, Steve Brody asked Evelyn to dance and Russell turned to Jane, but she was already stepping out with Quentin. The only woman left was plump little Mrs. Taylor and she carefully avoided Russell's glance.

He sat for awhile, smoking and watching the dancers, but when the orchestra played the same number over again and no one came back to the table, he cleared his throat and mumbled, 'Care to dance, Sally?'

For a moment he thought she wasn't going to answer, then she turned with a nervous smile and said, 'Oh, no, thank you. I—I think this one's a bit too fast for me.'

'The next waltz, then?'

'I—I'm sorry, Russell, but I promised the next one to my husband,' she answered and then got up abruptly, murmuring, 'Will you excuse me, please? I think I'll go powder my nose.'

Russell got to his feet when she did, but he didn't sit down again. He stood, gripping the back of his chair, fighting down an almost uncontrollable impulse to throw the chair at her, to tip over the table, to break furniture. His knuckles were white when he finally let go and slowly and carefully walked into the bar.

'Rye and soda,' he said to the bartender.

'Yes, *sir,*' replied the bartender cheerfully. He was a new man who hadn't been at the Club long. He didn't know the names of many of the members. With a curious feeling of relief, Russell realized that he didn't know him. He tossed off the small glass of whisky, held out his glass.

'Another, please. Make it a double one, this time.'

'Right you are, sir.' The bartender had a hearty Irish face, his voice was friendly.

The second whisky began to creep over Russell pleasantly, warming him, relaxing his tense muscles. He ordered a third, but this one he took slowly and then he began to talk.

'I suppose you're a hard-working fellow, trying to get ahead in the world,' he said to the bartender.

'Well, sir, I do my best,' he grinned.

'Pay your bills. Never beat your wife. Go to church. Get to work on time. All the rest of it.' Russell waved his hand.

'That's right, sir.'

Russell shook his head. 'Doesn't pay, Joe. Doesn't make a bit of difference. What is respectability? It's a house built on sand. It's a shell and if you touch it, it'll go to pieces.' He finished his drink slowly, then he gazed sadly at the bartender. 'Go ahead — work hard. Try to be decent and respectable. Make a place for yourself in the community. No good. No good at all. Want me to tell you why?'

He gave the bartender a long look. 'Because society . . . society is made up of wolves, just waiting for a chance to pull you to pieces. Think you're safe? You're not, Joe. Nobody's safe. Know why? I'll tell you why. Because we live in a jungle. A damned jungle.'

The bartender had a fixed smile on his face and he was looking over Russell's head. Russell turned and saw Jane Brody, Steve and the Quentin Lewises at the door, about to come in. They looked pained and embarrassed and Jane started to say something to her husband.

Russell laughed drunkenly. 'There they are, Joe. All my friends, my dear, dear friends. That's what you think. Know what they are? They're wolves. Wolves!'

He picked up his empty glass and threw it with all his might against the wall, shattering it. Jane Brody screamed and he saw Evelyn running toward him, her face white. He lurched away from the bar and there were tears in his eyes. 'Come on, Evelyn,' he said, 'let's go home.'

*(From '47 — The Magazine of the Year)*

# CARMENCITA

## BY WAVERLEY ROOT

BACK IN the early twenties, the uninhibited and unrepressed souls who made up the Paris edition of the *Chicago Tribune* gathered nightly in a dark and dirty *bistro* on the Rue Lamartine. There, across the street from the newspaper office, editorial workers and proofreaders, with an occasional stray from the business offices, met every evening for dinner, bringing with them the girls of their temporary choice. None of these young men had yet reached the point of marrying. Few had even acquired *petites amies;* those who had, owed that situation to the determination of the ladies rather than to any constancy of their own.

There was thus a heavy turnover in the feminine population of the *bistro,* or what might be termed a constant internal redistribution. To put it more bluntly, when one of the boys tired of Gaby or Elvire or Vivienne, another was very likely to inherit her. But sooner or later even those young ladies who enjoyed widespread popularity drifted away. The affairs that began there were strictly ephemeral.

Against this background, it required a considerable amount of amorous diligence for any one person to stand out. By common consent, nevertheless, Ray Farquharson did. The accolade was awarded him on no vulgar quantitative basis. After all, the sports editor had managed for a number of years to pick up a different girl every evening. Farquharson's distinction was qualitative. For him, each new affair was the one great love of his life. The average duration of his amours was about a fortnight, but while they lasted they were, every one of them, unparalleled passions.

In the throes of love, Farquharson was a man without memory. If, during one of his hymns of praise to the current favorite, he was reminded of similar words uttered a week earlier in praise of another, he dismissed the earlier with an offhand reference to puppy love. If you persisted in skepticism, he became really angry, with the righteous anger of the lover who is devoted unto death and resents the scoffing of baser souls.

Farquharson was older than most of his colleagues and the only one who, in that early period, was married. But his marriage weighed lightly upon him. Familiarity had finished by breeding not so much contempt as indifference. The current marriage was either his fourth or his sixth, the difficulty in assigning it a number resting in his own haziness as to which of his previous liaisons had been dignified by public authority. All except his last marriage had taken place in the United States. The final episode had been Parisian.

It was probably just as well that Farquharson had left America for a country where breach of promise suits were rare, where alimony was less easy to secure, and where neither public opinion nor police authority was ordinarily exerted to curb amorous exuberance. One theory current in the office was, indeed, that Farquharson had originally come to Paris for the sake of these advantages. The story ran that his ever-increasing obligations to pay alimony had finally outrun his income.

It was no secret that his French marriage had long since lost its savor, first for himself and, soon thereafter, for his wife. His reason for maintaining the fiction that he was married he explained by saying, during a lucid interval between affairs, 'What's the sense of my getting divorced? As long as I have one wife, I can't get hooked by another.'

The marital establishment also came in handy as a place in which to live between periods of sharing apartments with his successive girls. Setting up house with them was a measure of his sincerity, of his own belief in the genuineness of each new love. He was not only willing to try housekeeping with each new inamorata, but even willing, though chronically penniless and therefore seldom able, to pay for the necessary equipment. Unfortunately the bills usually continued to come in after the idyl had ended.

There was one occasion on which Farquharson only barely escaped having his marriage legally dissolved, and another union, from which he would have found it difficult to slip out, fastened on him. On that occasion he made the mistake of becoming enamored of a young lady many cuts above his usual taste, one of a species rare in the Paris of that date, a woman lawyer. She was one of the few for whom he established a joint apartment, although in this instance, to be exact, the lady footed most of the bills. And this time his customary protestations of a desire for a divorce fell on the ears of someone capable of doing something about it. The woman advocate was well on the way to freeing, and re-caging, him before the affair ended.

It was a near thing, for Farquharson's plans had become so definite that a date had been set at which he was to be introduced to the young lady's innumerable and strictly old-fashioned relatives at a formal dinner. It was probably dread of this ordeal which caused Farquharson, no very sober individual at best, to overindulge to such an extent that he wound up in a suburban railroad coach at almost the exact hour set for the dinner. Stumbling out of the train at the next stop, he telephoned his intended that he had just discovered he was in Versailles and would be a trifle late for dinner. On leaving the phone booth, he realized that he was actually in St. Germaine-en-laye. This so unnerved him that he never got to the dinner at all.

Undiscouraged, the girl covered up for him by telling her family a story of sudden illness, which they pretended to believe. The dread of marrying irrevocably into an orthodox French family probably also accounted for the sudden cooling of Farquharson's affections and his abrupt departure. A wandering American promoter had turned up in Paris as shepherd of a dance marathon, which had just proved a resounding flop in France. Anxious to try Spain, he engaged Farquharson as publicity man, and Farquharson, quitting the paper briefly, took off for San Sebastian, leaving with only an abbreviated note to the sharer of his home.

A few of the wanderer's artful love letters came through, but at increasingly greater intervals, and finally ceased altogether. Fighting the realization that she had been jilted, the girl appealed to Jim Plant, the news editor of the paper, to write to Farquharson. But before he had time to write, Plant received a letter from Farquharson. It appeared that the rover had met in Spain the great passion of his life, the one woman to whom he could cleave until death did them part. This, at last, was the real thing! The reason for the letter itself was a request that Plant do a little job of amatory arson and burn Farquharson's bridges behind him — in short, break the news that the Paris affair was over.

Plant had little taste for the assignment, but he finally called at the lady's apartment — formerly hers and Farquharson's — and broke the news as delicately as he could. There were, as he had anticipated and feared, tears. Never a man able to resist feminine weeping, Plant found himself lending the girl enough money to go to Spain to win Farquharson back. But a little later in the evening he also found himself consoling her in the classic fashion. The project for a trip to Spain somehow lapsed. The lady lawyer did not offer to return the loan, but Farquharson's ex-apartment came in handy, and considering one thing and another, Plant did not regret the outlay.

Meanwhile, it had not taken long for the American promoter to discover that Spain agreed with France about dance marathons. Farquharson, after previously wiring for (a) his old job back, and (b) a sufficient advance to pay his fare, returned to Paris. For a time, curiously enough, he exhibited a certain coldness towards Plant, who, he seemed to feel, had somehow done him out of something.

But he did not return alone. He had brought back the great Iberian passion.

She was preceded by samples of Farquharson's pressagentry which made it clear why he had been picked for the job of trying to persuade Spaniards to abandon bullfights for dance marathons. The girl was, Farquharson explained, a member of one of the most aristocratic families of Spain. The details of the story were vague, but one gathered that courting her had involved running the gauntlet of a host of duennas. The couple's departure had involved not so much an elopement as an abduction. Farquharson was not sure that the police weren't looking for him in Spain; he was certain the girl's brothers were.

The girl, when Farquharson's colleagues finally got a look at her, did not appear to live up to the advance billing. If one could overlook the fact that she was more than a trifle over-padded, one might have called her voluptuous. She might have been considered the baby-face type had it not been for her make-up, which in thickness was more likely to remind one of a Van Gogh than a baby. The rouge was brilliant, the lipstick was a wild-colored crust, and a question-mark of jet black hair lay coiled on her forehead, to which it was apparently glued.

The most alarming feature about her, however, was her eyes. The lids of these were weighted down with a coating of green paint so thick that merely looking at them fatigued the average beholder. The brows were imbedded in mascara, and each separate eyelash was so thickly embalmed in the same substance that there was a minute bead at the tip of each. The general effect was that of an actress about to appear in a stadium seating 40,000 persons.

Her name, inevitably, was Carmen.

Her appearance invoked a variety of skeptical comments concerning Farquharson's account of her origin. To all these he retorted heatedly, adding details of her exalted lineage. Knowing that none of his colleagues had been to Spain, he maintained that the heavy use of cosmetics was normal among pillars of society there, and attributed all slurs on Carmen's gentility to her critics' ignorance of Spanish standards.

Firsthand bulletins on the habits of Carmen, all unfavorable, were soon available, for Farquharson, with what may have been either *jemenfoutisme* or malice, established himself with his Carmencita in a hotel room just across the courtyard from another he had occupied, three romances back, with a member of the editorial staff, Edna Keen. Edna was still living there. As neither Carmen nor Farquharson ever appeared to discover that their windows were provided with shades, Farquharson's ex-favorite could provide a blow-by-blow account of the Carmen-Farquharson romance—which she did with relish.

Blow-by-blow seemed to be an exact description, for almost all of the private contacts of the couple were of a belligerent kind. The fortunate occupants of rooms whose windows were located at the proper angle across the court enjoyed almost daily the sight of a display of Spanish temper accompanied by the crash of crockery. From the stage of throwing (on Carmen's part) and dodging (on

Farquharson's), the pair progressed regularly to in-fighting, in which Carmen used all the weapons with which nature had endowed her — principally nails and teeth. This phase of the combat ended ordinarily with Carmen reduced to immobility by being pinned down on the bed by Farquharson's slightly greater weight. This was not the final stage of such encounters, but it is the last which may be set down here.

A little later the two could be seen moving about again, Farquharson applying court-plaster to his face and Carmen restoring her make-up. Occasionally the tranquil and contented strains of a languid Spanish song would float from the open window.

Compared with the accounts of these set-tos, the more routine details of Carmen's life held less savor. The office knew, from its conscientious observer on the spot, that Carmen's life followed a regular pattern of sleep, applying make-up, fighting Farquharson, succumbing to him, restoring make-up, emerging briefly for dinner, and returning to sleep again. It realized that this was a full day, for it had been informed that in preparing her beauty for the outer world, Carmen devoted a full hour to each eye alone. But such items were greeted with not quite so much interest as were the accounts of the battles royal between Farquharson and his Castilian aristocrat.

When he arrived at work bearing the scars of honorable combat, Farquharson was wonderful fun to bait. One day he arrived with a sizable section of his cheek raked open by Carmen's nails. This rowelling had missed his left eye by not more than an eighth of an inch. Unabashed by the closeness of Farquharson's escape from becoming a one-eyed lover, the boys pounced upon him and the witticisms flew thick and fast.

'Goddamn it!' Farquharson shouted at last. 'What do you fellows know about love? None of you ever had a woman who loved you enough to scrape half your face off.'

In calmer moments, he would exhibit his wounds complacently, even boasting about the fierceness of the Spanish temperament, a fury which, he implied, was active in love as well as in combat. In this he was backed by Carmen, who explained to Edna Keen, in one of the few English sentences she ever managed to utter: 'In Spain, no fight, no love.'

She did not get even this far in French. In spite of having managed to pick up a few English phrases, mostly obscene, from Farquharson, she never succeeded in getting anywhere at all with French. Even Edna, who had no reason to love her and, indeed, did not, once took pity on what she decided must be her lonesome and boring existence, and went to the trouble of buying her a Spanish novel.

Carmen responded queerly to the gift, failing even to thank Edna for it. Edna ascribed this to the absence of any common language, and thought no more of it. That is, she thought no more of it until the day when she found herself entertaining a friend who spoke Spanish. Feeling that it would relieve Carmen's loneliness if she could meet someone who knew her language, Edna suggested that they visit the Spanish girl. When they entered Carmen's room, they found her seated before her dressing table, about to start work on her second eye.

Very quickly the two girls exhausted the ordinary subjects of conversation. Falling back desperately on the first thought that came into her head, Edna asked her friend to inquire how Carmen had liked the book she had given her. Carmen hesitated for a moment. Then she replied in a voice pitched far below her usual strident tones. The interpreter relayed her information to Edna in a tone of surprise: 'She says she can't read!'

'What?' Edna cried. 'Can't read? What does she mean?'

'She doesn't know how,' the interpreter explained. 'She never learned to read or write. She says she comes from a very poor family. She never went to school.'

'So *that's* his aristocratic lady love!' Edna exploded. 'So *that's* what he sneaked away from a duenna! . . . No! there's something wrong. It can't be! I know she gets letters from home and answers them. Ask her how she does that if she can't read or write.'

The interpreter asked the questions and then explained: 'She goes to the Berlitz School. When she gets a letter, she takes it there. They read it to her and she dictates the answer.'

Carmen spoke up again. The interpreter listened and then said: 'She says she has one now. She doesn't want to take it there because the last time she was ashamed. She wants to know if I will read it to her. Should I?'

'Oh, boy!' Edna exulted. 'Should you? I wouldn't miss it for worlds!'

The letter was from Carmen's family. It bewailed the fact that señor Farquharson, who had made such generous promises when he was in San Sebastian four months ago, was now three months behind on the forty pesetas per month he had promised them in exchange for the companionship of Carmencita. If he could not pay, would he not at least send her back, so that she might again help support her large family?

With whoops of glee, Edna broke into the office half an hour later to blast forever the fable of Carmen's noble birth. Since Farquharson was broke, as always, the staff raised the money to ship her back to Spain and also to pay off, along with a little interest, the arrears in the rent charged for her person.

Farquharson was not angry at this intervention in his personal affairs. He had just become interested in a dancer at the Moulin Rouge. This time it was the real thing.

(*From Story*)

# THE TRAGEDY IN JANCIE BRIERMAN'S LIFE

## BY DOLPH SHARP

I *THOUGHT* it would be a lucky thing for Banjy and me that Jancie was already in love with Rudolph at the time we got our movie machine.

Mama once said, 'She'd be so happy if he would only spit on her, but he can spit on Mae Murray, he can spit on Pola Negri. Why should he come spit on Jancie Brierman, fifteen years old, who goes to Stogstead High School and seldom helps her mother with the dishes?'

So I said to Jancie, 'You know what I got for my birthday?'

'I know.'

'You really ought to see our movie, Jancie, one of these nights, if you can manage to stay in.'

Jancie got a real allowance every week. She blew it all in on stuff like face powder and ice-cream sodas and magazines and she never saved a penny.

'What do you mean? Everybody's always kicking about me, even the kids. To satisfy them I would have to live in a prison. You'd think I wasn't entitled to any freedom or the pursuit of happiness.'

I tried to get her back on the subject. 'But these movies, Jancie, they're as good as the Fulton Theater.'

'Oh yeah? It's probably cowboys and horses.'

'It is not,' said Banjy. 'There's only one cowboy and he doesn't go anyplace.'

That Banjy! It was the 'unending continuous strip' that came with the machine and went around and around so the horse kept galloping.

'As soon as we can I want to get one of those Rudolph Valentino pictures.' I was watching Jancie's face.

It got white like she had put on too much powder. 'What are you giving me, Rudolph Valentino? That kid machine—'

'Huh,' I said to Banjy, 'some kid machine. Every kid should only have such a machine. That machine will show anything. Jancie, we want to make *The Brierman All-star Theater of the Cinema* a real good place.'

'Who's stopping you?'

'We just thought maybe you'd like to help us.'

'Why should I? I got enough expenses without bothering with kid stuff. There's something very essential—'

'Gee, Jancie, I think a real movie picture of Rudolph Valentino would be better than just pictures from magazines pasted into a book.'

Jancie jumped up and grabbed me by the sides of my face. She looked into my eyes so that I couldn't tell a lie without her seeing it, and she yelled at me, 'What have you kids been doing in my room? Didn't I tell you kids never to go into my room?'

I tried to pull her claws off. 'Lemme go, Jancie! It's my room too!'

'And mine too,' said Banjy.

'But you're not supposed to get into my dresser!' She sat down at the table and began crying a little. 'When am I ever going to get a room of my own where I can have some privacy? When am I going to get rid of these damn kids?'

Mama stuck her head out of the kitchen. 'Act your age, Jancie. You think I like being crowded in this house? And they're not damn kids. Don't make such a solemn occasion.'

'We weren't really sneaking, Jancie,' I said. 'Why don't you see our movie sometimes? We need music. You could play.'

Jancie wiped her eyes. 'Can you really get pictures of Rudolph, Davie?'

'You can get anything,' I told her, 'Charlie, Bill, Douglas, Mary, Richard, and Rudolph. It costs a penny a foot.'

I could see Jancie was figuring it out. Then she shook her head.

'I'd like to help you kids out, but I'm saving up for something.'

'For what?'

'Oh, just for something.' She wouldn't tell us.

'O.K., Jancie, whenever you're all saved up, let us know. Then we'll get some real pictures of Rudolph into this house.' I started to go out. It couldn't be powder or magazines or other crip-crap because she got those all the time. It must be something important.

'Davie.' Jancie called me back.

'Yes?'

She stood up and got her pocketbook. 'Here's five cents I can spare. Buy five feet of Rudolph Valentino.'

I grabbed my head. 'Five cents! You couldn't buy a pig's whistle for that. You couldn't buy a smell. Twenty-five is the littlest you can get.'

She was thinking it over. She closed her pocketbook. Then suddenly she nodded her head, opened up the pocketbook again and counted me out twenty-five cents. I saw all she had was a few pennies more. 'I'll just have to save a little harder. Get the Valentino and let me know when you get it.'

Mr. Blitzen was leaning on the glass counter over the boxes with pictures of kings on the inside.

I started putting out the money on the counter. 'We'd like some movies.'

'This is not a theater,' he spoke slowly, still dreaming. 'It is a cigar store. Maybe I could interest you in a cigar?'

Couldn't he see we were only kids? 'You know, we bought the machine here. You got movies for sale, not like in a theater, but to show. . . .'

He swept the money all into one pile and then into his hand. 'What do you want, comedy or drama?'

'Rudolph Valentino.'

'Listen to him, he wants Valentino! The biggest of the day. It don't work that way. How can I tell what you get? You know and I know, the big companies, they cut up old pictures into cans. Maybe some is Charlie Chaplin, maybe some is Mary Pickford, but after all this is not their main business. All they stamp is *comedy* or *drama*. We ought to be thankful for that. They could stamp nothing. If you want something like Valentino, all you can do is take drama and keep on trying. What do you want?'

'Charlie Chaplin,' said Banjy.

'Give us drama, then,' I said quick, 'but could we have it with words?'

'Douglas Fairbanks,' said Banjy.

'With twenty-five feet you want words? Words don't come with less than a hundred. You got a dollar?'

As we went out, he said, 'When you got a dollar come back for the picture with words. And keep on trying for Valentino.'

Jancie stayed home that night. She even helped Mama with the dishes.

'Are you sure it's Valentino?' she asked. 'I wonder what picture? *The Four Horsemen of the Apocalypse, The Conquering Power, Uncharted Seas, Blood and Sand, Beyond the Rocks, Monsieur Beaucaire, Camille, The Sheik?* That has a wonderful sense of restraint and emotion of which he is a master in it. He's wounded, rescuing her, and they think he's going to die, but he doesn't let anybody know how he's suffering, and he tells her . . .'

'Tells who?' asks Mama.

'Agnes Ayers. She's a white woman. He's kidnaped her into his tent, and she can't stand him because he's dark-skinned. Of course, nobody knows he's really the son of an English duke. I think they could have done better than giving him Agnes Ayers, but he was just wonderful. I hope it's that scene. I think it's still my favorite. I could see that scene over and over. It couldn't be *The Son of the Sheik*. That just played in New York. He made a personal appearance, and he's going to do it in Brooklyn too.'

I didn't know what to say to let her know that it might not be Valentino. I began piling the rest of the dishes and Banjy helped me. In one trip you could take them all into the kitchen. 'Lazy-man's load!' yelled Mama. 'Stop it or there won't be no show! If I wanted to break them I could do it right away and save time. A stitch in time breaks everything.'

'Those kids are smart,' said Jancie. 'They make so much trouble you never make them work.'

'Jancie,' said Mama, 'you ain't so dumb yourself.'

'We want to help with all our heart,' I said, 'only nobody ever lets us.'

'With all our heart,' Banjy said after me.

'They tell the truth. The heart is good only it's covered with bad flesh, and the fingers are smeared with butter.'

Jancie corrected her, 'You mean, *The spirit's strong, but the flesh is weak*. That's from the Bible.'

'Yes,' said Mama, 'that's it. And the fingers are smeared with butter.'

The steam was rising from the dishpan and Jancie was poking around with the brush on a stick. 'You sure it's Valentino?' she said. 'I can hardly wait to see from what picture. I just know I can recognize it right away. There's a wonderful scene of heart-breaking tragedy in *Blood and Sand*. He's spent the night at the farmhouse with the wealthy widow, Nita Naldi, who pretended her carriage broke down. She's the other woman. You wouldn't think he could care for someone like that. And then his wife, Lila Lee . . . she's really ugly. . . .'

'Jancie, it's not their main business.'

'What is not whose main business?' Jancie stopped washing and looked at me, squinting down her eyes to half size.

'You know and I know, the big companies, they cut up pictures. They only got two kinds of cans—'

'Is it Valentino or isn't it Valentino?'

'Stop yelling,' said Mama. 'It's Valentino, it's Valentino. Maybe he'll spit on you.'

'Jancie,' I said softly, *'it's* a drama.' Well, I did my best.

So we all went in and sat down. Jancie was at the piano.

'Lights,' I yelled.

'Lights,' yelled Banjy, and they went out.

First I put in the slide from Papa's store and made it clear. It showed a picture of two men pulling a pair of overalls and underneath it said, 'You Can't Tear a Pair of Bim's Overalls.' Then there was a blank where you could write the name of your store in.

Mama clapped very loud. 'It's just like a real theater,' she said.

'Do we have to sit through all this junk?' asked Jancie.

'It's only your living,' said Mama. 'For shame on you.'

'The best part comes last, Jancie. Why don't you play?'

'Yes,' said Mama, 'play music. Something sweet.'

So Jancie began playing *Rock of Ages Let Our Song.* In a way it kind of fitted.

The next slide was a picture of a great big shoe and it said, 'Gripwell Work Shoes, You Can't Wear Them Out.'

Mama said, 'So you wear them in.'

'And what kind of music would you like for this one?' asked Jancie. She was making fun.

'A marching song would be good,' said Mama.

So Jancie played *Tramp, Tramp, Tramp, the Boys Are Marching, Cheer Up, Comrades, They Will Come.* Jancie knew a lot of music.

Then we showed the unending continuous reel. The cowboy began riding on the horse and didn't stop.

'I've sure seen this one before,' said Mama.

Jancie began playing real good riding music. It was just like the Fulton Theater, *dar-a dar-a dar-ara ra.* But I kept it going so she began playing *The Sheik of Araby, Your Love Belongs to Me.* It went good. It was horses galloping over the Sahara and you feel it in your blood.

'How long does this movie go on?' asked Jancie.

'It could go on all night,' said Mama.

'Not with me around.' Jancie stopped playing.

'Lights,' I yelled.

'Lights,' yelled Banjy and they went on.

I put the new one on the machine and announced, 'And now the big picture of the evening. Rudolph Valentino.'

Jancie played like trumpets on the piano.

'I only hope it is,' I said, but Jancie was playing louder than ever *Your Love Belongs to Me, At Night When You're Asleep, Into Your Tent I'll Creep.* Mama didn't like that song much.

And then it came on the screen. Jancie stopped. I pulled the nose out until it got clear. There was a man sitting by a table. You couldn't tell yet if it was Valentino because he had his head bent down into his hands like he couldn't hold it up. His shoulders were shaking and he had a glass of beer in front of him.

Jancie said, 'I thought it was going to be Valentino.'

'Maybe yet,' I said. I felt bad for Jancie. Suppose it wasn't, how would she feel?

Jancie began playing *It's Three O'clock in the Morning, And We Danced the Whole Night Through.* That Jancie sure could play.

Whenever she came to the middle part she would play four notes three times that sounded just like a great big clock striking. *Ding Dong Ding Dong There Goes the Three O'clock Chimes.*

The film rolled all out on the floor, the plain light showed, and the movie was through. Banjy turned on the lights.

Jancie just sat there, not playing, not saying anything. But it was only a minute. 'Is that all? Is that a movie? I thought it was going to be Valentino. You kids!' She was yelling now.

'Jancie, control yourself,' said Mama. 'Valentino, Schmalentino, it was a movie. A drunken man sat at a table and he couldn't hold his head up. There was a lot of work in it. Imagine what a man like that goes through.' She got up and started to lock up things for the night.

'You robbing kids,' screamed Jancie. 'You said it would be Valentino. Where's my twenty-five cents? I haven't money to throw out like that. I need money desperately.'

I didn't know whether to fly for my life or to stay and try to reason with her. I started moving but I wanted to stay friends with Jancie. 'Jancie, the man said it might be Valentino. There was only one way to know.'

'Well, why didn't you know then? Why didn't you?'

'The way was to show it. That's what Mr. Blitzen said. The only way. Keep buying it. It could be Valentino, it could be Mary Pickford.'

'It could be Charlie Chaplin,' said Banjy.

'But it wasn't!' cried Jancie. She was coming toward me, what for I didn't know. 'It was an actor I never saw, I never heard of.'

'You ought to be lucky,' said Mama. 'You know a new one.'

Jancie turned to her. 'There'll never be anyone like Valentino. This one is no actor, he's nothing.'

'He's worse than nothing,' said Mama. 'He's a drunk.'

Jancie got hold of me. I could of got away but God knows what she'd do to the machine. 'Give me twenty-five cents! False pretenses!'

'I ain't got a penny.' I didn't want to hit a girl, but I was getting mad myself. This was no way to act. It wasn't my fault.

That Jancie sure could get mad. She shook me so hard by the shoulders that my voice went uh-a-uh. I grabbed her hands, I kicked her shins. Banjy got hold of her leg. Then Mama grabbed

Jancie and pushed her in the face. Just then Jancie let go and began to cry. 'You always take their part. They pull a trick like that on me. I need that twenty-five cents. I'm desperately short.'

'So you'll kill people for it, your own brother?'

Jancie was just sobbing and she sat down on the floor. She almost sat on the film, the drama. When she noticed it, she grabbed it.

'It's mine,' she said, 'I paid for it. I can do what I like with it.'

'Look Jancie, you'll get your quarter back. As soon as we can save it up.'

'I don't want the quarter!' Now she was being like a devil. She tore the film in half. 'I think I like it better in two parts. It was too long.'

I was mad. 'Nobody will ever kiss you because you're a cold cup of coffee and you have no dignity.' In a magazine Rudolph Valentino said kissing a stupid woman was like a cold cup of coffee, and they ought to have dignity.

Jancie got up. 'It's mine. I can do what I want.' She closed the piano with a bang and started up the stairs.

Mama yelled after her, 'Take your movie with you, both parts.'

Banjy went to the piano. 'Let's break it,' he said. He would have, too.

'And I'll break you,' said Mama.

Before Jancie was all the way upstairs, Mama began talking. 'When she was in the carriage, people told me she would grow up to be a spitcat. At nine months a certain Miss Milikan told me choke her now or you will suffer all your life. Everything she wanted and when she didn't get something she would cry till she was blue in the face. Just roll on the ground and kick her feet. And always some kind of craziness. Lipstick . . . Valentino. . . . But you're good kids. Thank God I got you.' Then she changed the subject. 'You got to admit that movie didn't come to much.'

'Well, we only bought twenty-five feet. With one hundred feet you'd really see something. Even words. That's like in the real movies. It's what day it is and whereabouts and how many years since the movie started.'

'That cowboy picture, no words, and look how many years that can pass.'

'If we only had one dollar-buck.'

'Never be like Jancie,' said Mama. 'She's my own child, but I must say it though it breaks a mother's heart. Never satisfied, never helps her mother, one craziness after another, and her father's temper.'

Jancie stayed mad at us a whole week. *She* had a right to be mad! We were saving up to pay her back, though, so she wouldn't throw it up to us the rest of our lives. And then, one day we found her scrapbook. It wasn't in her bottom drawer or in the closet in the back underneath the rags. You'd never guess where. It was underneath the mattress. How do you like that! And from a piece cut out of the paper we figured out what she was saving for.

Jancie's book was a wonderful thing if you liked that kind of stuff. Banjy and me put it on the bed and looked through it. There was no counting the pictures. In one he was all undressed naked with only a little piece of pants and two feathers in his head and it said: *Why Not a Motion Picture of One of the Legendary Indian Love Tales. . . . With Rudolph Valentino as the Hero!*

'Shame, shame,' said Banjy.

There was one of him in a flat hat and baggy pants like balloons, dancing sideways with a lady in a shawl, only a picture of Jancie's face was pasted on the lady. Another was in a striped sheik suit, smoking a cigarette out of a long hose, and under it, it said in fancy printing: *'Pale Hands I Loved Beside the Shalimar, Where Are You Now, Who Lies Beneath Thy Spell?'* That was a song Jancie played too.

In another he was with a towel around his head and his eyes popping out at a lady he had hold of and she looked sick. Somebody made her look sicker with pencil scribblings on the face.

Then there were the stories about him and his sayings, so Banjy lay down and I read him one called *Phrenological Study of the Sheik*. It had a drawing of him with the head marked out into forty-two parts with each part something different like seven was *benevolence,* and I read: *'The head of Valentino — with its pyramidal structure combined with his somewhat heavy features, and the distance from his ears to the back of his head — place him at once in the physical-romantic type. His emotions are ardent but inclined to be short-lived because too intense.'*

'How do you like that kind of a guy?' I asked.

Banjy just rolled over and buried his face in the bed. 'I don't like that kind of a guy,' he said, muffled.

And there in the scrapbook between the pages of Valentino dressed up in a lady's white hair with his hands on his hips looking straight at you and Valentino dressed up in a Russian suit with a hat like a pot and a coat like a wooly bathrobe was where we found the piece cut from the newspapers.

*Brooklyn Premiere! In Person, The Sheik himself. The Greatest Lover's Greatest Picture! The Sheik is back! Watch out! His wild band is thundering down those luring moonlit desert sands! RUDOLPH VALENTINO, THE SON OF THE SHEIK! See it! See him!*

It was foolish to put all that money into just one night when you could buy over three hundred feet and see them to your heart's content. But anyhow, that's what Jancie was saving for.

Banjy and me opened up our barrel banks that only the First National was supposed to open and got our money out.

Jancie was sitting at the piano playing a very interesting song. *Sleepy-time Gal, You're Turning Night into Day, Sleepy-Time Gal, You Dance the Evenings Away.*

We stood alongside the piano until Jancie finished it once. Usually she started right over. And she had the right to complain about seeing the cowboy over!

She saw us, and while she didn't stop, she slowed down just playing the in-between part. 'When people play the piano, they don't like to be disturbed,' she said loud. The only way she talked to us yet was off of a wall.

'Jancie . . .'

'Mom!' she yelled, 'call your brats off!' and began playing very loud, *Just Give Me One Little Kiss, And Then Let Us Whisper Good Night.*

I slipped the eighteen cents on to the keys, a piece at a time. Jancie hit one penny and it went flying. She stopped. 'What's this?' Banjy picked up the cent and brought it back. He had to put it on a black key.

'We know you need money bad. We ain't got twenty-five cents, but maybe you can't wait. A stitch in time helps a little bit.'

She left the money right on the keys and kept playing right over it, softly. 'I'm sorry I tore your film.'

'That's all right. Maybe you ain't a cold cup of coffee.'

*Sleepy-time Gal, When All Your Dancing Is Through, Sleepy* . . . It struck up loud and then came low again. 'But you shouldn't have told me it was Valentino.'

'Jancie, we didn't.'

*I'll Build a Cottage for You. You'll* . . .

'You did. You said it was a drama with Valentino. You even said he would spit on me.'

'Jancie, I never. All they put on the cans is drama and comedy. If you keep buying drama long enough, some one of these days it will be Valentino.'

*To Cook and to Sew, What's More You'll Love It, I know* . . .

'Well, let's forget it.'

I held out my hand. 'Should we not shake hands?'

Jancie kept playing with one hand and shook with the other. She was very talented. *Stay-at-home, Play-at-home, Eight O'clock Sleepy-time Gal.*

Banjy had to shake hands too. 'Merry Christmas,' he said. It was the end of July and hot, but Banjy liked to say something sweet when he shook hands.

'Now we are friends again.'

Jancie sighed and stopped playing altogether and turned around on her whirling stool. 'Yes, we are friends, only don't pull any more stunts.'

'Why, Jancie, it was no stunt. We was hoping it would be Valentino as much as you.'

'Charlie Chaplin,' said Banjy.

'All right. Forget it.' Jancie put away the piece and got down another. *The Pal That I Loved Stole the Gal That I Loved; That's Why We're Not Pals Any More.* Jancie specialized in love and sadness. They were the same things, Mama said.

'We wouldn't give you the eighteen cents — and more — if we pulled stunts, Jancie. Jancie . . .'

'Yes?' She had to stop playing again. 'This friendship is going to keep me from perfecting my technique.' That's what Jancie was doing on the piano.

'Jancie, that money you are saving . . . you almost got enough?'

'I don't think I'll ever have enough.'

'Jancie . . . what else will you do in Brooklyn besides see Rudolph Valentino?'

She was so surprised she banged down on the piano with both hands like hammers and didn't play any more. 'How did you know I . . .'

'Why, Jancie, we was . . . how did we know what?' The piano was still ringing.

'Where did you find it? I thought I told you never to touch it. Take your filthy lucre!' And she swept the eighteen cents to the floor. Bad money was lucre.

Banjy began picking it up and putting it into his pockets.

'Aw, Jancie . . .'

'Don't *aw* me!' She slammed down the top of the piano. It made a crash and then a *nnnnnn* ringing that went on for a long time.

Mama came out of the kitchen. 'Who is wrecking the house?' she wanted to know, 'The piano?'

'Oh, those hyenas!' Jancie swore.

'Aw, like you say, you can't be good to Jancie. She's crazy.'

'She throwed the money on the floor but I picked it up,' said Banjy.

'Brothers! Sisters! Pots! Kettles!' cried Mama. 'Shame on you, calling yourselves hyenas! You're the oldest, Jancie, why do you act like such a Bronco Billy? If they do something bad, you teach them better.'

'When am I going to get a little privacy?' Jancie began crying. 'I can't even hide my personal belongings from these little brats. . . .'

'What personal belongings? What have you got that's so personal? Boys, what did you do?'

'It's Jancie's book on Valentino.'

'Under the mattress,' said Banjy. 'We happened to find it there.'

'Oh, Jancie, when are you going to get over being such a baby? And when are you going to get over ruining the bed? It troubled me why it stuck up so.'

Jancie spoke out, 'It's important to me. It's the finest thing I have in my life, something greater than myself, something pure. It is the only way I can survive in this madhouse!'

Banjy went to the piano and opened it up. Bang! he slammed it down, harder than Jancie. 'You crazy kids!' yelled Jancie, 'What are you doing?' Banjy was listening. Inside the piano was going *nnnnnm.*

Maybe Jancie would make it, but it was hard to see how. One week there was a new bottle of perfume and a *Photoplay* on her dresser, the next week a fancy pin for her dress and a *Motion Picture Classic.* We looked through both magazines and there were two spaces cut out. What else could it be and where else could it go? But you couldn't get to Brooklyn on that kind of business. Like Mama always told Jancie, 'You ain't cut out to save. You want to with all your heart, but you see a cripcrap and you can't resist it, so in the end you have lots and lots of cripcrap.'

And then one day, the papers said:

VALENTINO COLLAPSES IN APARTMENT
UNDERGOES DOUBLE OPERATION

Then for days it said he was grave, and Jancie was very worried. She could hardly eat and she didn't pay much attention to anything, and, I bet, she prayed a lot.

Then one day the paper said:

VALENTINO BETTER; PASSES CRISIS.

Doctors say the Screen Star is Now on Road to Recovery.
Patient Makes Plans for Convalescence.

And Jancie was so happy.

Two afternoons later Jancie came home looking like the cat dragged her in. Rudolph Valentino was dead.

Mama said, 'See, a beautiful face and body, he makes the girls, little ones and old ones, get hotsy totsy, but in the end, it's like anybody else. When it comes to being chopped down, ashes is dust.'

Jancie said, each word like a round pearl on a string, 'I shall always cherish the memory of the noblest of them all.'

'Cherish, schmerish. What you was doing is not cherishing, and if Valentino had to live on what you cherish, he might as well be dead.'

You would expect Jancie to raise hell because she had Papa's temper, but Jancie just suffered quietly like holy people when bad people come into the holy place and break things.

'Ha!' said Mama, 'Mrs. Bernhardt the Second. The tragedy of Jancie Brierman's life!'

Jancie's face was sad and gray. It was as if her heart was broken and she didn't want to go on because she had nothing to live for but she would live anyway in a dead sort of a way.

The next day Jancie went out to the Five and Ten to get herself some *Kolorit, black.* Then Mama was grumbling in the kitchen about telling papa, and Jancie was locked in the bathroom. We tried to peek in, a bad thing it was, to see what the heck she could be doing, but you couldn't see through that keyhole very well.

When Jancie came out and locked herself in the bedroom, you could see the sink was all black and there was some on the floor and the whole room was so steamy you could die. We looked through the bedroom keyhole but you couldn't make out much. Jancie was not crying the kind of crying you could hear, but you could feel that thick sadness.

At night when Papa came home, Mama asked him to do something to make that girl act reasonable. Papa ate through his dinner, reading the paper half aloud because it was too much news to read quiet.

'Three women commit suicide in grief over "sheik." Crazy women! Crazy Women!' he kept on saying.

'Crazy women, crazy women,' said Mama making fun of him. 'Never mind about the whole world. You got a crazy daughter upstairs.'

Papa gave her a look to keep quiet, and read another part.

Thousands in riot at Valentino coffin.

*More than* 30,000 *persons tried to get a two-second glimpse of the body of the great lover of the movies playing his last scene lying in state at Campbell's Funeral Church last night. As a result the police were wholly unable to control the situation for several hours. The police estimate that at least one hundred persons suffered injuries. Two large plate glass windows were smashed, and damage was done to the inside of the Campbell establishment.*

'She doesn't help, she doesn't eat, she carries on like a lunatic with some mysterious business all day long. What kind of father are you? Do something!'

Papa was so mad he shook his paper. 'What are you bothering me for! I haven't got time for craziness. It's your job, raising the children, and you spoil them! *Time after time during the afternoon a dozen mounted policemen were forced to charge the crowd, while women shrieked and yelled in terror and tried to scramble away from the horses' hoofs. Twenty-eight separate shoes were gathered up by the police at one time after the crowd had been driven back. In the midst of this tumult, women knelt in prayer on the cold wet pavement . . .* crazy women! Crazy women!'

Mama thumped the table six times. 'It's a father's place too. I can't do nothing with her. Why? Because she's a devil like you. You, go on up and lay down the law to her. Temper you got, but braveness no. What's the matter, are you afraid of her?'

Papa threw down the paper and Banjy got on his hands and knees to find the funnies. 'Aw, shut up! I ain't afraid of nobody! Do your own business! I got to go to the store.'

Banjy was reading *Boob McNutt,* but he still had to put in his two cents. 'Crazy women. All day she stays upstairs. Why is she so crazy? Does she still want to be spit on? Cold cup of coffee.' It was like he was singing a song to himself.

'You shut up or I'll give you a beating!' Papa yelled and he raised back his arm.

Banjy grabbed up the paper and ran out of there fast.

Jancie had to let us in the bedroom to go to sleep that night. We all lay in the hot dark with a mosquito zizzing around, she lay in her bed and we in ours. A long time went by and though she didn't make a sound I could tell she wasn't asleep. At last, 'Jancie,' I called to her, 'don't feel so sorry,' but she didn't answer anything and not long after that, she got up and went out.

I got up too and followed her downstairs, and Banjy followed me. It was too hot to sleep anyway, and we didn't need slippers or bathrobes. Maybe Jancie would run away forever.

The stairs creaked and the floor. I was afraid it would wake Mama.

Jancie was sitting at the white kitchen table in the yellow light cut out in the darkness, drinking some soda. I half expected that her hair would be white, but it was as black as ever. She was still wearing her white blouse and not in any black for the dead. Her face was fat like with the mumps and her eyes were puffed like bees stung them and red.

Quietly Banjy and me sat down on the other chairs. Nobody said anything. I got glasses and I poured Banjy a drink and one for myself. We drank up our milk and put the glasses down. Jancie was sobbing like she couldn't control it any more. It was so sad it made you want to cry yourself.

At last I said, 'Don't cry, Jancie, you can't help it,' but that made her cry all the more.

'Don't cry,' said Banjy.

'You can still go to New York as soon as you save up a little money. It ain't so much. You can even see him.'

Jancie shook her head. 'No. I want to remember—' but she couldn't finish because she was going uh-uh.

It was beginning to cool off and I was sleepy. 'Why don't you get yourself a good night's sleep, Jancie? Sleep makes the world seem beautiful. It's like a stitch in nine.'

We got up to go.

'Here,' said Jancie. She reached out something to me in her hand. It was a crumpled-up dollar-buck. 'Get a hundred feet. Try and get—' She had to stop awhile and take some breaths, but I knew. 'It will be a memorial. We can show it all . . .'

I shook my head and straightened the dollar out nice and smooth and laid it down on the table and flattened it there. It was a hard thing to say. 'It's a Chinaman's chance like a snowball in hell. Don't break your heart some more.'

'I don't care,' said Jancie, 'I won't blame you.'

'Boy, oh boy!' I yelled, and I went running over the floor, back up the steps to put the dollar-buck in a safe place. 'One hundred feet with words!'

Banjy came racing after me. 'With words! With words!'

Mama came out of her room in her nightgown with her hair all hanging down. 'Witch!' she yelled at Jancie who was coming up the stairs, 'now you got them crazy too.'

Jancie didn't say a word but went right into the bedroom.

During the night we could hear her sobbing in her sleep and the next morning we saw what Jancie had made black. There it was, hanging on the foot of her bed. Her underwear. That was really being remembering of the dead.

After that Banjy wanted to make himself some black underwear too, but I talked him out of it. It was a lot of trouble, Mama would only raise hell, and, after all, what was Valentino to him?

This time I put a whole dollar-buck on Blitzen's counter. 'One hundred feet, please, drama, and try to make it Valentino.' It was a very important moment.

'Valentino! I told you I can't tell. Look. They got two kinds of cans. Drama they put up in one can, comedy in the other. Not one word about Valentino. Not one word about anybody.'

'Mr. Blitzen, couldn't we just look inside the cans a little? We wouldn't make no mess, and we would put them all back. It's for our sister. Her heart's broken. Maybe she will die unless something is done, and the only thing that can help her is to see Valentino pictures over and over. Doctors can't help her any more. When we find a can with Valentino, we will buy it right away for cash.'

'I'd honestly like to help your sister out,' said Mr. Blitzen. 'I can see what's happening to women all over, older than your sister, smarter — if that's possible. They break in funeral-parlor windows. God knows what they'll do next. Do you boys have any idea? Now, about your suggestion, you can understand, being smart boys, once I explain. If I let one do it, everybody in town would come in and want to look at the films before buying. You'll be careful, but will the next? The pictures would get mixed up, scratched up, dirty, torn. I got kids of my own. Now, if that happened to my business, those kids would starve.'

It was so. It was just the way things were.

'I admit it's buying blind, but there's nothing else you or I can do about it. You want a picture, you pay your money and you walk out of the store and it's yours. One of these days you'll be nicely delighted and your sister will be cured to see Valentino making love on your wall. It might take ten years, but it'll happen — if any of us are still here.'

It was a hell of a big gamble, but we took it. And because we had twenty-seven cents left over, we bought Jancie an extra present.

That night we set up the living room. Jancie was there. She didn't sob or cry any more, but her eyes were sad and something in them said they would be sad forever. For all we knew, she was still wearing the remembering-the-dead underwear.

Mama said, 'It'll be like a ghost, him laying dead as a dog in the ground and here on our walls moving, eating, kissing.'

'Kish, kish,' said Banjy, laughing. 'Kish me on the mouth with a cold cup of coffee.' He always thought kissing was funny.

'Aw, Banjy, this is no time. Act your age.'

'And don't crawl,' said Mama.

'Jancie, will you play the piano?'

Jancie shook her head no. She still didn't talk much.

'Aw, come on.'

'Give them a break,' said Mama. 'You're going to see it anyway. What's a show without music?'

'If it's Valentino, I'll play for it.'

'Aw, Jancie, play from the start.'

She sat down at the piano.

Banjy passed out the *admit one* tickets. We didn't like to spoil new ones on the roll, so we used the same ones over each time.

'Lights.'

'Lights.'

It went dark, the machine lit up the sheet, and the first thing came on, the slide with two men pulling the overalls: *You Can't Tear a Pair.*

Jancie just said, 'Sweet God!'

'They always do this in the real movies, Jancie. It wouldn't be like a show.'

So Jancie began playing *Rock of Ages.*

Then we had the Gripwell Shoes with *Tramp, Tramp, Tramp.* Then the cowbody with *dar-a dar-a dar-a.* But we didn't run it long. We were anxious to see the new one.

Next came the twenty-five foot drama. We had to show it in two parts. The man sat at the table holding his head up.

'He didn't get over it. He's still drunk,' said Mama.

And this time Jancie played, *Show Me the Way to Go Home.* That Jancie sure knew a lot of music. But fast or slow, somehow there was a sadness in the music tonight.

And then, 'Lights.'

'Lights.'

'*The Brierman All-star Famous-Players Motion Picture Theater of the Cinema Incorporated* takes great pleasure in presenting the new feature picture, one hundred feet in length, a picture not only with pictures but also with words, one hundred feet with words. A picture that may turn out to be Valentino, the great movie actor of the movies who just had a sad experience but will live on in the hearts of people, especially girls. Lights.'

Mama clapped and Banjy joined in. 'He'll be a public speaker someday,' said Mama. 'Now, a hundred feet or Valentino — that is a question.'

Then the movie came on. It didn't start with words. A door opened in a dark house. The man wasn't such a young man. He wasn't Valentino, but you could never tell. Maybe he was going to meet Valentino.

Jancie wasn't playing at all now. She was taking deep breaths, anxious to see what it would be. The first time the picture really didn't need music. The excitement itself was enough.

There wasn't any words yet, but one hundred feet always had words. That's what Mr. Blitzen said.

The man came into the room and sat down on a chair.

'Next thing,' remarked Mama, 'he'll get himself a glass and start drinking.'

But he didn't. A little girl came running up to him. She was cute! She wore a little dress that came almost up to her belly, and she had long golden curls. The picture wasn't really golden but you could tell it would be.

'A darling!' said Mama.

The little girl came and stood against the man's knees. She looked up in his face with a shiny blue-eyed face. You could tell it would be blue eyes. And then the words came, nice clear white like-little-pearl words.

I read them over three times. Mama read them aloud: *'Why did you make my mother cry?'* Then she asked, 'Yes, why? Why should anybody make the mama cry? Let us see what he answers her, the loafer.'

The words went off and the girl was looking up into the man's face, but the man was not looking down into the girl's face. He was looking at a wall. He looked at the wall awhile, and then the last of the film rolled on to the floor and the pure light showed on the sheet to hurt your eyes like snow light.

Banjy turned on the lights.

'What? What?' asked Mama. 'It comes to nothing. Is that what they call a picture, a picture of one hundred feet? I was just getting interested what would happen next.'

There should have been more words for one hundred feet.

I was afraid Jancie would get real mad now, and tear the pictures up and endanger the machine. But Jancie just sat at the piano and softly and sadly she played *The Stars That Shine Above Will Light Our Way to Love You'll Rule This Land with Me. . . .* It didn't gallop. It was like the horses were dragging themselves home half dead.

'I'm sorry it wasn't him, Jancie,' I said. Jancie shook her head to show that it wasn't my fault, and she kept playing and playing like she was playing her heart out and she had a big heart. She only stopped when I gave her the present all wrapped up. When she opened it, it was a picture of Valentino with darkness all around and him looking out very mysterious, and below it was a poem. Jancie read it out loud:

*In Memorium, Guglielmi Rodolpho Alfonso Raffaelo Pierre Filbert di Valentina d'Antonguolla*

*By Margaret Sangster*

*His feet had carried him so very swiftly*
*Into the lands of wonder and romance*
*And yet, although they had traveled far, they never forgot to dance.*
*His lips had learned to speak a stranger language*
*His smile had warmed the wistful, lonely earth —*
*Yet fame had never taken from his spirit*
*The gift of mirth!*
*Although his eyes glimpsed bitterness and sadness,*
*They saw a dream that few folks ever see —*
*God grant the dream may tinge with lovely color*
*Death's mystery!*

The feeling in Jancie's voice made it beautiful, and the whole thing came inside a frame for twenty-five cents.

When Jancie finished, she looked at me through her tears. 'That's the sweetest thing anybody has ever done,' she said.

It was worth everything to hear her say that. I think her great sorrow had made Jancie a better woman.

*(From Harper's Magazine)*

# BEYOND THE GLASS MOUNTAIN

## BY WALLACE STEGNER

SOMEONE had left a funny paper in the booth, and while he waited with his ear intent on the regular buzzing rings, Mark let his eye follow the pictured squares. I know somebody that likes your new hat, Emmy, Kayo's balloon said, and Emmy's pleased balloon said, Well, for thirty-nine fifty they ought to, who is he? and Kayo's balloon said It's Beefy McGuire, he'd like it for his birdsnest collection, and on the fourth ring the line clicked and Mel's inquiring voice said, 'Hello?'

The voice was as familiar as yesterday, a voice whose wire-filtered flatness Mark had heard over telephones ten thousand times. The rising hairs prickled on the back of his neck; he felt as he might have felt if a door had opened and the face of someone long dead had looked casually out.

And he noted instantly, in refutation of his fears, that the voice was sober. He found himself leaning forward, grinning into the mouthpiece.

'Hello, you poop out,' he said. 'This is Canby.'

The old password came naturally, as if he were back seventeen years. In their college crowd everybody had called everybody else Canby, for no reason except that someone, probably Mel, had begun it and everyone else had followed suit. There had been a real Canby, a sort of goof. Now he was a CPA in Denver, and the usurpers of his name were scattered from coast to coast.

'Well, Canby!' the filtered voice said heartily. 'How's the boy?'

There was a pause. Then Mel's voice, more distorted now, beginning to be his clowning voice, said suspiciously, 'What was that name again?'

'Canby,' Mark said. 'Cornelius C. Canby.' He raised his head, grinning and waiting for the real recognition.

'Cornelius C. Canby?' Mel's thickening, burbling voice said. 'I didn't get the name.'

'It's a hell of a note,' Mark said. 'Your old friend Canby was here, and you didn't even get the name.'

Mel's voice was thick as glue now, like something mired down, except that on occasional syllables it fluttered upward like a mud-heavy bird, It was a maudlin, wandering, caressing voice, very convincing to strangers and drunks, and it always made any drunk his instant pal. *'Canby?'* it said. 'D'you say *Can*by? Cornelius Canby? Well my God. Wonnersnevercease. *Canby,* after all these years! Come on over here and shake my hand. Where are you? Hire a car. Wait a minute, I'll come and get you myself.'

'Don't bother,' Mark said. 'I can walk over in five minutes.' He grinned again into the mouthpiece. 'Are you at home or out at some bar?'

'Just down at the corner pub having a little drink,' Mel said. 'But I'll be home in minute, home quick as you are. Not far away.' There was another pause. 'What was z'name?'

Mark was beginning to feel a shade uncomfortable. The clowning was routine, but there was a point where it should have stopped. It left things uncertain. 'You stinker,' he said, 'this is Aker. Remember me?'

The drunken voice was an amazed buzz in the ear piece. Out of the buzz words formed. 'You mean Belly Aker, the basketball player, erstwhile holder of the Big Ten scoring record?'

'The same.'

'Not Mark Aker, the eminent penicillinologist.'

'It is he.'

'Well my God,' Mel said. 'I remember you. Seen your name in the Alumni Magazine.'

The words degenerated into a buzz, then became articulate again. 'You old sporepicker. How's the boy?' Then in a moment the earphone bellowed, 'What the hell you standing around there for?'

'Hold it,' Mark said. 'I'm on my way.'

He hung up and stepped out of the booth self-consciously, looking around to see if anyone had been close enough to hear the nonsense he had been talking. As he walked through the drugstore and out into the street he found himself explaining as if to some critical stranger. Just to listen to Cottam, you'd think he was a maudlin sot, but that's just a manner he wears. He puts it on for the same reason some people put on dark glasses . . .

He found himself at the corner of College and Dubuque Streets in Iowa City, at a little past ten on a Sunday morning in May, and as he stopped on the corner to let a car pass, the utter and passionate familiarity of everything smote him like a wind. Mel's voice on the wire had prepared him for nostalgia. Now the past moved up on him in a wave; it was as if he had never left here, or had just awakened from a long confused dream and found the solid and reassuring edge of reality again.

The brick street ran warm and empty down across the powerhouse bridge and up the other side, curving under big elms and hickories. On the crown of the hill across the river the Quadrangle's squat ivied towers barely topped the trees, and over on the other hill to the right the stone lace of the hospital tower rose above the massive rectangularity of the medical buildings. The lawns below Old Capitol were almost deserted, and the locusts were shrilling in the streetside trees.

Odd compulsions moved him. He found himself reciting the names of all the main university buildings. Crossing the river, he ran his hand along the cool cement rail as if establishing a contact, and halfway across he looked back to see how the union and the reserve library strung out along the riverbank, and the footbridge arched across to the experimental theater. The banks of the river had been landscaped since his time, but otherwise he saw no change. The highway traffic west poured across the Iowa Avenue bridge, and the law commons clung to the limestone bluffs. Mark looked curiously at the few students he met, wondering if they felt as he felt the charm and warmth that lay in the brick streets and the sleepy river and the sun-warmed brick and stone of the university. Probably no one appreciated things like that until they were gone and lost and irretrievable.

On his left as he stepped off the bridge he saw the little eating shack where he and Mel had had long johns and coffee practically every morning for four years. The mere look of its outside, patched with coke signs and Baby Ruth signs and Chesterfield signs, filled his nostrils with the peculiar and unique odors of the place: coffee and smoke and slightly rancid fat, oily-sweet doughnuts and baked paint and the reek of the bug-spray they used on the cockroaches, and under all the watery, tarry, wet-mud smells of the river.

The metal rasping of the seventeen-year-locusts rose loud as a crescendo in a symphonic poem as he climbed the hill, and it struck him as amusing that he too should return here at the end of exactly seventeen years. He couldn't quite imagine where those years had gone; it did not seem that either he or the town had changed a particle. The tennis courts he passed reflected hundreds of remembered mornings like this, and in the field house beyond them were whole lifetimes of recollection.

He would have liked to go in under the big round roof just to soak himself in the sensations he remembered: smell of lockers opened on stale gym clothes and stiff sweated socks; steam and thumping radiators and liquid soap smell; sweat and medicated foot baths and the chlorine smell and the jiggly reflecting chemical blue of the pool; splat of naked feet on concrete, pink of bare flesh, lean bellies and tiptoe bunching calves, the bulging triceps of the gymnastics team working out on the horses. Most of all, the barnlike cold of the basketball floor, and the tiny brittle feeling of coming out before a game to warm up in front of that crowd-faced emptiness, and the clubbing roar of crowd-sound as you drove in for a set-up. It was the same roar whether you made it or missed it.

All of it was still there — unimaginably varied smells and sounds and sights that together made up the way he had once lived, the thing he had once been, perhaps the thing he still was. He was in all of it, and Mel with him. It came to him like a pang that never since the days when he and Mel used to fool around after lunch in the Quad cafeteria, throwing rolled-up paper napkins at water tumblers, had he had a completely relaxed and comfortable ability to enjoy himself. They had made games out of everything; whole Sunday mornings they had spent throwing curves with pot covers in Mel's mother's kitchen. In those Damon-and-Pythias days there had been a sharp and tingling sense of identity and one intense and constant comradeship, and those were the best days of his life. Passing the field house he passed himself and Mel as they had used to be, and the feeling that he had not merely lived this but was somehow contained in it was as pervasive as the mild spring morning, as insistent as the skirring of the locusts. It was like sky-writing on the big warm sky.

The light over the whole hill was pure, pale, of an exaggerated clarity, as if all the good days of his youth had been distilled down into this one day, and the whole coltish ascendant time when he was eighteen, nineteen, twenty, had been handed back to him briefly, intact and precious. That was the time when there had been more hours in the day, and every hour precious enough so that it could be fooled away. By the time a man got into the high thirties the hours became more frantic and less precious, more needed and more carefully hoarded and more fully used, but less loved and less enjoyed.

Then he was pushing the doorbell button, bracing himself obscurely for something — for joy? for recognition? for a renewed flood of this potent and unexpected nostalgia? — and the door opened. Mel stood there in his shirt sleeves, a little mussy as usual, still deceptively round-armed and round-faced, with his beaked nose and his tender child's mouth.

He was either drunk or playing drunk. He smirked, and his eyes blinked in owlish amazement. 'Let me shake your hand!' he said, and hauled Mark inside.

Tamsen got up off the couch where she had been sitting with a highball in her hand. As she came forward, smiling, transferring the glass to her left hand, Mark noted how she adjusted her face for greeting. She was probably prettier than she had ever been, her hair in a long bob with sun-bleached streaks in it, her face smoothly tanned, her eyes candid, her smile white and frank. Presumably the two of them had been drinking together, but where Mel was frowsy and blinking, with red-streaked eyeballs, she was smooth and sober and impeccable.

'Of all the unexpected people!' she said, and gave him a firm hand. She left him in no doubt who was in command in this familiar house, who had established dominance.

Mel's hand pulled him around. 'Canby, you old snake in the grass, where you been? I've tried to call you up every night for ten years.'

'You did,' Mark said. 'Twice. Once in New Haven and once in New York. Both times at two in the morning.'

Tamsen laughed. 'Old Melly,' she said, almost as if affectionately. 'Every time he gets tight he wants to call somebody up. The further away they are, the more he wants to call.'

Mel was standing spraddling, a little flickering smile on his mouth. One hand was on Mark's shoulder. With the other he captured Mark's right hand again and shook it slowly. His breath was heavy with whiskey, and Mark felt dismayed and half sick. He had been so sure at first that the thickening voice had been put on as part of the old clowning act. Now he was bothered precisely as he had been bothered by those telephone calls. Even while he laughed at the ponderous solemnity, the incoherent, bumbling, repetitive nonsense, the marvellously accurate imitation of a soggy drunk, Mark backed away, because he couldn't be quite sure that the act was conscious any more. The act had become the man, and he went around living and acting out a grotesque parody of himself; or if it hadn't become the man, then it had been put on defensively so much that communication was no longer possible. Nothing had come of those telephone calls except a mumble of doubletalk and affectionate profanity, and yet Mark felt that there had been in each instance a need, a loneliness, a reaching out. He felt that there was the same thing now, if Mel would let it show. The old comradeship was there; this drunken parody was embarrassment as much as anything, the defense of a thin-skinned organism.

'Been peeking down those microscopes,' Mel said solemnly, pumping Mark's hand. 'You biological old pot licker. D'you invent penicillin?'

'I'm a modest man,' Mark said. 'Two or three other people helped.'

He got his hand free, and as his eyes crossed Mel's there was almost communication between them, a flash of perfectly sober understanding and warmth. Mel's delicate, bruised-looking lips pursed, but then the look slipped and was gone, and he was pawing for Mark's hand again, saying, 'Canby, you old Rhodes Scholar, slip me the grip.'

Tamsen was amused. 'You should charge him. Remember when he paid a barfly a dollar an hour to shake his hand down at Frank's?'

'Kept me poor,' Mel said, with a sweet imbecilic grin. 'Lose all your friends, got to buy more.' He smiled into Mark's face, hanging to hand and shoulder, and Mark looked deep behind that idiot alcoholic smile trying to compel expression of what he knew was there: the recognition and the pain. Mel beamed at him.

Tamsen too was staring, tipping her head sideways. 'I can't get over how much you've changed,' she said. 'You used to be such a string bean.'

'Cheer up,' Mark said. 'I'm still a string bean at heart.'

'No fooling,' Mel said. He plucked the cloth of Mark's sleeve, sniffed his fingers. 'Where'd you get that jacket?'

'Montreal,' Mark said, and immediately felt an obscure guilty shame, as if he had been betrayed into boasting, rubbing in the fact that he had gone up and out in the world and Mel had been marooned behind. 'I was up there a couple weeks ago at a genetics conference,' he said lamely, in extenuation.

For an instant he was furious at Mel, so furious he shook. In college it had been Mel who had everything — money enough, and clothes, and a car, and a home where starveling students could come like grateful sidling dogs off the street. And he had been brought up well, he had good parents, his home was full of music and books and a certain sense of social grace and personal responsibility. Mel had taught the whole unlicked lot of them something, how to win and how to lose, how to live with people and like them and forgive them. He had never owned a dime's worth of anything that he wasn't glad to share. Now the shoe was on the other foot. Now Mark had gone higher and farther than any of them had ever aimed, and it embarrassed and enraged him to know that he could give lessons to Mel. And it was unjust that having shared everything for four years in college, they couldn't share this trouble that Mel was in now.

Tamsen's level blue eyes were inspecting him, and it struck him that here at least was something they had never shared. He had always known more about Tamsen than Mel had. When he stood up as Mel's best man he could have told the bridegroom the names of four people who had slept with the bride. He wished now that he had; he had wished it a hundred times. And catching Tamsen's eyes, twinkling with a little spark of malice, he knew she understood precisely what he was thinking. She had always been shrewd, and she had been all her life one of the world's most accomplished and convincing liars. When she went after Mel she had fooled even the people who knew her best, made them believe she was infatuated. . . .

'I tell you for sure,' she said, 'if you'd been as good looking then as you are now I'd never have let old Melly take me in to church.'

'Maybe there's still time,' Mark said.

Mel's tugging hand hauled him around. 'You've *changed,* you know that, you damn Yale professor?'

'So have you,' Mark said, but his attempt to hold Mel's eye was unsuccessful, and he added, 'I stay in nights, now. Once I got free of your influence I steadied right down.'

'That's fact,' Mel said. 'Terrible influence. Half stiff ten thirty Sunday morning. Blame that boy of mine. Got his old man out playing baseball with a hangover before breakfast. You ever meet that boy?'

'Never did.'

'Where is he, Tam?'

'He's around,' Tamsen said. 'How about me getting you two a drink?'

Mark let her go. It was a way of getting Mel alone. It seemed to him that some of the drunken pose fell away from Mel as soon as his wife left the room. He looked into the streaked eyes and shook his head and grinned. 'How are things going, anyway?'

The eyes were round and innocent. 'Things going wonderful. I run the business now, since my dad died. My dad was a good business man, you know that, Canby?'

'I know that,' Mark said. 'It wasn't business I was thinking about.' With a quick estimate that he might have only two minutes more before Tamsen returned, he opened his mouth to say what he had come to say, and found that his tongue wouldn't go around it. In that instant it was clear that you did not come in on an old friend and say, 'I hear your wife's been playing around with a golf pro. I could have warned you about her that way. Probably I should have. But I hear you found out all right, and were all set to get a divorce. Bailey told me that much, a year ago. Then I heard that instead of getting a divorce you went down to St. Louis, you and Tamsen and the boy, and stayed six months, and came back home and no more said about any divorce. Get rid of her. She'll cheat on you all her life, and break you in the process. If she's pulled some lie out of the bag and convinced you that you were mistaken, don't believe it, she could lie her way out of hell. For the love of God, get that divorce, for the sake of the boy and for your own sake. She'll suck you dry like an old orange skin. You're already so far gone I could cry — soggy with alcohol and with that comedy-routine front on all the time. Come and stay with me, I'll line you up with Alcoholics Anonymous if you want. Give me a chance to pay some of what I owe you.'

You simply did not say things like that. Even thinking about them made them sound self-righteous and prying. Instead, you looked uneasily at your oldest and closest friend, trying to surprise in his eyes the things you knew were there, pain and shame and bitterness and defeat. But there was too thick an insulating layer between. Seventeen years were too many. Mel was like the elk in Jim's Bridger's Yellowstone story. He grazed on the other side of the glass mountain, clear and undistorted, looking only a hundred yards away. The hunter's gun went off, and the elk didn't even raise his head, didn't even hear the report. He just went on grazing, with blankness like a membrane over his eyeballs and an unpierceable transparent wall between him and the world.

Mel's lips twitched. He lurched forward, looking puzzled and solicitous. 'Whazza name?' he said, besotted and polite, and turned his ear sideward like a deaf man.

Mark pushed him away angrily just as Tamsen came in with glasses. Mel took two and handed one to Mark with a crooked grin. 'Here, rinse your mouth,' he said.

Tamsen raised her glass. 'Here's to the local boy who made good.' They clicked glasses elaborately all around. Irritated, baffled, frustrated, gnawed by that odd obscure shame, Mark drank with them to himself.

'I was thinking about you the other day,' Tamsen was saying. 'We were down watching the spring canoe race and two kids went over the falls by the power plant just the way you and Mel did once.'

'I hope they didn't swallow as much water as I did,' Mark said.

'Yeah, but this the other day was an accident,' Mel said. 'You, you pot-licker, you put us over there just to duck me.'

'I was along,' Mark said. 'I went over too. Remember?'

Tamsen shook her head. 'You were a pair,' she said. 'I guess I'd forgotten what a pair you were.'

They sat nursing their drinks, the door open upon the street and the locust noise, and groped carefully backward for the things to remember and laugh about, gleaning the safe nostalgic past. But it was not the canoes over waterfalls, the times Jay Straup tried to climb Old Capitol steps in his old Model T, the picnics on Signal Hill when all the farmer kids used to creep up and spy on the college kids necking, that Mark wanted to remember. People who recalled such things and shook their heads over them bored him. He kept looking at Mel in search of that spark of understanding, and he kept wanting to say—

Remember the times we used to go out on dates and come in late in your old Ford, and stop down along one of the river joints for a pork tenderloin and a ginger beer, two or three o'clock in the morning, only a truck driver or two on the stools? How good sandwiches tasted at that hour, and how late the moon would be over the bluffs when we came out yawning and started up to your house? Remember the mornings we woke up in this house, this very house seventeen or eighteen or twenty years ago, and found the sun scrambled in the bedclothes, and had a shower and breakfast and went out onto the sidewalk, not for anything especially, but just to be outdoors, and walked under those trees out there up to the corner and back again, loafing, alive to the fingertips, talking about anything, nothing, girls, games, profundities? Remember? It isn't what we did, but what we were, that I remember, and I know that what we were is still here, if we'd peel off the defenses and the gaglines and the double-talk routines and the Montreal jackets.

The porch thudded with feet and a chubby boy of twelve came

in with a bat in his hand. He stood forward gravely when Mel introduced him, shook hands with polite indifference, coasted into the kitchen and came back gnawing on a cookie.

'Canby, my friend,' Mel said to him, 'you'll be as fat as your old man.'

The child was a curious blend of his parents, with Tamsen's deceptively clear eyes and Mel's twisting delicate mouth. He looked at his father over the cookie, grinning.

'Stay away from pappy,' Tamsen said. 'Pappy started out to cure a hangover and behold he's swizzled again.'

A grunt that sounded almost like an angry outburst escaped Mel. He lunged for the boy. 'Come here!' he said, as the boy eluded him. 'Come here, and I'll knock your two heads together.'

Still grinning, the boy banged out onto the porch. 'How about another drink for the two old grads?' Tamsen said.

'Why not?' Mel said, but Mark rose.

'I've got to catch a train at twelve thirty.'

'You don't have to go,' Mel said. 'You just came, Canby.'

Mark put out his hand to Tamsen. 'Goodbye,' he said. 'If you ever come east don't forget me.'

He was trying to decide whether the look in her clear eyes had been triumphant, or whether there had actually been any look at all, as he and Mel went out to the sidewalk and down to the corner. They did not speak on the way down, but on the corner, under the warm shade, their voices almost lost in the incessant shrilling of the locusts, they shook hands again. Mark knew there was no use in trying to say any of what it had been in his mind to say. But even so he gripped Mel's hand and held his eyes.

'I wish you the best, you bum,' he said, and his throat tightened up as it sometimes tightened at an emotional crisis in a play. 'If you're not so stiff you can't listen straight, listen to this. I wish you the best, and if there's ever a time I can . . .'

He stopped. Mel was looking at him without any of the sodden fuzziness that had marked him for the past hour. His eyes were pained, intent, sad. On his delicate bruised lips there was a flicker of derision.

(*From The Kenyon Review*)

# THE PLAN

BY SIDNEY SULKIN

NEW people had arrived early in the morning. They could be seen walking toward the registration office, trailing humbly behind one of the UNRRA officers. One of the girls in the group — there were four, all rather plump with dark stringy hair and shapeless legs and hips — lingered at the very end and seemed to be struggling uncomfortably with the waistline of her dress. No doubt, like most of them, she had sewn a packet of American money in her clothes and was now afraid that she might be searched. A few yards from the wooden house which served as registration office, bank, records room and postoffice, she paused, waited for the others to enter and then quickly stooped as if to fix her shoe. Instead she dug something hastily into the ground, then straightened and disappeared into the building.

From his customary seat on the hard wooden bench alongside the dining hall — which with his exact knowledge of English he had pointed out many a time, and very cleverly too, the Americans appropriately enough called a 'mess hall' — Dr. Felix Allstein watched this phenomenon with only casual interest. Now as the girl vanished, he shifted his gaze back to where it had been, to the long low fields that rolled downward from the camp's edge to the tiny village below and then rose again on the other side and spread in slow undulations away to the horizon. He looked south across the beams of the sun so that everything, the cluster of roofs that made up the village, the occasional farmhouse, the fields and even the clumps of trees in the far distance, everything was without shadow ever but seemed always to be clear, even luminous, as if he were sitting above and could look down and gaze on all things from all sides at once. He came here continuously, it was his place and he had developed a philosophy about it. This was a domain—perhaps even his domain, though his imagination touched on that exquisite assumption only with temerity. It was a domain which had been purged by fire and sword, wrung to purity and goodness by the utter horror which had been perpetrated within it. So deep had been its ugliness that now, cleansed, it was beautiful. And for him it was unpeopled. He took no notice of the specks that moved in the valley or, for that matter, even of the shapes that trudged closer up the hillside. For, sitting up here at the tip edge of it, he dreamed that this domain would indeed one day be peopled, but in a special way. It was a plan he had created carefully, piece by piece. Yet, though it had many parts, though sometimes it required replies to many questions to state it, nevertheless, its virtue was, as one might expect of a great plan, its simplicity.

He looked long and softly southward and then sighed and rose and walked toward the registration office. Coming from another direction were two of the officers who had brought this morning's group in. Dr. Allstein glanced toward the uniformed men and reflected that their job was something like rounding up stray dogs. He had intended to nod a polite greeting to them but they seemed immersed in conversation and hardly noticed him. He stood before the registration office until they had passed. Then he dropped to his knee, pretending to tie his shoelace but groveling quickly in the dirt with one hand. It took some scraping around before his fingers closed on what he was after. It felt like a ring. He rose, brushed his trousers carefully and walked away. When he reached the barracks where he slept, he sat on his bed and drew the ring from his pocket. The stone flashed beautifully. It was probably very valuable. He held it in his cupped palms for a while and then carefully tucked it away in a corner of his mattress.

In the afternoon, Josephson brought two of the newcomers to meet him. He had expected it. He sat on his bench with his writing block resting on his lap and watched them moving across the path toward him. One was a terribly thin, emaciated man who walked with a stoop and an odd jerking of his neck that made him look like a scrawny chicken. The other was a girl. She wore men's shoes and dragged them clumsily. Josephson, as always, led them, half turning back as if to be sure they were following. Dr. Allstein waited somewhat impatiently. He had wondered just when Josephson would show up with the newcomers and it had delayed his work. Now only two of them had put in an appearance. He supposed the others would show up later just when he had settled himself to his writing again. Dr. Allstein sighed and bent toward his pad. He let a scowl of concentration grow on his face and pretended not to hear the footsteps approaching.

'Dr. Allstein, please excuse me.'

He raised his head slowly, the scowl still written painfully on his forehead and eyes.

'Excuse me, Dr. Allstein. I have brought some new friends who would like to hear your ideas.'

He glanced at last from Josephson to the others and now a benevolent smile took the place of the frown. 'My ideas? Every man has ideas. Don't you have ideas, Josephson?'

The young man blushed a deep color and then pushed the girl forward crudely. 'She heard about your plan so I brought her to meet you.'

It was the girl who had lingered behind the others at the registration office. She stood just in front of Dr. Allstein — he had risen in politeness to shake her hand — and gazed at him, not timidly, but with a shy inarticulateness. Her hair was, as he had noticed in the morning, stringy and dull, but her face was clear, almost pretty, and her body did not seem to have become overplump and spongy the way so many of them had soon after the liberation. Her eyes kept looking into his, waiting for him to say something, and he knew that she had no idea that he had followed her to that spot in front of the registration office. Perhaps, though, she had not yet gone back to look. Perhaps she was waiting for the darkness. He looked down at her shoes.

'Why do you wear men's shoes here? They will give you women's shoes.'

'I tried them. They're too small.' She stepped back and began to fidget with her dress.

The thin man, who had been waiting politely in the background, stepped forward and took the doctor's hand. 'I am Rutman. They gave me this suit in one of the camps two months ago. It is too big but the pockets are good.' He stabbed his fists into the jacket pockets to demonstrate.

'Six people came this morning,' Josephson said. 'The other four weren't Jews.'

'They were Hungarians,' the girl said.

Dr. Allstein sat down on the bench and the others gradually arrayed themselves on both sides of him.

'What are you, a writer?' Rutman asked peering down at the block of paper.

Dr. Allstein smiled, 'What are we all? If we have paper and patience we are writers.'

Josephson leaned forward to see if this sampling of the doctor's paternal wisdom had invoked sufficient response in the others. 'Give them your ideas, Mr. Doctor,' he begged.

'I suppose you have ideas about us Jews,' Rutman said.

Josephson motioned to him to be quiet. 'Dr. Allstein has a plan.'

The doctor shook his head. 'It is not any longer I who have a plan, Josephson. There is a plan. It has been written to the authorities and since then it is theirs. It no longer belongs to me.'

The young man jumped up and glared excitedly at the newcomers. 'You see, the authorities have it!' he cried triumphantly as if this were the final culmination of his faith.

'I suppose it is about us Jews,' Rutman repeated. He held out his hand, palm up. 'See, there is the world.' His fingers closed into a tight fist. 'And there, yes, there is the little Jew inside.' He held his fist, the knuckles straining white, under their noses.

'With good fortune,' Dr. Allstein said, ignoring him, 'we shall be moving from here.'

Josephson's face could no longer express his joy. Tears brimmed in his eyes. He stood with his back to them and gazed toward the fields. 'We shall begin moving soon. We shall take our country over. The Germans are moving out. They are walking and riding in carts.'

'Josephson, come sit down,' the doctor bade gently. The young man turned and sat himself at the edge of the bench near the girl. He put his hands to his head and began to run his fingers through his hair. The girl patted him on the back as if he had something in his throat.

'The plan,' began Dr. Allstein, 'is a simple one. All that you see before you and many miles to the east and west, as far as the Austrian border, all this will be cleared of the Germans. They will be moved out with their families and their clothes. Jews will take over their houses, their fields and their factories. This will be the land of the Jews.'

He leaned back against the side of the building and closed his eyes. There was a long silence. Then Rutman stood up and began walking back and forth, pressing his fists against each other and murmuring something in a singsong which no one could understand.

Josephson looked up. 'And what,' he inquired very deliberately, 'will happen to the Germans who are moved?' He gripped the girl's shoulder and made her lean forward with him to hear the happy reply.

'The Germans,' Dr. Allstein answered, still with his eyes closed, 'will go into camps for displaced persons where they will wait until the rest of the world has decided what to do with them.'

The girl looked down at the ground and began to tug at her finger as if she were twisting a ring, but the ring was no longer there and so she simply dropped her hands by her side and leaned back.

A great many people had heard about Dr. Felix Allstein's plan. Some had heard of the plan and found out only much later that it was his. And others had talked about it, thought about it and argued for it so long that in some instances they even declared that they had learned about it in other camps long before coming here. It was a beautiful plan, they all agreed, and sometimes they sat in the darkness and spoke in cheerful whispers about it. They imagined themselves already tilling the ground or opening little shops. Some put their children to sleep with old lullabies to which they had composed verses that said, 'Sleep, sleep, little one, for tomorrow you'll have school again. . . .' It hung about them, the plan did, like a faithful dog which could be touched and patted and called in to lie at one's feet for comfort. They sometimes walked by the dining hall in the afternoon and gazed from a respectful distance at the doctor working. On these occasions, when he caught sight of them out of the corner of his eye, the wrinkles of concentration grew quickly on his forehead and he leaned nobly over his pad. A few of them, watching this, decided that he was putting together the laws that would rule the new land; others declared that he was replying to a letter from the authorities; and still others whispered that he was writing his life's story, including the story of how he had conceived of the plan in the first place. They strolled away smiling and shaking their heads slowly with deep satisfaction written on their faces.

But there were some who were not pleased. These were the followers of Eliash, the young, hard-tempered, black-eyed Jew who, it was said, had been slipping from camp to camp like a thief, arguing for action, for action. Most of the young men — and some young women — could always be seen clustered about him. They drew maps on the ground with sticks or their heels and the rumor spread that they were an underground, that they were a link in a chain that lay sprawled all over Europe but which connected up in Palestine. They spirited people away, it was said, and from time to time one of the young men did disappear as if into thin air. 'Who? Rubin? He left long ago, months ago. There was a letter from him. He's in Palestine.' That was the answer they gave to inquirers. No one ever saw the letter and Rubin had been seen just yesterday in the dining hall breaking his bread over his soup nervously. But it was a dream. If you walked up to Eliash and said under your breath, 'It is warm in Palestine this time of year,' and made believe you were putting your hand into your pocket for money, he simply replied, 'In Palestine it's always warm, they say,' and walked off. It was a dream. At dinner time many people sat near the doctor and perhaps stood up to pass him the salt even though it had been passed to him three or four times before and even though he said, 'Thank you, I don't like too much salt, it makes me thirsty.' But Eliash and his group sat apart and ate heartily, banging the table and laughing coarsely, often glancing with sly meaning toward the doctor as if their jokes were about him. But the doctor didn't mind, Josephson told people.

Dr. Allstein never stated out loud that he disliked Eliash. That was one of the things that several people pointed out repeatedly whenever one of Eliash's crude remarks got around. It was a sign of the doctor's tolerance and standing. In truth, he had never told himself that he disliked Eliash. But he watched him. He had known his kind. They used to come from the eastern parts, from Poland or Russia, always burning with excitement, and they were usually dark. The early cartoons, he used to think — though he never condoned them — were meant to be about them. They hardly ever thought clearly or exactly. They seldom spoke the language well but chopped it, laughed at it and chopped it up. He dismissed Eliash, then, fairly easily. But he watched him closely.

One day Eliash came up to him. Josephson, who was sitting on the bench beside him saying something about the new girl, saw Eliash coming and stood up and left. This annoyed the doctor because it looked as if Josephson was deserting him. He turned his eyes down to his writing and waited for Eliash to arrive and start speaking.

'Why are you always writing here?' Eliash demanded as soon as he was near enough.

Dr. Allstein raised his eyes. This was a good question. He did not have to answer if he didn't want to because it had nothing to do with the subject.

'Any time anyone goes by you're sitting here writing,' Eliash went on. He had come up to the bench and stood glaring down at the doctor.

'What harm does it do?' Dr. Allstein murmured. 'If we have paper and patience we are all writers.'

Eliash sat down on the bench and began cracking his knuckles. 'Are you always writing about this plan of yours?'

The doctor looked carefully at Eliash. Truthfully, he had been nervous about him almost as if he feared him. But the sight of him sitting here now looking dejected and helpless gave him new courage. He began to feel a soft glow. 'It is an idea. As you may know, all things are ideas. If the ideas are strong the things are real. I have an idea that keeps growing stronger and stronger.' He watched Eliash continuously but the man simply sat staring at the ground working his palms and his fingers against each other. And so, feeling safe, the doctor told his plan, briefly, as he often told it to new people who came. When he had finished, Eliash looked up at last and asked, 'But who said the authorities agreed to it?' The doctor shrugged. 'Everybody,' Eliash went on, 'everybody keeps saying we are going to move soon.' He stood up and walked away.

Dr. Allstein lifted his pad and fumbled with the pages. His mind was blurred by a rush of triumphant gladness. He seemed to be sitting high on a hill, looking down, far down, farther and deeper than the village before him, to people below.

Josephson came around the corner and sat on the bench. 'Eliash is unhappy,' he said.

'You should tie your shoelaces. Look at them.'

Josephson looked away and drew a hand across his mouth. He had been standing just around the corner of the house and heard everything and now he was ashamed to have the doctor reprimanding him after talking so kindly to Eliash, even to Eliash. 'The new girl said she lost a ring. Somebody stole it.'

The doctor turned an angry face toward him. 'What is she making such a fuss about? She probably stole it herself. Tell her to stop making such a fuss. Pretty soon nobody will have to steal.'

Josephson stood up. He had never seen the doctor get so angry. 'I'll go tell her.'

Dr. Allstein closed his eyes. His annoyance with Josephson faded away quickly as he recalled the look on Eliash's face. He had enjoyed this feeling long ago on the day his book appeared. It was a feeling of floating. His wife, who had been plump — and sharp — had remarked, 'Bubbles float, too, and when they burst there's nothing in them.' It had been a thin book, so thin that after a while the covers bent in at the corners and touched each other. *Hegel's Idea* was the title. He had sat in a café once when the galley proofs were sent to him for corrections and had worked over them in a corner, sipping coffee and letting the long sheets hang over the edge of the table. He had seen this done by others many times and now here he was doing it himself. That was how the pleasure built up gradually, first the editor's note saying that the manuscript had been brought to his attention by a friend of the firm — that was his wife's father who had given one of the owners some money a while back — anc then the note that said they would publish it, then the proofs and later the finished, smooth and fresh-smelling book with tiny bits of clean paper falling off the edges of the pages where they had been cut. He had sent out fourteen signed copies and reeived nine polite letters, three of them very polite. There was a nention of it in the press, too, the day it appeared, giving the tite, author, publisher and price. He cut it out of two papers. Hescoured the other papers and the literary journals after that but there were no reviews. His wife reminded him of the bubble. He walked down the street to the café and sat in his corner. He haddreamed of coming here after the reviews appeared so that anyone who wanted to come and talk about Hegel would know whre to find him. No one came. Except the waiter to show him the picture of an actress in the newspaper and tell him that sh used to eat here before she went to Berlin. The book faded awy. No one even bothered to burn or ban it.

Long afterwards, however, it came to e again in a strange way. It was like dreaming. He was walkingon a road crowded with people. They trudged along tiredly, sor of them carrying boxes full of vases and lamps and dishes on thir shoulders, others dragging mattresses piled with shoes, sts, pillows, hats, chairs and anything else they had been ableo pick up on the way. Josephson walked beside him and told hn that now the war was over he was thinking of going to Amca. A young girl, dragging a bedsheet full of things, shouted om across the road that she was going there, too, and if he wou help her she'd give him half the things she had collected. Josnson stopped and made her untie the sheet so he could see wher it was worth it. The doctor stood beside him while he runaged. There were only pots and pans, some picture frames, a all head carved in stone, three or four women's dresses and a fevooks. Josephson snorted and told her to go to the devil. But thector stooped and picked out a book and then the tears started aming down his cheeks. Immediately the girl snatched it out his hand and declared,

'It's mine.' Evidently she had decided that it must be valuable if the doctor cried about it. Josephson slapped her hand and gave the book back to the doctor. A few people stopped to watch the argument and by now the doctor was smiling instead of crying. He explained that it was his own book, that he had written it long ago before the war and le showed them his name on it. They all congratulated him on fiding it and one or two asked to hold it. One man nodded wisely und said it was a good omen, it meant that they would all start gettig back the things that belonged to them. The girl told the doctor le could keep the volume as a gift. Josephson helped her tie her bndle and whispered to her that it was a famous book, he rememered when it came out. The doctor, he said, was a famous man. The movement along the road had been stopped by the incident and there was great congestion. Now everyone walked on agai talking cheerfully as if each of them had suddenly found a treasu of his own past.

That was the beginnig of Dr. Allstein's fame. When he came into a camp he carried nly this tiny book under his arm and people pointed him out each other. Whenever there was a discussion he sat in the ddle and smiled and nodded his head. One day Josephson ca to him and said, 'I think I'll go to America.' The doctor rugged and replied, 'You can go. But there'll be room for yo here.' Then he explained to Josephson a plan he had been thiing about lately. That was how it first became known. Later decided that one day he would write another book called, *Mydea.*

Dr. Allstein opened heyes and looked out on his domain. For the first time it did norouble him to think of it boldly as his domain. For now evenliash was conquered.

The story spread thatey were soon to move. It was a rumor at first and many refus to listen to it. But the story persisted. A few went to the doc and asked him about it but he merely smiled and shrugged l shoulders. An argument broke out in one of the barracks wl a man declared that many trucks had been ordered from a cant point, from Frankfurt, and that as soon as they arrived thntire camp was to be moved. Someone told him he was fooliso expect anyone to believe that he had heard such a story especially since he couldn't understand a word of English himself. He insisted that he had heard it and they argued until they were too tired to shout any longer. A boy reported that all the papers in the registration office were being packed. He took two others with him and they crept around the side of the building and peered in one of the windows. But all they saw were two soldiers sitting on metal boxes smoking. The soldiers did nothing but sit there and smoke and so the others slapped the boy and told him he was a liar. Three strange officers appeared one day, evidently important men because all the Americans saluted them and conducted them on a tour of the camp. Groups of people followed at a distance and tried to catch what they were saying. They left after spending the entire day there.

Finally a delegation came to Dr. Allstein and requested that he go speak to the Americans. He refused at first. 'It will come,' he assured them. But the delegation begged him to go to the Americans and so at last he consented. He walked down the path to the other end of the camp and entered the administration building. He asked the girl at the desk, very carefully in English, if he could see an officer. She led him into a room where a young man in uniform sat at a desk and smiled at him. He waited until she had left and then, very carefully in English again, he asked if it was true that they were going to move. The young man said yes, they were going to move to a bigger camp about eighty kilometers away. It was a much more comfortable camp, the young man assured him. The doctor thanked him and thanked the girl outside and then walked up the path toward the dining hall, smiling and nodding his head to the people who watched him from the edges of the barracks buildings. At his bench the delegation waited for his report. He hardly looked at them but gazed out at the fields and hills with teary eyes and then, at last, said slowly, 'Yes, we shall soon leave the camp.'

At first there was a hush at dinner. People came in and sat down and hardly ate and one could tell by their eyes that they had been weeping in private for gladness. A woman took the doctor's hands, looked into his eyes and then left the room quickly with tears streaming down her cheeks. Each one of them had taken the news to himself and wrung from it his own personal happiness. Some had gone straight to their bunks after the doctor's announcement in the afternoon and had lain back with their hands behind their heads and thought and thought. Now, sitting at the dinner table, they were still clinging to these thoughts. But gradually, in the company of the others, their joy began to unloosen. They began to talk about silly things. 'How many suits will you have for your stock?' someone asked Berman who used to own a clothing shop in Berlin. 'Listen to me, it will always be raining,' declared Goldstein who used to make umbrellas in Lodz. And Margolies who had been studying to be a dentist cried, 'Everybody needs new teeth!' The chattering rose quickly. People stood up and walked excitedly from one end of the table to the other. They touched the doctor's shoulder and he laughed with them. Once or twice he accepted a hand and shook it heartily. But he kept his eyes most of the time on Eliash. Eliash sat apart in a corner and brooded. The new girl sat beside him and occasionally touched his head. They seemed not to hear the laughing and the doctor was troubled. He didn't like the way the girl sat over there with Eliash. He wished that she, at least, would come over here and join the talk. Most of Eliash's friends had already done so. Josephson noticed them, too. He jumped about with the others but every once in a while he ran over to those two and glared at them and once or twice he gripped the girl's arm roughly and tried to pull her away. She paid no attention to him.

But no one else bothered about them. The happy ones laughed and called to each other and rattled their plates and talked all at once. There was no wine, no cake, but the babbling mounted in excitement. After a while it seemed to have a rhythm. To someone listening from afar it might have been singing. It might have been the sound of Chasidim dancing and clapping hands. Perhaps it was, perhaps inside of them a melody welled, leaped from mind to mind and united them in a single rhythm. La la la-la muzel tov. . . . The full and utter joy. The Pharaoh's lash was broken. The walls of the temple were rising once more. Jeremiah had changed his tune. The Golem had gone back to darkness. The ashes that still blew over the Ghetto of Warsaw were laid to earth at last, and the odor that drifted for many miles around Belsen and Buchenwald and Auschwitz had faded away at last. The lime pits were sealed forever. The Rebs and Zadiks danced in them. The Hillels and Rambams sang again.

Dr. Allstein, smiling constantly and nodding his head as if in time to this strange scherzo that tied the voices together, nevertheless did not feel a part of it. It was somewhat barbarian for him, it smacked of the eastern flavor which long ago in his youth he had noticed and rejected as uncultured. He despised them a little for the hubbub and the noise they were making. And yet it satisfied him, as if he were a man holding the strings and these were his puppets dancing grotesquely at his will. At the same time, he became more and more annoyed with those who did not join, as if they were defying his will. He kept his eyes on Eliash and the girl and finally he could restrain himself no longer. He rose and went to them and asked, 'Why are you sitting here?' Eliash merely looked down at his hands. The girl pulled at her finger. 'You should join the others,' the doctor said more sternly. He put his hand on the girl's arm and pulled her up from the chair. 'Yes,' Eliash said as if he agreed with the doctor. He rose and started toward the larger group. The doctor kept his grip on the girl and even tightened it because, oddly enough, she didn't seem to notice it at all. Her unconcern angered him and he dug his fingers into her flesh through her sleeve. But she still didn't seem to mind a bit. She allowed him to lead her to the other table in silence. He gave her arm one last angry squeeze and then pushed her roughly into a chair beside Josephson so that she was removed from Eliash. Josephson looked at her and Eliash triumphantly but neither of them said anything.

No one else had noticed what happened. The noise went on, as loud and foolish as ever.

The excitement lasted for three days. Nobody minded the time passing. They packed their bundles and prepared themselves for the trip. Then when a line of trucks did indeed appear, they scrambled into them with their belongings and sped along the road chattering and shouting and laughing. They rode for a few hours and then entered the gates of another camp and piled out. No one cared that they had come to a camp. It was understandable that they would have to stop somewhere for a rest. They couldn't just go on in one day. The drivers were probably tired and the trucks probably had to be fixed anyhow. They did not unpack their bundles but left them as they were for the next move. When they were assigned bunks they guessed that they would have to stay the night here so they settled down to wait. The next day they were asked to line up at another registration office to check in. Some grumbled that it was silly to do this if they were going to check out so soon. But they stood in line and waited, told their names and went back to their bunks.

The doctor found a bench under a tree and spent most of the day there making notes on his pad. Josephson came toward him but he pretended not to see him and so Josephson stood around for a few moments and left. The doctor went into dinner late and sat to one side pretending to read the notes he had written all day. One or two people approached him but he kept turning his pages and ignored them. They ate their food and waited. There was little talk.

After a few days some people unpacked their things and hid the valuable items under their bunks as they had done in other camps. Others extracted only what they needed and repacked everything else just in case. But after a while they, too, unpacked everything. Slowly, very slowly they all stopped waiting. Rutman began going around again holding out his palm and then closing it slowly into a fist and muttering, 'That's the little Jew.' Eliash moved away from the main table at meals and gradually his friends drifted back to him. A few other people sat near them to listen to the talk. Finally, Josephson began edging toward them, too. But no matter how many times he changed his seat he was always at the periphery of the circle. No one paid much attention to him.

Dr. Allstein appeared to take little notice of what was going on. He passed his day by himself under the tree. He could see a great distance from here, too, except that on the left almost everything was obstructed by a forest which grew very close to the camp. But he found it difficult to concentrate. Hardly anyone disturbed him now and yet he couldn't seem to get his ideas straight. The forest, he felt, was a distraction. He moved his seat to the other side of the camp where the view was cleared. It looked out on the highway and trucks rumbled by rather frequently; but there was no forest and in the distance he could see what looked like the spires of a city. Still, it was not easy to think even here. He took to pacing up and down with his hands behind his back as if he were faced with knotty problems which he would have to settle soon. The wrinkles of thought spread over his forehead and his cheeks screwed up into little balls of concentration. But there was no one to see it. Except occasionally Josephson, who sat on the ground a short distance away and watched him. This annoyed the doctor more than anything. He called to him once or twice, 'What are you sitting there for?' But Josephson just looked away and made no answer. The doctor walked up to him finally and touched him on the shoulder. 'The girl went away,' Josephson said, and then as though he hoped to hurt the doctor he added, 'Eliash sent her.' But Dr. Allstein merely shook his head sadly. 'You see, she didn't find her ring and still she went away,' he said as if that was to prove how silly she was in the first place. Josephson said, 'I may go to America.' But the doctor was already moving away.

For some reason after this Dr. Allstein began to feel better. He held the ring in his hand occasionally and when he did so it made him feel rich and satisfied, almost as if he had always been a man of affluence. But it was even more than that. Looking across the road at the distant city, he began to have the feeling that here indeed was the domain he had been seeking. In his mind he measured off the distances to left and right and made notes. And then one day he noticed a newcomer to the camp sitting under a nearby tree. The doctor began to pace up and down rapidly. Then he stood at the edge of the grass and strained on his toes as if he were gazing at something on the horizon. The stranger, an elderly man with sunken cheeks and thin, squinting eyes, approached and inquired if anything was wrong. The doctor pretended not to hear him at first and then turned and smiled and murmured, 'It depends what ideas we have.' The man nodded gravely. 'I have ideas all the time,' he said. The doctor took his arm firmly and led him to the edge of the grass. 'There is an idea,' he began happily pointing to the grey mists that seemed to shroud the distant landscape. 'As far as you can see, the hills and the towers and the sky will be ours. . . .' The man nodded and began to repeat the words in a murmur.

(*From Harper's Bazaar*)

# THE WHOLE WORLD KNOWS

BY EUDORA WELTY

*MOTHER said, Where have you been, son?—Nowhere, mother.—I wish you wouldn't look so unhappy, son. You could come back to me, now.—I can't do that, mother. I have to stay in Sabina.*

When I locked the door of the Sabina Bank I rolled down my sleeves and stood for some time looking out at a cotton field across the way until the whiteness nearly put me to sleep and then woke me up like a light turned on in my face. Dugan had been gone a few minutes or so. I got in my car and drove it up the street, turned it around in the foot of Jinny's driveway (there went Dugan), and drove down again. I backed in a cotton field at the other end of the pavement, turned, and made the same trip. You know—the thing everybody does every day.

There was Maideen Summers on the corner waving a little colored handkerchief. She was at first the only stranger—then finally not much of one. When I didn't remember to stop I saw the handkerchief slowly fall still. I turned again, and picked her up.

'Dragging Main?' she said. She was eighteen years old. She promptly told you all those things. 'Look! Grown-up and citified,' she said, and held both hands toward me. She had brand new white cotton gloves on—they shone. Maideen would ride beside me and talk about things I didn't mind hearing about—the ice plant, where she kept the books. Fred Killigrew her boss, the way working in Sabina seemed after the country and junior college. Her first job—her mother could hardly believe it, she said.

It was so easy, too, out in the world, and nice, with getting her ride home with me sometimes like this and not on the dusty bus — except Mr. Killigrew sometimes wanted her to do something at the last minute — guess what today — and so on.

She said, 'This sure is nice. I didn't think you saw me, Ran, not at first.'

I told her my eyes had gone bad. She looked sorry. I drove, idling along, up and down Main Street a few times more. Each time the same people, Miss Callie Hudson and all, the people standing in the store doors or riding in the other cars, waved at my car, and to them all, Maideen waved back — her little blue handkerchief was busy. Their avidity would be far beyond her. She waved at them as she did at me.

'Are you tired out like you were yesterday? Today's just as hot.'

She knew what anybody in Sabina told her; and for four or five afternoons I had picked her up and taken her up and down the street a few turns, bought her a Coca-Cola and driven her home out by the Old Murray Forks somewhere, and she had never said a word except a kind one, like this. She was kind; her company was the next thing to being alone.

I drove her home and then drove back to the room I had at Mrs. Judge O'Leary's — usually, but on this day, there at the end of the pavement, I turned up the cut to the Stark place. I couldn't stand it any longer.

Maideen didn't say anything until we reached the top of the drive and stopped, and I got out and opened her door.

'Do you want to take me in yonder?' she said. 'Please, I'd just as soon you wouldn't.'

All at once her voice came all over me. It had a kind of humility.

'Sure. Let's go in and see Jinny. Why not?' I couldn't stand it any longer, that was why. 'I'm going and taking you.'

It wasn't as if Colonel Waters didn't say to me every afternoon, Come on home with me, boy — argue, while he forced that big Panama down on his head — no sense in your not sleeping cool, with one of our fans turned on you. Mabel says so, Mabel has something to say to you — and he waited a minute in the door before he left, and held his cane (the one Dugan and I had gone in together to buy him because he was president), up in the air as if he threatened me with comfort, until I answered him No Sir.

With Maideen, I walked around the baked yard to the porch, under the heavy heads, the too-bright blooms that hang down like fruits from the trees — crape myrtles. Jinny's mama, I saw, put her face to her bedroom window first thing, to show she'd marched right upstairs at the sight of Randall MacLain coming to her door, bringing who-on-earth with him too. After daring to leave her daughter and right on Easter Sunday before church. Now right back to her door, big as you please. And her daughter Jinny, Virginia, who once Shared His Bed, sent straight into the arms of Trash by what he did. One thing — it was Jinny's family home after all, her mother still kept alive to run it, *grand* old Mrs. Stark, and this outrage right under her nose. The curtain fell back, as on a triumph.

'I've never been invited to the Stark home,' Maideen said, and I began to smile. I felt curiously lighthearted. Lilies must have been in bloom somewhere near, and I took a full breath of their water smell as determinedly as if then consciousness might go, or might not.

Out in the front hall, Jinny stood with her legs apart, cutting off locks of her hair at the mirror. The locks fell at her feet. She had on boy's shorts. She looked up at me and said 'How do you like it?' She grinned, as if she had been preparing for me, and then she looked past my shoulder. She would know, with her quickness like foreknowledge, that I would come back when this summer got too much for me, and that I would just as soon bring a stranger if I could find one, somebody who didn't know a thing, into the house with me when I came.

I remember Maideen looked down at her gloves, and seemed to decide to keep them on. Jinny hollered at Tellie to bring in some cokes. A spell of remoteness, a feeling of lightness, had hold of me still, and as we all stood on that thin light matting in the Stark hall that seems to billow a little if you take a step, and with Jinny's hair lying on it, I saw us all in the mirror. And I could almost hear it being told right across me — our story, the fragment of what happened, Jinny's and my story, as if it were being told — told in the clear voice of Maideen, rushing, unquestioning — the town words. Oh, this is what Maideen Summers was — telling what she looked at, repeating what she listened to — she was like an outlandish little bird, being taught, some each day, to sing a song *people* made. . . . He walked out on her and moved three blocks away down the street. Now everybody's wondering when he'll try to go back. They say Jinny MacLain's got her sweetheart there. Under her mama's nose. Good thing her father's dead and she has no brothers. Sure, it's Lonnie Dugan, the other one at the bank, and you knew from the start, if it wasn't Ran, who else in Sabina would there be for Jinny Stark? They don't say how it happened, does anybody know? At the circle, at the table, at Mrs. Judge's, at Sunday School, they say, they say she will marry the sweetheart if he'll marry her, but Ran will kill someone if she does. And there's Ran's papa died of drink, remember, remember? They say Ran will do something bad. He won't divorce her but he will do something bad. Maybe kill them all. They say Jinny's not scared. And oh you know, they say, they run into each other every day of the world, all three. Poor things! But it's no surprise. There'll be no surprises. How could they help it if they wanted to help it, how could you get away from anything here? You can't get away in Sabina. Away from anything.

Maideen held the tinkling glass in her white glove and said to Jinny, 'I look too tacky and mussed when I work all day to be coming in anybody's strange house.'

She looked like *Jinny* — she was an awkward version of Jinny. Jinny, 'I look too tacky and mussed when I work all day to be always revealed contamination. I knew it after the fact, so to speak — and was just a bit pleased with myself.) I don't mean there was anything of mockery in Maideen's little face — no — but something of Jinny that went back early — to whatever original and young my Jinny would never be now. The breeze from that slow ceiling fan lifted their hair from their temples, like the same hand — Maideen's brown hair long and Jinny's brown hair short, ruined — she ruined it herself, as she liked doing.

Maideen was so still, so polite, but she glowed with something she didn't know about, there in the room with Jinny. She took on a great deal of unsuspected value. It was like a kind of maturity all at once. They sat down in wicker chairs and talked to each other. With them side by side and talking back and forth, it seemed to reward my soul for Maideen to protest her fitness to be in the house. I would not have minded how bedraggled she would ever get herself. I relaxed, leaned back in my chair and smoked cigarettes. But I had to contain my sudden interest; it seemed almost too funny to be true, their resemblance. I was delighted with myself, most of all, to have been the one to make it evident. I looked from Jinny to Maideen (of course *she* didn't guess) and back to Jinny and almost expected praise—praise from somewhere—for my true vision.

There were knocking sounds from outside—croquet again. Jinny was guiding us to the open door (we walked on her hair) where they were slowly moving across the shade of the backyard—Doc Short, Vera and Red Lassiter, and the two same schoolteachers—with Lonnie Dugan striking a ball through the wicket. I watched through the doorway and the crowd seemed to have dwindled a little. I could not think who was out. It was myself.

*Mother said, Son, you're walking around in a dream.*

Bella, Mrs. Judge O'Leary's little dog, panted sorrowfully all the time—she was sick. I always went out in the yard and spoke to her. Poor Bella, how do you do, lady? Is it hot, do they leave you alone?

*Mother said, Where have you been, son?—Not anywhere, mother.—I wish you wouldn't look so peaked. And you keep things from me, son.—I haven't been anywhere, where would I go?—If you came back with me, everything would be just like it was before. I know you won't eat at Mrs. Judge's table, not her biscuit.*

When the bank opened, Miss Callie Hudson came up to my window and hollered, Randall, when are you coming back to your precious wife? You forgive her, now, you hear? That's no way to do, bear grudges. Your mother never bore your father a grudge in her life, and he made her life right hard, I tell you, how do you suppose he made her life? She didn't bear him a grudge. We're all human on earth. Where's little old Lonnie, now, has he stepped out, or you done something to him? I still think of him as a boy in knee breeches and Buster Brown bob, riding the ice wagon, stealing ice — your lifelong playmate, Jinny's lifelong playmate — a little common but so smart. Ah, I'm a woman that's been clear around the world in my rocking chair, and I tell you we all get surprises now and then. But you march on back to your wife, Ran MacLain. You hear? It's a thing of the flesh, not the spirit, it'll pass. Jinny'll get over this in three, four months maybe. You hear me? And you go back *nice*. No striking about now and doing anything we'll all be shamed to hear about. I know you won't. I knew your father, was crazy about your father, just as long as he could recognize me, love your mother. Sweetest people in the world, most happily mated people in the world. Go home and tell your mother I said so. And you march back to that precious wife. March back and have you some chirren. How long has it been? How long? What day was it you tore the house down, Christmas or Easter? I said Easter, Mr. Hudson said Christmas — who was right? My Circle declares she'll get a divorce and marry Lonnie but I say not. Thing of the flesh, I told Mr. Hudson. Won't last. And they've known each other a hundred years! The Missionary Circle said you'd kill him and I said, You all, who are you talking about? If it's Ran MacLain that I knew in his buggy, I said he's the last person I know to take on to that extent. I laughed. And little Jinny. I had to laugh at her. Says — I couldn't help it. I says, How did it happen, Jinny, tell old Miss Callie, you monkey, and she says, Oh Miss Callie, I don't know — it just happened, she says, sort of across the bridge table. I says across the bridge table my foot. Jinny told me yesterday on the street, Oh, she says, I just saw Ran. I hope Ran won't cherish it against me, Jinny says. I have to write my checks on the Sabina Bank, and Lonnie Dugan works in it, right next to Ran. And we're all grown up, not little children any more. And I says I know, how could you get away from each other if you tried, you could not. It's an endless circle. That's what a thing of the flesh is. And you won't get away from that in Sabina or hope to. Even our little town. Jinny was never scared of the Devil himself as a growing girl, and shouldn't be now. And Lonnie Dugan won't ever quit at the bank, will he? Can't quit. But as I said to Mr. Hudson — they're in separate *cages*. All right, I said to Mr. Hudson, look. Jinny was unfaithful to Ran — that's what it *was*. There you have what it's all *about*. That's the brunt of it. Face it, I told Mr. Hudson. You're a train man — just a station agent, you're out of things. I *don't* know how many *times*.

But I'd go back to my lawful spouse! Miss Callie hollers at me through the bars. You or I or the man in the moon got no business living in that little hot upstairs room with a western exposure at Mrs. Judge O'Leary's for all the pride on earth, not in August.

After work I was always staying to cut the grass in Mrs. Judge's backyard, so it would be cooler for Bella. It kept the fleas away from her a little. None of it did much good. The heat held on. After I went back to the Starks, the men were playing, still playing croquet with a few little girls, and the women had taken off to themselves, stretched out on the screen porch. They called Maideen, I sent her in to them. It was the long Mississippi evening, the waiting till it was cool enough to eat. The voice of Jinny's mama carried — I heard it — her reminiscent one — but the evening was quiet, very hot and still.

Somebody called, You're dead on Lonnie. It was just a little Williams girl in pigtails.

I may have answered with a joke. I felt lighthearted, almost not serious at all, really addressing a child, as I lifted my mallet — the one with the red band that had always been mine. I brought Dugan to earth with it. He went down and shook the ground, fanning the air as he went. He toppled and sighed. Then I beat his whole length and his head with that soft girl's hair and all the schemes, beat him without stopping my mallet till every bone and little bone, all the way down to the little bones in the hand, flew to pieces. I beat Lonnie Dugan till there was nothing to know there. And I proved the male body — it has a too certain, too special shape to it not to be hurt — could be finished and done away with — with one good loud blow after another — Jinny could be taught that. I looked at Dugan down there. And his blue eyes remained unharmed. Just as sometimes bubbles a child blows seem the most impervious things, and grass blades will go through them and they still reflect the world, give it back unbroken. Dugan I declare was dead.

'Now watch.'

Dugan said that. He spoke with no pain. Of course he never felt pain, never had time to. But that absurd, boyish tone of *competition* was in his voice. It had always been a mystery, now it was a deceit. Dugan — born nothing. Dugan — the other boy at the dance, the other man in the bank, the other sweetheart in Sabina, Jinny's other man — it was together he and I made up the choice. Even then it was hard to believe — we were the choice in everything. But if that was over, settled — how could it open again, the destroyed mouth of Dugan? And I heard him say 'Now watch.' He was dead on the ruined grass. But he had risen up. Just then he gave one of the fat little Williams girls a spank. I could see it and not hear it, the most familiar sound in the world.

There was that breathless stillness, and the sky changing the way a hand would pass over it. And I should have called it out *then* — All is disgrace! Human beings' cries would swell in the last of evening like this and cross the grass in the yard before the light changes, if only they cried. Our grass in August is like the floor under the sea, and we walk on it slowly playing, and the sky turns green before dark. We don't say anything the others remember.

But at our feet the shadows faded out light into the pale twilight and the locusts sang in long waves, O-E, O-E. Sweat ran down my back, arms, and legs, branching like some upside-down tree.

Then, 'You'll all come in!' They were calling from the porch — the well-known yellow lamps suddenly all went on. They called us in their shrill women's voices, Jinny and all and her mama. 'Fools, you're playing in the dark! Come to supper!'

Somebody bumped into me in the sudden blindness of the yard. We laughed at their voracious voices. Across the dark the porch of women waited. It was like a long boat to me, or a box lighted up from within. But I was hungry.

I'd go down to Mrs. Judge O'Leary's to sleep in my little western room — that's the house where Mrs. Judge and the three other Sabina schoolteachers sit on the porch. Each evening to avoid them I ran through porch and hall both, like a man through the pouring rain. In the big dark backyard, full of pecan trees, moonlit, Bella opened her eyes and looked at me. They showed the moon. If she drank water, she vomited it up — yet she went with effort to her pan and drank again. I held her. Poor Bella. I thought she suffered from a tumor, and stayed with her most of the night.

*Mother said, Son, I noticed that old pistol of your father's in your nice coat pocket, what do you want with that old thing, your father never cared for it. Not any robbers coming to the bank that* I *know of. Son, if you'd just saved your money you could take yourself a little trip to the coast. I'd go with you They always have a breeze at Gulfport, nearly always.*

When you get to Jinny's, there are yuccas and bare ground — it looks like some old playground, with the house back out of sight. Just the sharp, over-grown yuccas with up and down them rays of spiderwebs glinting in the light — as if they wore dresses. And back up in the shade is a little stone statue, all pockmarked now, of a dancing girl with a finger to her chin. Jinny stole that from a Vicksburg park once and her mama let her keep it.

Maideen said, 'Are you taking me in yonder? I wish you wouldn't.'

I looked down and saw my hand on the gate, and said 'Wait. I've lost a button.' I showed my loose sleeve to Maideen. I felt all at once solemn — fateful — ready to shed tears.

'Why, I'll sew you one on, if you stop by my house,' Maideen said. She touched my sleeve for an instant. A chameleon ran up a leaf, and held there panting. 'Then Mama can see you. She'd be so glad to have you stay to supper.'

I opened the little old gate. I caught a whiff of the sour pears on the ground, the smell of August. I had not told Maideen I was ever coming to supper at any time, or seeing her mama.

'Oh, Jinny can sew it on now,' I said.

'Oh, I can?' Jinny said. She had of course been listening to me all the time from the half-hidden path. She looked out from under her shade-hat. She has the face, she has the threatening stare of a prankster — about to curtsey to you. Don't you think it's the look of a woman that loves dogs and horses best, and long trips away she never takes? 'Come in before I forget, then,' Jinny said.

We went ahead of Maideen. There in the flower beds walked the same robins, where the sprinkler had been. Once again, we went in the house by the back door. We took hands. We stepped on Tellie's patch of mint — the yellow cat went around the corner — the back door knob was as hot as the hand to the touch, and on the step, impeding the feet of two people going in together, the fruit jars with the laborious cuttings rooting in water — 'Watch out for Mama's —— !' That had happened a thousand times, the way we went in. As a thousand bees droned and burrowed in the pears that lay on the ground.

As Mama Stark almost ran over me, she shrank with a cry, and started abruptly up the stairs — bosom lifted — her shadow trotted up beside her like a nosy bear. But she could never get to the top without turning. She came down again and held up a finger at me. Her voice . . . Randall. Let me tell you about a hand I held yesterday. My partner was Amanda Mackey and you know she always plays her own hand with no more regard for her partner than you have. Well, she opened with a spade and Fanny doubled. I held: a singleton spade five clubs to the king queen five hearts to the king and two little diamonds. I said two clubs, Gert Gish two diamonds, Amanda two spades, all passed. And when I laid down my hand Amanda said, *O partner!* Why didn't you bid your hearts! I said Hardly. At the level of three with the opponents doubling for a takeout. It developed of course she was two suited — six spades to the ace jack and four hearts to the ace jack ten, also my ace of clubs. Now Randall. It would have been just as easy for Amanda when she opened her mouth a second time to bid three hearts. But no! She could see only her own hand and so she took us down two, and we could have made five hearts. Now do *you* think I should have bid three hearts? — I said, You were justified not to, Mama Stark, and she gave me a nod. Then she glared as if I had slapped her. How well she could turn up her discontent to outrage again, and go on upstairs.

We turned, Jinny leading me, into the little back study, 'Mama's office,' with the landscape wall-paper and the desk full-up with its immediacy of Daughters of the Confederacy correspondence. Tellie sashayed in with the work basket and then just waited, eyeing and placing us and eyeing the placing herself between us.

'Put it down, Tellie. Now you go on. Pull your mouth in, you hear me?' Jinny took the fancy little basket and flicked it open and fished in it. She found a button that belonged to me, and glanced up at Tellie.

'I hear you's a mess.' Tellie went out.

Jinny looked at me. She pulled my hand up and I shot. I fired point blank at Jinny—more than once. It was close range—between us suddenly there was barely room for the pistol to come up. And she only stood threading the needle, her hand not deviating, not even shaken at the noise. The little heart-shaped gold and china clock on the mantel was striking—the pistol's noise had not drowned that. I looked at Jinny and I saw her childish breasts, little pouting excuses for breasts, all sprung with bright holes where my bullets had gone. But Jinny did not feel it, the noise had veered off at the silly clock, and she threaded the needle. She made her little face of success. Her thread always went in its tiny hole.

'Hold still,' Jinny muttered softly between fixed lips. She far from acknowledged her pain—anything but sorrow and pain. Just as when she was angry, she sang some faraway song. For domestic talk her voice would lower to a pitch of utter disparagement. Disparagement that had all my life elated me. The little cheat. I waited unable to move again while she sewed dartingly at my sleeve; the sleeve to my helpless hand. As if I counted my breaths now I slowly exhaled fury and inhaled simple dismay that she was not dead on earth. She bit the thread. I was unsteady when her mouth withdrew. The cheat.

I could not, dared not say goodby to Jinny any more, and 'Go get in the croquet,' she told me. She walked to the mirror in the hall, and began cutting at her hair.

I know Vera Lassiter darted in the room and her face lighted. 'Mercy me,' she said, and in her mischief came up and fingered Jinny's hair, the short soft curls. 'Who're you being now? Somebody's little brother?'

But Jinny stood there at her mirrored face half smiling, so touchingly desirable, so sweet, so tender, vulnerable, touching to me I could hardly bear it, again I could not.

Old Tellie spat into the stove and clanged down an iron lid as I went out through the kitchen. She had spent so much time, twenty-seven years, saying she had brought Jinny into this world: 'Born in dis hand.'

'No use for you atall you don't whup her. Been de matter wid you? Where you *been?*'

I found Maideen waiting out in the swing, and took her arm and led her down to the croquet where we all played Jinny's game.

Dear God wipe it clean. Wipe it clean, wipe it out. Don't let it be.

At last Mrs. Judge O'Leary caught hold of me in the hall. Do me a favor. Ran, do me a favor and put Bella out of her misery. None of these school teachers any better at it than I would be. And Judge too tenderhearted. You do it. Just do it and don't tell us, hear?

*Where have you been, son?—Nowhere, mother, nowhere.—If you were back under my roof I would have things just the way they were. Son, I wish you would just speak to me, and promise*——

And I was getting tired, oh so tired, of Mr. Killigrew. I felt cornered when Maideen spoke, kindly as ever, about the workings of the ice house. Now I knew her mother's maiden name. God help me, the name Parsons was laid on my head like the top teetering crown of a pile of things to remember. Not to forget, the name of Parsons.

I remember your wedding, Old Lady Hartford said at my window, poking her finger through the bars. Never knew it would turn out like this, the prettiest wedding in my memory. If you had all *this* money, you could leave town.

Maideen believed so openly—I believe she told Miss Callie—that I wanted to take her somewhere sometime by herself and have a nice time—like other people—but that I put it off till I was free. Still, she had eyes to see, we would run into Jinny every time, Jinny and Lonnie Dugan and the crowd. Of course I couldn't help that, not in Sabina. And then always having to take the little Williams girl home at night. She was the bridge player; that was a game Maideen had never learned to play. Maideen—I never kissed her.

But the Sunday came when I took her over to Vicksburg.

Already on the road I began to miss my bridge. We could get

our old game now, Jinny, Dugan, myself and often the little Williams child, who was really a remarkable player, for a Williams. Mama Stark of course would insist on walking out in stately displeasure, we were all very forward children indeed if we thought she would be our fourth, holding no brief for what a single one of us had done. So the game was actually a better one.

Maideen never interrupted our silence with a word. She turned the pages of a magazine. Now and then she lifted her eyes to me, but I could not let her see that I saw her wondering. I would win every night and take their money. Then at home I would be sick, going outdoors so the teachers would not wonder. 'Now you really must get little Maideen home. Her mother will be thinking something awful's happened to her. Won't she, Maideen?'—Jinny's voice. 'I'll ride with you'—the little Williams. Maideen would not have begun to cry in Jinny's house for anything. I could trust her. Did she want to? She wasn't *dumb*.

She would get stupefied for sleep. She would lean farther and farther over in her chair. She would never have a rum and coke with us, but she would be simply dead for sleep. She slept sitting up in the car going home, where her mama, now large-eyed, maiden name Parsons, sat up listening. I would wake her up to say I had got her home at last. The little Williams girl would be chatting away in the back seat, there and back wide awake as an owl.

Vicksburg: nineteen miles over the gravel and the thirteen little swamp bridges and the Big Black. Suddenly all sensation returned.

Sabina I had looked at till I saw nothing. Till the street was a pencil mark on the sky, a little stick. Maybe outside my eyes a real roofline clamped down still, Main Street was there the same, four red-brick scallops, branchy trees, one little cross, but if I saw it, it was not with love, it was a pencil mark on the sky. Sabina wasn't there to me. If some indelible red false-fronts joined one to the other like a little toy train went by—I did not think of my childhood any more. Sabina had held in my soul to constriction. It was never to be its little street again.

I stopped my car at the foot of Vicksburg, under the wall, by the canal. There was a dazzling light, a water-marked light. I woke Maideen and asked her if she were thirsty. She smoothed her dress and lifted her head at the sounds of a city, the traffic on cobblestones just behind the wall. I watched the water-taxi come, chopping over the canal strip at us, absurd as a rocking horse.

'Duck your head,' I said to Maideen.

'In here?'

Very near across the water the island rose glittering against the sunset — a waste of willow trees, yellow and green strands that seemed to weave loosely one upon the other, like a basket that let the light spill out uncontrollably. We shaded our eyes to ride across the water. We all stood up bending our heads under the low top. The Negro who ran the put-put never spoke once, 'Get in' or 'Get out.' 'Where are we going?' Maideen said. In two minutes we were touching the barge. Old ramshackle floating saloon fifty years old, with its twin joined to it, for colored.

Nobody was inside but the one man — a silent, relegated place like a barn. I let him bring some rum cokes out to the only table, the card table out on the back where the two cane chairs were. The sun was going down on the island side, and making Vicksburg alight on the other. East and West were in our eyes.

'Don't make me drink it. I don't want to drink it,' Maideen said.

'Go on and drink it.'

'You drink if you like it. Don't make me drink it.'

'You drink it too.'

I looked at her take some of it, and sit shading her eyes. There were wasps dipping from the ledge over the old screen door and skimming her hair. There was a smell of fish and of the floating roots fringing the island. The card table smelled warmly of its oilcloth top and of endless deals. A load of Negroes came over on the water-taxi and stepped out with tin buckets. They were sulphur yellow all over, thickly coated with cottonseed meal, and disappeared in the colored barge at the other end, in single file, as if they were sentenced to it.

'Sure enough, I don't want to drink it.'

'You drink it. It doesn't taste bad.'

Inside, in the dim saloon, two men with black spurred cocks

under their arms had appeared. Without noise they each set a muddy boot on the rail and drank, the cocks hypnotically still. They got off the barge on the island side, where they disappeared in the hot blur of willow branches. They might never be seen again.

The heat trembled on the water and on the other side wavered the edges of the old white buildings and concrete slabbed bluffs. From the barge, Vicksburg looked like an image of itself in a tarnished mirror — like its portrait at a sad time of life.

A short cowboy in boots and his girl came in, walking alike. They dropped a nickel in the nickelodeon, and came together.

The canal had no visible waves, yet trembled slightly beneath us; I was aware of it like the sound of a winter fire in the room.

'You don't ever dance, do you?' Maideen said.

It was a long time before we left. All kinds of people had come out to the barge, and the white side and the nigger side filled up. When we left it was good-dark.

The lights twinkled sparsely on the shore — old sheds and warehouses, long dark walls. High up on the ramparts of town some old iron bells were ringing.

'Are you a Catholic?' I asked her suddenly, and I bent my head to hear her answer.

'No.'

I looked at her — I made it plain she had disappointed some hope of mine — for she had; I could not tell you now what hope.

'We're all Baptists. Why, are you a Catholic?' Oh, nobody was a Catholic in Sabina.

'No.'

Without touching her except momently with my knee I walked her ahead of me up the steep uneven way, to where my car was parked listing sharply downhill. Inside, she could not shut her door. I stood outside and looked, it hung heavily and she had drunk three or four drinks, all I had made her take. Now she could not shut her door. 'I'll fall out, I'll fall in your arms. I'll fall, catch me.'

'No you won't. Shut it hard. Shut it. All your might.'

At last. I leaned against her shut door, spent for a moment.

I grated up the steep cobbles, turned and followed the river road high along the bluff, turned again off into a deep rutted dirt way under shaggy banks, dark and circling and down-rushing.

'Don't lean against my arm,' I said. 'Sit up and get some air.'

'I don't want to,' she said in her soft voice that I could hardly understand any more.

'You want to lie down?'

'No. I don't want to lie down.'

'Get some air.'

'Don't make me lie down. I don't want to do anything, anything at all.'

'You're drunk.'

'I don't want to do a thing from now and on till evermore.'

We circled down. The sounds of the river tossing and dizzying and teasing its great trash could be heard through the dark now. It made the noise of a moving wall, and up it fishes and reptiles and uprooted trees and man's throwaways played and climbed all alike in a splashing like innocence. A great wave of smell beat at my face. The track had come down deep as a tunnel. We were on the floor of the world. The trees met and matted overhead, the cedars came together, and through them the stars of Vicksburg looked sifted and fine as seed, so high and so far. There was the sound of a shot, somewhere, somewhere.

'Yonder's the river,' she said. 'I see it — the Mississippi River.'

'You don't see it. We're not that close.'

'I see it, I see it.'

'Haven't you ever seen it before? You baby.'

'Before? No, I never have seen the Mississippi River before. I thought we were on it on the boat.'

'Look, the road has ended.'

'Why does it come this far and stop?'

'How should I know? What do they come down here for?'

'Why do they?'

'There are all kinds of people in the world.' Far away somebody was burning something.

'Do you mean bad people and niggers and all? Ones that hide? Moonshiners?'

'Oh, fishermen. River men. Cock fighters. You're waked up.'

'I think we're lost,' she said.

*Mother said, if I thought you'd ever go back to that Jinny Stark, I couldn't hold up my head.—No, mother, I'll never go back.—The whole world knows what she did to you.*

'You dreamed we're lost. We'll go somewhere where you can lie down a little.'

'You can't get lost in Sabina.'

'After you lie down a little you'll be all right again, you can get up. We'll go somewhere where you can lie down.'

'I don't want to lie down.'

'Did you know a car would back up a hill as steep as this?'

'You'll be killed.'

'I bet nobody ever saw such a crazy thing. Do you think anybody ever saw such a crazy thing?'

We were almost straight up and down, hanging on the bluff and the tail end bumping and lifting us and swaying from side to side. At last we were up. If I had not drunk that last drink maybe I would not have made such startling maneuvers and would not have bragged so loud. The car had leaned straight over that glimpse of the river, over the brink as sweetly as you ever saw a hummingbird over a flower.

We drove a long way. All among the statues in the dark park, the repeating stances, the stone rifles again and again on lost hills, the spiral-staired and condemned towers.

I looked for the moon, which would be in the last quarter. There she was. The air was not darkness but faint light, and floating sound—the breath of all the people in the world who were breathing out into the night looking at the moon, knowing her quarter.

We rode in wilderness under the lifting moon, Maideen keeping very still, sighing faintly as if she longed for something herself, for sleep—for going the other way. A coon, white as a ghost, crossed the road, passed a gypsy camp—all sleeping.

Off the road, under the hanging moss, a light burned in a whitewashed tree. It showed a circle of whitewashed cabins, dark, and all around and keeping the trees back, a fence of white palings. Sunset Oaks. A little nigger boy leaned on the gate this late at night, wearing an engineer's cap.

Yet it did not seem far. I pulled in, and paid.

'One step up,' I told her at the door.

I sat on the bed, the old iron bed with rods. I think I said, 'Get your dress off.'

She had her head turned away. The naked light hung far down in the room—a long cord that looked as if something had stretched it. She turned, then, with tender shoulders bent toward the chair, as if in confidence toward that, the old wreck of a thing that tonight held her little white dress.

I turned out the light that hung down, and the room filled with the pale night like a bucket let down a well. It was never dark enough, the enormous sky flashing with its August light rushing into the emptiest rooms, the loneliest windows. The month of falling stars. I hate the time of year this is.

If we lay together any on the bed, almost immediately I was propped up against the hard rods with my back pressing them, and sighing—deep sigh after deep sigh. I heard myself.

'Get up,' I said. 'I want the whole bed. You don't need to be here.' And I showed I had the pistol. I lay back holding it toward me and trying to frown her away, the way I used to lie still cherishing a dream in the morning and Jinny would pull me out of it.

Maideen had been pulling or caressing my arm, but she had no strength in her hands at all. She rose up and stood in the space before my eyes, so plain there in the lighted night. She was disarrayed. There was blood on her, blood and disgrace. Or perhaps there wasn't. I did not remember anything about it. For a moment I saw her double.

'Get away from me,' I said.

While she was speaking to me I could hear only the noises of the place we were in—of frogs and nightbirds, a booted step in the heavy tangle all around, and the little idiot nigger running up and down the fence, up and down, as far as it went and back, sounding the palings with his stick.

'This is my grandfather's dueling pistol — one of a pair. Very valuable.'

'Don't, Ran. Don't do that, Ran. Don't do it. Please don't do it.'

I knew I had spoken to her again in order to lie. It was my father's pistol he'd never cared for. When she spoke, I didn't hear what she said; I was reading her lips, the way people being told good-by do conscientiously through train windows. I had the pistol pointing toward my face and did not swerve it. Outside, it sounded as though the little nigger at the gate was keeping that up forever — running a stick along the fence, up and down, to the end and back again.

Poor Bella, it was so hot for her. She lay that day with shut eyes, her narrow little forehead creased. Her nose was dry as a thrown-away rind. The weather was only making her suffer more. She never had a long thick coat, was the one good thing. She was just any kind of a dog. The kind I liked best.

I tried to think. What had happened? No — what had not happened? Something had not happened. The world was not going on. Or, you understand, it went on but somewhere it had stopped being real, and I had walked on, like a tight-rope walker without any rope. How far? Where should I have fallen? Hate. Discovery and hate. Then, right after . . . Destruction was not real, disgrace not real, nor death. They all got up again, Jinny and Dugan got up. . .

Up and down, the little idiot nigger. He was having a good time at that. I wondered, when would that stop? Then that stopped.

I put the pistol's mouth in my own. It tasted, the taste of the whole machinery of it. And then instead it was my own mouth put to the pistol's, quick as a little baby's maybe, whose hunger goes on every minute — who can't be reassured or gratified, ever, quite in time enough. There was Maideen still, white in her petticoat.

'Don't do it, Ran. Please don't do it.'

Urgently I made it — made the awful sound.

And immediately she said, 'Now, you see. It didn't work. Now you see. Hand that old thing to me, I'll keep that.'

She took it from me. She took it over to the chair, as if she were possessed of some long-tried way to deal with it, and disposed of it in the fold of her clothes. She came back and sat down on the edge of the bed. In a minute she put her hand out again, differently — and touched my shoulder. Then I met it, hard, with my face, the small, bony, freckled (I knew) hand that I hated (I knew), and kissed it and bit it until my lips and tongue tasted salt tears and salt blood — that the hand was not Jinny's. Then I lay back in the bed a long time, up against the rods.

'You're so stuck up,' she said.

I lay there and after a while my eyes began to close and I saw her again. She lay there plain as the day by the side of me, quietly weeping for herself. The kind of soft, restful, meditative sobs a child will venture long after punishment.

So I slept.

How was I to know she would hurt herself like this?

Now — where is Jinny?

(*From The New Yorker*)

# THE SECOND TREE FROM THE CORNER

## BY E. B. WHITE

'EVER have any bizarre thoughts?' asked the doctor.

Mr. Trexler failed to catch the word. 'What kind?' he said.

'Bizarre,' repeated the doctor, his voice steady. He watched his patient for any slight change of expression, any wince. It seemed to Trexler that the doctor was not only watching him closely but was creeping slowly toward him, like a lizard toward a bug. Trexler shoved his chair back an inch and gathered himself for a reply. He was about to say 'Yes' when he realized that if he said yes the next question would be unanswerable. Bizarre thoughts, bizarre thoughts? Ever have any bizarre thoughts? What kind of thoughts *except* bizarre had he had since the age of two?

Trexler felt the time passing, the necessity for an answer. These psychiatrists were busy men, overloaded, not to be kept waiting. The next patient was probably already perched out there in the waiting room, lonely, worried, shifting around on the sofa, his mind stuffed with bizarre thoughts and amorphous fears. Poor bastard, thought Trexler. Out there all alone in that misshapen antechamber, staring at the filing cabinet and wondering whether to tell the doctor about that day on the Madison Avenue bus.

Let's see, bizarre thoughts. Trexler dodged back along the dreadful corridor of the years to see what he could find. He felt the doctor's eyes upon him and knew that time was running out. Don't be so conscientious, he said to himself. If a bizarre thought is indicated here, just reach into the bag and pick anything at all. A man as well supplied with bizarre thoughts as you are should have no difficulty producing one for the record. Trexler darted into the bag, hung for a moment before one of his thoughts, as a hummingbird pauses in the delphinium. No, he said, not that one. He darted to another (the one about the rhesus monkey), paused, considered. No, he said, not that.

Trexler knew he must hurry. He had already used up pretty nearly four seconds since the question had been put. But it was an impossible situation — just one more lousy, impossible situation such as he was always getting himself into. When, he asked himself, are you going to quit maneuvering yourself into a pocket? He made one more effort. This time he stopped at the asylum, only the bars were lucite — fluted, retractable. Not here, he said. Not this one.

He looked straight at the doctor. 'No,' he said quietly. 'I never have any bizarre thoughts.'

The doctor sucked in on his pipe, blew a plume of smoke toward the rows of medical books. Trexler's gaze followed the smoke. He managed to make out on of the titles, 'The Genito-Urinary System.' A bright wave of fear swept cleanly over him, and he winced under the first pain of kidney stones. He remembered when he was a child, the first time he ever entered a doctor's office, sneaking a look at the titles of the books — and the flush of fear, the shirt wet under the arms, the book on t.b., the sudden knowledge that he was in the advanced stages of consumption, the quick vision of the hemorrhage. Trexler sighed wearily. Forty years, he thought, and I still get thrown by the title of a medical book. Forty years and I still can't stay on life's little bucky horse. No wonder I'm sitting here in this dreary joint at the end of this woebegone afternoon, lying about my bizarre thoughts to a doctor who looks, come to think of it, rather tired.

The session dragged on. After about twenty minutes, the doctor rose and knocked his pipe out. Trexler got up, knocked the ashes out of his brain, and waited. The doctor smiled warmly and stuck out his hand. 'There's nothing the matter with you — you're just scared. Want to know how I know you're scared?'

'How?' asked Trexler.

'Look at the chair you've been sitting in! See how it has moved back away from my desk. You kept inching away from me while I asked you questions. That means you're scared.'

'Does it?' said Trexler, faking a grin. 'Yeah, I suppose it does.'

They finished shaking hands. Trexler turned and walked out uncertainly along the passage, then into the waiting room and out past the next patient, a ruddy pin-striped man who was seated on the sofa twirling his hat nervously and staring straight ahead at the files. Poor, frightened guy, thought Trexler, he's probably read in the *Times* that one American male out of every two is going to die of heart disease by twelve o'clock next Thursday. It says that in the paper almost every morning. And he's also probably thinking about that day on the Madison Avenue bus.

A week later, Trexler was back in the patient's chair. And for several weeks thereafter he continued to visit the doctor, always toward the end of the afternoon, when the vapors hung thick above the pool of the mind and darkened the whole region of the East Seventies. He felt no better as time went on, and he found it impossible to work. He discovered that the visits were becoming routine and that although the routine was one to which he certainly did not look forward, at least he could accept it with cool resignation, as once, years ago, he had accepted a long spell with a dentist who had settled down to a steady fooling with a couple of dead teeth. The visits, moreover, were now assuming a pattern recognizable to the patient.

Each session would begin with a résumé of symptoms — dizziness in the streets, the constricting pain in the back of the neck, the apprehensions, the tightness of the scalp, the inability to concentrate, the despondency and the melancholy times, the feeling of pressure and tension, the anger at not being able to work, the anxiety over work not done, the gas on the stomach. Dullest set of neurotic symptoms in the world, Trexler would think, as he obediently trudged back over them for the doctor's benefit. And then, having listened attentively to the recital, the doctor would spring his question: 'Have you ever found anything that gives you relief?' And Trexler would answer, 'Yes. A drink.' And the doctor would nod his head knowingly.

As he became familiar with the pattern Trexler found that he increasingly tended to identify himself with the doctor, transferring himself into the doctor's seat — probably (he thought) some rather slick form of escapism. At any rate, it was nothing new for Trexler to identify himself with other people. Whenever he got into a cab, he instantly became the driver, saw everything from the hackman's angle (and the reaching over with the right hand, the nudging of the flag, the pushing it down, all the way down along the side of the meter), saw everything — traffic, fare, everything — through the eyes of Anthony Rocco, or Isidore Freedman, or Matthew Scott. In a barbershop, Trexler was the barber, his fingers curled around the comb, his hand on the tonic. Perfectly natural, then, that Trexler should soon be occupying the doctor's chair, asking the questions, waiting for the answers. He got quite interested in the doctor, in this way. He liked him, and he found him a not too difficult patient.

It was on the fifth visit, about halfway through, that the doctor turned to Trexler and said, suddenly, 'What do you want?' He gave the word 'want' special emphasis.

'I d'know,' replied Trexler uneasily. 'I guess nobody knows the answer to that one.'

'Sure they do,' replied the doctor.

'Do *you* know what *you* want?' asked Trexler narrowly.

'Certainly,' said the doctor. Trexler noticed that at this point the doctor's chair slid slightly backward, away from him. Trexler stifled a small, internal smile. Scared as a rabbit, he said to himself. Look at him scoot!

'What *do* you want?' continued Trexler, pressing his advantage, pressing it hard.

The doctor glided back another inch away from his inquisitor. 'I want a wing on the small house I own in Westport. I want more money, and more leisure to do the things I want to do.'

Trexler was just about to say, 'And what are those things you want to do, Doctor?' when he caught himself. Better not go too far, he mused. Better not lose possession of the ball. And besides, he thought, what the hell goes on here, anyway — me paying fifteen bucks a throw for these séances and then doing the work myself, asking the questions, weighing the answers. So he wants a new wing! There's a fine piece of theatrical gauze for you! A new wing.

Trexler settled down again and resumed the role of patient for the rest of the visit. It ended on a kindly, friendly note. The doctor reassured him that his fears were the cause of his sickness, and that his fears were unsubstantial. They shook hands, smiling.

Trexler walked dizzily through the empty waiting room and the doctor followed along to let him out. It was late; the secretary had shut up shop and gone home. Another day over the dam. 'Goodbye,' said Trexler. He stepped into the street, turned west toward Madison, and thought of the doctor all alone there, after hours, in that desolate hole — a man who worked longer hours than his secretary. Poor, scared, overworked bastard, thought Trexler. And that new wing!

It was an evening of clearing weather, the Park showing green and desirable in the distance, the last daylight applying a high lacquer to the brick and brownstone walls and giving the street scene a luminous and intoxicating splendor. Trexler meditated, as he walked, on what he wanted. 'What do you want?' he heard again. Trexler knew what he wanted, and what, in general, all men wanted; and he was glad, in a way, that it was both inexpressible and unattainable, and that it wasn't a wing. He was satisfied to remember that it was deep, formless, enduring, and impossible of fulfillment, and that it made men sick, and that when you sauntered along Third Avenue and looked through the doorways into the dim saloons, you could sometimes pick out from the unregenerate ranks the ones who had not forgotten, gazing steadily into the bottoms of the glasses on the long chance that they could get another little peek at it. Trexler found himself renewed by the remembrance that what he wanted was at once great and microscopic, and that although it borrowed from the nature of large deeds and of youthful love and of old songs and early intimations, it was not any one of these things, and that it had not been isolated or pinned down, and that a man who attempted to define it in the privacy of a doctor's office would fall flat on his face.

Trexler felt invigorated. Suddenly his sickness seemed health, his dizziness stability. A small tree, rising between him and the light, stood there saturated with the evening, each gilt-edged leaf perfectly drunk with excellence and delicacy. Trexler's spine registered an ever so slight tremor as it picked up this natural disturbance in the lovely scene. 'I want the second tree from the corner, just as it stands,' he said, answering an imaginary question from an imaginary physician. And he felt a slow pride in realizing that what he wanted none could bestow, and that what he had none could take away. He felt content to be sick, unembarrassed at being afraid; and in the jungle of his fear he glimpsed (as he had so often glimpsed them before) the flashy tail feathers of the bird courage.

Then he thought once again of the doctor, and of his being left there all alone, tired, frightened. (The poor, scared guy, thought Trexler.) Trexler began humming 'Moonshine Lullaby,' his spirit reacting instantly to the hypodermic of Merman's healthy voice. He crossed Madison, boarded a downtown bus, and rode all the way to Fifty-second Street before he had a thought that could rightly have been called bizarre.

# BIOGRAPHICAL NOTICES

ALEXANDER, SIDNEY. A native New Yorker, thirty-five years of age, Mr. Alexander served for three years with the Army Air Force, part of the time as a public relations man. He is the author of two books of poems, *The Man On the Queue* and *Tightrope In the Dark*. His poems and short stories have appeared in many magazines and anthologies, including *Harper's Magazine, Harper's Bazaar, Mademoiselle, Accent, Common Sense, War Poems of the United Nations, Anthology of Flight,* and *Virginia Quarterly Review*. He is the winner of several prizes for his short stories, one of which was the *Charm Magazine's* annual award of a thousand dollar bond. Mr. Alexander has also written both for radio and the legitimate theater. One of his stories appeared in *The Best American Short Stories, 1944.*

BOWLES, PAUL. Born in 1911 in New York City, Mr. Bowles was first published at sixteen in *transition,* then edited in Paris. He turned seriously to composing, and visited for a summer with Gertrude Stein in Bilignin. In 1938 he married Jane Auer, already having written chamber music, several musical scores for Orson Welles, and one for the American Ballet. Since then he has written the musical scores for two of William Saroyan's plays, *My Heart's In the Highlands* and *Love's Old Sweet Song,* the Helen Hayes-Maurice Evans *Twelfth Night,* the Theater Guild production of Philip Barry's play *Liberty Jones,* José Ferrer's adaptation of *Cyrano de Bergerac, Jacobowsky and the Colonel,* and *The Glass Menagerie.* His opera, *The Wind Remains,* was first given at the Museum of Modern Art in 1943. For a time he was music critic for the *New York Herald Tribune.* In 1945 Mr. Bowles returned to short story writing after a lapse of twenty years, and is continuing to be interested in this form of expression.

BRADBURY, RAY. A resident of California, Mr. Bradbury was born in 1920 in Waukegan, Illinois. He has written a large number of short stories, twenty-seven of which appear in the collection *Dark Carnival.* While working on his first novel he has continued writing shorter fiction, his stories having appeared in *Harper's Magazine, The New Yorker, American Mercury, Collier's, Mademoiselle, Charm, Touchstone,* and the Cornell University Quarterly *Epoch.* His story, 'The Big Black and White Game,' appeared in *The Best American Short Stories of 1946,* and in 1947 he was selected for the O. Henry Memorial Award *Prize Stories.* He has written several plays for CBS and NBC, and recently Dodd, Mead and Company chose his radio drama *The Meadow* as one of the *Best One Act Plays of 1948.*

CANFIELD, DOROTHY. One of America's most distinguished writers, Dorothy Canfield was born in Lawrence, Kansas, in 1879. Her father was a well-known educator and president of several universities. Mrs. Fisher (in private life she is the wife of John R. Fisher) graduated from Ohio State University and received a Ph.D. in Romance Languages from Columbia University. She also studied in France. In 1912, her first novel *The Squirrel Cage* was published. Twenty-five more books followed, including novels, juveniles, non-fiction, translations of foreign works, collections of her short stories, and a play. Her short stories have been printed in many magazines and anthologies. Among the most widely known of her novels are *The Bent Twig, The Brimming Cup, Raw Material, Her Son's Wife, The Deepening Stream,* and *Seasoned Timber.* These books have also received wide acclaim abroad. Mrs. Fisher is a judge of the Book-of-the-Month Club and is active in educational work. Her home is on a farm near Arlington, Vermont.

CHEEVER, JOHN. This writer was born in Quincy, Massachusetts, in 1912, and received his education at Thayer Academy in South Braintree. He served in the Army for four years with the Fourth Division, and has worked in Boston, Washington, Saratoga Springs, and New York, where he lives at present. He has written a great many short stories, some of which have been collected in the volume called *The Way Some People Live,* and most of which have appeared in *The New Yorker.* His story *The Pleasures of Solitude* was reprinted in *The Best American Short Stories, 1943.* His first novel will appear in the fall of 1948.

CLAY, GEORGE R. Born in Philadelphia in 1921, Mr. Clay was educated at Groton School and Harvard University where he achieved the honor of being elected editorial chairman of the *Harvard Crimson* and associate editor of an intercollegiate magazine, *Threshold.* Enlisting in the Navy in 1943, he served in both the Atlantic and Pacific areas on a World War I 'fourstacker' which hunted German U Boats, acted on convoy duty, carried an underwater demolition team, and assisted in almost every major Pacific invasion. After discharge, he attended Columbia University where he studied short story writing under Martha Foley and novel writing under Caroline Gordon. He entered the University of Pennsylvania Law School for one term, at the end of which, with the encouragement of a contract from Little Brown and Company for a novel based on his story 'That's My Johnny-Boy,' he gave up law to devote all his time to fiction.

CLAYTON, JOHN BELL. Born in Craigsville, Virginia, in 1906, Mr. Clayton entered the newspaper business soon after taking his degree at the University of Virginia, and has spent most of his working life in editorial and news departments. One of his short stories published in *Esquire* was made into a two-reel movie comedy, and in 1947 he held the distinction of winning first prize in the O. Henry Memorial Award *Prize Stories.* He is married, has one son, and at present is living in California.

COUSINS, MARGARET. Miss Cousins, who is well known both as writer and editor, comes from Texan pioneer stock, and received her B.A. degree from the University of Texas in 1926. She began her New York career with the *Pictorial Review* and in 1939 joined the staff of Hearst Magazines as copywriter. In 1943 she became associate editor of *Good Housekeeping,* and for the past three years she has been its managing editor. Miss Cousins sold her first magazine story in 1936, and has contributed fiction, articles and verse to the popular magazines for the past ten years.

FISHER, M. F. K. Miss Fisher received her early education in Southern California where she now lives with her husband, Donald Friede, and their two small daughters. She has recently completed a new translation of *The Physiology of Taste* by Brillat-Savarin for the Limited Editions Club. A novel *Not Now, But Now* was published in 1947, and a year earlier an anthology of her writing appeared under the title *Here Let Us Feast.* Other books include *Serve It Forth, Consider the Oyster, How to Cook a Wolf,* and *The Gastronomical Me.* Between the two World Wars, Miss Fisher lived for more than a decade in France and Switzerland, and owned and worked a small vineyard near Vevey, France, with her former husband Dillwyn Parrish who died in 1941. She has contributed fiction and articles to leading American magazines for the past twelve years.

GARRIGAN, PHILIP. Born in 1914 in Medford, Massachusetts, Mr. Garrigan has lived most of his life at Lowell, and is at present a social worker for the Bureau of Old Age Assistance there. He served with the Air Corps for more than three years during World War II. At one time he was business manager of the poetry magazine *Alentour,* and about forty of his poems have appeared in that magazine, *Harper's Magazine, The University Review, the* Grinnell College *Tanager,* and others. The selection by which he is represented here, 'Fly, Fly Little Dove' appeared as an *Atlantic* 'First' in the June, 1947, *Atlantic Monthly.* He is at present working on a novel, *At the Morning Star,* and continuing with short story writing.

GELLHORN, MARTHA. Miss Gellhorn has proved herself to be at the same time an outstanding foreign correspondent and a fiction writer. Born in St. Louis, Missouri, in 1908, and educated at the John Burroughs School and Bryn Mawr, she first worked on *The New Republic* and the Albany *Times Union.* From 1937 to 1941 she covered the war in Spain and the Russian invasion of Finland for *Collier's* and from 1943 to 1945 she returned to Europe as a correspondent in France, Italy, Germany, and England. Until recently she was married to Ernest Hemingway. She has contributed to many magazines, and her books include *What Mad Pursuit, The Trouble I've Seen, A Stricken Field, The Heart of Another,* and *Llana.*

GRENNARD, ELLIOTT. Although living at present in Los Angeles, Mr. Grennard was born in New York City in 1907 and resided there until he motored west in 1944. He has had a number of songs published and has written special material for night club performers. When *The Black Crook* was revived by Harry Wagstaff Gribble and Tony Sarg, he wrote a new set of lyrics for it. For three years he was music editor for *Billboard,* the show-business trade paper, and has had articles published in *PM* and *Music and Rhythm.* Since 1944 he has been writing creative fiction, and has just completed his first novel.

GUSTAFSON, RALPH. Mr. Gustafson is a Canadian, born in 1909 in Lime Ridge, Quebec. He received his B.A. and M.A. degrees from Bishop's University in Canada and from Oxford University, England. After graduation he taught for a year in a boys' school in Ontario and then returned to England where he did private tutoring. A first volume of poems, *The Golden Chalice,* was published in London and given the Quebec Government Literary Award for 1935. After living abroad for four years, he came to New York City where he is at present engaged in free-lance writing. His short stories have appeared in *Atlantic Monthly, Story, Cross Section, 1948,* and *Epoch.* His second book of poems, *Flight Into Darkness,* was published in 1944, and another volume, *Rivers Among Rocks,* is scheduled for 1948. He has also edited *Anthology of Canadian Poetry, Canadian Accent I* and *II* and *A Little Anthology of Canadian Poets.*

HERSEY, JOHN. Mr. Hersey was born in Tientsin, China, in 1914, and attended primary and grammar schools there before moving to Briarcliff, New York, in 1925 where he continued his education until entering Hotchkiss School, then Yale, and finally Clare College, Cambridge. His first job was in 1937 as private secretary to Sinclair Lewis. Since then he has worked as writer and correspondent for *Time, Life,* and *The New Yorker,* and during World War II he distinguished himself as a war correspondent, visiting the Pacific Theater on *U.S.S. Hornet,* Guadalcanal in 1942, North Africa and Sicily in 1943, Russia in 1944 and 1945, and China and Japan in 1945 and 1946. As well as numerous shorter pieces of fiction and articles which have appeared in American magazines, he is the author of *Men On Bataan, Into the Valley, A Bell for Adano* (for which he won the 1945 Pulitzer Prize), and *Hiroshima.* He is a contributor and editor for *'48, the Magazine of the Year.*

JEFFERS, LANCE. Immediately after Pearl Harbor, Mr. Jeffers enlisted with the Army and served as 1st Lieutenant in Medical Administration in England and Germany. Born in 1920 at Fremont, Nebraska, he attended public and high school in California, and entered the University of California as a pre-medical student (working after class hours as a redcap) and in summers as a merchant seaman. He is now living in New York City, where he has done some newspaper writing, and is free-lancing.

LINCOLN, VICTORIA. Asked recently what she would most like to be, Miss Lincoln answered, 'an author and the mother of a household.' She is a steady contributor of short stories, poems, and sketches to magazines, as well as author of the novel *February Hill* published in 1934 and dramatized a few years later as *The Primrose Path;* a collection of sketches, *Grandmother and the Comet,* published in 1944; and three novelettes published in book form in 1946 under the title *The Wind At My Back*. Her story 'Down in the Reeds By the River' appeared in *The Best American Short Stories, 1947*. She is the wife of Victor Lowe, a professor of philosophy at Ohio State University, and the mother of three children. She was born in Fall River, Massachusetts, in 1904, educated at Radcliffe College, and has lived abroad for short periods, as well as in various parts of the United States.

LOWRY, ROBERT. From 1942 to 1945, Mr. Lowry served as a G.I. with the Army, two years of which were spent with a photo reconnaissance unit in Africa and Italy. George Davis, fiction editor of *Mademoiselle,* discovered his stories in three books printed privately in Italy, and since then his stories have appeared regularly in that magazine. In 1945 Mr. Lowry became production manager and book designer for New Directions Press. A novel, *Casualty,* published in 1946, has appeared in French, Italian, and Swedish translations. A second novel, *Find Me In Fire,* is being published by Doubleday and Company in 1948. Mr. Lowry was born in Cincinnati, Ohio, in 1919, and attended the University of Cincinnati for six months before leaving to hitch-hike around America. He returned to Cincinnati when still only eighteen to publish the *Little Man Books* for three years, using his own printing press. One of his short stories 'Little Baseball World' was reprinted in *The Best American Short Stories, 1947*.

LYNCH, JOHN A. This twenty-six-year-old writer received his B.A. degree from the University of Notre Dame in 1943 shortly after he had enlisted with the Army. For several summer vacation periods he was copy boy at the Detroit *Times,* and while at Notre Dame he held such jobs as mailman, office clerk, library handyman, and student secretary to Richard Sullivan, whose class in creative writing he also attended. His Army service was with the 88th Division in Italy as a member of a machine-gun squad and as a litter bearer. He was wounded and spent fifteen months in various army hospitals before his discharge in 1946. Since then he has attended writing classes at the University of Oklahoma, at Columbia University where he came under the direction of Martha Foley, and at Stanford University under Wallace Stegner. His story, 'The Burden,' reprinted in this anthology, was also included in the O. Henry Memorial Award *Prize Stories of 1947*. He has been published in several Catholic periodicals including *Concord* and *The Holy Name Journal.*

MCHUGH, VINCENT. Born in Providence, Rhode Island, in 1904, Mr. McHugh has also lived in New York, Los Angeles, and San Francisco, and is at present Assistant to the Dean at New York University. He is the author of five novels and a book of verse, including *Sing Before Breakfast, Caleb Catlum's America,* and *The Victory,* published by Random House in 1947. His writing has appeared in Edward J. O'Brien's collection, *The Best Short Stories, 1934, A Quarto of Modern Literature,* and Clifton Fadiman's *Reading I've Liked*. He has also contributed to *Atlantic Monthly, The Nation, The New Yorker, Story, '47,* and many others. During World War II he was a member of the Writers' War Board and the War Shipping Administration, and was writer-director for the Office of War Information.

MORSE, ROBERT. Mr. Morse divides his time between painting, specializing in portraits, and writing. He has had several exhibitions in New York, and has written critical articles connected with painting for such magazines as *The Symposium* and *The*

*Nation*. A number of his poems appeared in Oliver Wells' *Anthology of the Younger Poets* published in 1932, and two long narrative poems were published in book form by Creative Age Press in 1942 under the title *The Two Persephones*. Only recently has Mr. Morse turned to fiction, the story reprinted in this collection being the second to appear in magazine form. He was born in Toledo, Ohio, in 1906, and graduated from Princeton University in 1928. He is married and has one son.

PORTUGAL, RUTH. Since the close of the War, Miss Portugal has traveled as correspondent in the Pacific and the Far East. She was formerly an author's representative in New York City, and was assistant editor on *Harper's Bazaar* for a number of years. Her first published short story 'Neither Here Nor There' appeared in *The Best American Short Stories, 1944* and the following year another story, 'Call a Solemn Assembly,' was reprinted in the same collection. Her stories have also appeared in the O. Henry anthology. Miss Portugal is a native Long Islander, and a graduate of Barnard College at Columbia University.

POST, MARY BRINKER. Born in Seattle, Washington, in 1906, Mrs. Post has three children and one granddaughter. Two of her sons are at Harvard University. She married Harry Grant Post, an ordained Episcopalian minister, in 1924, and at present is living in New Milford, Connecticut. Mrs. Post's first published short story appeared in *Frontier and Midland* in 1931. Since then her stories have been printed in *Prairie Schooner, The Forum, Woman's World, Household Magazine, Good Housekeeping, Woman's Home Companion, Cosmopolitan, Today's Woman, Seventeen, Chatelaine,* and many other magazines, including periodicals in England, Australia, South Africa, Denmark, and Sweden. She has appeared four times on the O'Brien 'Roll of Honor.' Her novel, *Annie Jordan,* is being published in 1948 by Doubleday and Company, and is the Dollar Book Club selection of July for this year. She was contract and free-lance writer for the radio programs *Valiant Lady, Grand Central Station, Chaplain Jim,* and was for a time associate editor of *Woman's Day* Magazine.

ROOT, WAVERLEY. Born in Providence, Rhode Island, in 1903, and educated at Tufts College, Medford, Massachusetts, Mr. Root was European correspondent for the Chicago *Tribune,* United Press, *Time* Magazine, and the Mutual Broadcasting System, and was well known as a news analyst and syndicated columnist on international politics during World War II. In 1945 his book, *The Secret History of the War,* was published by Scribner's. The following year *Casablanca to Katyn* was also published by Scribner's. He is at present operating a five-hundred-acre farm in Vermont and working on a volume about American foreign relations and a novel with an interwar Parisian background.

SHARP, DOLPH. Mr. Sharp, who is in his early thirties, was born in Stogstead, Long Island, and attended the University of Michigan, with graduate work at New York University and the University of Arizona. For a short time he worked as a reporter on a weekly newspaper, until advancing spinal arthritis forced him west to Arizona and then south to the Mexican border. He is now living in Burbank, California, with his wife and two-year-old daughter, and is working on a book for The Story Press in which 'The Tragedy in Jancie Brierman's Life' will appear.

STEGNER, WALLACE. The present reprint is the fifth of Mr. Stegner's stories to appear in *The Best American Short Stories,* and he has also won the O. Henry Memorial Award. His first book, *Remembering Laughter,* brought him the Little Brown novelette prize of $2000, and *One Nation,* written in collaboration with *Look Magazine,* won the 1945 Life in America Award from Houghton Mifflin Company, and shared the *Saturday Review of Literature's* Anisfield-Wolfe prize. His other books include *On a Darkling Plain, The Potter's House, Fire and Ice, Mormon Country, The Big Rock Candy Mountain,* and *Second Growth.* He has had stories and articles published in numerous magazines, and is professor of English and director of the creative writing program at Stanford University, California. He was born in Iowa in 1909, and educated in Canada, Montana, Utah, California, and Iowa, where he received his Ph.D. degree in 1935.

SULKIN, SIDNEY. Mr. Sulkin was born in Boston in 1918 and was graduated from Harvard in 1939. While still at college, his story, 'Reunion,' was listed by Edward J. O'Brien among the Distinctive Stories of 1937. Before enlisting he worked for a New York book publisher, and his army service included the positions of chief of English language broadcasts to Europe, chief of news for the American Broadcasting Station in Europe, and member of a SHAEF mission into Holland. After a severe accident he was invalided back to America, only to return to Europe shortly after as director for an international book association with headquarters in Stockholm, traveling throughout Europe as foreign correspondent and commentator on international affairs for CBS. He has written numerous magazine and newspaper articles in America and abroad, for *Harper's Magazine, Virginia Quarterly Review, New Republic,* and others. 'The Plan,' reprinted in this anthology, is intended as one of a group of post-war stories on the theme of exile.

WELTY, EUDORA. Born in Jackson, Mississippi, Miss Welty is a graduate of the University of Wisconsin, and has done post-graduate work at Columbia University. She has held various publicity jobs and was copy ready for the New York Times Book Review Section for a short time recently. Her stories have appeared in *Atlantic Monthly, Harper's Bazaar, Harper's Magazine, Accent* and other magazines. One of them, 'Asphodel,' was reprinted from *The Yale Review* in *The Best American Short Stories, 1943.* Her novels include *The Robber Bridegroom, Curtain of Green,* and *Delta Wedding* published in 1945. She lives in Jackson, Mississippi, and currently is devoting all her time to fiction.

WHITE, E. B. Born in Mt. Vernon, New York, in 1899. He was graduated from Cornell University in 1921, and began work as a reporter. Since 1927 he has been on the staff of *The New Yorker,* and for about a decade wrote the 'Notes and Comment' page of that magazine's 'Talk of the Town' department. Following this, he moved to Maine, and wrote essays regularly for *Harper's Magazine* under the heading of 'One Man's Meat.' During the war he returned to New York and to writing some of the editorials for *The New Yorker,* and he writes essays, verse, and stories for this and other magazines. He is the author of a number of books, including *One Man's Meat, Stuart Little,* a book for children, and, most recently, *The Wild Flag,* a collection of his editorials on World Government. Mr. White divides his time between New York and Maine. He is married to Katharine S. White, an editor of *The New Yorker,* and they have one son.

# THE YEAR BOOK OF THE AMERICAN SHORT STORY

January 1 to December 31, 1947

# ROLL OF HONOR

## 1947

### I. *American Authors*

Aistrop, Jack
Three Christmases. '47.
Alexander, Sidney
Part of the Act. Story.
Angoff, Charles
The Lodge Doctor. University of Kansas City Review.
Ayalta, J.
The Eternal Values. Commentary.

Babb, Sanora
Reconciliation. New Mexico Quarterly Review.
Baizer, Ashur
Living Amoeba. New Republic.
Barrett, Catherine
When They Cast Their Leaves. Yale Review.
Bartlett, Paul Alexander
Barley Water. Southwest Review.
Behrman, S. N.
Mr. Wolfson's Stained Glass Window. New Yorker.
Benson, Sally
Lady With a Lamp. New Yorker.
Bonowsky, Phillip
The Ladybug. Story.
Bowles, Paul
A Distant Episode. Partisan Review.
Boyle, Kay
Army of Occupation. New Yorker.
Bradbury, Ray
I See You Never. New Yorker.

Cadle, Dean
We Have Returned. Tomorrow.
Canfield, Dorothy
The Apprentice (appeared under title 'Once and For All'). Ladies' Home Journal.
Casper, Leonard
Least Common Denominator. Southwest Review.
Cheever, John
The Enormous Radio. New Yorker.
Clay, George R.
That's My Johnny-Boy. Tomorrow.
Clayton, John Bell
Visitor from Philadelphia. Harper's Magazine.
The White Circle. Harper's Magazine.
Cousins, Margaret
A Letter to Mr. Priest. Good Housekeeping.
Curley, Daniel
The Ship. Accent.

De Pereda, Prudencio
Home Is the Soldier. Tomorrow.
Dreher, Carl
The Early Million. Good Housekeeping.

Fast, Howard
Departure. Mainstream.
Fifield, William
Glory Sunday. Accent.
Fisher, M. F. K.
The Hollow Heart. '47.
Freitag, George R.
The May Walk. Atlantic Monthly.

Garrigan, Philip
'Fly, Fly, Little Dove.' Atlantic Monthly.
Gellhorn, Martha
Miami-New York. Atlantic Monthly.
Gibbons, Robert
The Brothers. Collier's.
Goldberg, Emanuel
Many More Than He Saw. Pacific.
Gordon, Caroline
The Petrified Woman. Mademoiselle.
Greene, Mary Frances
The Silent Day. Mademoiselle.
Grennard, Elliott
Sparrow's Last Jump. Harper's Magazine.
Gresham, William Lindsay
The Dream Dust Factory. Atlantic Monthly.
Griffin, William J.
The Best Kind of Night. Mainstream.
Gustafson, Ralph
The Human Fly. Atlantic Monthly.
Surrey Harvest. Epoch.

HERSEY, JOHN
Why Were You Sent Out Here? Atlantic Monthly.
A Short Wait. New Yorker.

JACKSON, SHIRLEY
Men With Their Big Shoes. Yale Review.
JEFFERS, LANCE
The Dawn Swings In. Mainstream.
JOHNSON, JOSEPHINE
Christmas Morning in May. Harper's Bazaar.

KARCHMER, SYLVAN
The Fano Club. University of Kansas City Review.

LINCOLN, VICTORIA
Morning, A Week Before the Crime. Cosmopolitan.
LOWRY, ROBERT
The Terror in the Streets. Mademoiselle.
The War Poet. Western Review.
LYNCH, JOHN A.
The Burden. Atlantic Monthly.

MACKENZIE, RACHEL
The Thread. Harper's Magazine.
MARQUAND, JOHN P.
Close to Home. Good Housekeeping.
MARSHALL, LENORE G.
Unknown Artist. Virginia Quarterly Review.
MCGILL, RALPH
She'll Talk Later. Harper's Magazine.
MCHUGH, VINCENT
The Search. '47.
MCLAUGHLIN, ROBERT
I'm in the Middle. New Yorker.
MORRIS, EDITA
A Ball of Yarn. Western Review.
MORSE, ROBERT
The Professor and the Puli. Harper's Magazine.

NEWHOUSE, EDWARD
Put Yourself in My Place. New Yorker.
NIN, ANAIS
The Sealed Room. The Tiger's Eye.

O'HARA, JOHN
Pardner. New Yorker.
OWENS, WILLIAM A.
Hangerman John. Southwest Review.

PETRY, ANN
The Necessary Knocking at the Door. '47.
PORTUGAL, RUTH
The Stupendous Fortune. Good Housekeeping.
POST, MARY BRINKER
That's the Man! Today's Woman.

ROOT, WAVERLEY
Carmencita. '47.

SCHORER, MARK
The Shame of the Man on the Egg. Harper's Bazaar.
SHARP, DOLPH
The Tragedy in Jancie Brierman's Life. Story.
SHELTON, WILLIAM R.
The Snow Girl. Atlantic Monthly.
STAFFORD, JEAN
The Tunnel with No End. Harper's Bazaar.
STEGNER, WALLACE
Beyond the Glass Mountain. Harper's Magazine.
SULKIN, SIDNEY
The Plan. Kenyon Review.

TANNER, JACK
Home for an Indian. Western Review.
TAYLOR, ELIZABETH
A Sad Garden. Harper's Magazine.

WELTY, EUDORA
The Whole World Knows. Harper's Bazaar.
WEST, JESSAMYN
Horace Chooney, M.D. Mademoiselle.
WHITE, E. B.
The Second Tree from the Corner. New Yorker.
WOOD, ANNA
A Dull Servant. Northern Review.

## II. *Foreign Authors*

COLETTE
The Sick Child. Mademoiselle.

GREENE, GRAHAM
Proof Positive. Harper's Magazine
A Drive in the Country. Harper's Magazine.

HITREC, JOSEPH G.
Life, How Simple It Is. Tomorrow.

MCCLAVERTY, MICHAEL
The Wild Duck's Nest. '47.

MORAVIA, ALBERTO
The Island of Dreams. Chimera.

O'CONNOR, FRANK
The Babes in the Wood. New Yorker.
My Da. New Yorker.

O'FAOLAIN, SEAN
The Man Who Invented Sin. Harper's Bazaar.
Up The Bare Stairs. '47.

PRITCHETT, V. S.
The Sailor. Harper's Magazine.
The Collection. Harper's Magazine.

TABORI, GEORGE
Grete. Today's Woman.

# DISTINCTIVE VOLUMES OF SHORT STORIES

## Published in the United States

## 1947

ALGREN, NELSON. The Neon Wilderness. Doubleday and Company, Inc.
ASWELL, MARY LOUISE, Editor. The World Within. Whittlesey House.
BEER, THOMAS. Mrs. Egg and Other Americans. Alfred A. Knopf.
BRICKELL, HERSCHEL, Editor. O. Henry Memorial Award Prize Stories of 1947. Doubleday and Company, Inc.
DREISER, THEODORE. The Best Short Stories of Theodore Dreiser. World.
FOLEY, MARTHA, Editor. The Best American Short Stories, 1947. Houghton Mifflin Company.
FORSTER, E. M. Collected Tales. Alfred A. Knopf.
HARPER, WILHELMINA, and PETERS, AIMEE M., Editors. The Best of Bret Harte. Houghton Mifflin Company.
KIELTY, BERNADINE, Editor. A Treasury of Short Stories. Simon and Schuster.
LAMPMAN, BEN HUR. The Wild Swan and Other Sketches. Thomas Y. Crowell Company.
LAUGHLIN, JAMES, Editor. Spearhead. New Directions.
LAVIN, MARY. At Sallygap and Other Stories. Little, Brown and Company.
LINSCOTT, ROBERT N., Editor. The Best Short Stories of Bret Harte. Modern Library.
McCLAVERTY, MICHAEL. The Game Cock and Other Stories. Devin-Adair Company.
NABAKOV, VLADIMIR. Nine Stories. New Directions.
POWERS, J. F. Prince of Darkness and Other Stories. Doubleday and Company, Inc.
PRITCHETT, V. S. It May Never Happen and Other Stories. Reynal & Hitchcock, Inc.
PUDNEY, JOHN. Edna's Fruit Hat and Other Stories. Harper & Brothers.
SCHORER, MARK. The State of Mind. Houghton Mifflin Company.
SWALLOW, ALAN. Anchor in the Sea. William Morrow & Company.
WARNER, SYLVIA TOWNSEND. The Museum of Cheats. Viking Press.
WEIDMAN, JEROME. The Captain's Tiger. Reynal & Hitchcock, Inc.
WELTY, EUDORA. A Curtain of Green and Other Stories. Harper & Brothers.
WESTON, CHRISTINE. There and Then. Charles Schribner's Sons.
YARMOLINSKY, AVRAM, Editor. Best Short Stories of Maxim Gorky. Grayson and Grayson, Ltd.

# DISTINCTIVE SHORT STORIES IN AMERICAN MAGAZINES

## 1947

## I. *American Authors*

AISTROP, JACK
Three Christmases. '47, Dec.

ALEXANDER, SIDNEY
Part of the Act. Story, Jan.-Feb.

ALPERT, HOLLIS
The Partition. Mademoiselle, Sept.
The Sound of Doom. Matrix, Fall-Winter.

ALTULER, H. B.
The Harnessery. Western Review, Summer.

AMEJKO, EDWARD
War In Peace. New Mexico Quarterly Review, Spring.

ANGOFF, CHARLES
The Lodge Doctor. University of Kansas City Review, Spring.

ANNIXTER, PAUL
The Lynching. Collier's, Oct. 25.

ARNOLD, MAXWELL
Never Hit a Cripple. Harper's Magazine, Nov.

ATTAWAY, WILLIAM
Death of a Rag Doll. The Tiger's Eye, Oct.

AYALTI, J.
The Eternal Values. Commentary, Dec.

BABB, SANORA
Reconciliation. New Mexico Quarterly Review, Summer.

BACON, PEGGY
The Peculiarity of Mr. Morton. New Yorker, Oct. 25.

BAHR, JEROME
Bannon's Pavilion. Harper's Bazaar, Jan.

BAIZER, ASHUR
Living Amoeba. New Republic, Apr. 21.

BAKER, DENYS VAL
River of Light. Western Review, Spring.

BARNA, MICHAEL
A Couple of Old-Timers. New Yorker, May 31.

BARNARD, MARY
The Cat. Today's Woman, March.
A Character Must Have a Name. Yale Review, Winter.

BARRETT, CATHARINE
When They Cast Their Leaves. Yale Review, Spring.

BARTH, LAWRENCE
The Right Shade of Blue. New Masses, Feb. 11.

BARTLETT, PAUL ALEXANDER
Barley Water. Southwest Review, Autumn.

BEAUCHAMP, D. D.
The Cruise of the Prairie Queen. Cosmopolitan, Feb.

BEHRMAN, S. N.
Mr. Wolfson's Stained Glass Window. New Yorker, June 28.

BELL, THOMAS
The Man Who Made Good In America. Mainstream, Winter.

BEMELMANS, LUDWIG
The Antlers of the Alpenrose. New Yorker, May 24.

BENSON, SALLY
Lady With a Lamp. New Yorker, Jan. 18.
A Number of Things. New Yorker, Nov. 1.

BERNHARD-COHN, EMIL
The Striving of Saul Morteira. Menorah Journal, Winter.

BLAIR, HOWARD R.
The Rooming House. Chicago Review, Spring.

BLASSINGAME, WYATT
The Atonement. Cosmopolitan, May.

MALAQUAIS, JEAN
The Inspector. Commentary, March.
MALKIN, RICHARD
Pico Never Forgets. Town and Country, Dec.
MALONEY, RUSSELL
Fitzgerald and Son. Good Housekeeping, Jan.
MARKFIELD, WALLACE
Ph.D. Partisan Review, Sept.-Oct.
MARMUR, JACLAND
Proved by the Sea. Blue Book, Apr.
MARQUAND, JOHN P.
Close to Home. Good Housekeeping, Nov.
MARRIOTT, ALICE
El Zopilote. Southwest Review, Summer.
MARSH, WILLARD
The Rival. Southwest Review, Autumn.
MARSHALL, LENORE G.
Unknown Artist. Virginia Quarterly Review, Winter.
MARTIN, PATRICIA
Accident. University of Kansas City Review, Winter.
McCOY, ESTHER
The Male Grapes. New Yorker, July 5.
McCUNE, HELEN
Seedling. Story, Sept.-Oct.
McGILL, RALPH
She'll Talk Later. Harper's Magazine, Oct.
McHUGH, VINCENT
The Search. '47, July.
McKENNA, VINCENT
Room for a Stranger. Good Housekeeping, Nov.
McKENNEY, RUTH
Grandpa's Sign. Atlantic Monthly, Aug.
McLAUGHLIN, ROBERT
I'm in the Middle. New Yorker, June 14.
MELLINGER, EDWARD D.
Incident of the Marital State. Story, Sept.-Oct.
MEMLING, CARL
Strong Man. American Hebrew, March 4.
Invitation to a Bar Mitzvah. American Hebrew, July 4.
MORLEY, CHRISTOPHER
Time of Life. '47, June.
St. Bypass-Under-the-Bridge. '47, Dec.
MORRIS, EDITA
A Ball of Yarn. Western Review, Winter.
MORSE, ROBERT
My Name is Trouble. Tomorrow, March.
The Professor and the Puli. Harper's Magazine, June.
MOSELEY, EDWIN
Art Nook. Accent, Winter.
MOSS, HOWARD
The Paris Dog. Accent, Autumn.

NEIDER, CHARLES
Conquest. Hairenik, Jan. 2.
Success. Pacific, June.
The Carp. Mademoiselle, Sept.
NELSON, STEVE
El Fantastico. Mainstream, Spring.
NEWHOUSE, EDWARD
Put Yourself in My Place. New Yorker, Feb. 15.
The Light Across the Hill. New Yorker, Apr. 5.
Choice of Weapons. New Yorker, May 10.
NIGGLI, JOSEPHINE
A Visitor from Dominguez. '47, Aug.
NIN, ANAIS
The Sealed Room. Tiger's Eye, Oct.
NOONAN, CATHERINE
Good Neighbor Gerrity. Woman's Day, Sept.
NORFORD, GEORGE E.
Peace on Earth. Common Ground, Spring.

O'BRIEN, BRIAN
The Last Canoe. Saturday Evening Post, Dec. 27.
O'CONNOR, EDWIN
The Gentle, Perfect Knight. Atlantic Monthly, Sept.
O'DONNELL, MARY KING
A Pair of Shoes. Good Housekeeping, Apr.
O'HARA, JOHN
Not Always. New Yorker, Jan. 11.
The Moccasins. New Yorker, Jan. 25.
Pardner. New Yorker, Feb. 22.
Someone to Trust. New Yorker, March 22.
Drawing Room B. New Yorker, Apr. 19.
Miss W. New Yorker, May 3.
The Lady Takes an Interest. New Yorker, June 28.

Royster, Myrtle
And She Wore Diamonds in Her Teeth. Harper's Magazine, Sept.

Salinger, J. D.
A Young Girl in 1941 with No Waist at All. Mademoiselle, May.

Sandoz, Mari
Martha of the Yellow Braids. Prairie Schooner, Summer.

Satterthwaite, Alfred
The Uncelebrated Case. American Hebrew, Aug. 29.

Schorer, Mark
The Shame of the Man on the Egg. Harper's Bazaar, Feb.

Schrag, Otto
A Town Is Born. '47, Apr.
Wedding in Vernois. '47, July.

Schramm, Wilbur
The Voice in the Earphones. Saturday Evening Post, March 29.

Seager, Allan
Sham. Good Housekeeping, June.

Seghers, Anna
The Saboteurs. Mainstream, Summer.

Seifert, Mary Harris
Clouds Over Canaan. Common Ground, Spring.

Selvin, Paul
The Blotter Woman. Antioch Review, March.

Seymour, Harold
Mota. Sewanee Review, Summer.

Sharp, Dolph
The Tragedy in Jancie Brierman's Life. Story, March-Apr.

Shattuck, Katherine
The Answer. Sewanee Review, Summer.

Shaw, Irwin
The Passion of Lance Corporal Hawkins. New Yorker, March 29.
Widows' Meeting. New Yorker, Apr. 19.
The Single Brute. Esquire, Oct.
The Man With One Arm. '47, Nov.

Shedd, Margaret
Couple Hundred Thousand Als. New Yorker, Feb. 15.

Sheean, Vincent
Snowbound. Cosmopolitan, Feb.

Shelton, William R.
The Snow Girl. Atlantic Monthly, May.

Smallwood, Effie
Major Albert-Surgeon. Canadian Forum, Oct. 27.

Smith, William J.
The King of the Jungle. Chicago Review, Spring.

Sorensen, Virginia
The Talking Stick. New Mexico Quarterly Review, Winter.

Stafford, Jean
The Tunnel With No End. Harper's Bazaar, Jan.
A Slight Maneuver. Mademoiselle, Feb.

Starr, Roger
The Harbin Club. Furioso, Spring.

Stavisky, Samuel E.
Ma Didn't Like Handsome Men. American Hebrew, Aug. 1.

Steegmuller, Francis
Snapdragons. New Yorker, Jan. 11.

Stegner, Wallace
Beyond the Glass Mountain. Harper's Magazine, May.

Steig, Henry
A Man Has to Eat. Tomorrow, Feb.

Stevens, Helen
The Black Shawl. Southwest Review, Summer.

Stock, Irvin
A Box of Candy. Antioch Review, March.

Storm, Hans Otto
Twelve Hundred Pesos. Southwest Review, Summer.

Strong, Austin
All on a Winter's Night. Atlantic Monthly, Jan.

Strong, Joan
Terence Died. Chimera, Spring.

Stuart, Jesse
Evidence Is High Proof. Esquire, June.
Huntress and the Hunted. Western Review, Autumn.

Suhl, Yuri
I Find a New Landsman. New Masses, Feb. 18.

Sulkin, Sidney
The Plan. Kenyon Review, Summer.

Summers, James L.
The Sling. New Mexico Quarterly Review, Spring.
Trumpet in the Sky. Southwest Review, Winter.

Summers, Richard
Oldest Inhabitant. New Mexico Quarterly Review, Spring.
Swift, Arlene
I Can't See You Anymore. Husk, Dec.

Tanner, Jack
Home for an Indian. Western Review, Spring.
Tarcov, Edith
An Open Window. Antioch Review, Fall.
Taylor, Elizabeth
The School Concert. Harper's Bazaar, July.
The Light of Day. Harper's Magazine, Dec.
A Sad Garden. Harper's Magazine, Dec.
Thompson, Lawrence R.
Last Week-End. Story, Sept.-Oct.
Towers, Frances
The Golden Rose. Charm, Sept.
Tracy, Honor
A Romance in Paris. Harper's Bazaar, Nov.
Tucci, Niccolo
Free Ride. Harper's Bazaar, Feb.
The Evolution of Knowledge. New Yorker, Apr.
War and Peace. Harper's Bazaar, July.
The Truce. New Yorker, July 5.
Twigger, Beth
The Beautiful Life. New Yorker, Nov. 8.

Van Doren, Mark
The Man Who Had Died a Lot. Touchstone, Nov.
Van Pragg, S.
Songs Are Sung. American Hebrew, Feb. 21.

Wagner, Eliot L.
Garden of Eden. Antioch Review, Winter.
Wahl, Betty
Martinmas. New Yorker, Nov. 5.
Wainwright, Loudon S.
Clean Jersey. New Yorker, Nov. 1.
Watson, John
Black Market Monkeys. Southwest Review, Spring.
The Gun on the Table. Harper's Magazine, July.
Benny and the Tar-Baby. Harper's Magazine, Dec.

Wassell, Irma
Wade in the Water. New Mexico Quarterly Review, Winter.
Weaver, John D.
A Sign for Selina. Harper's Magazine, Apr.
Wedeck, Harry E.
Temptation. American Hebrew, Jan. 17.
Weismiller, Frances
Mrs. Mallon and the Octopus. New Yorker, March 22.
Welty, Eudora
The Whole World Knows. Harper's Bazaar, March.
West, Gertrude
Sweet But Tartish. Household, Sept.
West, Jessamyn
Horace Chooney, M.D. Mademoiselle, Feb.
Another Word Entirely. New Mexico Quarterly Review, Spring.
Alive and Real. Harper's Bazaar, Sept.
White, E. B.
The Second Tree from the Corner. New Yorker, May 31.
White, Milton
To Remember These Things. Seventeen, May.
Wilcox, Wendell
Seventh Heaven Doesn't Describe It. Harper's Bazaar, Jan.
Wilder, Charles
Image in the Summer Air. University of Kansas City Review, Autumn.
Williams, Elva
Temptation. Cosmopolitan, Feb.
Williams, Tennessee
The Yellow Bird. Town and Country, June.
Wilson, Sloan
Check for $90,000. New Yorker, Feb. 2.
Bearer of Bad Tidings. New Yorker, March 8.
Wimberly, Lowry Charles
Merry Christmas, Prof. Western Review, Summer.
Winterich, John T.
None of Is (Or Are) Perfect. New Yorker, May 24.
Wiseman, Max
The Lesson. Partisan Review, Sept.-Oct.
Wood, Anna
A Dull Servant. Northern Review, Oct.-Nov.

Woodburn, John
The Better Part of Valor. Esquire, Jan.

Woodford, Bruce P.
The Necessary Illusion. New Mexico Quarterly Review, Spring.

Woodhouse, W.L.
The Visit With Jimmy Baxter. New Mexico Quarterly Review, Spring.

Woods, Donald
Bella: Pioneer. Tomorrow, March

Woulff, Sholem
Bar Mitzvah. American Hebrew, June 6.

Wykes, Alan
The Holiday. Tomorrow, Feb.

## II. *Foreign Authors*

Babel, Isaak
The Awakening. Commentary, Spring.

Berridge, Elizabeth
Woman About the House. Accent, Autumn.

Blunden, Geoffrey
The Indian Game. Atlantic Monthly, Nov.

Colette
The Sick Child. Mademoiselle, July.

Evslin, Bernard
The Red Pays. Tomorrow, Jan.

Greene, Graham
Proof Positive. Harper's Magazine, Oct.
A Drive in the Country. Harper's Magazine, Nov.

Hitrec, Joseph G.
Life, How Simple It Is. Tomorrow, Jan.

Hughes, Cledwyn
The Stepping Stones. Virginia Quarterly Review, Summer.

Johnson, Olive
The Soldanella Field. Atlantic Monthly, Sept.

Kersch, Gerald
The Scene of the Crime. Esquire, June.
The Epistle of Simple Simon. Tomorrow, June.

Maugham, W. Somerset
The Romantic Young Lady. New Yorker, June 21.
A Man from Glasgow. Town and Country, July.

McClaverty, Michael
The Wild Duck's Nest. '47, July.

Moravia, Alberto
The Island of Dreams. Chimera, Spring.

O'Connor, Frank
The Babes in the Wood, New Yorker, March 8.
My Da. New Yorker, Oct. 25.
The Cornet Player Who Betrayed Ireland. Harper's Bazaar, Nov.

O'Faolain, Sean
The Man Who Invented Sin. Harper's Bazaar, March.
The Woman Who Married Clark Gable. '47, Apr.
Up the Bare Stairs. '47, Oct.

O'Flaherty, Liam
Two Lovely Beasts. Story, Nov.-Dec.

Phelan, Jim
Pinkeen. Story, Sept.-Oct.

Pritchett, V. S.
The Sailor. Harper's Magazine, March.
The Collection. Harper's Magazine, Sept.

Slavin, Lev
Crossroad Madonna. Mainstream, Fall.

Tabori, George
Grete. Today's Woman, Apr.
Two Inches on Top. Tomorrow, May.

Weston, Christine
Her Bed Is India. New Yorker, May 31.

Z,Oscar Castro
(Translated by Alexander B. Morris)
Lisandro Pozo and the Soil. Southwest Review, Spring.

# ADDRESSES OF AMERICAN AND CANADIAN MAGAZINES PUBLISHING SHORT STORIES

Accent, P.O. Box 102, University Station, Urbana, Illinois
Adventure, 205 East 42nd Street, New York City
American Hebrew, 48 West 48th Street, New York City
American Magazine, 250 Park Avenue, New York City
American Mercury, 570 Lexington Avenue, New York City
Antioch Review, Yellow Springs, Ohio
Argosy, 205 East 42nd Street, New York City
Arizona Quarterly, University of Arizona, Tucson, Arizona
Atlantic Monthly, 8 Arlington Street, Boston, Massachusetts
Bard Review, Annandale-on-Hudson, New York
Blue Book, 230 Park Avenue, New York City
Canadian Forum, 16 Huntley Street, Toronto, Ontario, Canada
Canadian Home Journal, Richmond & Sheppard Streets, Toronto, Ontario, Canada
Catholic World, 411 West 59th Street, New York City
Charm, 122 East 42nd Street, New York City
Chatelaine, 481 University Avenue, Toronto, Ontario, Canada
Chicago Review, Reynolds Building, 5706 University Avenue, Chicago, Illinois
Chimera, 265 West 11th Street, New York City
Collier's, 250 Park Avenue, New York City
Commentary, 425 Fourth Avenue, New York City
Common Ground, 20 West 40th Street, New York City
Commonweal, 386 Fourth Avenue, New York City
Cosmopolitan, 57th Street and Eighth Avenue, New York City
Country Gentleman, Independence Square, Philadelphia, Pennsylvania
Crisis, 69 Fifth Avenue, New York City
Decade of Short Stories, 3642 North Pacific Avenue, Chicago, Illinois
Direction, 500 Fifth Avenue, New York City
Elks Magazine, 50 East 42nd Street, New York City
Epoch, 252 Goldwin Smith Hall, Cornell University, Ithaca, New York
Esquire, 191 North Michigan Avenue, Chicago, Illinois
Everywoman's, 1790 Broadway, New York City
Folio, 1212 Washington Street, La Porte, Indiana
Foreground, Warren House, Quincy Street, Cambridge Massachusetts
'48, The Magazine of the Year, 68 West 45th Street, New York City
Furioso, R.F.D. 1, Madison, Connecticut
Glamour, 420 Lexington Avenue, New York City
Good Housekeeping, 57th Street and Eighth Avenue, New York City
Hairenik Weekly, 212 Stuart Street, Boston, Massachusetts
Harper's Bazaar, 572 Madison Avenue, New York City
Harper's Magazine, 49 East 33rd Street, New York City
Holland's Magazine, 3306 Main Street, Dallas, Texas
Household Magazine, Topeka, Kansas
Hudson Review, 39 West 11th Street, New York City
Husk, Cornell College, Mount Vernon, Iowa
Instead, 1 East 53rd Street, New York, New York
Interim, 1536 Shenandoah Drive, Seattle, Washington
Jewish Life, 35 East 12th Street, New York City
Kansas Magazine, Box 237, Kansas State College, Manhattan, Kansas
Kenyon Review, Kenyon College, Gambier, Ohio
Ladies' Home Journal, Independence Square, Philadelphia, Pennsylvania

Liberty, 37 West 57th Street, New York City
MacLean's Magazine, 481 University Avenue, Toronto, Ontario, Canada
Mademoiselle, 122 East 42nd Street, New York City
Mainstream, 832 Broadway, New York City
Matrix, 828 Gerard Avenue, New York City
McCall's Magazine, 230 Park Avenue, New York City
Menorah Journal, 63 Fifth Avenue, New York City
Neurotica, 4438½ Olive Street, St. Louis, Missouri
New Mexico Quarterly Review, University of New Mexico, Albuquerque, New Mexico
New Republic, 40 East 49th Street, New York City
New Yorker, 25 West 43rd Street, New York City
Northern Review, 3575 Durocher Avenue, Apt. H, Montreal, Quebec, Canada
Nuances, 121 Madison Avenue, Apt. 6-K, New York City
Opportunity, 1133 Broadway, New York City
Pacific, Box 467, Mills College, Oakland, California
Pacific Spectator, Stanford University, Stanford, California
Partisan Review, 1545 Broadway, New York City
Perspective, 216 Menges, University of Louisville, Louisville, Kentucky
Phylon, Atlanta University, Atlanta, Georgia
Prairie Schooner, 12th and R Streets, Lincoln, Nebraska
Profile, 106 Student Union Bldg., University of Cincinnati, Cincinnati, Ohio
Quarterly Review of Literature, 1928 Yale Station, New Haven, Connecticut
Queen's Quarterly, Kingston, Ontario, Canada
Reader's Scope, 114 East 32nd Street, New York City
Redbook, 230 Park Avenue, New York City
Salute, 19 Park Place, New York City
Saturday Evening Post, Independence Square, Philadelphia, Pennsylvania
Script, 548 South San Vicente Blvd., Los Angeles, Calif.
Seventeen, 11 West 42nd Street, New York City
Sewanee Review, University of the South, Sewanee, Tennessee
Southwest Review, Southern Methodist University, Dallas, Texas
Story, 116 East 30th Street, New York City
Sybylline, 33 Phillips Street, Watertown, Massachusetts
Tanager, Grinnell College, Grinnell, Iowa
This Week, 420 Lexington Avenue, New York City
Tiger's Eye, R.F.D. 4, Westport, Connecticut
Today's Woman, 67 West 44th Street, New York City
Tomorrow, 11 East 44th Street, New York City
Touchstone, 17 East 42nd Street, New York City
Town and Country, 572 Lexington Avenue, New York City
12th Street, New School for Social Research, 66 West 12th Street, New York City
Twice A Year, 509 Madison Avenue, New York City
University of Kansas City Review, Kansas City, Missouri
View, 1 East 53rd Street, New York City
Virginia Quarterly Review, One West Range, Charlottesville, Virginia
Viva, 404 West 115th Street, New York City
Western Review, Rm. 211, Fraser Hall, University of Kansas, Lawrence, Kansas
Weird Tales, 9 Rockefeller Plaza, New York City
Woman's Day, 19 West 44th Street, New York City
Woman's Home Companion, 250 Park Avenue, New York City
Yale Review, P.O. Box 1729, New Haven, Connecticut